SHOT THROUGH TIME

SHOT THROUGH TIME

RICHARD MODLIN

HARTSIDE PUBLISHING
OWENS CROSS ROADS, AL

Shot Through Time
A Novel

Historical sites in Boston, Concord, Lexington, Massachusetts, as well as in Newcastle-upon Tyne and Gateshead, England, UK are real. Characters involved in the Battles of Concord and Lexington and Bunker Hill are also real. But this is a book of fiction. Any resemblance to real people, living or dead, is purely coincidental. Most of the characters appearing in this work are fictitious.

Copyright © Richard Modlin, 2023
Hartside Publishing
Owens Cross Roads, AL 35763

All rights reserved. No part of this book may be reproduced (except for inclusion in reviews), disseminated, or utilized in any form or by any means, electronic or mechanical. This includes photocopying or using any informational storage and retrieval systems, or the Internet without expressed permission of the author or publisher.

For further information please contact www.richardmodlin.com.
Printed in the United States of America

Hardback ISBN: 978-0-9985427-2-0
Trade Paperback ISBN: 978-0-9985427-4-4
Hartside Publishing, Owens Cross Roads, AL 35763

Acknowledgments

The editorial comments, criticisms, suggestions, and encouragements of my wife, author, literary editor and photographer, Marian Moore Lewis, enhanced *Shot Through Time* and kept the project in line. I would also like to pay tribute to Elizabeth Ridley, who professionally edited my novel, and provided insights to the development of the characters and dynamics of the plot. My writers' group, Rusty Bynum, William Case, Dr. William Goodson, and Sara McDaris, all published authors, added to the improvement of *Shot Through Time*. My tributes also go to Danna Mathias Steele, who created the enticing cover image and formatted the manuscript for publication.

"The best thing about the future is
that it comes one day at a time."

– ABRAHAM LINCOLN

Wednesday, April 19, 1775

Sergeant Noland Black woke just after midnight on April 19, 1775, a day that for him would end in total and astounding confusion. He rubbed his eyes, yawned. *Damn, another boring day,* he thought, rolled out of his cot, and stood. Incoherent voices and clamors of men in the enlisted men's quarters, readying themselves for the day's mission, penetrated the walls of the sergeant's cubicle. *Greenhorns. Wish I could get a company of veterans. I feel like a wet nurse to these damn recruits.*

Sergeant Black, a young-faced, square-jawed, strapping thirty-year-old grenadier in the 10th British regiment, drew up his trousers, stuffed his blouse down around his waist, belted the pants, sat, and tugged on his boots. He stood, grabbed a thin leather necklace from which dangled a silver Celtic cross imbedded with four gold-colored gems and hung it around his neck. After the sergeant put on his waist-coat and buttoned it, he stood in front of a mirror and brushed his long, dark-brown hair, which he tried to maintain at roughly the ten-inch regulation length. He grasped the hair and pulled it together into a queue, and tied it so that one inch of hair would hang below the lanyard. The sergeant then donned his red coat, adjusted his queue to hang down the back of the collar, straightened, and stepped out of his compartment into the barracks. The clamor ended and the soldiers came to attention next to their cots. From an inside pocket in his coat, Black removed a sheet of paper, examined it, and stuck it back into the pocket.

"Today's expedition should not be different from the others you've been on," Sergeant Black announced in an authoritative, deep, gravelly voice. "That is if those damn rebels don't get edgy." He stiffened his stance. "Our mission today is to march to Concord. Find, confiscate, and destroy any stashes of arms and ammunition those damn rebels have hidden. We have searched this village before, and little has been found, but Concord's a long trek. About twelve miles. Need to get there about 0800. And back here to Boston for supper. Keep alert, stay calm, and remember Lieutenant Colonel Smith's command, 'Do not fire on the rebels.' Now grab your muskets and join the lieutenant colonel's regiment outside." He scanned his men. A surge of apprehension tightened his stomach. Lieutenant Colonel Smith awaits. Grab your muskets and fall in outside. Dismissed!"

Another mundane trip, if everyone keeps a cool head, Black thought as he followed his men out of the barracks to begin the twelve-mile march to Concord and Lexington.

C H A P T E R 2

Wednesday, April 19, 1775

Mission accomplished. As expected, little illegal weaponry was found. Sergeant Black and his recruits gathered at Wright's Tavern in Concord to gain sustenance before the return trip to Cambridge. They followed him into the tavern.

Inside, the sergeant stood and scanned the interior. His men seemed to scatter about. When the door opened, allowing a gust of warm, humid air and a burst of sunlight to flush in, Black thought, *unusual temperature for mid-April.* He watched two late comers materialize through the brilliant beam of light that filled the doorway. They stumbled to a nearby table and collapsed into chairs.

Unconsciously Black fumbled the Celtic cross. *Poor fellows. Marched almost double-time through the night. Then Lexington at near sunrise and some damned fool had to take a shot. And for the moment. All hell broke loose. My troops seemed to forget Lieutenant Colonel Smith's command not to fire on the colonial rebels, but the boys emptied their muskets of their loads—protecting themselves. Killed a few rebels. Lucky only one of our men got injured. Been a hard morning searching for contraband. And, they have not eaten. They are hungry and tired.*

With his back to the bar, Sergeant Black seated himself on a nearby stool, and removed his hat. He scratched his full head of dark brown hair, and grunted, "Mr. Wright, bring some vittles for my men. Like me, they are hungry. And we still have a long trip back to the barracks."

Amos Wright, the tavern manager, bent toward Sergeant Black. "Aye. I'll take care of your men as I always do for all who enter my tavern." Amos started back to the kitchen, but turned. "You just missed the Massachusetts militia commander and his men, sergeant. They filled their bellies and headed for the hills without a word."

"Too bad," Sergeant Black replied. "My men, recruits they are, would have enjoyed meeting a parcel of rebels."

Again, the tavern door burst open and more soldiers stumbled in. Several had their muskets pointed forward and others had their musket barrels pointed upward. A couple of men sprawled onto the sawdust-covered floor, while others dropped their butts into chairs. Several of the Redcoats nodded at Sergeant Black.

"Water and beer!" Black yelled, stepped off the barstool, stood tall, and faced the motley troops. "Proud of you. You did well today."

Upon the sergeant's words, the tavern filled with a cacophony of sighs, coughs, grunts, and moans. Then, from the floor, someone grumbled. "Fourth of these damn, useless missions I been on—when's Gage gonna realize, colonials don't have weapons—o'll they know is, we're a comin'."

"General Gage, soldier...." Sergeant Black barked. He reached around, grabbed his mug, and swigged the remaining beer. "Don't want to hear any disrespect for our commander. Remember, soldier, he's a general." His eyes narrowed for a moment. Then he looked down at the floor, raised his head, pursed his lips, and gritted his teeth. "Know you're tired. Frustrated. But you men found two large cannons buried on Barrett's farm. Broke off their trunnions. Rendered them useless. Burned the gun carriages that were found in the barn. Seized some rusted muskets around the town. And, that five hundred pounds of musket shot you dumped into the lake, I would say you men did well."

"Shot a few of them rebels too," a soldier mumbled.

"Aye, that you did." Black returned to his stool at the bar. But before he seated himself, he turned back to his men. "We need to heed Lieutenant Colonel Smith's command to resist shooting colonials. Fire only if you're fired upon. Killing those crazy bastards could cause them to revolt. We only faced little resistance in Lexington. Almost none here in Concord. In fact, helping the colonials extinguish the fires and saving that barn seemed to gain their respect." He paused, took a breath. His voice softened. "Eat the grub these fine folks provided us. And do not forget, we each pay our reckoning. After, we will fall into ranks, meet with Captain Laurie's company at North Bridge, and march back to Boston."

The weather on April 19, 1775 at 11:30 in the morning was still comfortable. The British troops had completed their search of Concord and were given a couple of hours to rest and refresh themselves. Once outside Wright's Tavern, located on the south side of the village, Sergeant Black ordered his troops to stay nearby. "I expect the lieutenant colonel and his company of regulars to join us. Doddle about, but don't stray." A look of concern crossed the sergeant's face when he glanced about at the men. *They are tired. Novices in this business. Never have they faced battle.* He bent down and pulled a blade of grass, stuck it into his mouth, and lay back against the trunk of a stout oak tree. The grass stem calmed him as he twirled it with his tongue. Unconsciously his fingers touched his neck. They slowly pulled the thin leather cord from under his blouse and began to fumble the cross that hung from it. Though a gift of remembrance from a young lady he left behind, to Noland, this Celtic cross became his talisman. He came to believe it had special powers that kept him safe in moments of danger. While wearing it in several battles, he had only received a single superficial wound from a musket shot. While in the midst of chaotic combat where swords clashed, bayonets stabbed, and arrows flew, only his saddle and uniform received ravaging blows. He prized the amulet and never went anywhere without it.

Since his arrival at the Boston command, Noland had led six or seven similar raids on nearby colonial farms and villages, searching for hidden caches of weapons, ammunition, and gunpowder. These forays resulted because colonists loyal to Britain informed on their traitorous neighbors. Rarely were any significant amounts of armament found. But, with the unsettled atmosphere that surrounded the American Colonies at this time, these informants' information instilled paranoia in the British high command. Normally, these expeditions were more of an outing for the soldiers, but today was different. Shots were fired at Lexington. Colonists were injured, killed. Sergeant Black's anxiety was momentarily quelled when the horse carrying Lieutenant Colonel Francis Smith came to a halt near the stoop of the tavern. A patrol of about thirty men followed.

"Get your men in rank," the lieutenant colonel shouted. "We need to make for Boston. The forests are coming alive with rebels. Our return may be troubled."

Sergeant Black ordered his troops to fall into a two-by-two column on the road.

Smith's regulars mixed with the sergeant's soldiers.

"Not much resistance in Concord," Lieutenant Colonel Smith said, "but I suspect the local minutemen[1] are amassing along the Boston Road. Stay alert."

"Forward! March!" Sergeant Black yelled, and the company trudged off toward North Bridge.

They hadn't gone more than a hundred yards when shots were heard. Muskets were raised in readiness. The sergeant signaled the company to separate and move along the perimeter of the road, instead of down the

---

1   **Minutemen,** forerunner of present-day National Guardsmen pledged to serve at a moment's notice. They were organized before the American Revolution began, gained military training through periodic exercises, wore uniforms or an identifying logo, and were supervised by militarily trained officers. Recruits came from all walks of life and were promoted based on experience and training.

middle. Then, from around the curve, soldiers came running, stumbling, waving their muskets. Several appeared to have torn their cross belt, which allowed their red coats to fly open and cartridge pouches to trail behind them. And, dashing behind the frightened, confused company of Redcoats, Captain Walter Laurie, whom Lieutenant Colonel Smith had put in charge that morning to guard North Bridge, was waving his sword and trying to catch up.

"Rebels crossed North Bridge!" one of the men cried. "Takin' cover on the hills, those damned colonials are!"

"Drummer! Beat to quarters," Lieutenant Colonel Smith howled. He yanked the reins of his horse. As it reared, he brandished his sword and began waving it over his head. "Captain Laurie, have your men come to order!"

With the rat-tat-tat of the drum, Sergeant Black's and Captain Laurie's shouts, and the lieutenant colonel's sword flashing about, the disorder calmed.

"Fall into ranks an' stand your ground!" Sergeant Black yelled.

Lieutenant Colonel Smith lowered the sword, attained control of his horse, and galloped to the center of the company of soldiers. "Captain Laurie, take control of your men. Have a patrol of fifteen flank the road to the right. Sergeant Black, send some of your men along the left flank." Smith trotted his horse to the middle of the road. "The rest of you men follow behind me. I believe we are going to have a tough go ahead."

"Break rank!" Black yelled and motioned his men to the left side of the road. "Stay alert! Mind what you have been trained for."

CHAPTER 3

Wednesday, April 19, 1775

Sergeant Black pushed his cap back and scratched his forehead. As he passed less than a hundred yards from North Bridge, the sergeant and his men flanking the road came upon corpses of their comrades who were killed during the skirmish at the bridge. Several of his troop yelled to scare away flocks of crows that were congregating near the fallen soldiers. Black stopped, bent down, and examined the body of a young recruit. When he rolled the corpse over, he gasped. "My god! What a grotesque sight." The musket ball had blown away part of the man's face. Sergeant Black straightened and swallowed hard. "Fellow was no more than eighteen years old."

The sergeant turned, looked toward North Bridge, and saw a group of militiamen on the far side. They were watching him and the scatter of British soldiers tromping eastward through the grassy, muddy morass. Some of the colonials had shouldered their muskets. Others had their gun barrels pointed skyward. They were out of range. After a moment the colonials turned and headed up the road toward Concord.

Sergeant Black continued to observe the militiamen[2] until they went out of sight around a curve. Unknowingly his fingers began to fondle the metal cross that hung around his neck. He trudged on after his men through the mire covered by brush and knee-deep weeds. "Goddamn," he growled when he stepped into a ditch and the water poured over the top of his boot. Snowmelt and recent spring rains had turned the fields to quagmires. He shook his head and glanced to the rear. *I don't understand these colonials. Like pesky mosquitoes they are. If they continue, they'll start a war that they cannot possibly win. Our regiment is only a speck in the forces of Great Britain—a fragment of the mightiest army in the world—and our navy controls the oceans. There's no way in hell that these rebels can win. Why don't they just tolerate King George's rules—stop the bloodshed and live peaceably. If they continue, I'll shoot the next rebel bastard that attacks any of my men…*

The pounding hooves of Lieutenant Colonel Smith's horse ended Sergeant Black's vexing thoughts. "Sergeant!" the lieutenant colonel yelled. "Call your men in from the flank. Have them fall into rank on the road. There's a narrow bridge ahead we have to cross."

"Aye, Sir." Black waved his right arm toward the road several times as he simultaneously shouted, "Fall in! On the road."

His men slogged toward the road, across several flooded ditches, and fell into two columns. They were quickly joined by Captain Laurie's troops, who had trudged in from the fields to the south. Reorganized, the regiment began its return toward Boston at a more hurried pace.

When Lieutenant Colonel Smith's expeditionary force had left Boston the night before, it contained seven hundred men. Though Captain

---

2   **Militiamen** were militarily untrained able-bodied citizens, who rarely wore military uniforms, and were led by a charismatic, somewhat more experienced individual who was identified by some military rank. They comprised the **Militia,** which was the whole of able-bodied citizens declared by law as being subject to call to military service as needed to protect their domain from jeopardy.

Walter Laurie's company had lost a few men at the North Bridge encounter, the lieutenant colonel's contingent appeared to be a formidable red line that stretched about three-quarters of a mile along the road. Upon reaching the narrow bridge that crossed a small stream, and with a daunting colonial militia amassing behind, Lieutenant Colonel Smith realized it would take his troops too long to safely move across the bridge. He commanded the column to fall in, three abreast.

The colonial militia began shooting irregularly and inefficiently from a distance. Most of their shots flew over the heads of the British troops or to their sides. But as the colonials came within range, their shots hit their mark, killing and wounding several near the tail end of the Redcoat infantry. When the last of Lieutenant Colonel Smith's regiment, who were being led by Sergeant Black, crossed the bridge, they turned and returned fire. This caused the militiamen to retreat into the surrounding forests. The sergeant's men maintained their position until the British expeditionary regiment had distanced itself a few hundred yards ahead.

"Catch up with our company!" Sergeant Black shouted, waving his arm down the road. "Stay low. Widen the distance between yourselves. Watch your backs." The sergeant and two nearby men knelt. They kept their muskets trained on the bridge until the retreating men moved out of musket range. Then the defenders carefully raised to a stooped position and stealthily made their way toward the vacating regiment.

Within a mile, the Redcoats encountered another bridge. They crossed it without incident. But ahead, a quarter of a mile, the Boston Road curved north around the base of a forested ridge, and birds could be seen darting and flitting about the limbs. The birds' disturbance alerted the soldiers. Though still out of range, they became cautious and moved warily. Some stopped. Checked their muskets. As they moved closer to the ridge, jets of orange fire and white smoke spurted from behind trees and boulders from all levels of the meadows and knolls. The soldiers dove for whatever cover they could find.

From about two hundred yards to the rear, Sergeant Black heard the shooting and saw Lieutenant Colonel Smith's horse rear, twist its head to the left, and, with the lieutenant colonel tight in the saddle, gallop into a field across the road out of musket range. He heard the lieutenant colonel shout, "Charge!" Then the men at the head of the column, about three hundred of them, yelled and dashed forward, up the slope, their guns blazing toward the forest.

Minutemen and local militia, hiding behind trees, boulders, and rock piles, held their ground and responded with full force. Lead balls whizzed through the air, ricocheted off boulders, thudded into trees, and thunked into the bodies of the charging Redcoats. Wounded soldiers in the lead twisted, snapped backward, and fell. The men behind them jumped for cover. Both sides kept firing. A pallor of smoke rose from the roadside and the weald.

"Flank those bastards!" Sergeant Black shrieked at his men. "Our mates need help!"

Rather than charge in a solid reddened line, the sergeant and his patrol scattered into the field, which ran to the base of a knoll. They dashed toward the field, swinging or holding their muskets high. When they got within range, they dropped to the ground and took cover behind bounders, log piles, and in ditches. They began to shoot with accuracy, hitting several of the closest militiamen. Several colonials hiding in trees were shot and fell just as the sudden sound of a drumbeat began to fill the air.

"What in the hell is going on?" Sergeant Black shouted. "Retreat is being signaled!" Dumbfounded at this command, he watched as the attacking Redcoat company withdrew out of the meadow to the road while the colonial rebels broke their cover and ran up the hill. "Bloody hell! We've gotten the upper hand. Why did that idiot call a retreat?"

In the few moments of confusion, the shooting stopped.

"Let's get to the road," the sergeant called to his men, "and get our arses back to Boston."

Sergeant Black's troops began scuttling from the field just as the colonial militia regrouped again on the hillside. The sergeant looked back and saw the ragtag horde of militiamen swarming, like angry ants, down toward the retreating Redcoat company.

"Damnit. Form an attack line!" Sergeant Black yelled, "We're outnumbered. Start shootin'."

Fortunately for the sergeant's men, a rock wall lined the south side of the road. They didn't have to defend from an unprotected line. Instead, the men jumped behind the wall and began firing on the approaching onslaught.

Sergeant Black crawled to the stone fence, removed his hat, and scrunched down. He dragged himself to the edge of the wall and glanced over it toward the hillside. Several musket balls ricocheted nearby, sending rocky splinters around him. He wiped the dust from his forehead and eyes, and slid down. "Spread out along this fence and shoot at those rebel bastards," he yelled. "Stay down. Crawl toward that ledge." He raised his arm and pointed to the right. "As you move, get up, take a shot. Be careful. Stay low. This wall will cover us till we get to the ledge. The road curves there. Those rebels can't shoot around corners."

Black's company did as commanded. They crawled quickly. Rose up periodically and fired their muskets. Then they'd prostrate themselves on their backsides, reload, flip over, and continue to pop up while they creeped forward behind the cover of the stone wall.

As Sergeant Black moved, he noticed that most of the regiment had reached and negotiated the curve in the road. His men would be safe. This pleased him, but seeing dead and injured soldiers scattered about appalled him. *Goddamn officers, decided not to bring any surgeons. No provisions for wounded. Determined that the colonial militia wouldn't attack. And damn it, they usually didn't. But we've never killed any before.* He crept along the wall. Laid back against it for an instant and shrugged. *What I would not give to be at home at this moment, in the barn with father, grooming our horses.*

Suddenly he heard a cry for help. Looking in the direction from where the call came, he saw a wounded soldier sitting in a soggy depression on the far side of the road. The young man was trying to staunch the blood oozing from the side of his waist.

The sergeant raised himself slightly, glanced behind and up the rise. He looked ahead at his men. Most had reached the ledge and were protected. No one was shooting. He started to inch across the road on his knees, using his left hand for support and balance. The stock of the musket on his right side, which he gripped tightly by the barrel, scraped over the gravel as he moved. When he reached the shallow gulley, he warily stood and started to descend toward the wounded man. Within seconds after a musket was fired from the nearby coppice, Sergeant Black felt a hot, stinging pain in his right shoulder. His body twisted and snapped back. His weapon flew out of his hand as he began to fall. A second shot grazed the side of his forehead. Another hit his side. Then the pain came. It felt as if a mass of hornets were stinging his back. Impulsively he flung his hand toward the wounds. His thumb caught the choker that held the talisman hanging around his neck. Feeling a tightness, his eyes closed, but jagged, lightning-like flashes blazed about behind his eyelids. The thought, *I am dying*, raced through his mind. *I will never see my England again.* The flares joined, then smoothed and spiraled counter-clockwise to a central point as he fell. The light blipped off to total darkness when his body hit the muddy ground.

CHAPTER 4

Saturday, April 19, 1975

The little boy heard a muted *whoomp* behind him, turned, and ran across the road.

"Mommy, Mommy, there's a soldier lying in the ditch! I think he's hurt."

Sergeant Black heard the child's voice; it sounded some distance away. Disoriented and distraught, he raised his head and curled his body to the right, compressing his shoulder. Sharp pain made him wince. He continued to force himself to roll onto his back, which caused his head to hurt and throb. He pushed himself to a sitting position, then moved his left arm toward the agonizing wounds. His hand scraped the painful area. Then he reached to his forehead where a musket ball grazed his head. It felt cold and slimy. *Damn! Fell into a muddy ditch.* He opened his eyes. The eye-fog blurred his vision. After a couple of blinks, it cleared, enabling him to resolve the position of his outstretched legs. He tightened the leg muscles and then raised his knees. *My clothes are wet and muddied.* The sergeant glanced around. *Hell. There's no mud or water. I'm sitting on grass…an' it's dry.*

"Mommy, Mommy, come quick. He's moving."

Still feeling as if he were in a dream, Sergeant Black blinked his eyes, kept his head low, and took inventory of the immediate surroundings.

Where is the injured soldier I tried to help? There should not be a child on a battlefield. Several muffled musket shots startled him. He raised his head and looked toward the hillside. Then he saw a boy of about eight years of age standing on the brink of the ditch looking down at him.

The boy jumped back when he realized he had been seen. Then a brunette woman appeared next to the boy. She put her hand on his shoulder.

Sergeant Black grabbed for the barrel of his musket, thinking to use it as a brace, but it wasn't there. He shrugged, worked himself into a stable position, and sat up with shoulders drooped.

The woman noticed the blood on Black's face and the reddish-brown gore that stained the right side and shoulder of his coat. "Please stay where you are," the woman said. "My husband went for help."

"Madam," Black said in a muddled voice. "There's a battle going on. The hillside behind you is full of colonial militia and you are in their line of fire."

"Indeed. There is a battle going on. It is on the green." The woman looked up and to the right. "Boys over there are having a little war…"

What the bloody hell is going on? The sergeant tried to move forward, but with each move the pain intensified. He pushed his right hand onto the ground and slumped to the side.

The woman twisted and looked behind her around the bend in the road. "There is no one at Bloody Angle. As I said, they're playing their wargames on the green. There's no one shooting over here." She glanced back at Sergeant Black, who was doddering where he sat.

The woman started to descend the grade toward him. "You appear badly injured. Please sit still before you pass out and exacerbate your injuries. Something terrible has happened to you. Help is coming. Please sit."

Totally confused and feeling nauseous, Sergeant Black relaxed and slowly lay back. He raised his head, then lowered it and exhaled deeply. *What the hell is going on? Where am I? Where's my regiment?* He shivered. His muscles tensed. Then he perceived a rhythmic sound that grew louder. As the sound intensified, he heard metallic creaks and squeaks mixing with the roar. Then a loud, gravel-scraping noise brought the thunder to a stop. Black glanced up and saw only a cloud of dust rising from the roadway. *Where the bloody hell am I?*

Bewildered, Black closed his eyes and slowly shook his head. His muscles began to clench tighter, until he realized the woman was next to him. He looked up, gasped, and tried to skid himself backward. *My god! She wears only a corset and an under blouse.* Dismayed at her near nakedness, he recoiled and blinked his eyes.

Towering beside him stood a lean, healthy woman devoid of "decent" clothes and what Sergeant Black considered nothing but underclothes. She finished pouring some fluid from a transparent bottle onto a cloth and stooped next to him. She moved the cloth toward his face.

Black snapped his head to the side.

"It's okay. I'm not going to hurt you. It's only water. I'm going to try to clean the blood and dirt from your face." She gently put the wet cloth on Black's cheek and began to wipe. She could feel his face tense.

He pushed her hand away. "You're unclothed! Where are your garments?"

The woman was taken aback. She dropped to her knees and straightened her back.

From above, Sergeant Black heard what sounded like boots stomping on the road, and then he saw several men hurrying down toward him and the woman. The two descending men wore British army uniforms. *Officers*, Black guessed. Three other men were dressed in the garb of colonial militiamen, and another wore basic colonial clothing. Narrow-brim tricornes covered the heads of three and one wore a cap Black had never seen before. No one carried a musket, but one of the British officers held a white, leather satchel with a large red cross printed on its side. The sergeant didn't recognize this insignia.

As the woman rose and started to ascend to the roadway, the officer with the satchel dropped to his knees. He reached into the bag and pulled out a pair of large scissors. "Going to have to cut away your coat to expose the wound," he said.

Identifying the shears as a weapon and instrument that could destroy his regiment coat, Sergeant Black swung out his good arm. But the second officer caught and gently restrained Black's arm. Confused and combative, the sergeant straightened and groaned, "I'll remove it. My commanders will charge me six months recompence if the jacket is destroyed." Black twisted about, moaned, and squinted as he attempted to remove the coat by pulling his right arm from the sleeve. The pain in his shoulder intensified as he bent and, with the aid of the kneeling officer, slipped the appendage free.

"Yes, yes. Of course," the officer said. "It is a fine piece of tailoring. Your coat can be easily cleaned, and the tears and bullet holes repaired." The British officer took the red military jacket and handed it to another fellow standing nearby who was also dressed in a British officer's garb. "Take good care of this man's coat."

Fellow's gentle, Black thought as his stressed body began ease. *Believe this man may be the company surgeon that has come with reinforcements.* "You may cut off my shirt," Black said.

When the tip of the scissors touched his skin, the sergeant's body tensed. The officer worked to keep his patient calm. So rather than unbutton the shirt, he slowly cut the blood-soaked portion of the shirt and sleeve away. As he did, his voice softened. "I see you are wearing the uniform of a sergeant. My name is Andrew Gorski, Sergeant, and I live in Boston." Andrew removed the bloodied portion of Black's shirt, laid it on the ground, and looked into Black's eyes. "And whom do I have the privilege of serving, Sergeant?"

Black gritted his teeth and straightened. He recognized the uniform Andrew wore had the designations of lieutenant. "Sergeant Noland Black, grenadier in His Majesty's Tenth Regiment, Lieutenant Gorski, Sir." He tried to raise his wounded arm but couldn't. "Sorry, Sir, I am not able to salute."

"I do not warrant a salute, Sergeant Black," Andrew said. "I am a physician, but not a military officer. Where are you stationed?"

Gorski's latter statement confused Black. He shifted his chin to the left. "Charlestown," he mumbled softly. "The fifth barrack. Where the Mystic and Charles Rivers meet."

Andrew Gorski scratched his head. "Will you tell me who your commander is?"

"Lieutenant Colonel Francis Smith."

Dr. Gorski tore open a packet containing an alcohol swab and began wiping away the crusted blood from around Black's wounds. The sergeant winced from the chill and sting of the alcohol.

"Besides the bullet holes in your shoulder and biceps, you have many small punctures that penetrate your back…" Dr. Gorski said. "It's as if you were also hit with buckshot. Those wounds need to be examined. Any imbedded pellets or debris will have to be removed. I don't have the equipment nor the sterile conditions to do that here. You will have to be taken to a hospital." He turned and spoke to the man who was holding Black's regiment coat. "John, this man needs immediate attention. The jeep has a two-way radio. Call the police watching the reenactment. Have them call for an ambulance."

John handed Sergeant Black's coat to one of the minutemen nearby and stepped away.

Black watched John turn and run up toward the road. *What's a jeep? What's a two-way radio?*

"On its way," John yelled as he ran back.

Andrew returned his attention to Black. "I know this sounds impossible, but the only real battle ever fought on this road was years ago when the colonials attacked the British troops returning from Concord and Lexington." Gorski scratched his head. "How did you get shot?"

Black took a deep breath. "Was crawling across the road to aid one of my wounded men, I attempted to stand, and that's when a rebel's musket shot found its mark. The devils were hiding on the hillside."

Andrew gasped, furrowed his brow. "What day is today, Sergeant Black?"

Lowering his head, Black raised his left hand and rubbed his forehead. He then slowly looked up, confused. "Wednesday, the nineteenth day of April, in the year of our Lord, 1775…"

A couple of the men standing nearby heard the sergeant's answer and snickered.

Andrew's eyes widened and a grin crossed his face. "Right," he said. "Today, my friend, you are exactly two hundred years out of date." He looked up at the men standing by him. "Bring down the stretcher. I believe our injured soldier is hallucinating. John, have our registrar check the list of reenactors for a Noland Black. I suspect this fellow is more badly damaged than we think."

"What's he doing here anyway?" John asked as the other four men scampered to where the jeep was parked. "Our reenactment is over a quarter mile away. Maybe someone had a ball in their musket." He scratched his head, then shook it. "Do you suppose a musket shot could travel so far?"

"Don't think so," Dr. Gorski replied. "Perhaps some boys in the forest near Bloody Angle were trying to poach squirrels."

"Yeah, maybe. Today's Saturday. Kids are out of school."

Dr. Gorski looked west, down the road. "Aah. Don't think so. Parking lot's been empty all morning. Don't believe anyone's poaching in the area." He glanced around and saw the men bringing the stretcher.

Sergeant Black also heard the group approaching, raised his head, and twisted toward the sound. He recognized the canvas slung between two long poles for what it was. *Aye. They're bringing a litter.*

"Okay, guys," Dr. Gorski said. "Pretend like you're rescuing a fallen man in the field. But! Be careful with this man. He's really injured."

Still totally bewildered, Sergeant Black stretched his legs forward. But, when the men gathered around him, he felt his muscles tense as his rescuers tried to help him onto the stretcher. "Belay that," he grunted. "I can get myself on the litter." With the aid of his left hand, he shifted next to the stretcher, flipped his buttocks onto it, and lay back. Then he raised his head and glanced around. *Where's the man I tried to aid?* "Did you rescue the other?" he asked.

"There are no other wounded soldiers or people here," Dr. Gorski said. "You're the only one." He gestured for the men to move up the rise. "Get him to the road. John, bring my bag."

While the litter bearers lifted the stretcher, one of them winked. Though Sergeant Black didn't see the bearer do so, he did overhear him ask, "Think this guy is for real? Come from the past? Does have a strong British accent…"

"Oh yeah," another gibed in a quirky, deep voice, as the litter bearers mounted the rim of the ditch. "Strange things happenin' around here."

"Yeah, sure," a third said. "We probably crossed into the Twilight Zone." Then the litter bearers chuckled and began to hum and whistle a haunting tune the sergeant had never heard before.

Before the litter bearers placed Sergeant Black down on the road, he noticed the woman and child standing next to a man wearing similar skimpy clothing. All were standing next to a pair of bicycles. One had a child-carrier over the rear wheel. *Velocipedes. Saw such conveyances in France.* The sergeant's mind raced. *Am I in France? But no one is speaking French.* He attempted to focus his eyes on the bicycles. *Those velocipedes are not made of wood.* Then the sergeant saw Andrew walk toward the couple.

From where he lay, Sergeant Black could only see the little boy clutching the leg of the man beside the woman. However, he could hear the man ask, "Is the fellow okay?"

"Yes and no," Andrew said. "He's been shot and seems to be hallucinating. I called for an ambulance to transport him to Mass General Health Clinic in Charlestown. It's the closest to where we are. The clinic doesn't have an emergency room, but there are doctors there that can take care of gunshot wounds. By the way, my name is Dr. Andrew Gorski. I'm a physician at Mass General. Your son found the man, did he not?"

"Good to meet you, Dr. Gorski. I'm Jim Cooper," the man said, "my wife, Sandra, and son, Tommy." Jim placed his hand on Tommy's shoulder. "Yes, Tommy did indeed find the fellow."

Dr. Gorski frowned and bit his lip. "I'd like to thank you for informing us. If you don't mind, I want to ask you a few questions."

"Yes. Of course. Sandra and I don't mind. We bicycle this road every weekend and nothing like this has ever happened before. Is he one of your reenactors?"

"He did give us a name, Sergeant Noland Black," Gorski said. "Says he's with some British regiment that was being attacked by colonial rebels. But his injuries may be playing havoc with his brain. I don't recognize him as one of our reenactors."

Sergeant Black nervously shifted about on the stretcher. *Bloody hell, I'm no actor. My company was attacked. We're in a bloody battle. Where is my company? Where's my regiment? Where am I?*

⌇

Dr. Gorski's eyes locked on Jim Cooper's. "Do you know of anyone by the name of Noland Black?"

"Never heard of anyone by that name," Jim said. He nodded toward Sandra. "She knows many folks in Concord. That's where we live." He glanced at Sergeant Black. "Saw his face, though it was bloodied…" He shook his head. Didn't recognize him either." He glanced at his wife. "Honey, ever hear of this fellow or see him around town?"

Sandra raised her eyelids and shook her head.

"Hear anyone shooting around Bloody Angle?" Dr. Gorski asked.

"No. Only the shots you guys made earlier."

Dr. Gorski looked down at the boy. "Hi, Tommy. Hear you had a little excitement this morning, didn't you? You did a great job finding the injured soldier. What made you cross the road and look into the ditch?"

The little boy pulled closer to his father.

"It's okay," Jim said. "Tell Dr. Gorski how you found the man."

The boy relaxed his grasp on his father's leg, straightened, and smiled. "We stopped our bicycles, 'cause Daddy wanted to look at them little yellow flowers over there on the hill—"

"Daffodils," Jim interrupted. "First flowers of spring. They're a few weeks early. Go on, Tommy. Tell the good doctor what you saw."

Tommy stepped away from his father, clasped his hands, and shyly looked up at Dr. Gorski. "Bright light. Then a boom. I crossed the road to see. And, in that ditch, there he was just layin'. Not movin'. Looked hurt. I called Mommy. When she come, she looks scared. She called Daddy. Tol' him to get some help."

"You didn't see anyone else around?"

"Nope."

Dr. Gorski shrugged. "The injured man doesn't seem to have any recollection of what happened, except that someone here shot him when he was trying to help an injured colleague. The sergeant thinks he was shot by the colonial militia; he called them rebels. As you can see, there are no other injured or dead men around here; no one else close by except visitors and reenactors. And they're quite a distance away. It's been exactly, to the date, two hundred years since any battle has occurred here. We have no idea who Mr. Noland Black is or how he got here, or who shot him."

Dr. Gorski's interrogation ended as the siren of the approaching ambulance became apparent.

Dr. Gorski's friend, John, sidled next to him and whispered, "No one by the name of Noland Black is on our list of reenactors."

The strange, shrill wailing of the siren, getting louder and louder, triggered Sergeant Black's muscles to again tighten. He furiously began to twist about and grope for the sides of the stretcher to rise and bring himself to a sitting position. "What the bloody hell is that?"

"Relax, man! It's only an ambulance," one of the bearers called out.

Black snapped around toward the sound and saw, roaring toward him like a monster from hell, a shining, white box with flashing red eyes and trailing a cloud of dust. He jumped up off the stretcher and onto his feet. The adrenaline surge locked his thighs and calves. He stood erect, combative, ready to face this screaming demon. His arms flailed about, trying to grip a weapon. Not finding one, he whirled and fell.

Hearing the commotion occurring around Sergeant Black's litter, Dr. Gorski spun around and said, "I believe I'm needed. Thank you for your help." He quickly shook Jim Cooper's hand, nodded to his wife, patted Tommy's head, and hurried to Sergeant Black's side to assist John and the two litter bearers who were trying to subdue the sergeant.

The sergeant's arms lashed about as the litter bearers tried to hold him down. One of Black's fists smacked the leg of a bearer. The man cried, dropped to the ground, and clutched his calf.

"My bag!" Andrew shouted.

John dropped it next to his friend, bent over, and opened it.

"Hold him down." Dr. Gorski reached into the bag, pulled out a syringe, and flipped it into his left hand. He reached back into the satchel, removed a vial, examined it, and stuck the syringe needle through the vial's cap. Filling the syringe and pulling it out, he pushed the needle into Sergeant Black's left bicep. "He'll relax in a moment. Keep a hold on him. Don't want him to injure himself more."

The sergeant struggled, but felt his muscles weaken as several other men in blue uniforms lifted him onto a gurney. When they started to push him toward the shining, white monster, his muscles momentarily tensed. He felt himself being jostled about but could not respond. He noticed that Dr. Gorski was on one side of him and John on the other. Then the daylight dimmed. He heard a muffled thump as the ambulance door closed, then Sergeant Black's world went dark.

CHAPTER 5

Saturday, April 19, 1975

Sergeant Noland Black began to regain consciousness as the ambulance approached the clinic. Though he heard the siren wail and its sound diminish, he remained in a dreamlike state. The ambulance came to a stop in the back of the clinic. The driver came around and yanked the rear doors open. Dr. Andrew Gorski and his friend John rose. They followed the four individuals dressed in white lab coats, who entered the ambulance and removed the gurney upon which the sergeant lay.

Noland opened his eyes as he was jostled about during the exit from the ambulance. Then he felt a surge, then the sensation of drifting forward. He turned his head to the side and blinked. A misty vision of a pair of robust spirits appeared to be moving next to him along a vaporous, whitish tunnel, but a periodic flash of light from above blinded him. Noland felt his body shift and then a jolt, as if the forward end of the cot hit a barrier. But the cot upon which he lay continued to move as if it had passed through a solid wall. Anxiety stiffened the sergeant's body, but he had little control when he tried to raise his arms.

Beyond the obstacle, the cot stopped. A brilliant, silvery brightness invaded Sergeant Black's vision. He blinked. Then more angels seemed to surround him. When one or another closed in to look at him, he saw only the eyes. A mask covered the lower portion of the face. Other ghostly images appeared to move randomly around him.

"The patient is getting tense," he heard one of the spirits say. "Why did you bring him here? The clinic doesn't have an emergency room or an operating room."

Then Sergeant Black heard Dr. Gorski say, "Taking this fellow downtown would have created too much commotion. I'll explain later. For now, please tend to him."

A female voice said, "We'll have to work in this room. It's not an OR, but it has monitoring instruments. Remove what clothing he's wearing. Administer a mild anesthetic. Got to get that buckshot out of him, before infection sets in."

No sooner were the words spoken, when a group of the apparitions moved next to him. He tried to tighten his muscles. A muffled groan escaped his mouth when his trousers were removed. A sudden chill surrounded the sergeant's body. But then he saw one of the spirits snap open a sheet and cover the lower half of his body. Several others attached objects to his chest and ankles. When these spirits finished, Noland began to hear a rhythmic beep. He flinched when something stung his left bicep. He lay back for a moment. The beeping continued.

His eyes began to clear, and he recognized the image standing over him. *A human female. "A healer?"* She had short, auburn hair and gray-greenish eyes. He squirmed as she bent toward him and placed something cold on his chest. She moved this object around his chest, then paused for a moment, looked at him, and smiled. He tensed. Then the woman looked up. "Roll him on to his left side." Noland twisted his head and saw a rack of gray boxes with blinking lights, glowing numbers, and moving lines. He noticed that the numbers changed, and the moving lines spiked with each beep he heard. He twisted his head back toward the woman. The healer was staring at his back and continued to touch different parts of him with the cold thing. "Attach the IV…" he heard the healer say. "Put him to sleep. Those pellets have to be removed."

Sleep? IV? What in the hell are they doing to me? Noland felt his left hand being secured. "Huhh," he groaned when he felt the sharp sting penetrate a vein and a momentary burn spurt into his blood. The fingers of his left hand stiffened. He recoiled and, within a moment, his mind drifted back into bewilderment and oblivion. Again, his world went black.

"Dr. Morris," Dr. Andrew Gorski said. "Being only a GP, I have very little surgical experience. You're a surgeon. I'll be happy to assist."

"It's warm in here. We're not in an OR," Dr. Carol Morris, a confident woman in her mid-thirties, said. Irritated by the perspiration on her brow, she motioned for the attending nurse to pat it away. Strands of her auburn hair, exposed below her surgical cap, covered her ears. She nodded and gave Andrew a serious look. Her eyes, emphasized by the white mask covering the lower portion of her face, engaged Andrew's. "Yes…though this man's injuries are not severe and the surgery minor, it will take some delicate probing not to damage more tissue than the shots did. He seemed to be hit by not only pellets, but also by a mess of other debris. It's as though whoever shot him used not only musket balls, but also bits of gravel—like buckshot. How did this happen?" She turned to Mia, her attending nurse. "Please swab my brow."

"Don't really know," Dr. Gorski said. "Colonial patriots, if they didn't have sufficient shot, packed their muskets with whatever they could push down the barrel. When we found this man, he identified himself as a Redcoat sergeant by the name of Noland Black. He told me he was shot while trying to help an injured man. His company he said was being attacked by a bunch of rebels."

Dr. Carol Morris turned and ordered one of the resident assistants to wheel in the X-ray machine. "That junk imbedded in his tissue will be easier to find with a couple of photos." She looked over at Dr. Gorski. "Did someone in your group shoot this man?"

"No! None of the reenactors load their muskets with shot. Sergeant Black was found several hundred yards from where the reenactors were, but he was wearing the uniform of a British military soldier. He was found by some bicyclers." Dr. Gorski shook his head slightly. "The only time reenactors fully load a musket is when they are in a marksman competition. And then, the load is a lead ball, not refuse."

"Have you notified the authorities?"

"Haven't yet. This fellow is unusual." Dr. Gorski scratched his head and adjusted his face mask. "He's a special case. I don't want you to jump to conclusion about his mental conditions when I tell you about him."

Dr. Morris glanced at Andrew.

He saw her eyelids rise.

"You're saying he may be a nutcase, Dr. Gorski? Perhaps he *is* from your reenactment group? Maybe he energized himself with a shot of 'Jack' or something stronger before trying to join your troop?"

"No! When we found him, he was in no way inebriated. Except for his injuries, he was acting perfectly normal. Though a shot appeared to have grazed his head. That may have caused something…" Dr. Gorski paused, pursed his lips. "But here's the kicker—"

"Excuse me, Doctor," Dr. Morris interrupted as she accepted the X-ray photos from her nurse. She attached them to the lightbox on the wall and scanned them. "He's got two clean-looking musket balls. One imbedded in the right bicep and the other in the teres major. Caught a lot of debris in the bicep, teres, and intraspinatus muscles…" She pointed out several larger fragment and pellets. "Luckily none of that junk penetrated any major arteries. Few pieces are lodged in the upper backside intercostal muscles, but none broke any ribs. This guy was shot in the back a least three times. Forceps!" Dr. Morris accepted the forceps, bent down toward Sergeant Black, and began to remove the first musket ball lodged in his bicep muscle. It clanked loudly when she dropped it into the pan Dr. Gorski was holding. "What's the kicker? Is he a nutcase?"

Dr. Gorski saw Dr. Morris's cheeks and eyes raise. "Hmm." He cocked his head to the side. "When I asked him what day it was, he answered, 'April Nineteenth, 1775...'"

"Huh?" Dr. Morris took a slow, deep breath. "You're saying this man is from the past? A British soldier, who was involved in the attack on Concord and Lexington? That happened two hundred years ago."

"Could be. What I've heard and seen, seems to suggest that. This is why I don't want to bring this matter to the attention of the authorities just yet. Getting them involved will alert the media. You've seen it on television, an alien from space or from another time appears, and *wow*, all hell breaks loose. The police and media are relentless. They'd be all over the poor fellow. I certainly don't want him psychologically destroyed. He's already showing signs of major cultural shock."

Dr. Gorski nervously moved from Dr. Morris's right side to her left. The pan he held clattered as the musket ball rolled around it. "Today is the bicentennial of the first shot fired that began the war that won America's independence. Our reenactment is part of the celebration at the Minute Man National Park. We found Sergeant Black where the road makes the Bloody Angle bend—a couple hundred yards from where the reenactment was taking place—at about the time the British regiments were, back on April Nineteenth, 1775, marching down Boston Road on their retreat to Boston. And they were indeed being attacked. When we came upon him, he was confused and appeared overwhelmed." Dr. Gorski paused. "As we carried him from the ditch where we found him, he saw a bicycle. Called it a velocipede. That's what the French named the two-wheeled contraption they invented in the early eighteenth century. When the ambulance arrived, he become frightened and belligerent. I gave him a sedative..."

"Good god!" Dr. Morris dropped the second musket ball she removed from the sergeant into a pan Dr. Gorski held. "Do you think this is for real?"

"Don't know." Dr. Gorski shrugged. "His words and some circumstantial evidence seem to point to that possibility."

"From what you have told me, it does indeed." Dr. Morris continued to concentrate on removing the other bits of debris from the sergeant's back and shoulder muscles and tick off their location on the X-ray. When she finished, she turned to Mia and said, "Please swab the blood from his back and shoulder."

"I plan to have the musket balls and the shot debris analyzed." Dr. Gorski jiggled the pan holding the bullets and fragments. "We have his red military jacket, his trousers, and several other items he had on him when we found him. I want some expert to examine all these objects for authenticity before I make that call. I'll need a lot of solid evidence to verify we have a live British soldier from the past among us or I too may be considered a nutcase. This is crazy, but I've got a gut feeling that this man may have somehow been shot through time."

"Finished," Dr. Morris said as she stitched up the last of the larger wounds. She turned to Mia. "You can bandage the wounds on the shoulder and back, give him a shot of amoxicillin and one for tetanus. Then have a couple of male nurses remove what clothes he's wearing and put him in a hospital gown." She looked at Dr. Gorski and began to remove her gloves. "Well, Doctor, you've created an interesting quandary, one that has some difficult consequences. Not notifying the police of a gunshot wound could jeopardize your career. Let's hope your secret can be contained and your assessment is correct. But once the media finds out, they'll have a field day with you and the sergeant." Dr. Morris removed her mask. "When he awakes, we'll get him into a private room where I'll post Mia to watch over him. She's extremely loyal and can keep a secret. I'll look in on him and I expect you will too, Dr. Gorski. Now you need to gather some 'solid evidence,' as you put it." Dr. Morris threw her gloves into the medical waste container, looked up at Gorski with raised eyelids. "That evidence needs to be strong. Time travel is still science fiction."

"I hear you."

"Oh! You should know, I have to record the procedure I just preformed and note whom to charge. Do you think the sergeant has medical insurance?" Dr. Morris grinned.

"Thank you for taking care of my patient. You can bill me for his expenses." Dr. Gorski removed his gloves and mask. He raised the pan containing the musket balls and shot fragments and glanced at them. "Can I use your office to make a few calls?"

Dr. Morris nodded. "The hour is getting late. I'll check on the sergeant's recovery while you make your phone calls. I assume you'll return in the morning?"

"I will. Maybe I will have some answers by then." Dr. Gorski left.

About an hour after Dr. Gorski departed, Dr. Morris looked in on Sergeant Black. Mia, her attending nurse, told her the patient had awakened from anesthesia, seemed a bit agitated, but then fell back to sleep.

"He needs to be watched during the night," Morris said. "He should sleep through the night. But make sure I'm notified if anything should happen. I'll be back here at eight in the morning."

Mia nodded. "You can count on me, Dr. Morris."

CHAPTER 6

Sunday, April 20, 1975

Sergeant Black slept peacefully through most of the night, but his sleep became fitful. He'd awakened momentarily, thrashed about, grunted, then fell back to sleep. Toward morning his dreams became nightmarish, more disturbing, causing him to become frantic. In his delirium the air seemed viscous as he crawled across the road toward the blurry image of the wounded soldier lying in the gulley. It felt as if he were fighting against a mysterious force, because as he crept forward, his movement met with greater and greater resistance. He could see the soldier's image. But it seemed to be shrouded in a curling mass of smoke. The image waxed and waned the closer he got. Black tried to maintain his focus, but the specter became vignetted, began to glow then faded into the haze. The sergeant felt himself rise to his knees and fan his hands into the vapor. As he crawled to where the injured soldier seemed to lie, the image of a bloody arm stretched toward him from the smokiness. He reached forward to grasp the arm as he started to stand, but he heard a dull pop. Instantly, he felt pain whiz through his shoulder. His right arm swung away from the appendage reaching toward him. His body twisted to the left. Another muffled pop. Then another. His back stung as if being attacked by a swarm of angry bees and the muscles on his right side burned like they had been penetrated by hot pokers. The sergeant felt himself jerk forward. His arms flung about. He rolled onto the grassy morass. Then he felt a pressure on his chest and a tightness gripped his wrists; his hallucination ended.

Mia, who was attending Sergeant Black, had momentarily stepped out of his room to talk to an orderly, a slim, eighteen-year-old by the name of Joel, who was returning the sergeant's red coat. She heard the commotion inside and dashed back into the room. Joel followed. They saw the sergeant's head and torso partially raised and his arms thrashing through the air. Had the gurney's rails not been raised, the patient would have been lying on the floor. She pushed against his chest to force him back to a reclining position. "Call the desk! I need two strong male nurses immediately," Mia commanded, and then cried out as Black's left hand whacked her in the side.

Within moments, two brawny, crewcut men wearing white scrubs dashed into the room. They were followed by a couple of female nurses. The male nurses grabbed Sergeant Black's wrists, pressed his arms to his sides, and quickly belted them to the rails of the gurney.

With her eyes closed and teeth gritted to stifle the pain in her side, Mia continued to press down on the sergeant's chest. She felt his muscles relax and heard him gasp. "Someone call Dr. Morris." She looked at Joel. "Why are you holding that jacket?"

"Yesterday Dr. Gorski told me to take the jacket to be repaired. He said the holes needed sewing up and the jacket needs cleaning. When that was all done, I was to take it to his office. But I hadn't had a chance, 'cause my shift ended. So, I left it hanging in the nurses' station overnight."

"Hang it on one of those folding chairs. It can be taken care of later."

"Yes, ma'am."

Seeing the British red coat Joel hung on the chair, one of the male nurses asked, "He the reenactor that was injured?"

Mia nodded, then asked, "Please leave the room, but stay nearby. He's quiet now. I'll tend to him until Dr. Morris arrives." Mia glanced at the others in the room. "Thank you all for your help. I believe it would be better if you all leave. This patient apparently has some psychological problems. It will be better if the room is quiet when he awakes." She smiled. "Joel, did you call Dr. Morris?"

"Yes," he said from the doorway. "The doctor said she'd be here as soon as she's free."

"Thank you." Mia rubbed her side then moved next to Sergeant Black and adjusted the blanket covering him as everyone left the room. The pain in her side had lessened.

Twenty minutes had passed before Dr. Morris returned to Sergeant Noland Black's room. "How's our patient?" she whispered to Mia.

"He became agitated and began thrashing his arms as he was waking from anesthesia," Mia answered in a low voice. "It seemed as if he were having a nightmare. Lucky the rails were up on the bed or he may have fallen off. The male nurses secured his arms." She looked over at Noland. "He seems to have dozed off."

Noland opened his eyes, turned toward the voices, and recognized Dr. Morris. "I'm not asleep," he mumbled and began to squirm. "Where the bloody hell am I? What is this place? What day is this?" He pulled his arms against the restraints, gasped, and relaxed in frustration.

"Full of questions, aren't you?" Dr. Morris said and turned to Mia. "Go to the kitchen. Have them prepare a hardy breakfast; eggs, toast, bacon, home fries, coffee, and anything else they can toss in. I'll call to tell you when to bring it to the room." Her nurse nodded and exited the room as Dr. Morris walked next to the sergeant's bed. Her grayish eyes focused on him. "I guess I'd have many questions too if I were in your situation. I have one for you. Do you recognize me?"

The sergeant stared back, paused, and then nodded. "You are the 'Healer' who treated my wounds."

"Hmmm," Dr. Morris said. "Healer? You called me a Healer. That is interesting. It's an antiquated word people used to identify medically trained and untrained persons—medicine men, midwives, witches, who supposedly had an ability to cure someone's malady..." She smiled. "There may still be some witches around, medicine men for sure. The American Indians and the Aborigines of other countries believe in them. Today, one needs to be properly educated and have a license to publicly practice any form of medicine. These persons are known as medical doctors, nurses—surgeons and sisters in Great Britain. I'm Dr. Carol Morris, your doctor—or Healer, if you prefer to call me that. The person I sent to get you some food is Mia. She is my attending nurse." She bent down and fingered the straps that restrained Noland. "You seem fairly lucid. Will you remain calm if I remove the straps from your wrists?"

"Aye," he mumbled.

Dr. Morris began to unbuckle the restrains that held the sergeant's arms and as she did, she calmly responded to his questions. "Today is Sunday, the twentieth of April, 1975. You were brought here yesterday with gunshot wounds in your right shoulder, right bicep, and, what appeared to be a scatter of puncture wounds across the right side of your back. From them I removed much detritus. It's as if you were shot with a load of gravel. You are presently in a second-floor outpatient recovery room at Mass General Health Clinic here in Charlestown..."

Noland moved his left arm across his abdomen, clenched his fist, relaxed it, and worked his fingers. "I've not seen a place as this. Not in London or Boston. Bright lumination from the ceiling. Beds with bright metal rails. Soft pillows that smelled clean. No odor of decay. No moaning. No Screaming. A room of warmth and comfort." He paused for moment. Looked around. "A clinic, you say? I have not heard of such a place." He grabbed the bed rails and tried to pull himself to a seating position.

"Do you know what an outpatient is? Have you heard of a dispensary?" Dr. Morris asked as she lowered the rails on the bed.

"Aye. Outpatient. A person with a minor injury. Such a person would go to a dispensary for treatment." The sergeant slowly nodded. "Aye. Dispensary is what you call a clinic."

"Yes." Dr. Morris assisted Noland and readjusted his pillow. "It would be best if you did not exert yourself for a few days; allow your wounds to heal. I'll examine them shortly. Dr. Gorski brought you here to the clinic because he wants to keep you a secret. I'm skeptical of his desire to keep you concealed. He seems to believe you came from the past and, he's trying to prove it. Oh well, we'll see what he comes up with." She put her hand on the sergeant's left shoulder and then stepped away from the bed. "When was the last time you had a good meal?"

"My last…" He scratched his head. "I ate at a tavern owned by a fellow named Wright on the Lexington Road. My company finished searching Concord for weapons. Wright's wife makes a hardy venison stew. Wright brews an ale that tastes much like what comes from the British Isles. My men needed a hardy meal. We faced a twelve-mile march back to our barracks." Noland watched the doctor move to a table near the door and put her hand on a white object from which a tiny red light glowed. "Why does Dr. Gorski want to keep me a secret?"

"The police get excited when someone is treated for gunshot wounds. They're always full of questions, wanting to know how the victim got shot.…" She paused and removed the white object from its carriage. Returning her attention to Noland, Dr. Morris said, "Also, we're not sure where you came from. Getting the police involved creates many complications. Dr. Gorski wants to investigate you. He thinks your accent, appearance, and behavior are unusual." She looked at the object, held it in front of her, pressed some buttons on its face, and raised it to her ear. She paused and glanced in Noland's direction. "You must be quite hungry if your last meal was more than twenty-four hours ago. I know of this tavern where you say you had eaten. Wright's Tavern. It's a historic site, but it's not a restaurant. It is now owned by a religious group who turned it into a place of worship."

Noland stared back and saw a momentary grin cross the doctor's face. His expression didn't change. Dr. Morris's comment about the tavern did not catch his attention, but the object she held to her ear did. "What is that that you hold?"

Rather than answer Sergeant Black, Dr. Morris turned, faced the window, and spoke into the object, though she had heard his question. "This is Dr. Morris. Please ask my nurse to bring up the meal I ordered. Our patient needs food." She then returned her attention to Noland. "Your meal should be here shortly."

The sergeant rearranged himself. "Something to eat would be good. I am hungry."

Rather than return the object to its carriage on the table next to the bed, Dr. Morris held it out in Noland's direction. "To answer your previous question, what I'm holding is the receiver of an instrument called a telephone. The telephone allows a person to communicate with someone else in the world within seconds if they answer the call." She showed Noland the telephone receiver and laid it into his hand.

With an inquisitive expression, he slowly turned the receiver about in his hand, examining the mysterious thing. Inhaling and exhaling slowly.

Dr. Morris pointed to the telephone carriage and explained the touch tone buttons and their function. She slid a finger over the front of its plastic case and the twelve buttons, numbered boldly from one to nine, with zero in the middle of the bottom set of three buttons.

Noland lifted the receiver to his ear, like he saw Dr. Morris do, shook his head, and drew the receiver away, when he heard the buzz of the dial tone, and dropped it. As the receiver slid toward the edge of the bed, Noland attempted to grab it to keep it from falling to the floor. When he did, the back of his hand accidentally hit the keypad. Though he caught the receiver and returned it to his ear as he rolled back onto the bed, the dial tone stopped. As if he had done something wrong, Noland snapped the phone around to the front of himself. Disturbed, his dark marble eyes enlarged. Nervously, he handed the receiver back to Dr. Morris. "The sound I heard, it stopped. Have I damaged it?"

A smile lit her eyes. "I don't think so. The sound you heard is called a dial tone. It means the telephone is ready for use. You must have pressed one of the buttons on the carriage and activated the telephone. Activation ends the dial tone and allows the caller, who punches in the code of the person they are calling, to signal them to answer on their telephone."

Dr. Morris lifted the carriage and held it toward Noland and continued her explanation. "Every telephone has an exclusive set of numbers, a code. To communicate with another person, you have to know that person's telephone number. The number is entered by pressing the proper buttons. When your telephone connects with the one you are calling, that person's telephone will alert them. Then they will answer and the two of you can communicate with each other."

Noland's eyelids raised. He stared at Dr. Morris and extended his hand toward her. "What a magnificent invention!" he blurted. "Can anyone have such a device?"

"Yes…" she paused for a moment, placed the telephone back in Noland's hand and the carriage in his lap.

He accepted it.

"Everyone has a telephone."

He examined it, lifted it, held the receiver to his ear, and again heard the dial tone. "A telephone? I have never seen or heard of such a tool. It must be very new. No one in the regiment has one. Pray tell, has this invention of communication been given to the military?"

"Yes, it has."

Noland's curiosity and excitement grew. "Then General Gage must have one." He held the telephone in front of himself. "I can inform the general of the expedition's disastrous situation. He can then send reinforcements." The sergeant raised the receiver to his ear, heard the dial tone, touched a keypad button, then heard tone end. He scratched his head. "How do I communicate with the general? Get his—what did you call it? Telephone number?"

"Huh? I'm afraid that is not possible." Dr. Morris said. "The telephone was not yet invented in the seventeen hundreds when the British held Boston. It was only invented about a hundred years ago."

"What? My god. What has happened to me? Where am I?" A fit of fear and depression enveloped Black. His hand released the remote telephone. It fell next to him as he seemed to melt into the hospital bed. He closed his eyes. "I have no way to help my regiment."

Dr. Morris moved next to the bed, laid her hand on his forehead, and picked up the telephone. "I'm afraid you and I are thinking in two different time periods. The battle you say you fought, happened two hundred years ago. Either that wound you received to your head, which appears to be minor, is not, and it's disturbing your mind, or, we have another mystery on our hands, which everyone thinks is highly doubtful, that you somehow came from the past. Don't know if that's possible, since such events only happen in science fiction. Dr. Gorski, the person who found you, enjoys a challenge and is investigating your dilemma." She moved around and looked at him. "There is a new procedure to examine your brain for injuries, but it cannot be done here. You'd have to be taken to Mass General Hospital. That hospital has the instrumentation that allows doctors to look at the condition of a human brain. It's relatively new, but it can show if there is any damage to your brain."

Noland's brow furrowed as he raised his head. Doubt showed in his eyes.

"But given a little time and rest, your mental problem may cure itself," Dr. Morris said with a masterful glance. "In the meantime, Dr. Gorski is examining your clothing, the musket balls, and other debris I removed from your wounds. Your behavior and the things you have told us seem a bit unbelievable. But Dr. Gorski enjoys history and would, I'm sure, love to prove you fought in the Battles at Concord and Lexington."

Sergeant Black's face flushed. He threshed his fist onto the bed. "But I was—I was at Lexington and Concord. The regiment was attacked on its return to Charleston. Our barracks are here in Charlestown. My company is housed at the temporary stronghold on a rise that over-looks the Charles River. You must believe me!"

The doctor pursed her lips and nodded. "Yes, yes, I'm sure."

Black squirmed, then sat up. His face reddened; head straightened as his hands grabbed the back of his neck. "You do not understand. I cannot forsake my men. They are under attack. I must return."

"Please relax! You have to relax! Nothing can be done at this moment. Let us see what Dr. Gorski learns."

Noland took several deep breaths, slackened his arms, and slowly lay back. His eyes closed for a moment.

Dr. Morris moved to the head of the bed. She lifted the edge of the blanket, and covered Noland's chest. "Please lie quietly. A good meal is on its way. Hopefully, it will help you come to grips with your situation."

Doctor Morris's attending nurse, Mia, entered Noland's room. Immediately he responded to the aromas of breakfast foods. His nose caught whiffs of hickory-smoked bacon and toasted bread. His stomach began to grumble and his mouth moistened. He adjusted himself to a sitting position. "Such wonderful smells you have provided," he said as Mia placed the tray crosswise over his legs, turned, and left the room. "Military food is substantial, but...such fragrances, such foods..." He lifted a slice of toast. He generously covered it with grape jam that he found in a ceramic condiment ramekin located to the right of the breakfast plate, passed it below his nose, then tasted. "Oh, such flavor. At the barracks, toast is not served with jam. Bread and jam—when jam is available—service is usually done at the end of a meal, as a pudding. I'll forgive you for this oversight." With the jellied piece of toast in his right hand, the sergeant used it to guide a glob of scrambled eggs onto the fork.

Dr. Morris noticed Noland held the fork in his left hand, and rotated it upside down. He then used a morsel of toast as Europeans do to push a bit of egg onto the backside of the fork.

He then inserted the fork's tines in the bit of toast and put it and the egg fragments into his mouth. He savored their flavor for a moment, then slowly chewed, swallowed, and then took a bite of bacon. His head lifted. A grin of pleasure crossed his face. "I'm accustomed to a porridge breakfast. What you are providing me is unusual. Eggs, I have never had. Oh, several of us collect seagull eggs, but learned that because of their flavor, they were inedible. And the bacon is special. It is usually only served to the officers…" He sighed. "These eggs are from what bird?"

"Chicken," Dr. Morris answered.

"A partridge for the royalty. Never served to the military." Noland shook his head and licked his lips. He then smiled. "This red fruit you call tomato is new to me. It is sweet, tasty, but tart. The juice of an orange? This fruit I have seen, but have never eaten any. A tropical fruit enjoyed by the wealthy. The military does not serve such delicacies."

"It is good you are enjoying hospital food. The eggs are from the common chicken. And the orange is a citrus fruit related to the lemon. Oranges are sweeter. I do believe limes were provided to your sailors to combat scurvy. The breakfast is nothing special. Designed to nourish the patient," Dr. Morris said. "Most patients don't even taste it. Find it flavorless; dump piles of salt and pepper on it, and gulp it down. By the way, if you need any salt or pepper, there are some packets on the tray."

"Aye, the Royal Navy and occasionally the army does serve the juice of lemon. Lemon is very sour." Noland fingered the packets lying next to the dish. Examined them. "Salt…pepper," he mumbled and looked toward Dr. Morris. "I have never seen spices provided in such a manner."

"If you have come from where you say you have, there is much you have not seen or will recognize." Dr. Morris adjusted the pillow behind Noland's back. "Yet, there are things in the past with which you may be familiar or you may have used, but they are greatly improved." The doctor moved to the window and looked out. "The musket, for example, was familiar to soldiers in the eighteenth and nineteenth centuries, and I am sure these men were able to load and shoot one quickly, but the weapon was very inaccurate."

"Yes. Yes," Sergeant Black said as he forked the remaining morsels of egg into his mouth and shifted himself to a more confident position. Then continued, while swallowing and puffing out his chest, "I am able to load and shoot thrice in one minute."

"Perhaps you can," Dr. Morris said. "But the musket has been greatly improved. Today we call them rifles and they can be loaded and shot within seconds. Many bullets can be discharged within a minute." She stared out the window and shook her head. "So much has been improved or invented since the eighteenth century…it baffles the mind." The doctor returned her attention to Noland. "When the food tray is taken away, I'll examine your wounds, and Mia will apply fresh bandages. Then I want you to come to the window, look out, and tell me what you see. If your mind is somewhat confused now, I believe, if you really are from the past, what you see beyond the glass will be wilder your mind even further."

Sergeant Noland ståraightened himself after a teenaged candy-striper took the breakfast tray away. He looked up at Dr. Morris, who was glancing out the window. He belched. "Beggin' your pardon, Ma'am."

Dr. Morris turned her head back toward the sergeant. A slight smile crossed her face.

Satiated, the sergeant's anxieties calmed. He scanned the room, took a deep breath, and raised his head a little. Seeing lustrous chrome rails and fixtures, the telephone, a darkened table lamp, but no candles, instead overhead florescent lighting, unusual sounds, and Dr. Morris's strange clothing, his nerves continued to quiver. "I don't know where I am—nothing in this room is familiar," he said. But his confusion turned to immediate concern. "I need to relieve myself. Madam Doctor, could someone direct me to the latrine?"

Momentarily surprised by the request, Dr. Morris gasped and nodded. She scurried to the door, opened it, and shouted for Joel, who was idling at the nurses' station. He came running into the room. "Assist Mr. Black to the lavatory and explain to him how everything works."

A questioning expression crossed Joel's face. "What's with this guy? Doesn't he know how to flush a toilet?" he mumbled under his breath, but loud enough to be overheard by Dr. Morris.

"Do as I say!" she grumbled.

"Yes, Ma'am." Joel blushed as he moved to help Sergeant Black from the bed. Seeing that the sergeant's feet were bare, the orderly shifted to a set of drawers and removed a pair of anti-slip socks. He handed them to Noland. "Please put these on your feet. The floor is cold."

Sergeant Black swung himself around and dropped his feet toward the floor. When he bent down, he grimaced from the pain in his wounds as he pulled the socks on. He stood and, when a gust of air chilled his completely naked backside, realized that the hospital gown he wore was open. His glutes tensed and he sat back down. "What is this I wear?"

"A hospital gown," Joel said. "All patients wear them when they are being treated. The pants you wore are hanging safely in the closet." He pointed to a closed door on the opposite wall. "The shirt you wore was pretty much messed up, so the guy who brought you here put it in a bag and took it with him." He moved next to Noland's bed. "If you stand, I'll tie the ties on the gown tighter. That'll close up the gap."

It didn't. When Noland followed Joel out of the room and down the hallway to the men's room, a cool breath whiffed around him as he walked.

Joel pushed the door to the men's room open and allowed Noland to enter first. Then he followed.

The sergeant raised his head and sniffed as the men's room door closed. Unlike the dim, dark-walled, mud floor barrack's latrine with a central pit from which issued odors of urine and other bodily wastes, the atmosphere in this clean, bright men's room had a flowery scent. He froze in the middle of the tiled floor and stood astonished. On his right was a mirrored wall above a sink. To his left was a white marble urinal and commode, both with chrome fixtures. And, in front of him was a cubicle with various chrome fixtures. Its door was closed, so he didn't examine it. Slowly turning his head to the right, his mind analyzed the image in the mirror. He rolled his head to the side and stared at himself. *I am who I am, but I rarely see myself.*

The urge to relieve himself intensified. "What's this? Where do I go?"

Joel snickered. "Sorry." He walked to the urinal and placed his hand on the flush lever. "Empty your bladder here…" he pushed the lever down, "then flush."

The jets of water that squirted momentarily startled Noland.

Joel swung his arm to the right. "Sink and soap to wash your hands when you finish. Lever on top turns the water on and off and controls its flow. Push it back to turn on, pull toward you to it turn off. Hot, push the lever to the left lever and cold, push it to the right. If you keep it in the middle, water temperature should be right."

Noland felt his glutes contract. "What you have told me is all very informative, but, *damn it*, I need to take a shit. You understand my English?"

"That's direct." Joel stepped around the sergeant and pointed to the toilet. "Expose your behind, sit on the commode…"

"I don't see a woman's headpiece, a chamber pot!" Noland barked.

"Oh yeah, you're British, aren't you?" The orderly chuckled. "That seat is called a water closet in London." He glanced at the sergeant.

"Know what that is? You sit on it and drop your load. When you're done, use a piece of the toilet paper hanging on the right to clean your bottom, drop it into the commode, then push the lever behind you and all the crap will flush away." Joel stepped aside. "I'll be outside the front door to take you back to your room. If you need something, yell." He shook his head, chuckled, and walk out of the men's room.

Noland satisfied his urge, stood, cleaned himself with a piece of toilet tissue as told, turned, and stared into the mirror. His image was clear, not distorted like he saw himself in the mirror on the wall of his room at the barracks while he brushed his hair. Astonished and confused, he tilted his head to the side, sighed, then strolled next to a urinal. Fascinated, he pushed the flush lever. A blast of water squirted down the back of the fixture and disappeared through a white mesh lying on the bottom. He cocked his head to the opposite side, gritted his teeth, then strolled forward and returned to the toilet. He saw that the bowl below the seat contained water and his feces. Examining the commode, he found, protruding from the chrome pipes behind the toilet, the flush lever. Bending toward it, he pushed the lever down. The immediate rush of water and rapid swirling in the bowl shocked him. In a moment the whirlpool ended. The water in the toilet bowl became serene and returned to its original level. He pushed the flusher again and the same thing happened. He grinned and nodded. "Ah huh. That's how the bloody shit is removed," he grumbled.

Noland returned to the countertop and put his hand under the sink's spout. The on/off lever was down and in the middle. He slowly pushed it up. Water began to flow. It streamed faster the farther he pushed the lever back. He slowly placed his fingers into the stream to test its temperature. Then he tapped the lever to the right and left. Water temperature responded as Joel said. *This is all a dream. How did I get here?* He shook his head and pushed the on/off lever to the left and snapped his hand away from the hot water. "Ow! Goddamn, that hurt. I am alive," he growled. "Where the hell am I? Can I get back?"

Using his hospital gown to dry his hands, he pushed the bathroom door open, and shouted, "Get me out of here. I'm done."

Joel stepped away from the wall he was slouching against and moved to the middle of the hallway. "Everything come out okay, man?" he said flippantly as he walked in front of Noland. "Come on, I'll get you back to your chamber." Entering the room, Noland noticed that Mia had returned.

Dr. Morris looked up. "Please sit on the bed. Mia will remove your bandages so I can check how healing is progressing."

Sergeant Black did as he was told. Within a matter of moments Mia had all the dressings removed.

Dr. Morris stood to his side. "Move to the left so I can take a look."

Noland shifted himself. Dr. Morris untied the gown, spread it open, and touched his back. Her cold fingertips made his skin twitch.

Dr. Morris stepped back and straightened so she could look into the sergeant's eyes. "You're healing nicely." She then turned to Mia. "I don't see any signs of infection. Clean the injured area and spread on some bacitracin, then bandage the wounds." She raised her head, clasped her hands, and moved toward the room's window. "When Mia is finished, please come to the window, look out, and tell me what you see."

The cold felt more intense when Mia wiped the area with alcohol. His skin relaxed when the wounds were dabbed with antibiotic cream and covered with bandages. Sergeant Black sighed, straightened, and stood. With his brow furrowed and eyes narrowed, he strolled to the window, and looked out. While gazing for a moment, a continuous diminishing roar from above caused him to look skyward. He saw a large, strange object pass eastward.

"What do you see?" asked Dr. Morris. "Or better, what don't you see?"

Sergeant Black looked down. He turned his head slowly to one side then the other. His hands grasped the window frame as he stared ahead and took a deep breath. The airplane had gone out of sight.

Shaking his head, his grip tightened. He then stepped away from the window. His eyes closed. "I should not be here. A strange object in the sky. I know of nothing I see." He clasped his head as it dropped forward. Noland breathed deeper, opened his eyes, and straightened. His face looked muddled, in disbelief. After several blinks, he scanned the hospital room. "I must get back." His arms lowered to his sides and his fists clenched tightly. Raising his head, his chest muscles became tense as he locked his eyes on Dr. Morris. "Return me to where I was found. This is not my world. I know not where I am. My men? I need to find my men."

"Your first request can easily be done, but the other will be a challenge," Dr. Morris said as she gently took hold of his right arm and attempted to guide him back to the bed. "Finding your men—that may not be possible."

"What is this place? There are no—horses—carriages…" he slouched onto the bed. "People in queer dress. There are no boardwalks. Unusual carriages move on a black path. Others sit idle on the side. What means of transport are these? An object moving where birds should fly." His head snapped up. "And there are distant towers on the horizon. What are they?"

Dr. Morris took a quick glance out the window and nodded. "Automobiles—motor cars." She sighted between the buildings across the street. "The skyline of towers is the city of Boston. And you saw an airplane approaching the Boston airport."

Noland shook his head. His fingers fondled his neck. *My medallion. It is not about my neck.* "I am not wearing my amulet," he bawled and looked up at Dr. Morris, then at Mia. "Where is it?"

Disturbed, Dr. Morris's body crooked upward and away from the window. "Do you mean dog tags? Were you wearing a dog tag?" She answered her own question. "You weren't wearing any dog tags or, for that matter, any identification at all."

Sergeant Black looked confused.

"Sorry. A charm, perhaps. Did you have a medal or something like that hanging from your neck?"

"Aye." The sergeant's fingers massaged the area where the Celtic cross once hung. A distant look crossed his face. "I must find it," he mumbled. "It keeps me safe." Suddenly his body stiffened. It was as if he had, while sitting, snapped to attention. "That is my coat! On the back of that chair. Is it not?" His eyes locked on the red coat. "I am Sergeant Noland Black, grenadier in the Tenth Regiment of the Royal Army, from Newcastle, England, posted to Boston duty September, 1772." He remained stiff, as if facing an interrogator. "I am billeted at the Bunker Hill barracks. I wish to be returned to my regiment. It is my duty. If I do not, I will be considered a deserter, disgraced, and removed from service. And at the worst, hung!"

Sunday, April 20, 1975

John, Dr. Andrew Gorski's reenactor friend, met him for lunch at the Cambridge Common, a popular restaurant on Massachusetts Avenue near the Harvard Museum of Natural History in Cambridge. The two seated themselves at a table near the back wall. The diner had just opened, but about half the tables were taken. Both ordered the fish of the day, because their waitress told them that today's fish was American shad caught fresh last night in the Connecticut River.

"Love shad, crispy fried," said Dr. Gorski. "Can only get them this time of the year. Masses of them swim up the Connecticut to spawn, and the state allows a few commercial fishermen to set drift nets in the lower part of the river during the night. I think that may be the only commercial shad fishery in the country. But it's a big deal…"

"Yeah," John interjected. "Like grunion on the California beaches. But there is no commercial fishery for these fish. However, one can always go down to the beach, when the grunion are running, and buy a bucket. Don't get your feet wet that way." He chuckled. "Heard of folks eating shad roe—but never eating the fish. Too bony, they say. Ever eaten the roe?"

"Yeah. It's different. Supposed to be a delicacy." He sat back and released the silverware rolled in the napkin. "You'll find no bones in a shad fillet. An expert filleter gets rid of all the bones," Gorski said as the waitress put two pints of beer on the table. "Met a woman once who could fillet a shad in thirty seconds. She and three others worked in a shack near the mouth of the river and cleaned the catch brought to them. Sure wouldn't want to get in a knife fight with her." He shook his head and gritted his teeth.

"Your orders will be here shortly," the waitress said as she passed their table.

"Wait a minute, please." Dr. Gorski looked at John. "Ever try shad roe? I can order a side dish. Something new for an Ohio boy. Whaddaya say?"

John shrugged, then nodded. "Sure."

"Bring us a dish of shad roe. Have to indoctrinate my friend to old New England cuisine."

"I'm sure it'll be an experience." John arranged his knife and fork, placed the napkin in his lap, then picked up the salt shaker. "Why'd you decide to meet here for lunch?" He sprinkled a little salt into his beer.

A queer look crossed Dr. Gorski's face. "Why did you do that? Put salt in your beer."

"Don't know, really. My dad and all his buddies in Ohio used to do it. They said that it keeps you from dehydrating. Supposedly beer depletes minerals from your body, which can cause muscles to cramp. Think it's an ol' wives' tale. Salt does increase your thirst. Dad's friends did drink more beer. Ah, beer companies probably started the rumor. They'd tell you anything to get you to drink more beer. Who knows?" John grinned and took a sip of his beer. "Does nothing for the taste." He set the glass back on the table. "So why are we meeting here?"

"Bob Ericson asked that we meet here. You know Bob. One of our reenactors. Works at the Harvard Museum of Natural History. Bob's kind of an expert on muskets and the ammunition of the time. Asked him to look at the musket balls Dr. Morris extracted from our mystery man's shoulder." Dr. Gorski lifted his glass and sipped the beer. "The only thing Bob, nor I, realized was that getting here would require being confronted by an ongoing demonstration."

"Yeah. Everyone tired of the Vietnam War, a war for no reason." John took a drink of beer. "We're losing a lot of fine young men. It's ridiculous. A few days ago, President Ford ordered the evacuation of Saigon. Hope this puts an end to the war." He set his glass down and looked at Gorski. "How's the mystery guy doing?"

"Don't know. Haven't seen the supposed British soldier since the musket balls and debris were removed from his shoulder. Anyway, Bob called this morning and said the musket balls were old, but oddly new. Said he'd explain when we met. Sure made me curious. Something very strange going on, if those balls are real." Dr. Gorski took a longer swig of his beer.

"Hey, guys." Bob Ericson pulled a chair away from the table and seated himself. "Order yet?"

"Yes," Gorski said. "Charred shad fillet. They're supposed to be fresh from the Connecticut River."

Bob raised his hand to attract the waitress. As she approached, he asked her to bring him an ale. She nodded.

John took a swig of his brew as Dr. Gorski asked, "Well, what's the contradiction with the musket balls? Over the phone you said they were new, yet old."

"Yes. They have all the markings of being made using some old method of molding a lead ball, but their shape isn't spherical. They're deformed, sort of pear-shaped. And there are no mold seam ridges. Instead, the lead surface is imbedded with particles of clay and other debris, as if the hot lead was poured into a hole punched into wet dirt. Also, the apex of the balls are scratched and scraped, indicating that the pour sprue had been cut off and filed down. The balls are the size that would fit down the three-quarter-inch barrel of a British Brown Bess musket. One of the balls has roughly a diameter of zero point six nine inches; the other's max diameter is zero point six eight. Excuse me a second." Bob sucked off the foam from the top of the glass of ale the waitress set in front of him and took a drink. "Excuse me, ma'am, could you bring me a scrod sandwich and an order of fries?"

The waitress nodded. Bob returned to instructing his buddies.

"Now here's the interesting part. The musket balls could have been poured yesterday. But if they are recent, whoever made them would have used a proper mold and the balls would be spherical, with a seam ridge around the middle, like the equator around the earth. Their size would be zero point six nine three, the exact size of a mold-made musket ball. The British didn't use the method poor colonials did, even though proper musket ball molds were available in the eighteenth century. Too expensive. The majority of the colonials couldn't afford them, even if they could get them. And, if the shot had to be made in a hurry, it's easier to shove a finger in the dirt and pour in the lead. Lead and pewter are soft metals that melt at low temps, and easily filed to fit into the barrel of a musket.

"Musket ball molds used by the military were made of iron and of the exact size to produce shot that fit into a British Brown Bess musket." He took another swig of beer.

Bob placed his glass back on the table and continued. "The lead on the surface of a two-hundred-year-old musket ball would be darkened; covered in an oxidized patina. The ones you brought me are not oxidized. On yes, there's some blackish bits of crud on their surface, but the exposed metal has the grayish sheen of recently molded lead or pewter. If those balls were removed from the body of an animal, I suspect the crud is dried blood and tissue. Didn't do any metallurgical analysis on metal. Though the musket balls look new, I do believe they're old. And, recently extracted from something that got shot. You guys didn't shoot anyone, did you?"

Dr. Gorski shook his head.

Bob grinned and relaxed against the back of the chair. He reached into his coat pocket and brought out the box that Dr. Gorski gave him that contained the musket balls and other debris Dr. Morris extracted from Sergeant Black's muscles. He put the box on the table and shoved it toward Gorski.

"Thank you for the lecture on musket-ball making, Bob," said Dr. Gorski. "Did you get a chance to look at the debris that was used as buckshot?"

"Yes. Had the plant and soil expert look at that stuff. Except for some bits of lead particles, spattered, probably, the soil guy said that the debris was what would be commonly found in any barnyard in the area. The stuff is local dirt."

"Thank you for looking at the musket balls and detritus I gave you," Gorski said. "Your information may help in solving a mystery that's confronting me. But I need more concrete evidence."

"What's the mystery?" Bob questioned. "You didn't dig those balls out of the mud. That much is evident. Perhaps they came from an old airtight box?" Bob looked to his side. "Do you know anything, John?"

John glanced at Dr. Gorski, then shook his head.

"Don't want to say anything at this time, Bob," Dr. Gorski said. "But I'll keep you informed."

The waitress brought the men's lunches and saved Dr. Gorski from Bob Ericson's further inquiries.

"Bon appétit, gentlemen," Dr. Gorski said while he rearranged his plate to suit himself.

"Okay," Bob said. "I've got to wolf this sandwich down and get back to my office. Got some unfinished stuff that needs to be done. You're going to keep me apprised of what you are doing, aren't you, Andrew?"

"Yeah, sure. Hey, today's Sunday. You're supposed to be off." Dr. Gorski licked his lips after he'd put a piece of shad into his mouth. "That's very tasty." He swallowed the morsel. "Yes, I too have to hurry. Got to get to Mass General clinic in Charlestown. Seems there's a patient there that needs my attention."

The three men finished their meals and saw each other off. Dr. Gorski motioned for John to stay for a moment. "Thanks for not answering Bob's question. I rather not give out any information about that fellow we found yesterday. If he turns out to be who he says he is, we've got some real problems on our hands."

"Yeah, the media will be all over you." John stepped off the curb. "You really believe the guy came from the past?"

"Well, he doesn't belong to our group. And wearing that uniform. Where else would he have come from? Strange things do happen." A slow smile appeared on Gorski's face. He raised his eyebrows. "I'm willing to hold my decision until I get more evidence."

"I'll accept that." John chuckled and waved as he crossed the street and headed toward his car. In the middle of the street, he snapped around and yelled to Dr. Gorski, "Hey, shad roe is like rolling a bunch of BBs around in your mouth." He continued on to his vehicle, laughing.

Andrew Gorski met Dr. Morris in her office when he returned to the clinic after lunch. "How's the patient?" he asked upon entering.

Dr. Morris motioned for Dr. Gorski to sit. She briefed him on Black's condition. "He's healing well, but distraught." Her face tensed and brow furrowed. She shook her head. "He demanded I return him to his regiment. Seems he wore a Celtic cross around his neck, his fetish. When he learned it was missing, he became agitated. Seeing his red coat hanging on the back of a chair, he relaxed. Then, for some reason, his behavior changed. At that point, I became dumbfounded. He did claim he was from Newcastle, England." Dr. Morris slid back in her chair and sighed. "Then my nurse came in with lunch and I realized I had to get my head together. So, I patted him on the shoulder and left him to eat his lunch."

"I don't know what to say." Dr. Gorski tightened his lips and nodded. "He may be telling the truth."

"Another incident happened this morning." She straightened and bent forward. "Noland asked to use the latrine. I had Joel, the orderly, take him down the hall to the Men's Room. The orderly returned and said, 'Man, that guy's strange. Became totally confused when we walked into the john. Didn't know how to use anything. Had to try everything.'"

"Asked to use the latrine? Only a military man or a Boy Scout would ask for a latrine."

"That's what I thought." Dr. Morris relaxed back into her chair. "Why did you say he might be telling the truth? Did you learn something?"

"Sort of," Dr. Gorski said, "Showed the musket balls and other debris you extracted from the supposed sergeant's wounds to my friend Bob Ericson, who is in town visiting colleagues at Harvard. He's a curator of early American weaponry at the US Naval Museum in DC. And his answer to the musket balls was that they resemble those that would have been made by colonials, but by their appearance suggests they could have been poured yesterday. He said the balls had all the markings of being poured in makeshift molds..." Dr. Gorski tapped his index finger on Dr. Morris's desk, "like a finger-sized hole punched in the mud. Helps our case somewhat, but not really. Circumstantial evidence at best." He shrugged. "As for the dirt you pulled out of the wounds, Bob asked one of his friends, a soils expert at Harvard, to look at it. Results, its common local dirt, except for some BB-sized bits of lead—buckshot or spatter particles. However, for lack of real ammunition, it was common for American rebels to stuff debris down the barrel of their muskets."

Dr. Morris pursed her lips and looked directly at Dr. Gorski. "When the man looked out the window, he did not recognize the skyline of Boston. Called the skyscrapers, towers..."

"It is doubtful that two hundred years ago you'd have seen the skyline of Boston from here," Gorski interrupted.

"Guess not. I suspect Boston didn't have much of a skyline back then. But that doesn't prove anything. He could be lying." Dr. Morris looked at her wristwatch, sighed, and then reached for a clipboard. "Let's go back to Sergeant Black's room and see how he's doing."

"By the way, did anyone examine his red coat?"

"No. It is hanging on the back of the chair in his room. The orderly hung the coat there and it sort of got forgotten until Black saw it."

"Does that orderly know who Black claims to be?"

"No. The only other person who knows is Mia, my attendant nurse. And that lady won't tell a soul."

"Okay. Then let's go to his room. I do want to take a look at that coat. If he's from the past, his clothes should show signs of being manufactured in the past."

When Drs. Morris and Gorski entered Sergeant Black's room, they saw him standing at the window looking out, his arms apart and hands grasping the window frame. The doctor's attending nurse stood next to the bed, adjusting and straightening the sheets. The nurse straightened and looked at the doctors. Dr. Morris raised her eyebrows, glanced at Mia, and twitched her head toward the sergeant, questioning his behavior.

"After he ate his lunch, he got out of bed, walked to the window, and stared out," Mia said in a quiet, gentle voice. "He's been there for about the last fifteen minutes."

Sergeant Black, hearing voices, pushed back from the window, but kept both his hands grasped to the frame. The others heard him take a deep breath, saw him stretch, then retract and remain transfixed on the view beyond the glass, gripping the frame as if his life and the view were about to vanish.

Dr. Gorski moved into the room. Seeing Noland's military red coat hanging on the back of the chair, he rushed to it, took it off the chair, and handed the coat to Mia. "Take this to Dr. Morris's office and put it somewhere safe," he whispered to her.

She folded the coat over her arm, nodded, and exited the room.

Dr. Gorski turned his attention to Noland Black. He carefully walked to him and put his hand on the sergeant's shoulder. He felt the man tense and spoke with care. "All is well. I'm Andrew Gorski, the man who found and brought you to this hospital. It appears Dr. Morris has been taking good care of you. You appear to be feeling better."

Noland slackened his grasp of the window frame. His body and the air around him loosened. His left hand released itself. He dropped it to his side. He held his right hand against the window to stabilize himself and turned away from the window to face Dr. Gorski. "Aye, the doctor has been very kind…" He shook his head and looked to the floor. "But I am totally confused. This is not my world. I see things here that are very unfamiliar—transport vehicles, but no horses. Roadways that are not mud or gravel. People dress in unusual clothing. In the distance I see buildings that rise into the sky. Dr. Morris said that those buildings are in the city of Boston. That is not the Boston I know. I do not know where I am." Noland raised his head, lifted his hands, and rubbed his temples. "May I move to the bed?"

Dr. Gorski held the sergeant's arm while he made his way to the bed. "I have examined the musket balls that Dr. Morris removed from your shoulder and arm. The markings on them suggest that those two shots were poured in a mud hole. A process that perhaps a colonist may have used." Dr. Gorski steadied Noland as he laid himself onto the bed.

"Aye," Noland said. "The rebels are farmers. That is the usual procedure they use, fore they have no proper musket ball molds. We forbid the trade of them to colonists. Some have made the molds of wood, but wood molds scorch when hot lead is poured into them and can only be used once or twice before a new one must be carved."

Dr. Gorski grinned softly and nodded. "Though the musket balls have characteristics from the past, they do not look two hundred years old. It is as if they were poured recently."

"No! Two hundred years? No! I have only been away for a day or so. The musket ball could have been fashioned the morning of the attack."

"Yes, you told me that rebels attacked on the road from Concord. We found you where the road makes a tight bend—a recent name given to that bend is Bloody Angle, because of a bloody ambush that took place along that part of the road. The fields off the road are full of boulders and knolls. As a matter of fact, that attack took place yesterday, but two hundred years ago, the day that began the American Revolution." Dr. Gorski pulled a chair next to the bed and sat down. He placed his hands on his knees. "Quite a few British soldiers were killed by the colonials hiding in the fields." He stared into Noland's eyes. "Could you have been in that battle?"

"Aye! My regiment was ambushed. I was hit when I tried to help a confederate across the road."

Dr. Gorski twitched his head suspiciously. "Fascinating story, but there is a problem." He glanced at the sergeant. "How did you get here?"

"That I do not know." Sergeant Black gritted his teeth and clenched his fists. His face reddened with anger.

Dr. Morris poured a glass of water, stepped over to the bed, stood next to Dr. Gorski, and with a smile, handed the glass to Noland. "Sergeant Black's story sounds impossible, but it could be probable. We really have not learned all the secrets of the universe, though sometimes we believe we have," she said, trying to lighten the tension. "A new novel that just came out is about a man from the future who is unknowingly transported into the past because he pines for a nine-teenth-century actress whose image he found. The novel is *Bid Time Return*, written by Richard Matheson." She shrugged. "So perhaps it's possible to come forward in time." She bent toward Noland and patted the pillow. "Drink the water."

Sergeant Black took a deep breath, raised the glass to his lips, drank a swallow of water, and relaxed against the pillow. His face faded from anger to confusion.

"Yes, we need to stay cool about this matter," Gorski said as he relaxed back against the chair. "You seem like a lucid man, Noland, but we're in the twentieth century and time travel has not yet been discovered or invented. Nature is a strange mother. Who knows what she has in her bag of tricks? I could use a shot of Jack." He bent forward. "You understand, we have to find more significant evidence. Though tantalizing, the musket balls really don't substantiate that you fought in the Battles at Concord and Lexington."

Noland nodded and stretched back against the pillow. He glared at the ceiling.

"Dr. Gorski, I believe Mr. Black would like to relax," Dr. Morris said. "He needs to mull over what he has seen and heard. I'll have Mia look in on him and change his bandages. Perhaps you should go to my office." She pushed the nurse's call button.

"Yes." Dr. Gorski stood and moved next to Noland's bed. "Take it easy, my friend. I'll check back with you when you have rested." He walked to the door that opened onto the hall as Mia entered.

CHAPTER 8

Sunday, April 20, 1975

r. Andrew Gorski was sitting behind Dr. Morris's desk, holding the sergeant's coat spread open in front of him, when she walked into the office. "Did you learn anything from the coat?"

"Yes, ma'am." He folded the coat and laid it upon the desk. "As far as I can tell, this coat is old and authentic. It is made of dense broadcloth wool, and it has a lining of wool." He lifted the bottom of the coat, spread it open so a portion of its inner side was exposed, and ran his fingers along the inner edge. "There are no hems. The wool is specifically shrunk to pack the fibers, making the cloth dense. If cut, the edges don't fray. So, they don't have to be hemmed. Also, the lining has been hand-stitched to the coat. This is not the way a modern-day reenactor's coat would be made. Reenactors' red coats are a mixture of wool and other fabrics, making them more comfortable. Linings are some sort of polyester. And all the edges are hemmed." Dr. Gorski closed the coat. "And here…" he pointed to the edges along the front of the coat, "the facing, it's yellow and lined with white. The color of the facing identifies the regiment to which the sergeant belongs, the regimental colors. Reenactors don't pay much attention to regimental colors—of course, if you're a purist, you might. But normally, reenactor coats have white facing."

"He's a grenadier," Dr. Morris said. "Told me he belonged to the Tenth Regiment. Is yellow the regimental color?"

"Indeed, it is. Called my buddy, John, and asked him to look up the regimental colors of Great Britain's Tenth Regiment of Foot. It's yellow."

Dr. Morris put her hand on the coat. She then moved it to the bullet holes in the right shoulder. "Need to get these fixed. Mia said she could sew up the holes. This coat isn't really red."

Dr. Gorski nodded. "Yes. It has seen some wear. The dyes used in the seventeen-hundreds were made from vegetable extracts. The color fades with weathering. Unlike the modern military, where uniforms are issued, a British soldier or sailor had to purchase his own uniforms. And uniforms weren't cheap, and the military didn't pay well, so the guys tried to get the most mileage out their uniforms. Too bad we didn't find his hat. Its design would identify him as a Grenadier."

"Didn't he wear a tricorne?" Dr. Morris questioned.

"No. Grenadiers wore a short, stovepipe-like hat, called a shako; a headpiece decorated with various bands, ribbons, medals, which identify his rank. I believe he was wearing a cross belt."

"The rest of his clothing is in the closet in his room. Believe there is what looks like a pair of white leather belts that are connected by a metal buckle."

Dr. Gorski nodded. "The buckle is usually inscribed with the soldier's regiment. If it is, it would be a piece of strong evidence. Soldiers usually carry their bayonet and an ammunition cartridge hooked to the belts. He didn't have either." Gorski looked up from the coat. "He was in a battle. Probably had the bayonet attached to his musket and may not have been carrying an ammo cartridge. He had no weapons when we found him."

"Do you have enough evidence to suggest Mr. Black is from the past?"

"What we have sure sounds convincing."

"Not to me." Dr. Morris pursed her lips and tilted her head. "I'm still suspicious. He could be a reenactor who either stole the coat or bought it at a yard sale. And, for some unknown reason, got himself shot. Coming from the past is still a fantasy.

"Wow! You're going to be hard to convince."

"As your friend at the museum said, all the evidence you have is circumstantial." Dr. Morris shrugged.

Dr. Gorski lifted the coat from the desk. He shrugged. Holding the coat by its shoulders, he lifted it in front of himself and scanned it inquisitively. His body suddenly jolted back. "Whoa! What's this?" He carefully laid the coat back on the desk, reached forward, and touched the corner of a piece of parchment that was sticking out the front left side of the coat near its collar. Carefully he turned back the lapel and removed a paper from an inner pocket. "Didn't know the coat had inner pockets," he mumbled. Dr. Gorski carefully unfolded the parchment and tried to scan it, but the message was apparently written in a light-colored ink and the illumination in the office was dim. "Need more light to read this. This note is a bit scribbled in old eighteenth-century script."

Dr. Morris moved around her desk. "Slide over please," she said. When he did, she reached in a drawer, removed a magnifying glass, and then flicked on the desk lamp. "Perhaps this will help." She moved to the side.

"Yes—yes. Just what I need." Dr. Gorski slid the parchment into the light. With the magnifying glass he examined what was written. "Looks like the day's orders to the sergeant, though it's not addressed directly to him, but to his regimental field commander, Lieutenant Colonel Francis Smith. The message reads, 'By order of Lieutenant General Hugh Percy, Regimental Commander, Lieutenant Smith, you are to march your regiment to Concord. Search out any ammunition, powder, and weapons in the possession of the Colonials or hidden by them. These are to be confiscated and destroyed. As has been done on previous expeditions, I urge you to maintain a semblance of a passiveness. Do not fire upon the rebels, unless you are fired upon. Remember, the Colonials you encounter, though they may respond with stubbornness and defiance, are citizens of Great Britain. Keep this mission peaceful.' This portion of the message is signed by General Percy. It is readable." Dr. Gorski examined the message more closely. "There is an additional sentence below the general's signature and seal." He paused, then continued. "It's written in a different hand and more scribbled. I'll try to read it. 'Sergeant…company south'—next word looks like Concord—search farms…barns'—a large ampersand, which is an 'and' in the old script—meet with Captain Laurie company at North Brid…and return to Boston.' This message is initialed, FS. Lieutenant Colonel Francis Smith, I assume."

Dr. Gorski rubbed his fingers on the paper the message was written on. "Not the kind of paper we have today. It's parchment. Crafters still make the stuff, but it was the writing paper of the eighteenth century." He lifted it, carefully folded the message, and slipped it back into the inside pocket of the sergeant's red coat. He then patted the pockets of the coat. "I feel something solid in this pocket." Gorski reached in and brought out two silver coins. He examined the coins. "Please, hand me the magnifying glass." He took a closer look at the engravings on the coins. "These are British shillings. Good god, I do believe we just found the solid verification we've been looking for." Dr. Gorski's eyelids widened and a grin flashed across his face. "Aren't the actual mission orders I just found more convincing?"

"Somewhat."

"Let's get back to the sergeant's room. I need to ask him about the mission orders." Gorski slipped the shillings back into the sergeant's red coat pocket.

"Before we do that, there are a couple of items that need to be considered," Dr. Morris said.

Dr. Gorski seemed to be locked in a trance as he stared at Sergeant Noland Black's red coat. "Huh? Sorry, my mind got caught up on what the sergeant must have experienced on that march back to Charlestown." He blinked and shook his head. "What do you think of that fellow?"

"He's healthy, handsome, muscular, but confused and vulnerable. At this moment, what I think of him is not important." Dr. Morris took a deep breath. "Tomorrow is Monday. This clinic will become busy and chaotic. The full staff will be present and some, I'm sure, will have some pointed questions. We have to get Sergeant Black out of here. His injuries are not life-threatening. He's healing well and able to travel, but to where? He also needs some modern clothing. His clothing, I mean uniform, needs cleaning and repair. Remember, I told you Mia can take care of that. But the poor fellow can't be running about town in his birthday suit."

Dr. Gorski grinned. "Yes, I understand. But first let's talk to him for a few minutes. I am of the assumption that he is who he says he is, but I still have a few questions. Anyway, he and I are about the same height and build. Afterwards, I'll run to my apartment and get him some jeans, a sweatshirt, and other things. I think I even have a spare pair of running shoes."

"Where can we take him?" Dr. Morris asked. "Your place, perhaps?"

"I have only a one-bedroom studio in Cambridge. It's too small to house two guys."

Dr. Morris nodded and gritted her teeth. She clasped her hands and anxiously rubbed them together. "Yes, and I have a house in Somerville, but I'm not in the habit of having a man stay overnight."

"If anyone asks, you tell them it's your brother or cousin from Denver or somewhere. If Noland is who we think he is, the guy's special. He has no place to go. His barracks have been torn down long ago. We just can't put him out on the street..." Dr. Gorski inhaled deeply. "Dr. Morris, you've got to help me out. Can you please house him 'til we figure out what to do with him?"

Dr. Morris bit her lip as she bobbed her head. "Yeah, I guess..." she sighed and put her hand on the edge of her chin, "under these circumstances. Okay. Let's go and ask our surreal traveler some questions." She turned toward her office door.

When Drs. Morris and Gorski came down the hall, Mia was at her desk in the nurses' station, writing, and examining medical charts. Dr. Gorski gave Mia Sergeant Black's red coat. She stood and hung it on a hanger attached to the wall behind her desk and sat down.

"How's our patient?" Dr. Morris asked.

"Physically, he's doing fine." Mia looked up from her task. "I cleaned his wounds, rubbed the injured area with a fresh layer of bacitracin and covered it with new bandages. He ate the dinner I was able to put together in the kitchen. You know Mrs. Martin, the cook, went home about noon. She and her aide work the kitchen on Saturday. Today is Sunday. The kitchen is normally closed except in emergencies. Sunday and Monday are Mrs. Martin's days off. But, because of our unusual medical situation, I asked her yesterday if she could come in today and put together a breakfast and lunch for the patient. Usually under special conditions she does, and today the sweet woman did." Mia laid the ballpoint pen she was holding on the desk and raised her eyes from the charts. "Anyway, our patient ate what I brought him, then he strolled to the window and looked out for a few minutes. He then returned, sat down on the bed, and covered his face with his hands. When I asked if he was well, he nodded and said he was all right." She looked up at the doctors. "He continued to sit, rub his face, and stare at the window, while I took the tray of dishes off the table. Will you be fine if I leave you alone for a while? I asked him, and he said he would be. I took a look into the room about ten minutes later and he seemed to be dozing." She turned and pointed to the red coat. "Sewed up the holes in the coat. Easy fix. The bullets didn't damage it too much. Those coats sure are sturdy. But I bet they really get hot in the summer."

"Thank you for the update, Mia. Dr. Gorski and I will look in on him." Dr. Morris turned to Dr. Gorski. "Got a feeling he's okay physically, but not so mentally. Let's go check in on him. If I were in his shoes, I'd be feeling totally confused, apprehensive, and distraught." She stepped behind the counter and removed the coat from the hanger and folded it. "Thank you for sewing up the bullet holes. I'm sure Mr. Black will be more comfortable when he sees that his coat has been mended."

The two walked down the hall to Noland Black's room. Dr. Morris quietly opened the door and peeked in. She saw the sergeant standing, looking out the window. He seemed intensely absorbed. He did not hear the doctors enter. His head slowly raised and the doctors heard him whisper, "I recognized you."

Dr. Morris moved her head to the side and saw a brownish, speckled moth walking up the outside of the windowpane. She watched as the sergeant followed the moth move, then she saw the sergeant glance upward and heard him say, "I know what you are, too. Time has not changed you either."

"What did you see?" she asked as she hung the red coat on the back of the chair.

Noland snapped his head around and faced the doctors. "Seagull!" He slapped his thighs, shrugged, returned to his bed, and sat down. Glancing up and, with an appearance of cool confidence, said, "The world may have changed, but not all. What I touch here and what I see outside are beyond my understanding. Yet, a common moth has not changed. Trees still have leaves. And seagulls fly in from the ocean. So, I am still on earth." He ran his fingers through his long, dark hair. "As a schoolboy, I once saw drawings of Leonardo da Vinci's flying machine. To us, the images were absurdities. Something to laugh at. I am sure the brilliant man was jesting when he created them." The sergeant looked at Dr. Gorski and grinned. "Birds still fly. Man does not. But I suppose next, you will tell me that he now does."

Dr. Gorski swallowed, cocked his head, and raised his eyelids. "What can be conceived in the human mind, eventually becomes reality. Yes, though some may have looked upon da Vinci's drawings of flying machines as fanciful doodling, his images stimulated the minds of future inventors." The doctor bit his lip. "Yes. Humans can fly. Flying machines, or what today are called airplanes, have been invented. They are the fastest means of transportation from one place to another…"

Sergeant Black's mouth opened. Confusion crossed his face. "Aye. I saw such a flying object earlier today. Dr. Morris called it an airplane."

"Yes. Where two hundred years ago it took anywhere from seven weeks to seven months to travel from Boston to London, today a trip across the Atlantic takes six to seven hours." Dr. Gorski paused to allow Noland to process what he had just been told. "And something more astonishing, humans not only fly all over the earth, but six years ago, three men, for the first time, landed and walked on the moon. There have been several more visits since. They flew, not on an airplane, but on an Apollo rocket."

"This cannot be not real." Sergeant Black's hands covered his face. He shook his head in disbelief.

"Can I get you a glass of water, Mr. Black?" Dr. Morris asked.

"No. No. What you say, cannot be true." Sergeant Black stared at the ceiling. His mind conjured the moon hanging in the night sky. "That is not possible."

"It is," Dr. Morris said quietly. "Two hundred years ago, a group of Americans, you called them rebels, frustrated by the way Great Britain was treating them, revolted. The war they started, theoretically, they should not have won, because two hundred years ago Great Britain was the greatest military force on earth—but the American rebels did win. Sergeant Noland Black, today is April the twentieth, 1975, and you are in Charlestown, Massachusetts, which is in the United States of America, a country totally independent from Great Britain…"

Disturbed, Noland's body tensed. His face reddened. He clenched his fists, jerked himself upright, and sat straight and tense. "You do not speak the truth. It cannot be. Motley groups of rebels did attack my regiment yesterday. They would have been overrun had they not ambushed us. And when reinforcements arrived, the rebels would have been destroyed. What you say is not true." His arms flung up, which caused him to shutter and wince. He shook off the pain that shot from his right shoulder down his back and flipped his legs off the bed. His feet thudded onto the floor. "My uniform, *please*. I need to be returned to my regiment! For if I do not, I will be marked as a deserter or spy and hung.

Dr. Morris pressed the nurse-call button. Within a minute, Mia's face appeared at the door. "Bring a sedative."

"I think the sergeant would rather have a glass of rum," Dr. Gorski said in a gentle, kind voice, then put his hand on Noland's shoulder. "What we've told you is true. I understand your anxiety, confusion, and disbelief. Somehow and some way you have come forward in time, two hundred years. I don't know how that happened, but everything we've learned so far, indicates you did. We need to talk, but first you need to calm down and get a hold of yourself." He turned to Dr. Morris. "Call Mia. Have her go to your office. In my bag, lying against your desk, she'll find a bottle of rum. I figured that the sergeant may need something familiar to him that will settle his nerves before this day ends, while he contemplates what has happened to him." Dr. Gorski smiled at Noland, while Dr. Morris hurriedly pushed the nurses' call button several times. Mia finally appeared at the door.

"Please go to my office and get the bottle of rum out of Dr. Gorski's bag and bring it here. Forget the sedative," Dr. Morris said.

In less than ten minutes Mia returned with the rum, some glasses, and a bowl of ice.

"That was quick," Dr. Gorski said. He opened the bottle and poured a shot into three glasses. "Mia, will you join us?"

Mia shook her head. "I'm still on duty but thank you." She went out the door and returned to the nurses' station.

Dr. Gorski grinned and handed a glass to Dr. Morris. He then turned and handed one to the sergeant. "It's certainly not old English rum, but it's the next best thing. This rum comes from Jamaica. Isn't that where the British in North America got their rum?"

"Aye. Indeed, they did." Sergeant Black sighed as he passed the glass under his nose, smelled the burnt sugary aroma, and then took a sip. He momentarily choked. "Definitely has the flavor of Jamaican rum." He took another swallow. Though he nodded approval and seemed to be relaxing, he continued to appear distressed. "We have been on many expeditions to search for weapons and ammunition the colonials had or may have hidden. There were skirmishes. Minor disputes and combativeness, but these wrangles ended in calmness and conciliation. No one was killed. But yesterday, on our return from Concord, we were ambushed."

"Yes," Dr. Morris said. "On the way to Concord, your expedition stopped in Lexington, where the troops fell into ranks on the town green. Then some damned fool, rebel or soldier, fired a musket, and all hell broke loose. Your guys started firing indiscriminately at the colonists assembled along the edges of the green. Several were killed, others wounded. That first shot has become known as the 'Shot heard around the world.' That shot started the American Revolutionary War…"

"Aye!" blustered Sergeant Black. "Recruits! Most of the men had never experienced battle. Young. Insecure. Uneasy. Never before been shot at. Became excited. Momentarily, they disregarded commands to cease fire." His muscles tensed. He exhaled deeply and clasped his fists. "These were the troops I had to contend with. The entire clash was an ill-fated mistake."

"It was indeed," Dr. Gorski said. "Unfortunately, several colonists died that day."

Sergeant Black slumped. "That first shot was not fired by the troops. But it threw them into disarray."

"To this day, no one knows who fired that first musket shot. But it was the catalyst that started the war for independence." Dr. Gorski lifted the bottle of rum. "Yes, it was an unfortunate mistake, but the pot was already boiling. All it took was that one shot to boil it over. Your regiment felt the brunt of the colonists' anger toward Great Britain on your return from Concord and Lexington—an anger that had been stewing for several years." He held the rum bottle toward the sergeant. "Can I give you another tot?"

Sergeant Black relaxed and held his glass out. Dr. Gorski poured him a couple of ounces more rum and looked over at Dr. Morris, stood, and walked to her. "What time is it getting to be?"

She looked at her watch. "Just about two o'clock. Have you another appointment?"

"No," he whispered for only her to hear. "Thought I'd run to my apartment and get a few pieces of clothing."

"Good idea. I'll keep the sergeant company until you return."

Dr. Gorski excused himself, stood, and left the room.

Noland became anxious when Gorski walked out of the room. "Why is he leaving?"

"Dr. Gorski has gone on an errand to get you some modern clothing. He'll return in about an hour. Since your clothing is not of our time, you'd look very conspicuous. Some might think you are an actor, but this is not New York City, where that is more common. So, you need to appear as someone who lives in the present. Also, tomorrow is Monday, and this place will be full of medical people and support staff who normally work here during the week. Many, if they come in contact with you, will have questions. Questions, that if answered, will create additional curiosity, confusion, and circumstances that can bring on unwanted consequences. So, we have to get you out of here tonight. You are well enough to leave. What care you may need can be done outside of a hospital."

"But to where?" The sergeant's anxieties increased. "You said, my barracks, my regiment, do not exist. I do not know where I am. Where will I go. I am lost…"

"We're not going to turn you out into the cold." Dr. Morris looked at the sergeant with care and concern. "Dr. Gorski and I will take you to my home, since he has only a small apartment. My house is not far away and large enough for us both to have private space. We decided it would be best for you to stay with me until we can determine what to do."

"How did I get here?"

"I don't know. That is a mystery humanity has yet to solve. If it is even solvable."

After Sergeant Noland Black showered and dressed in the clothing that Dr. Gorski brought for him, he and Dr. Morris left the hospital room. Instead of the British grenadier that he was, the sergeant resembled a spiffy twentieth-century young man dressed in a pair of Levi's. He wore a gray sweatshirt with UCONN printed in blue across the chest, and a pair of L.L. Bean scuffed hiking shoes. His anxiety peaked when he exited the medical clinic and stood in the parking lot contemplating Dr. Morris's green 1973 series 1300 VW Super Beetle. She opened the hood and motioned to him to come near. He stumbled toward her, shaking his head as he stared at the empty space at the front of the vehicle. She put his uniform into the trunk of the "Bug," closed the hatch, looked up at him, and smiled. She liked what she saw; the way the clothing he wore accentuated his muscles. To her, the tight-fitting sweatshirt gave him the rugged air of an adventurer. She also noticed his anxious eyes and nervous gestures. *A bit tall for this vehicle, but I'm sure he'll become accustomed to it and the other things this modern world has to offer,* she thought. The doctor motioned for him to follow her around to the right. She walked to the passenger-side door, stood next to it, and grabbed the door handle.

The sergeant, perplexed, kept his eyes on Dr. Morris as he inched along behind her. As he walked, he slid his hand along the side of the Bug. When he got to the door, he placed his hands onto the roof as if for support. He then gave the little car a slight push. The VW flicked back and forth. It seemed his uneasiness gave way to a sense of power and control, *'Tis indeed a sturdy object. But how does it move?*

"This is where the passenger sits." Dr. Morris opened the door. She then walked around the VW to the driver's side, opened the door, and slid into the seat.

"You have to get in if we're going to go anywhere," she said.

"Aye." A quizzical expression crossed the sergeant's face as he attempted to struggle into the VW. *My god, a woman in control of this strange vehicle. What has the world come to?* He put his left leg in, but his body got stuck between the door and back of the seat. Trepidation surged as he tussled about. Shaking his head, he pushed himself out, turned, and stood next to the Bug.

"Darn! Sorry. You're a big guy. Should have thought of that. Wait a minute." Dr. Morris reached down, grabbed the seat adjustment lever, and shoved the passenger seat back as far as it would slide. "Now, sit yourself into the seat and swing your legs in. Then grab the door handle and pull the door closed. There is a handhold above the door. It'll keep you steady when we are moving. Also, before we move, you have to wear a seat belt. Reach to the right next to the seat and you'll feel it. Pull the belt across your waist and push it into the buckle on the left of the seat."

Following the doctor's instructions, he crammed himself into the seat and closed the door. His knees were almost to the level of his chest. "A bit cramped," he protested. "A buggy has more space for my legs. And I can stand in it if I would so desire." He reached up and his hand vise-gripped the handle above the door.

"Seat belt!" Dr. Morris said and started the Bug's engine.

"Aye!" Noland winced when he heard the growl from behind. As he squirmed, his right hand scuffled about trying to find the seat belt. Finding it, he gripped it and pulled the belt across himself, but had trouble trying to connect the latch to the lock.

Dr. Morris reached over his lap, took hold of the belt, pulled it to the lock, and pushed it down. "Hear it snap," she said. "We're good to go." She shifted the car into reverse, slowly backed out of her space, turned, and pointed the car's nose toward the parking lot exit. Then shifting into first gear, she crept ahead to the street. "Dr. Gorski will follow, when he sees us come out onto High Street."

After negotiating the side street that led from the parking lot, Dr. Morris slowed the VW and turned the Bug onto High Street. Noland gasped and held the handle above the door in a white-knuckled grip as the centrifugal force swung him to the left.

CHAPTER 9

Sunday, April 20, 1975

Two eight-foot-tall excel lilac bushes, planted not far from Dr. Morris's gray-with-white-trimmed, two-story cape cottage, scented the afternoon air that came through the vents as she drove her Beetle into the driveway. When Noland wiggled out of the Bug, he stumbled, caught himself, then stretched. He took a breath, put his hands on the vehicle, and stepped away. "A very unusual experience." He smiled and sighed. "Ahh. A fragrance I have not smelled since childhood." He twisted his body several times to loosen his back muscles, relaxed, and looked at the house. "Is your spouse home, Ma'am?"

"I'm widowed." Dr. Morris exited the vehicle and walked to its front. She grabbed the handle and lifted the hood. "Norma, my friend who shares my house and takes care of it, is at home. She is also a good cook and lives in a cozy cottage behind the house. I'll introduce you as my cousin, who is visiting from England, when we get inside. That will explain your accent." Dr. Morris reached into the trunk and collected the sergeant's clothing. "By the way, you can call me Carol. Cousins are not usually formal."

"Aye, Mistress Carol. Then I should be known by the name my mother always called me before I volunteered for the military and left England. Please, I am Noland."

"Thank you, Noland, but drop the Mistress. No one uses that anymore. Here, take your coat. The bullet holes have been sewn up." Dr. Morris handed Noland his red coat, tucked the rest of his clothes under her arm, and closed the hood.

The two became distracted when Dr. Gorski pulled into the driveway and parked his 1970 Chevrolet Impala behind the Bug. They waited until he exited his automobile and joined them.

"Thank you, Dr. Morris…" Dr. Gorski said, "for giving me your contact information. It helped me find your place." Dr. Gorski gripped the handle of the briefcase he held and spread his arms. "Let me take that bundle of clothes."

Dr. Morris handed Noland's garments to Dr. Gorski. "Thank you. We're not at work. As I told Noland, we can be less formal. My name is Carol. Let's go into the house."

Norma, a plump, grandmotherly-looking woman of around sixty-five years of age, with a head full of tight, white curls, greeted the three as they entered the living room. "I see you brought some friends home, Carol. Welcome."

"This is Norma, a nurse friend who needed an activity after retirement. She agreed to tend my house and cook if I allowed her to stay in the little cottage out back," Dr. Morris said and introduced the two men. "Norma, this is Mr. Noland Black. Noland is a long-lost cousin; we haven't seen each other since we were children. He's visiting from London, England, and to my surprise, the medics brought him to the clinic. He ran into some problems in town, and we had to patch him up. He's okay now but has no place to stay. So, I asked Noland to stay with us for several days. He'll be our guest. I know the guestroom hasn't been used for a time, so could you…"

Norma smiled at Noland and offered her hand. "So nice to meet you, Mr. Black." She glanced up at Dr. Morris and nodded her approval of the young man. "Yes, I will prepare the guestroom. Does Mr. Black have any luggage?" She then looked back at Noland.

"Umm?" Dr. Morris paused for a moment. "Luggage?" She glanced at Dr. Gorski. "His luggage was lost—or stolen. Dr. Gorski is holding his clothes that were damaged in the scuffle, and the red coat Noland is holding are the only clothes he has at this time. Dr. Gorski was kind enough to lend the garments he is wearing. Lucky the guys are both about the same size."

"Oh, dear." Norma scanned him from head to toe. "Let me have your coat. I'll lay it across the back of this chair." Her eyes then turned to Dr. Morris. "Perhaps Mr. Black might fit into some of Mr. Morris's clothing. He seems to be of his size."

Dr. Morris raised her eyelids and shrugged at Norma. "Yes. I have yet to empty his closet. Some of Ray's casuals may fit Noland. I will check later. Thank you for the suggestion. Also, please excuse my lack of concern, Norma. I should have given you a warning this afternoon, that I was bringing guests home this evening. I hope we have something to offer our visitors?"

"It is not a problem, Ma'am. Yes, I made a small roast this afternoon, but I do believe there will be enough for all of you. I have eaten, but I'll make mashed potatoes and green beans. It'll only take a few minutes. We have plenty of wine. So, all will be fine. Now who is this young man?" Norma gestured toward Dr. Gorski.

"Ah, sorry. This is Dr. Andrew Gorski. He's a colleague who works at Mass General Hospital in Boston, and he's also a Revolutionary War reenactor."

Norma extended her hand. "Pleasure to meet you, Doctor."

Andrew nodded and sheepishly looked at the bundle he held. His right wrist ached from holding the briefcase in an odd position. "Yes, these are Noland's clothes. They need washing and mending."

Norma smiled and extended her arms. "Please let me take those things. I know a good seamstress. I sure she'll be able to repair the damage done to the shirt and pants and then clean them. Should only take a day or two."

"Thank you." Dr. Gorski let Norma take the bundle. He placed the briefcase next to a wingback chair and rubbed his wrist.

"Sorry to burden you with all of this, Norma." Dr. Morris bit her lip and apologized again. "I'm not being very kind to you."

Norma shook her head. "Not to worry, Ma'am." She laid the bundle of clothing in the chair next to the kitchen door. Straightening, she slid her hands down the side of her light blue dress covered in a pattern of small white flowers. "It is quite all right, my dear," she said with a smile. "Please excuse me. I had planned to retire early this evening. I have a new book to read that has just come out. An adult fantasy written by Richard Matheson titled *Bid Time Return*. It's about a young man who finds a photo of a beautiful young actress and falls in love with her image. His problem is that she lived long ago. But supposedly they do get together, because somehow, he is transported into the past and meets her. I'm anxious to read it. I'll leave you all, but first, I will stop by the kitchen to mash the potatoes and take care of what else needs to be done. Then, I'll go to the cottage and read my new book. It is a pleasure meeting you gentlemen. Hope you'll stop by again, Dr. Gorski." Norma touched Noland's arm as she turned to leave. "Expect a good breakfast in the morning. I'll see you tomorrow. Goodnight, all." Norma picked up Noland's clothes. Everyone wished Norma a good night.

"Such a fine, sweet woman," Dr. Morris expressed. "I think of her as my lost aunt. Cares for me and the house. She does a perfect job, is great company, and never has any complaints. Since the cottage doesn't have much of a kitchen, I let her use the one here in the house. Norma's husband died a few years before she retired. He was her only family. Now she's part of mine. Been with me for about four years." Dr. Morris paused. "Interesting, Norma picked up a copy of the book I mentioned earlier, Andrew. I'll have to read it later." She then moved to a dark, wooden cabinet next to an armchair, bent down, and opened it. "Can I offer you a glass of wine or something stronger? Then we can eat, and after, relax and discuss Noland's dilemma."

Satiated with leftover roast beef, mashed potatoes, gravy, and green beans that Norma had put together, all returned to the living room. Noland seated himself on the gray mohair-covered armchair across from the couch. Dr. Gorski dropped into a nearby wingchair, while Dr. Morris topped everyone's glass with red wine, then relaxed on the couch.

Though Sergeant Black appeared tranquil, his eyes and face reflected confusion and uncertainty. "A very satisfying meal," he said. "Please complement Madam Norma. I have not had such a dinner in many years. Military cooks do not have the skill to create such a simple, yet satisfying meal." He sighed. "I want to thank you both for tending to my injuries, but I am not in my world. I must return to my regiment, but I do not know where I am, nor where my regiment is, or how I came to be here, or…" he shrugged, "how to return. Mostly I feel you have doubts. I do not know how to convince you that I am who I say I am. I do not belong here." His body slumped as he inquisitively glanced back and forth from Dr. Morris to Dr. Gorski. His fingers slid insensibly along the area of his neck where the amulet once hung.

Humbled by a lack of answers, Gorski shrugged. "As I told you earlier today, you are in twentieth-century Charlestown. We found you exactly two hundred years, to the date, along the original Concord to Lexington Road where your regiment was attacked by colonial milia and minutemen. How you got here? I cannot say. I have no answer to that question.

"You see, in the past two hundred years, many great inventions and fantastic discoveries have been made. But time-travel is not one of them, though over the years a few authors have written of such possibilities. Like, for example, the new book that Norma is, at this time, probably lying in her bed and reading. These stories are science fiction. Perhaps someday, someone will discover a way to travel into the past and to the future. But at this time, that has not happened.

"And most of the time-travel stories are about characters that travel into the past to visit or attempt to change history. As far as I know, only one author has written a book where his character travels into the future. Just before the turn of the century, an Englishman by the name of H.G. Wells wrote a science fantasy titled, *The Time Machine*. His protagonist..." Dr. Gorski looked at Noland, who appeared detached. "Are you following me?"

"Aye! Most interesting. Please continue." Noland took a sip of wine.

"Yes." Dr. Gorski continued. "Mr. Wells's protagonist invented a machine that could take him forward or backward through time, but since the machine could not move from one place to another on its own, he kept the time machine in his laboratory near a window where he could see outside at the changes that supposedly would occur as he passed through time. He seated himself in the time machine. In front of him was a lever that controlled the direction in time he wanted to travel. Since the traveler was most interested in the future, he pushed a lever forward. A large disk behind his seat began to spin and, as he watched through the window, the scene outside changed. After he had traveled some years into the future, he stopped. The window had been boarded up, obstructing his view. He left the time machine, went outside, and tore the boards from the laboratory's window. His house stood, though timeworn, and he saw that most of the other windows on the house had also been boarded. After, he returned to the time machine and continued his travel. He stopped again when London was being bombarded. Again, he went outside, but quickly returned to the laboratory and the time machine and pushed the lever forward as far as it would go. The disk behind the traveler spun rapidly and transported him quickly many thousands of years into the future. When he finally eased back on the lever and brought his travel to a stop, he found himself in a world not like what he had left, but one totally different; a seemingly lush, peaceful, and serene world." Dr. Gorski ended and took a swallow of his wine. "It's an exciting story—but it's only a fantasy."

"Does the traveler return to his own time?"

Gorski grinned. "He does."

Dr. Morris took a drink. "Yes, though *The Time Machine* is a stirring story, Andrew, a few years ago another book was written about traveling into the future. A young-adult book titled *A Wrinkle in Time*. The book was written by Madeleine L'Engle, only her method of time travel has a scientific possibility. She uses the idea of a tesseract, a four-dimensional geometric concept of a small cube within a larger cube, with time as the additional dimension. The perception is that the tesseract would allow a traveler to go through time by passing through the space of the larger cube into the space of the smaller cube. The tesseract is sort of a time portal. This concept fits with Albert Einstein's Theory of Relativity. Since I'm not a physicist, I have no idea what that theory is all about. So that's as much as I can add to explain time travel."

The tesseract concept caught Dr. Gorski's attention. "Space-time warp!" he yelped. "Yes. Einstein's theory predicted this. The author of *A Wrinkle in Time* utilizes Einstein's prediction that there are folds in the space-time continuum. And if there was a hole, channel, bridge, or pipeline between two closely aligned folds, it would allow a time traveler to pass from the present into the future or past. The tesseract analogy describes such a portal, a doorway to the past or future. Neat idea, but this is pure conjecture. However, in reality, such portals have recently been theorized by other physicists. Einstein's theory also predicts black holes or dark stars in the space-time continuum. Writers of the television series *Star Trek* have hopped on this idea. They use black holes as the time portals that enable the Starship Enterprise to travel light-year distances in a short time. Of course, I imagine Scotty had to activate the ship's warp-drive too." Dr. Gorski chuckled and shook his head. "Black holes have never been seen or verified. Likewise, neither has L'Engle's use of the tesseract as a means to create time travel portals. Ah well…" Gorski scratched his head, "except in the minds of science fiction advocates and writers. Imagination is a great diversion." Dr. Gorski shook his head. "Since I'm neither a physicist, nor a writer, I'm not even sure if what I said is accurate."

"Please excuse me." Sergeant Black clasped and squeezed his hands. "Your attempts to explain my presence are confusing me terribly. The examples and manifestations you provide are, to me, farfetched. I know not of black holes, time portals, television, or how I got here, but I'm here, and I must return home immediately."

"The bottom line is, we don't know how you got here or if it's even possible you will ever return to your time." Gorski raised his eyebrows and gritted his teeth in apology for his ignorance. "Sorry, my friend…"

"With all the unknowns," Dr. Morris interrupted, "I'm still skeptical if you are telling us the truth about who you are and where you came from. Dr. Gorski found a message in the pocket of your coat which appears to be convincing. But we still feel uncertain, because to us, time travel does not exist. If you really are from two hundred years ago, there is no way to explain how you got here." She sighed in frustration.

"Yes," Dr. Gorski said, as he walked to where the coat lay over the back of the chair, reached under its lapel, and removed the message. "Noland, I examined your coat while Dr. Morris and I were still at the clinic. Little worn, but it appears as an authentic eighteenth-century British red coat. While I had your coat spread across Dr. Morris's desk, the corner of this communication…" Gorski reached into the coat and removed the parchment, "slipped into view. I read it. It's written in early English script. And it appears to be combat orders. It is signed by the Commander of Regiments in Boston, Lieutenant General Hugh Percy, and issued to your field commander, Lieutenant Colonel Francis Smith. How did you, a mere sergeant, get a copy of these orders?"

Noland gave Dr. Gorski an imposing stare. "Aye. The orders you have are the expedition's orders-of-the-day. Lieutenant Colonel Smith always scribed copies to inform company leaders. On expeditions where little military action is expected, as the one to Concord to locate hidden weapon and ammunition stores, an experienced grenadier is appointed to lead a company of recruits to ready them for more difficult missions. This happens when there are insufficient rank officers in the garrison. Since I have sufficient prior military experience, I was assigned a position of supervision. My charge is a company of fifty recruits at the Ferry Hill barracks. That is why I received the orders—"

"Ah yes." Dr. Gorski interrupted. "I apologize for being patronizing, but I wanted to hear your answer. I assumed that to be the case. In today's army you'd be rated as a Master Sergeant. I believe that would be the same in today's British army. It's a non-commission rate that allows one to lead a small company of men; usually they're recruits. Here in America, we call them drill sergeants."

Sergeant Black gave Dr. Gorski a curious look and proceeded with his explanation. "Aye. That may be so. I have been assigned to lead twenty such missions. They are boring outings. I would rather be assigned to a vanguard unit. But in the military, we rarely have a choice. Though on occasion, the recruit company does encounter colonial anger and bluster. This is good for beginners. Reduces anxiety. Keeps them alert. Strengthens their resolve. Usually, the show of rebel force comes as a brandishing of pitchforks, axes, rusted swords, clubs, and sometimes a musket that is shot into the air. Except for bruises and cuts, the men are not injured badly from their encounters…" Noland paused; pursed his lips in a show of depression, "but the Concord mission turned out not to be so. The expedition on its return was ambushed and attacked."

Dr. Gorski nodded. "Thank you, Sergeant. Your words clarified your position in the battle. Your company came upon a very difficult situation. An encounter that was unexpected. But the colonials were already on the verge of revolt. The pot, so to speak, had started boiling some years before. It is unfortunate that your men were less battle ready..." Gorski sighed and sipped his wine.

"Aye." Noland sat more upright. "My company was the least experienced. I do not feel they fared well. Most of Lieutenant Colonel Smith's regiment were experienced infantry. And they were ahead, but they too were surprised by an attack. I do not know how they managed."

"Perhaps I can ease your mind."

"Let me interrupt for a moment." Dr. Morris raised and shook an empty bottle. "I'll open another, while you two continue your conversation. Sounds like Dr. Gorski is convinced you have somehow traveled from the past." She looked at the two men.

Dr. Gorski nodded and Noland Black grinned. Dr. Morris took hold of the new bottle, cut off the wrapping around the neck, and cranked the wine screw into the cork.

"Sergeant Black," Gorski continued, "I enjoy learning about how Boston took part in the American Revolution. That is why I became a reenactor and have studied the history of America's war for independence. I am aware of Lieutenant Colonel Smith and Lieutenant General Percy and can inform you that Smith's expedition survived. By the time the regiment reached Lexington, word had reached General Percy's office and he sent a one-thousand-man reinforcement unit, double-time, to rescue the troops that came under siege. Without rapid communication, I don't know how your command in Boston was informed of the rebel attack. Perhaps Lieutenant Colonel Smith dispatched a man or two on horseback to obtain reinforcements. However, I did learn that the British lost a few troops. I don't know how many. And with reinforcements, your Lieutenant Colonel Smith was able to get the expedition back to Boston. For your information, the Battle at Concord and Lexington is marked in history as the battle that began America's War for Independence." Andrew held his glass toward Dr. Morris for a refill.

Dr. Morris nodded and poured some wine in Dr. Gorski's glass, turned, and aimed the bottle neck at Sergeant Black.

"Aye." He raised his glass.

Dr. Morris filled the sergeant's glass about half full and, while doing so, looked at his hair. "Noland, you have a fine head of hair. Does the military allow long hair?"

"Thank you." Sergeant Black brushed the hair off his right ear. "Aye. A soldier's hair must not exceed ten inches. That is the required length. It cannot be cut shorter. That is a regulation. And, when properly combed, the hair must be pulled to the back of the head and worn with a proper length queue." Using both hands, he pushed the hair along the sides of his head back, grabbed the bundle, and held it at the back of his head. "To stay in place, my queue would have to be tied at a proper length, one inch above its end. I cannot put my hair into a queue. My lanyard has been lost."

Dr. Morris smiled. "Today soldiers wear their hair brush cut."

Dr. Gorski beamed. "Another piece of trivia that almost no one knows, this business about hair length in the eighteenth-century British military. Noland is correct. Regulations in the British army at that time were quite stringent when it came to being properly coifed. While in rank formation, all the soldiers had to look the same from behind. They all had to wear their hair in a queue. Why, you ask? Because it looked good in a parade. This is not the case anymore. Most military personnel wear a buzz cut." Gorski gulped some of his wine.

"Buzz cut?" Noland looked confused. "I do not know what that may be."

Dr. Morris laughed. "It's a mark of machoism, manliness. It's also called a crewcut. The top of your head looks like a brush, so called a brush cut, and the sides of your head are almost bare."

"That would not have been looked upon favorably," Sergeant Black commented. "This war for independence, you speak of. How could there have been one? The rebels were not organized, lacked discipline. They fought with crude weapons, rusted muskets, pitchforks, axes, clubs. The village militias, nothing but ragtag gangs. If such a war had been waged against Great Britain, it would have been squashed in a matter of days. And the leaders hung for treason against King George. So how can you speak of such a war? Unbelievable, unbelievable…"

"Unbelievable?" Dr. Gorski grinned. "As unbelievable as you being here, two hundred years after that war occurred. The American Revolutionary War did happen. Great Britain lost. America—the ragtag gangs, as you called them, under the command of one dominant, dynamic leader, won. The Americans fought for and won their independence from Great Britain."

Noland grasped his head, then shook it in disbelief and shouted, "That cannot be true!" He glared at the floor. His head snapped up. He glowered at Drs. Gorski and Morris. "How can a disparate, untrained mass of disorganized gangs compete with the most superior military power on earth, the finest marksmen, most astute leaders and strategists, greatest naval force on earth…" Sergeant Black's hands covered his face and he mumbled, "this cannot be."

Andrew wiped his forehead and took a drink of wine.

"Dr. Gorski is telling you the truth," Dr. Morris said. "Remember, you are two hundred years in the future. The action of those small groups of untrained, undisciplined rebels, has, over the years, increased the fledgling thirteen colonies into an independent, democratic country composed of fifty-two colonies, now called states, known as the United States of America."

Noland raised his head. "This *cannot* be. Great Britain, the mightiest military force the world has ever seen, lost to a mass of rebels?" Shaking his head, he continued to mutter, "Unbelievable."

"Believe it," Dr. Morris said. "One can still consider that the sun never sets on the British Empire. Great Britain is still one of the mightiest military forces in the world, but so is the United States of America. And there are several others in the world that will argue that they have the mightiest military, but that's another story. Now, settle down, drink your wine, ask questions, and Andrew and I will try to bring you up to date."

"I have a question," Dr. Gorski said as he placed his wineglass on the side table, rose from the chair, and walked to the couch where Sergeant Black's bundle of damaged clothes had lain. His soiled white cross-belt was still lying there. Norma had not taken it. Dr. Gorski picked it up and examined the brass plate that was attached where the belts crossed. "This plate has an X inscribed on it. I assume the X is the Roman numeral for ten, the mark of the Tenth Regiment. It indicates that, as you said, you belonged to the Tenth Regiment of Foot."

Noland nodded. "Aye. That is correct."

"Your red coat, which has yellow facing, also signifies that regiment's color." Dr. Gorski looked at Noland with a happy smile. "I believe you are who you say you are." After one quick inspection, he laid the belt back on the couch. "I hope you brought your piece of white pipe clay. The belt needs a bit of a cleaning." Gorski returned to his chair.

Noland grinned. "You inspected my coat. I'm surprised you did not find it in the coat pocket. Now, please explain how an untrained force of motley rebels won a war over the mightiest army in the world. For me this is very hard to believe."

"If I were in your situation, I too would find that unbelievable. Welcome to the twentieth century. Now, let us sit back and enjoy the wine and I'll try to give you the highlights of the American Revolution for Independence and a summary of what has happened in the past two hundred years."

"Andrew, while you go into your history lesson, I'm going to excuse myself." Dr. Morris rose from where she sat. "I need to make sure the guestroom is ready and try to find some of my husband's things so Noland will have something to wear. I feel this is going to be a long evening. There is another bottle of wine and some snacks in the kitchen."

Both men looked up and smiled at her. Dr. Gorski asked that she return as soon as possible, because he felt he needed assistance and verification. Sergeant Black agreed.

"Yes," Dr. Morris said. "Also, Sergeant Noland Black does not really exist in the twentieth century. But, since he is alive and here, breathing in this room, we need to figure out what to do with him. And, how to integrate him into this century. Something to think about."

"No!" Noland grunted. "I cannot stay in this century. I have duties; I must see to my men. You say my arrival is a mystery. But something brought me here. Whatever it is, we must find it. We should go to where you found me. It may still be there, and I can return to my time."

"Perhaps so," Dr. Gorski said pensively. "To return to where you turned up is not a problem, but trying to locate the impetus of transport will be the challenge." Gorski pick up his glass of wine and took a sip. He nodded to Dr. Morris to continue on her errand. "For now, let's relax, enjoy the evening while I try to briefly bring you up to date on what has happened in the past two hundred years."

C H A P T E R 10

Sunday, April 20, 1975

Sergeant Noland Black sat mostly in silence as Dr. Gorski provided him with the highlights of the American War for Independence. He kept his eyes closed and, when he opened them, he gazed in disbelief. Or sometimes, they glistened in credence. For the most part, his hands covered his face. Occasionally he'd shake his head, especially when the doctor mentioned battles the British lost. Noland's face reddened and his fists punched the arms of the chair when Dr. Gorski told him about the blockade of Boston, which led to the British evacuating the city.

"My apology," Noland said. I almost lost my life fighting for my country and to lose a battle causes agony.

"I understand." Gorski continued.

When he mentioned how General William Howe and his brother, Admiral Richard Howe, invaded Long Island, chased George Washington and his troops off of Manhattan Island and hung a few spies, the sergeant raised his glass and toasted his comrades. "By the way, Great Britain held New York City for the duration of the war." Dr. Gorski smirked.

Noland smiled and asked, "How long did the war last?"

"Eight years and a few months," Gorski answered. "The war began yesterday two hundred years ago—remember the phrase that Dr. Morris reiterated, 'The shot that was heard around the world.' Someone, to this day no one knows who, fired the musket when you and your men stood in rank on the Lexington Green on the morning of April nineteen in the year 1775. And all hell broke out for a few minutes. But before the British commanders brought their troops under control and ordered them to cease fire, six or seven colonials were fatally shot. The rest of them ran away. You all regained your ranks and marched on to Concord. History refers to that 'shot' as the one that started the American War against Great Britain."

Noland straightened. "I sensed great tension among the men who stood in rank in the open on that day. They were not battle trained. Rebels, brandishing muskets and other weapons, stood on the edges of the green, harassed and jeered the British troops. Many of them had never been fired upon. When they heard that shot, those in the front ranks became alarmed, dropped to their knees, and, without being ordered, started shooting." He lowered his head. "The troops' reaction was a major blunder." The sergeant paused and sighed. "When the chaos was brought under control, there was no one to answer to. The rebels had scattered. It was later found that the musket shot came from behind a nearby barn." Noland's chest expanded. "This is why I need to return. Our recruits need more training. They need confidence and discipline."

Dr. Gorski nodded. "Anyway, that shot started a war, which ended at Yorktown, Virginia eight years later. Your General Charles Cornwallis surrendered his sword to General George Washington."

Sergeant Black shook his head. "I do not understand how a highly disciplined army could be brought to its knees by an ill-trained, poorly armed bunch of ragtag rebels. I cannot believe that Great Britain's superior military could lose such a war. I do not believe what you say." He gritted his teeth and, for a moment, stared at the ceiling. His head lowered and he glanced at his glass of wine. "Might you have something stronger?"

Dr. Gorski reached over the arm of the chair, unsnapped his briefcase, and removed the bottle of rum he had brought to the clinic earlier that day. "Indeed, you definitely need something stouter." He screwed off the bottle's cap and poured Noland and himself a shot of rum. Comforting himself against the back of the chair, Gorski lifted his glass and took a deep breath. "Drink up and I'll pour you another tot. You'll need a fortifier when I try to explain why the British lost the war, a war you guys should have won. Great Britain had the military advantages, skills, and resources. The colonials didn't."

Noland swigged down his drink.

"Though the British fought valiantly, your regiments used line-formation warfare. An effective method to get a lot of bullets in the air with inaccurate muskets, but also an excellent way to lose many troops if the enemy being attacked is undercover. Your military never adapted the guerrilla or irregular warfare methods the colonials learned from native Americans, the usage of stealth, hide and shoot, surprise attacks, retreat and run. General George Washington was a master strategist in using these techniques."

"Who is this General George Washington?"

"He was the Commander of the Continental Army, appointed to that position a month or two after the Battle of Concord and Lexington. Many of the men he commanded thought him a god. They believed he would never let them down. To everyone he encountered, he instilled the strong desire to fight for independence. Washington is one of the most honored men in America. After the war he was elected the first president of the United States of America." Gorski poured himself a shot of rum, took a sip, and continued his explanation. "Great Britain had other disadvantages that led to its demise. Geography and communication. Seems your commanders relied on orders from King George and Parliament. Those orders took much time to be delivered across the Atlantic. And, for the British commanders on this side of the Atlantic, there was a lack of knowledge. They didn't know how faraway places, like cities and towns, were from their bases. Nor did they know how to get to them or what sort of terrain lay between one place and another. America is a vast nation. There were rather few road maps back then. Geographic uncertainty created havoc to travel and to the movements of troops. But, I think, the greatest disadvantage was the desire to engage in a war so far from home. Your soldiers really didn't have the will and drive to fight, and essentially do battle against their own countrymen. To them that was a moral drawback. Whereas the determination of the colonials to fight for their ideas of freedom, the need to protect what they had built, and the supposed desire for the future of the country they were trying to create, was enormous."

Sergeant Black closed his eyes and rubbed them. He lowered his head, then raised it. "What you say does have merit. The men in my regiment were young recruits, but they were dedicated. Except for several small skirmishes they encountered with a few belligerents, they never had to avoid musket balls fired at them during an ambush. And being young, they longed for their home and family." He massaged his forehead and tussled his hair. "This is why I must return. The troops need more training, learn to fight as a unit, and stifle sentimentality."

"That sounds pretty rough, but that's how wars are won," Dr. Gorski said after taking a sip of his rum.

"Aye," Sergeant Black groaned. "Does Great Britain still exist?"

"It does indeed. As Dr. Morris mentioned earlier, 'the sun never sets on Great Britain.' Great Britain gained this acclaim when it won its long-lasting war with France a few years after the American Revolution, now known as the Napoleonic War. Your country took over many of the territories around the world that France governed. A much larger prize for Great Britain back then than the American colonies. Eventually the American colonies and Great Britain become strong commercial, military, and political allies."

Sergeant Black stretched forward in his chair, closed his eyes, and rubbed his legs. He squinted in utter confusion and stared at Dr. Gorski. "The America I know is not here. What you are telling me has bewildered my mind. I do not understand. The American rebels went to war with Great Britain, were victorious, gained independence, but did not claim sovereignty over Great Britain. Instead, the two countries became strong allies? This I do not understand. Are the British Isles independent? Is there still a monarchy? Who rules England, Great Britain?"

Dr. Gorski took another sip of rum. "The colonists, or rebels, as you call them, fought the war to gain independence. It was never a war of expansion.

"As years went by the United States and Great Britain realized they needed each other economically and militarily, so they formed an alliance." Dr. Gorski paused for a breath and then continued.

"To answer your other questions, Great Britain is still a monarchy, presently reigned over by a queen. But the British Isles themselves are democratic rather than feudal. The country is ruled by the people, somewhat like what we have here in America. In England, legislative officials, the Members of Parliament, are elected by the people. The political party with most members appoints the prime minister, who has authority over the various legislative branches of government. The monarch can agree with the prime minister, but if she or he does not, the prime minister doesn't lose his head." Dr. Gorski chuckled. "The present Prime Minister of Great Britain is Harold Wilson. I do not know to what party he belongs. But, since King George the third, there have been seven monarchs. The present one is Queen Elizabeth the second, coronated in 1952."

Befuddled, Sergeant Black glanced about the room, but not seeing anything. "Should I return to England today…" he squinted directly at Gorski, "I should find nothing of what I left." He lowered his head into his hands.

"Partially that would be true," Dr. Gorski answered. "Just as here, England has over the past two hundred years advanced, industrialized, and modernized. But it was doing that when you lived there. Remember, the culture of Great Britain has been evolving for thousands of years, whereas the development of the American nation roughly began the day the Pilgrims set foot on Plymouth Rock, only about four hundred years ago. If you were able to return today to Newcastle, where you say you came from, you'd find a contemporary city, a modern university, a recently built bridge over the River Tyne, and many other modernizations. Several years ago, I attended a conference at the university there. So, I got to see many places that have not changed and would still be familiar to you—Hadrian's Wall and other Roman ruins, the Castle Keep, the Black Gate, and several other medieval places that gave the city its history and name. The city's streets have not changed, but they have been improved to handle modern conveyances and no doubt many have had their names changed. The city has moved into the twentieth century, but much of what was present two hundred years ago is still there."

Noland raised his head. A momentary expression of longing crossed his face. Then it saddened. "If I were able to return, no one there would remember me, and I would not know anyone. Though the trip would be a long and arduous journey, I do want to return to Newcastle and my homeland. But would I be in my own time or in a time unknown to me? I do not know how to live in this new time." He shook his head and looked at Dr. Gorski. Confusion emanated from his eyes. "Is there a possibility that I could return?"

Dr. Gorski pursed his lips, slowly working them back and forth. Then he took hold of his glass, gazed at it, and slowly rotated it several times while contemplating an answer. He placed the glass on the table to his side. "If you were able to travel to Newcastle, you could leave today and be there tomorrow. But such a trip may not be possible. We live in an extraordinarily complex time, and you do not exist in it. Nowadays, to travel between countries one must prove their existence. Every country in the world issues their citizens some form of identification, a document that allows them to travel across borders. The document is called a passport. This passport contains your name, the date and place of your birth, your physical information, and a photo—opps, sorry, I mean picture—of you. Without a valid, formal passport issued by the country of residence, the individual is a person without a country and cannot legally travel."

Noland listened, pondered what Gorski just told him, and squirmed in his chair, then blurted, "But I do exist! I sit in this chair not as an impression, but as a man of flesh and blood."

"Yes, you do." Dr. Gorski's head nodded several times like a ball on a spring. "Indeed, you do, but not in 1975." He shrugged, stretched his arms forward, and pushed his clasped hands between his knees. "Remember what Dr. Morris said as she left to arrange your room, we need to figure out how to integrate you into our time. So, let's relax and wait until she returns. Can I top off your drink?"

Noland sat back and took a deep breath. "I do not believe so. Perhaps later."

"Well, did Dr. Gorski provide you with a two-hundred-year smattering of American history, Noland?" Dr. Morris asked as she returned to the living room.

"Aye, he did," Noland answered, his eyes tired, and clouded with confusion, suspicion, fatigue, and the effects of alcohol.

Dr. Morris glanced at Dr. Gorski. "Any ideas what to do with our guest? If anyone learns we are harboring a purported live visitor from the eighteenth century, reporters from every newspaper, TV station, and tabloid in the world, and not to mention agents from every federal agency in our government and that of Great Britain, will muster and camp on my lawn. It's not big enough to hold such a picnic."

"We kind of touched on that subject," Dr. Gorski said. "Noland expressed an interest to return to Newcastle, England." He shrugged, raised his right hand, and scratched behind his ear. "I really don't know what to do. Noland doesn't exist in the twentieth century. He has no identification. He's a man without a country. I tried to explain that no individual can travel internationally without a passport issued by his or her home country. Noland needs some sort of birth certificate." Dr. Gorski continued to fiddle with his ear. "We could try to find a printer, willing to risk arrest, to print a created identity for him."

Dr. Morris gritted her teeth and looked at Noland. "I don't think you want to dig into that can of worms." She tilted her head. "It's getting late. For now, Noland can pose as my long-lost cousin from England. He doesn't need any identification to prove that for now. I think my patient needs rest. He's had a couple of hard days and it appears that he's falling asleep. We need to give this problem clearer thought and work on it later." She glimpsed back at Gorski and saw his face express a moment of anxiety. "It'll be okay."

"Yes, I sure hope so," he said. "Good god, if anyone at your hospital begins to ask questions, we're in trouble."

"No. I'll say he's a psychiatric patient who thinks he's from the 1700s. Anyway, I have a few leave days coming and my schedule this week is light. There are several other doctors that can handle any problems that may arise."

Dr. Gorski nodded and sighed. "I'm concerned about that orderly named Joel. He noticed that Noland didn't know how to use a bathroom. He hits me as the kind of kid that makes jokes out of human shortcomings." Dr. Gorski stood, grabbed his bag, and turned to the others. He shook his head. "I don't know. It bothers me when someone makes light of a handicap. If someone picks up on his comments, they may become suspicious." He started for the front door. "I'll try to get some time off, so we can get together and mull over our thoughts. I'd also like to help you show our guest around in the modern world."

"That will help."

Dr. Gorski walked out the door, to his vehicle.

"It is about six o'clock," Dr. Morris said after Dr. Gorski departed. "I enjoy watching the local news. It'll be on in a few minutes." She noticed that Noland looked confused. "The news comes on a recent twentieth-century invention called a television set. When you see it, you'll be astonished; another gadget of communication like the telephone you examined this afternoon. Only this one receives live images that are sent through the air or on a wire that is called a cable."

Noland shook his head and yawned. "I do not know what you speak of, but I am very curious."

She nodded and walked to a walnut credenza where she lifted two small, framed photographs and held them for Noland to see. "This one is a photograph of my husband. His name was Raymond, Ray for short. The other photograph is of my favorite dog. I keep their images to remember them." Dr. Morris looked up at Noland. "You have never seen a photograph or heard of a camera, have you?"

"I have heard of a camera obscura, but do not know the word photograph."

"Photographs are pictures." She handed them to Noland.

"Pictures I know of. I have seen many. In London museums. Painted by great artists." Sergeant Black shook his head while he examined the photos. He touched the glass covering them and twisted his head, looked up, smiling. "Aye, paintings, they are. Excellent paintings. Yes? By an artist of great talent?"

"No. These are not an artist's paintings. They are images taken with a camera, another device of the modern world. The process is called photography. That is why the images, captured with a camera, are called photographs or photos; they are not paintings done by an artist. The images you see were taken with a modern film camera, which is like the box of a camera obscura. The modern camera also has a pinhole, like the camera obscura, that allows a light to enter its inner chamber. But on a modern camera, the little hole is covered by a lens that focuses the light onto a piece of film covered with light-sensitive chemicals. Exposure of the chemicals to light captures the image." She bent over and opened a cupboard door on the far side of the credenza and removed a Polaroid camera. "This is my camera. It makes an instant image of whatever I want to photograph." She handed the camera to Noland. "I'll try to explain how it works. Televisions work in a similar way, but they are too complicated."

The sergeant took the camera. Rotated it in his hands. Held it in front with the lens pointed toward his face. Scrutinized it for a minute, then touched the knob on the camera's top and pressed the little button to the right of the knob. Nothing happened. He started to touch the lens with his finger, but Dr. Morris caught his arm. Noland drew his finger away.

"You will leave your fingerprint on the lens that will damage the next photo. The lens should not be touched."

"This is a very strange object. There is metal on the camera, but the box is made of a material I have never handled."

"You wouldn't. It's a plastic material that wasn't discovered until the early 1800s. When I take you to see the city, the location where you fought your battle, and some other places that were present two hundred years ago, we can take some photos."

"How does the camera take a picture?" Noland handed the Polaroid back to Dr. Morris.

"I'll try to tell you, but I'm not a physicist or engineer. I can only give you a very simple explanation. The eye and camera work in about the same way. We see light, from wherever it comes. Light is visible because it hits our eyes as particles called photons that activate the retina. The retina is light sensitive. But then some geniuses made things more complicated. Supposedly, light also comes to our eyes in waves or vibrations. Not being a physicist, I cannot really explain this theory, but I do comprehend that everything we see reflects light in some form or fashion."

Noland squeezed the camera. He swallowed hard, gazed toward the fireplace, then back to the chair he had been sitting in. "Are all women in this century as learned as you?"

Dr. Morris eyes widened. "Are you asking if I have been formally educated? Like being able to attend a university?"

"Aye." Noland handed the camera back and mumbled. "You own a residence, and an objective of transport. You have shown me pictures of your husband and dog. Were they of your choosing?

Dr. Morris shrugged, then nodded. "Now that we are alone, are you uncomfortable in my presence" She placed the camera on a nearby table and put her hand gently on Noland's arm. "The rights of women have come a long way since the 18th century. You come from a male dominated culture where it was common for women to be considered chattel, subequal to men and subjugated by them. Today American women can enroll in universities, vote, enter politics, own land, choose their mate—I fell in love with my husband and we married—but women still have not achieved equality in the workplace." She squeezed Noland's arm and looked up at him. "Noland look at me. I don't want you to feel intimidated. We still consider a man as the hunter, knight in shining armor, and lover. Some of us have lost our domesticity, but we still cook, sew, care, and love."

Noland took a deep breath, relaxed and gazed down at her. "I understand. Culture and relationships between men and women have changed. But I come from a different time. It will be difficult for me to accept the new norms."

Dr. Morris held Noland's arm to steady him as he moved to the chair, sat, and smiled. "Let's take our time. You have been injured and you've only been here about a day and a half."

Noland seated himself and nodded.

Dr. Morris paused and fumbled with the camera. She raised it toward Noland in show-and-tell fashion. "Let's play with the camera for a moment. It's a mechanical device. It can only capture lighted images. This is a Polaroid and everything is done inside the camera."

Dr. Morris lifted the Polaroid to her right eye and aimed it at the fireplace.

Noland heard a click and whine and saw a piece of paper slide out the bottom of the camera. We'll have a quality image within about two minutes. A photograph is more precise that one painted by an artist."

Dr. Morris removed the paper card and for a moment fanned it in the air. "The chemicals are developing the image," she explained. "This photographic process was invented right here in Boston some years ago." She held the Polaroid photo for Noland to see and watched his expression progress from confusion to astonishment as an image of the fireplace began to emerge on the white card.

Noland shook his head. "It is like magic." With his eyes wide, he watched Dr. Morris remove a little object from a vial and swipe it over the photo. "A preservative," she explained and again fanned the photo in the air. "The photo is now preserved."

"The world has advanced considerably," Noland said with trepidation, "beyond my simple knowledge, but the camera and television set fascinate me. A photograph is a wonderful record. And I am curious to see the images on the television set. Dr. Morris, can we now see how that operates?"

"Yes, Noland, but will you please call me Carol?"

"Aye. Carol, I am enthralled by your modern world, but it is a very confusing world. I would much enjoy viewing the television set. Perhaps what I see will broaden my perspective of this future time."

Dr. Morris opened a set of center doors on the credenza and exposed an RCA color TV set with a twenty-six-inch screen. She punched the on/off button. After several black, white, and colored blips, the screen illuminated with the end of a Marlboro cigarette advertisement that quickly blipped to an introduction to a weekend news recap on CBS. Noland's eyes widened when the image resolved. He became transfixed on the animated images flashing across the screen.

"Would you like a cup of tea or coffee?" Dr. Morris asked.

"Aye. Tea would be wonderful, Ma'am," Noland answered without his eyes ever leaving the screen. The moving images fascinated him. He sat mesmerized as the news anchor's voice welcomed viewers to the recap of the week's news.

"The Vietcong," the anchor began, "have encircled the city of Saigon. This has prompted the removal of American diplomats, troops and some Vietnamese from the city." While the announcer spoke, videos of individuals attempting to scramble onto helicopters were being shown.

Awestruck by the chaos and confusion of individuals grabbing onto lifting helicopters, the sergeant shook his head, lowered it, and closed his eyes. An image of a wounded soldier Noland had left behind materialized in the darkness. Startled, he tightened his fists and lurched as Dr. Morris returned carrying a tray with two cups of tea.

"Is everything, all right?" She placed a cup on a coaster that lay on the table next to his chair.

"Nay," he grunted. "A terrible event. Is it a battle? I do not know or understand what I see. The people are frightened. Trying to escape. Some climb into that noisy mechanism. Others fall out. Is this a rescue? What is that mechanism?"

"That mechanism is a flying machine called a helicopter," Dr. Morris said. "What you're watching are the attempts of American Marines trying to rescue and evacuate the personnel from the American embassy before Saigon is invaded. The city is the capital of South Vietnam. It was being invaded by North Vietnam. This evacuation started a day or so ago."

"I do not know of this place, Vietnam."

"It is in Asia. A distant country in the South Pacific Ocean. America's involvement in this country has been long, difficult, and political. My husband and many others were killed there."

Noland shook his head. "I am sorry…" He was about to say something more, but the TV grabbed his attention when he heard the anchor mention Great Britain. He began to discuss Margaret Thatcher's struggles since becoming the leader of the Conservative Party. Since her election, England had been plagued by IRA bombings in London. The news anchor commented on the attacks for a moment, but then switched to two other pressing issues troubling London and the Conservative Party;

a June sixth vote to determine whether the United Kingdom would join the European Communities, and the beginning of the repairs to London's Moorgate Underground Station. Several days earlier, a train had crashed into a brick wall at this station, creating much damage.

Sergeant Black was most fascinated by the videos showing what London looked like. Unbelieving, he kept rubbing his eyes. He raised his arms to his head and ran his fingers through his hair. "What is this underground?"

"It is a method of transporting people around the city on trains that travel through underground tunnels," Dr. Morris said. "A mass transit system. Boston has a similar transport system, as does New York City and many other large cities. We call them subways. Subways are a quick way to get people from one place to another. I will take you into the city center of Boston on one. It should be an experience."

Noland nodded and smiled. "Aye." He gritted his teeth and continued to stare at the TV screen and absorb anchor's voice.

The news of Great Britain and Europe continued until a commercial break. An advertisement, highlighted by disaster-foreshadowing theme music and haunting images of giant sharks, publicized the forthcoming movie, *Jaws*. The clip boggled Noland's mind. But what followed, captivated him even more. The newsman returned, discussed, and presented a NASA video on the upcoming Apollo and Soyuz joint mission. But perplexing Noland even more, were clips of the 1969 Apollo mission, showing Neil Armstrong and Buzz Aldrin walking on the surface of the moon.

Sergeant Black slouched down in the chair as the news anchor signed off. "Tune in tomorrow to Walter Cronkite and the *CBS Evening News*. Noland's muscles seemed to melt. He sighed and took a sip of his tea, which had by then cooled. He gritted his teeth as his mind attempted to comprehend what he had seen. *Astonishing this future is, if it is true.*

Dr. Morris noticed Noland, though he appeared relaxed, remained transfixed to the highly animated, enticing commercials being broadcast across the television screen. Yet, his face showed concern. "What did you think of television and what you have seen?" she asked.

"Astounding indeed." Noland turned away from the TV and toward Dr. Morris. "However, I have little comprehension. This time period has many inventions and discoveries that make living cleaner, easier, and healthier. There is faster communication and transport, and, no doubt, other contrivances that I have yet to encounter that improve human life. There appears to be sufficient food, clean water, instant entertainment, many fascinating devices. And I have just seen on the television, man has walked on the moon…" Noland paused. Took a breath. He massaged the side of his neck with his fingertips. He lowered his head for a moment, then straightened. "This is difficult to understand. I see a world of unbelievable wonders, yet frenzied with discontent and turmoil. Wars continue. Disagreements are still present. Time has not changed humanity. It continues to be troublesome."

"Yes, Noland, you have come from a simpler time." Dr. Morris picked up the sergeant's empty cup. "It was a time when life was tougher, harder, and perhaps confusing, which made survival more difficult. Fortitude and self-reliance were the qualities that allowed humans to survive in your time. Today those qualities have weakened; individuals have become dependent on the conveniences that science and technology have provided. A person going from the twentieth century to the eighteenth century would find it difficult to adapt and survive. You, on the other hand, have the primitive instincts to adapt and endure in this time period."

Noland yawned, then stood. "My life is now a contradiction. I want to remain here in this future time. Learn. Experience. But I would greatly want to return to my time and inform those of the futility of fighting the rebels. Let Great Britain know it will lose America, but still will remain an empire and become allied with this country. That may be very difficult to make the military, parliament, and the Crown believe." The sergeant rubbed his forehead and thought for a moment. "Perhaps not. I would probably be hanged for heresy or treason."

"You've had a long day," Dr. Morris said. "I believe it is time for you to rest, get some sleep. You, Dr. Gorski, and I, I'm sure, will talk more in the days to come of the dilemma your unexpected visit has created. But for now, let me show you to the guestroom. Wait, while I put the teacups in the kitchen."

Sergeant Black stood and stretched. Dr. Morris returned and gestured for him to follow her as she walked into a hall that led to a staircase. She started up the stairs. "Your room is on the second floor. And just across the hall, you'll have your own bath. I laid out some trousers, shirts, a sweater, and other things on the bed. They are new and still in their original packaging. My husband bought them…" she paused for a moment and wiped a tear from her eye, "but never got a chance to wear them."

As the doctor entered the bedroom, she extended her right arm to the wall switch for the overhead light. She pointed out the switch to Noland and flicked it up. "Turns the ceiling light on." Then she snapped it down… "Off," and then flipped it up again.

They entered a warm, comfortable-looking, off-white, medium-sized bedroom. It contained a full-sized bed covered in a quilted plaid spread. A plush chair and a small writing table were located between the dormer windows. A small side lamp stood on each table to the side of the bed's headboard.

Dr. Morris walked to a bedside table and picked up the lamp, rotated it on its side, and pushed the on/off switch. The lamp lit. She showed the switch to Noland. "Every lamp has an electrical switch."

Noland nodded and laid his red coat across the back of the chair by the desk. "Candles are no longer used?"

"They are. Candles are used when the electricity goes out. They are also used to decorate birthday cakes. They are considered a fire hazard."

"Aye." Noland nodded. "Everything seems safer now and so much easier." A smile crossed his face when he saw Dr. Morris's late husband's clothing laid out on the right side of the bed. To him they looked unusual, but pleasing. Dr. Morris stood next to the bed and bent over to adjust the location of the T-shirts. Noland glanced at her back and felt his pelvic muscles stir. *A lovely woman, she is. And caring.* He shook his head. "How long has your husband been gone?"

"A little over a year." Dr. Morris dipped her head. "I miss him. Seeing his clothing depresses me." She sighed and straightened. "Sleep in, in the morning. Dress and come downstairs. Norma will prepare your breakfast. I need to leave early, but I will try not to disturb you. You should not hear me leave, because my room is on the first floor." She patted the bed, straightened, and turned to face him. "The mattress is hard. It has been rarely used. I do not have many guests. Before I leave for my bedroom, let me show you the bathroom." She walked out the door and reached into the room across the hallway and flicked on the light. Dr. Morris gestured for Noland to enter. "The light switch is on the wall just inside the door, just like the one in the bedroom. Everything works the same way it did in the men's room at the hospital. Take it slow. I'm sure you'll figure out how everything works." She bent over the bathtub and rotated the faucet. Water flowed into the tub. She then clasped the shower plug atop the spigot and pulled it. Water flow switched from the bathtub spigot to the showerhead. "This plug activates the shower. If you use the shower, test the water temperature with your hand before you pull this plug. Don't want to have you scald yourself."

"Aye. I will be cautious."

Dr. Morris stepped back into the hallway. "When I no longer hear the shower water, I will wait about fifteen minutes for you to dry off and put on the pajamas…"

The sergeant looked confused.

"Don't know if you noticed, but I laid out some night clothes on the bed—pajamas, we call them. They're of soft, brown-and-white checkered material. You can sleep more comfortably in them. But I don't know if you dress for sleep at night, or if you'd rather sleep without them, that's up to you. We may, in some ways, be more prudish than people were in the eighteenth century. Anyway, wear the pants when I come up and look at the shoulder where I removed the bullets and dirt. The old bandages will come off when they become wet. The injured area will need a new layer of antibiotic and dry bandages."

"Aye. Thank you, Carol, for being so kind. I will be in the proper attire upon your return to tend to my injuries."

With a grin, Dr. Morris turned and walked to the stairs.

After hearing Sergeant Black's footsteps as he moved from the bedroom to the bathroom and the clank of several items he dropped onto the floor, she heard the shower water come on and a curse. "Must have had the water on too hot," she mumbled. She went into the kitchen and put the used glasses and cups into the dishwasher. To her it seemed like a long time for the sergeant to be showering. An anxious urge to run upstairs and check on him came over her. But calmed when the water flow stopped. She looked at her watch. "I'll give him a few more minutes," she mumbled.

Dr. Morris called out before she went up the stairs. When she heard him acknowledge, she grabbed her medical bag and ascended. She found Sergeant Black sitting on the bed, wearing the pajama bottoms. She shook her head and raised her eyebrows. "Shift around so your back is toward me."

The sergeant did as he was told. It took only a few minutes to check the sergeant's wounds, apply the antibiotic, and rebandage the area.

"You can put your shirt on. I'm finished. You are healing very well." She looked at her wristwatch; it was nearly midnight. She returned the unused bandages and tube of antibiotic to her bag. "I believe you will sleep well. I will see you around lunchtime. I plan to take several days off work so Dr. Gorski and I can introduce you to the twentieth century. Norma will have your breakfast in the morning when you are ready."

"I appreciate what you, Carol, and Dr. Gorski are doing for me. Until tomorrow. May you also sleep well."

Dr. Morris left the room, walked to the stairway, and descended to the first floor. Noland moved toward the bed, but an object on the dresser he had never seen caught his eye. He picked it up and examined it. *Bracelet with an ornamental disk*, he thought and examined the disk further. *A chronometer on a bracelet. How unusual.* "On the morrow, I must ask Dr. Morris of this bracelet," he mumbled. "A timepiece to be worn on the arm? It must have been her husband's." Placing the wristwatch back on the dresser, he crawled into bed.

CHAPTER 11

Monday, April 21, 1975

A fresh scent engulfed Sergeant Black as he pulled the sheet and blanket over himself. His uncommon, wearisome day had tired him. He sighed and snuggled himself into a comfortable position. The clean, lavender aroma of the bedding overwhelmed his mind and caused him to fantasize pleasant, stimulating visions of Dr. Morris. He had had a few congenial encounters with women since being posted to the Boston area, but none had come to fruition. Unconsciously, he moved his left hand along his inner thigh and closed his eyes. But as soon as he did, exhaustion extinguished the provocative images his brain had generated.

The sergeant slept soundly for a couple of hours, but a backfire from a passing motor vehicle startled him. His eyes popped open. All he saw was the dim rectangular reflection of the outdoor lighting projecting through the dormer window onto the ceiling. Tensed, he listened for a moment and heard only the hissing in his ear. Relaxing his head into the pillow, he closed his eyes and again fell into sleep, but his slumber was fitful. The smell of lavender again stirred his subconscious. Only this time, the fragrance stimulated the image of a young, vulnerable-looking girl with long auburn hair. She lay in a meadow. The ruins of Ravensworth Castle decorated the field at the edge of a forest. Folds of her long dress splayed over a blanket. She rolled to her right side, picked a sprig covered with small bluish flowers from a clump growing nearby, turned back, and sat up. She passed the spray of lavender under her nose and looked up at Noland. With an affectionate smile, she offered the twig of flowers to him. As he bent toward her, her hand, holding the love offering, began to vaporize. In a moment, the beautiful girl was gone. His eyes had opened, and he was again staring at the reflections of light on the bedroom ceiling.

"Meera!" he cried. Shook his head, flipped onto to his belly, and pushed his face into the pillow. The pressure caused him to see nothing but blackness. Keeping his eyes closed tightly, he turned to the side, relaxed, and took a breath. After a few moments his mind began to detach itself from consciousness and he dozed off, but the grinding of an automobile engine attempting to start and several more backfires again threw his brain into bedlam. He lay for an hour glaring at the ceiling until sleep again encased him.

Noland trembled, snorted, but didn't wake. Instead, he heard muskets fire. They seemed a distance away. With hazy vision, he saw soldiers in his regiment crawling behind a stone fence along the edge of the road. Other than the cracking of the shots, the scene was soundless. He felt himself straighten. Then an arm poked through the mist and stretched out to him. As he moved to it, his body violently twisted, shuddered, and he fell. Suddenly the haze cleared. He saw Lieutenant Colonel Smith looking at a wounded man and gesturing. Noland tried to call to Smith, but he had no voice. The lieutenant colonel vaporized. Where his apparition stood, Noland saw two soldiers lift the injured man onto a wagon. He called to the corpsmen, but this time his attempt manifested as a loud moan, which woke him. He snapped up with a force that shot the pillow onto the floor. His body felt hot, sweaty, and tense. The blanket constrained his legs when he tried to move. He untangled himself from the twisted covers. Free, he rubbed his eyes. They darted about. The night had left the room. The radiance of the morning's twilight blurred and diminished the luminous projections on the ceiling. He exhaled deeply, and when he saw his red coat hanging on the chair, the frightening tension that had gripped him eased. *There is no battle here.*

The sergeant used his elbows to push himself up, roll to the side, retrieved the pillow from the floor, and adjusted it behind his head. He slid back down into its softness and pulled the blanket to his neck. A quick, discomforting stitch of pain shot through his shoulder and down his back. When he tried to move his right arm behind his head, the ache informed him that the bullet holes on his right side were still healing. The distress relented when he returned the arm to his side and relaxed. *Well, that at least tells me I am alive. But I do not know where I am, or how I got here. And I do not believe I can return. The doctors say I cannot.* He lay back and stared at the ceiling; his mind attempted to analyze his predicament. *They say I am near Boston. In the future. There are places and things I know and so many I do not. My mind is in complete confusion. I know not what to do.* The sergeant pushed his head into the pillow, rotated it back and forth several time, then glanced toward the window at the morning glow. "Ah, soft and warm." *This future place is more comfortable. Life is easier. It would not be hard to live in this future. I cannot go back, they say. Though I want to, to help my regiment. But why? Great Britain lost the colonies, the doctors say. Even so, Britain becomes a strong ally of the colonies. That makes no sense.* He scratched his head. *This, I still find hard to believe.* Noland shook his head, rolled to his other side, and stared at the wall. *If I could return, I would tell everyone of my unusual experience, what I have learned, and of the futility of harassing the colonials—Ah, no. No one would believe me.* "They would say I lost my mind." He continued to gaze at the wall. His stomach tightened, he fisted his hands, his mind created a darker scenario. *I have been absent from my regiment for two days. If I return unharmed, I would be considered a deserter.* The sound of a door closing somewhere downstairs caused Noland to flip onto his back and stifle the ominous thought.

The sergeant heard the muffled grinding of the VW's engine starting. The sound arrested the chaotic factfinding mishmash befuddling him. *Dr. Morris is returning to the hospital.*

It wasn't long before the aroma of fried bacon and coffee wafted to the second floor and into the bedroom.

"Before you sit at the table, please turn your back to me and remove the sweatshirt," Norma said when Sergeant Black walked into the kitchen. "Dr. Morris asked that I examine and clean your injuries. And then, put on some new bandages. Did you sleep well?" She moved to the kitchen counter where she had laid out what medical materials she needed.

"Aye, Ma'am." Noland did as she asked. "I did sleep well, though I had some unusual dreams."

"My, my, but you're a healthy young man." Norma turned and looked over Noland's muscular back. "Your dreams were probably caused by the anesthesia given to put you to sleep while Dr. Morris repaired your wounds. After-effects of the drug, no doubt." Norma removed the old bandages and began to swab the wounded area with alcohol.

Noland flinched. The effect of the astringent's evaporative cooling caused his upper back and shoulder muscles to tighten.

"Your wounds are healing nicely." Norma allowed a few minutes for the alcohol to dry. She then began to gently apply an antibiotic salve. "The injuries appear to be punctures. No one told me how you became injured."

This woman does not know that I am from the past. Neither of the doctors told her anything of my predicament.

Norma finished covering the wounds with clean bandages. "You can put the sweatshirt back on."

As Noland's head slipped through the sweatshirt's collar and his arms slithered into the sleeves, he gritted his teeth from the twinges he felt in his shoulder, and he said, "I do believe the doctors did not want to trouble you. I was ambushed. I did not see who the culprits were. Dr. Gorski and some men, whom he called reenactors, found me. I was not of good mind when they took me to Dr. Morris's surgery."

"It was so lucky for you that your cousin was the surgeon at the hospital."

Norma's use of the word "cousin" perplexed Noland. "My cousin?" His head twisted to the right. His body temperature rose. "Oh, oh—Oh yes." He ran his fingers through his hair and nodded. "A momentary lapse of my memory. Yes. Dr. Morris. I mean Carol. Yes. Fortunate that she was the healer there." He smiled.

"Healer. Yes." Norma smiled back. "You Brits have an unusual way of saying things. Come. Sit at the table. I'll fry some eggs and bacon and toast several slices of bread. And I do believe you English like to have a slice of tomato on the side. I'll cut one if you like."

"Aye, I experienced my first tomato at Dr. Morris's clinic. I would enjoy another taste. Their flavor is sweet and unusual."

"Tea or coffee?" Norma stepped to the range, moved a skillet onto an eye, and turned and faced Noland.

"Tea would be fine."

"How do you like your eggs?"

The sergeant cocked his head in confusion. "You said you were to fry them...."

"Oh. Sorry. The yolks. Do you want them soft, running—we call them sunny-side-up—or hard?"

"I have only eaten eggs prepared at Dr. Morris's clinic. They were called scrambled. So please fry them as you like."

She chuckled. "I will fry the eggs so the yolk is firm."

Noland smiled. "Thank you."

After Norma served his breakfast, Noland tasted the egg yolk and savored its creamy, rich flavor. He closed his eyes in delight. Adding the aroma and taste of hickory-smoked bacon, strawberry jam on the toast, and the tomato, Noland relished the breakfast. When he finished, he grinned and nodded at Norma, and pleasurably relaxed against the back of the chair.

"Can I warm your tea?"

The sergeant dipped his head and wrapped his hands around the cup as she refilled it.

"The damaged, soiled clothing you were wearing is unusual," Norma said as she poured. "It appears old and handmade."

Noland's body tensed. A furtive expression crossed his face. He wasn't sure how to answer her question. His eyebrows raised as he looked up. But as he was about to speak, the telephone rang.

"Sorry." Norma placed the teapot on the stove and scurried off to answer the phone.

Noland straightened and took a sip of tea. *If I tell her, it is a military uniform, she will ask many more questions.* He set the tea cup down and ran his fingers through his hair.

"It's Dr. Morris," Norma said as she returned to the kitchen. "She wants to talk to you. The telephone is in the den on her desk." She pointed the way. "Down the hall. Door on the right."

The sergeant sighed in relief and stood. *An opportune save.* When he got to the den, he saw the telephone receiver lying on the desk next to its cradle. Naturally, because of the receiver's design, he raised it in the proper orientation, microphone at his mouth and receiver next to his ear. "Dr. Morris? I am here."

"Did you sleep well, Noland?"

"Aye." Noland adjusted the telephone receiver closer to his ear. He looked toward the door. *Norma is remaining in the kitchen.* "Thank you. I must ask something," he whispered. "Just before you telephoned, Norma said the clothing she is to repair is unusual. To her, I am sure, it must be. She is not aware of from where I have come. You and Dr. Gorski did not mention my plight. I do not know how to answer her. What should I say?"

"Saved by the bell."

Noland squinted and shook his head. "How does a bell solve my problem?"

"Not important. It's just an expression. The telephone rang and interrupted Norma's inquiry…"

"Aye." Noland nodded and chuckled. "Telephone bells. Aye. Another American utterance—like sunny-side-up eggs."

"Yes, they are." Dr. Morris snickered. "Tell Norma you were wearing old-fashioned clothing because you are a writer. You felt that if you wore a British uniform, you'd catch people's attention, because you wanted to learn how modern-day Americans respond if they see a British Redcoat coming down the street. Tell her, you want to know if some Bostonians carry a bitterness or still hold a grudge. A Redcoat may make them curious and they'll ask questions. Others may view the uniform with humor or think you are an actor. I would imagine, most don't even remember that the American Revolution occurred. If Norma asks about your injuries, just say that you were attacked by someone who held a grudge against the British." Dr. Morris paused for a moment. "Anyway, I'm sure you will come up with something. But for now, we have a more critical problem. Seems word got out about the hospital mending an alien and holding him in isolation. I believe Joel, that foolish kid who sometimes volunteers here as a nurses' aid, probably flapped his jaw at a local hangout. He's the one who helped you to the men's room. A couple reporters from the *Enquirer*, a tabloid newspaper, were in the clinic this morning asking about the little green men that we are hiding." She snickered.

"Aye, Joel. I remember him. He is the one who guided me to the latrine. I had never encountered the place you called a men's room. In my confusion I must have acted quite irrational."

"Yes. But rumors, whether real or fictional, have a way of being exaggerated. This can create problems. But all is well for now. The reporters have left. But what I would like for you to do is stay in the house. Answer Norma's query as best you can. She'll believe you, but

don't get too absurd. I have freed the rest of my week so I can introduce you to 1975...."

"Aye! That is good," Noland interrupted. "I saw an unusual bracelet on the dresser. Are chronometers worn on one's arm now?"

"Yes. It's called a wristwatch. Ray, my husband, bought a Timex dive
watch before he shipped out to Vietnam. It's been on that dresser since
he left." Dr. Morris paused and sighed. "Anyway, we can talk later. I'll see
you around noon; blow the horn when I pull into the driveway. When
you hear it, come out and get into the car. Then we'll go to lunch."

About twelve thirty Norma heard Dr. Morris pull into the driveway
and blow the VW's horn. She alerted Noland and said, "Have fun."

"Thank you," he said, nodded, and went out the front door.
The sergeant breathed in the cool air as he walked to the car. "Ah.
Refreshing." He sighed and enter the vehicle. "It is good to be on the
move. I'm looking forward to what I will see. However, I feel uneasy
and have uncertainty of what I may encounter."

Dr. Morris put the VW in reverse, backed out onto the street, and
aimed the Bug forward. "You are. Your mind is telling you where you
should be. But now, in the daylight, what you see is contradicting
what should be. Last evening, when we drove from the clinic to my
house, the ride, I'm sure, was confusing; the darkness outside obscured
much of the view and you were inside a moving, motorized vehicle,
an experience unknown to you. Then, as probable now, I understand
your feeling of uncertainty. What has happened to you is a mystery.
Stay calm. What you are going to see as we drive and walk about will
probably overwhelm you; two hundred years has changed what you
knew as Boston. I empathize with your doubts and misgivings. But everything will be all right. You are an intelligent man. I know, because
for the short time that you have been here, you have quickly grasped
and accepted the newness that has confronted you."

Noland sighed and gripped the handle above the VW's passenger door as Dr. Morris wheeled out of her residential area onto a main thoroughfare and headed toward Charlestown. The traffic was more considerable than Noland had experienced the night before. His eyes widened; his hand tightened on the handle. He sat breathless staring at automobiles, trucks, buses, buildings, and lack of trees and open space. "So many means of conveyance, such abundance of construction and habitation." He shook his head in disbelief.

"Yes." Dr. Morris down-shifted and turned on to another main street. "Today is Monday, a work day. Many people now live in Boston. They move about the city, going to their place of work, make deliveries, some visit markets. The movement creates considerable traffic. Makes it hard to find a place to leave your vehicle; a place we call a public parking space where our vehicle can be securely deposited. So, we'll stop at the clinic and I'll leave the car in my reserved parking space, then we can go and stroll about. Maybe ride the subway or take a bus if we get tired."

Noland jerked to the side as Dr. Morris zipped next to an eighteen-wheeler. When the traffic light switched from red to green, the truck driver gunned the engine. "What is this monster?"

"Semi-truck," Dr. Morris said with a smile. "Hauls large, heavy loads of many things. Transports commercial wares from place to place. The noise is its large motor that makes the truck move."

"Aye. Like a monstrous wagon, but with no horses or mules."

"Yes. Interesting, the truck's motor is still likened to a horse's power of pulling a load. Where a wagon may be pulled by one horse or two, the pull-power would be one-horsepower or two-horsepower. The truck's motor may have the power of many hundreds of horses." Dr. Morris turned in to the clinic's parking lot and parked the Volkswagen.

"Aye. What you say, overwhelms my mind." Noland exited the car. "How many horses does it take to move your carriage?"

"I'm not sure," Dr. Morris said as she met the sergeant behind the VW. She reached down and opened the hatch on the VW's engine compartment. "There's a plate in here somewhere that should tell us." The doctor scanned the compartment. "Ah, here it is." She read the data on the little plate. "It says here that the engine is one point seven liters in size—I think that is the capacity of the internal cylinders—which produces sixty-two horsepower when it is pulling at its top speed. Take a look at the engine. But don't touch it. It's hot."

Noland peered into the compartment. The acrid smell of lingering exhaust irritated his sinuses. He gasped and rubbed his nose. "That devil-smelling contrivance, you call an engine, is indeed smaller than a single horse, but yet it produces such power." He raised his head and took a deep breath of fresh air. "What would the world be if there was such power in the time from where I have come?"

"Yes. Indeed," Dr. Morris said. "Our world would be different." She closed the hatch "Come, let us walk to Cambridge. It's a little over a mile. I'd like to show you Harvard University. It was in Boston for about one hundred years before you came to this continent. There are some buildings that still exist from the seventeen hundreds you might recognize on the campus. On the way we'll have a quick lunch. There is a McDonalds several blocks away where we can enjoy a hamburger, French fries, and a shake."

"Aye, the seminary I know. Two months after I arrived at my post in the colonies, I stood in rank in the Harvard Yard. The school that taught young colonial men to preach the word of the Lord. It still exists?" Noland looked surprised.

"Indeed, it does. I'm sure you'll be astonished by how it has changed from a small school of divinity to an internationally recognized university. The campus takes up much of central Boston and teaches every imaginable subject on earth. I guess its program still includes theology. Though American students are numerous, there are many that come from other countries."

Several vehicles honked as the two crossed High Street. Dr. Morris led Noland along several side streets to Main Street and then they walked north toward Washington Street. All along, the sergeant was awestruck by the houses, buildings, traffic, and people that passed. As they crossed onto Washington Street, Dr. Morris pointed toward a squat building enwrapped in large windows and surrounded by a blacktop parking lot that contained several cars. Along each side of the building stood a golden arch, and at the entrance to the parking lot a free-standing sign advertising "McDonald's Hamburgers Over 5,000,000,000 Sold," beckoned patrons. "Let's stop there for lunch," she said.

Noland gazed at the fast-food restaurant and shrugged. *I have never seen a public house with such a curious display.* He cocked his head; the fingers of his right hand pushed the hair off his ear as he followed Dr. Morris through the door. The vivid interior of the restaurant, with its white, gray, and black mosaic-patterned tile flooring, chrome-leg-supported chairs with pliable seat pads, plastic-top tables, and cushiony dark-varnished booths, bedazzled him even more.

"I'll order for the two of us," Dr. Morris said as she proceeded to the counter. Two customers were ahead when she entered the order line. "I'll get us something special, Big Macs, French fries, and milkshakes."

"Aye. I do not know what those foods are," Sergeant Black said. "I do not often have the pleasure of eating French food."

"The French fries are slivers of potatoes. I guess they were invented by some French chef, but they are an American fast-food snack. The potato strips are deep fried and salted. I'm sure you'll like them."

"The potato I know little of and have not eaten any. In England they are known as the Devil's apples. Many think they are dangerous to eat. Potatoes are not grown on manor-land for harvest. However, I have heard, they are grown in France, Germany, and elsewhere on the continent."

Dr. Morris smiled and turned to Noland. "Today, potatoes are the most staple side dish in the world and even throughout the British Isles. I don't think any household could do without them. What root plants did the common people in Great Britain eat in your time?" She turned her attention back to the order clerk.

"Turnips, swede, carrots." Noland glanced at the menu. "What is a hamburger? Is it a meat?"

Dr. Morris bent forward to place the order. "Two Big Macs, two medium fries, and two chocolate milkshakes."

The order clerk read the order back and then said, "That'll be two dollars and fifty-two cents."

Dr. Morris paid the woman, turned, moved to the side, and said, "I'll explain the hamburger when we find a booth. Now we wait for our order. It'll be here in a moment or two."

When the order came, Dr. Morris headed for a booth by a window. On the way, she picked up some straws, napkins, and a couple of packs of salt and pepper. The doctor allowed Noland to carry the tray. The restaurant had a few customers. But, since it was about an hour and a half after twelve o'clock, the lunch crowd had already eaten and left.

Dr. Morris served Noland and herself the Big Macs, French fries, and milkshakes, and pushed the tray to the side. She opened the box containing her hamburger and held it up, ready to take a bite, but for a moment held it in front of her. "This is a Big Mac hamburger," she said. "It contains *two beef patties, a special sauce, lettuce, cheese, pickles, onions, all on a sesame seed bun.*" She thought for a moment. "That's the Big Mac jingle. If someone can say that ditty in four seconds or less, they get their Big Mac as a prize. It's a promotional strategy." She cocked her head slightly, continued to smile, and took a bite.

Noland followed suit. Slowly chewed his piece. The moment he swallowed his face brightened and he licked his lips. "Quite delicious. A delectable version of a cottage pie, but not wrapped with crust, but rather the meat is pushed into a bap." He took another bite, chewed, and grinned. "Big Mac, I could learn to like it." He sampled a French fry and again his eyes lit up.

Dr. Morris nodded. "Thought you'd enjoy these foods." She stripped the paper cover from a straw, removed the little pipe, and then pushed it through the middle of the plastic cover into the milkshake.

Noland did the same and sucked some of the cool, creamy drink. His eyes closed in delight. "A taste of pleasure indeed." He sighed. "Food in the barracks is usually stale mutton and pudding, with bread and spruce beer. For a more delectable meal one would have to go to a tavern or public house. Though even in such places, the food is commonplace."

"The modern military is well fed with proper-tasting foods," Dr. Morris explained. "Today, there are many restaurants in Boston where different foods can be purchased, enjoyed, and eaten."

Confused, Noland asked, "What is a restaurant?"

"Sorry. A place where food is sold, served, and eaten," she said. "Like a tavern or public house, but more luxurious."

As the two ate, Dr. Morris described the breadth of restaurants that could be found in the city. "McDonald's serves what today we call fast foods. It allows for people who have only little time, to sit and eat quickly. Many working folks get only forty-five minutes to an hour for lunch. Hamburgers are substantial and have an appealing flavor. Fast foods are still provided by taverns and pubs in England, just as they did in your time. But now, they compete with Wimpy's, some fast food restaurants in your country. McDonald's is what is called a chain restaurant. If the desire is to eat a more sumptuous meal, with comfortable and attractive surroundings, then one goes to a deluxe or fine restaurant. This evening we'll meet up with Dr. Gorski and go to such a café." The doctor looked at her wristwatch. "It's almost two thirty. If we're going to get to Harvard, we need to move on."

Sergeant Black nodded. Dr. Morris collected all the trash onto the tray, rose, and headed toward the door. Noland followed, sucking up the last bit of milkshake. Smiling, he tossed the cup into the trash bin after the doctor laid the tray onto the shelf. They continued west on Washington Street.

Noland didn't have a problem keeping pace with Dr. Morris's rapid stride. However, when gazing at people, traffic, buildings, and ogling store windows, he'd fall behind and she'd have to pause a moment for him to catch up. When he did, he would shake his head in amazement at what he was seeing. Washington Street eventually blended into Kirkland Street. After walking for about twenty minutes, the two reached the north side of the Harvard campus after passing the engineering complex. In another few minutes they had reached the curve where Kirkland Street turned ninety degrees to the north and became Oxford Street. The sergeant followed Dr. Morris across the junction to a pedestrian way that passed between the Science Center and Memorial Hall to the Plaza over Cambridge Street, and then progressed to Meyer Gate, the entrance to Harvard Yard, the university's earliest complex of structures.

They strolled past Holworthy Hall and onto the green that made up the Old Yard. Cutting diagonally across the yard, they headed toward a path that led into a small northwestern quadrangle, which was ringed by six buildings, most constructed during the nineteenth century. A walkway into the middle of this quad passed between Hollis Hall, on the south, and Stoughton Hall, on the north. It ran toward a small, rectangular, red brick building centrally located in the quad. "Holden Chapel." Dr. Morris pointed. "You must recognize that building? It was built in the 1740s."

"Aye." Noland scanned the little structure's façade, then turned and looked at Hollis Hall. "Not long after I arrived in the colonies, my regiment marched on the green we just came through." Extending his arm, he motioned eastward toward the Old Yard, then to Hollis Hall. "That building was also present, though it has been changed. Also, another..." His arm gestured even more southernly, down the middle of the quad, toward Harvard Hall. "There were two other constructions. One where that building stands..." he pointed toward Harvard Hall, "I do not recognize the one there. It has a larger edifice and it is more elaborate. I believe there was another just beyond."

"Yes. That is Harvard Hall," said Dr. Morris. "It's obstructing your view. Though it dates to the eighteenth century, it has been enlarged and reconstructed. I believe the one you are referring to is Massachusetts Hall, the oldest building on campus. It is just beyond. It contains the offices of the university president."

They walked around Harvard Hall and faced a green space that separated the two original classrooms/dormitories. A series of pedestrian ways crisscrossed the area. The main one, which was down the center, connected the Old Yard with Johnson Gate and Peabody Street to the west. The others accommodated foot traffic between the northwest quad and a small southwest quadrangle. Massachusetts Hall was at the head of the lower quad.

Sergeant Black gazed at the long, rectangular, three-story, red brick edifice, with its six tall chimneys projecting above the roof line and nodded. "It is just as I saw it." A grin lightened his face. "Aye. I know this student barracks. I was told that it has a telescope. Students who attend, study the doctrines of Christianity and are given the occasion to view the heavens. That is so inspiring. Perhaps some may even see the Christ. What an opportunity..." He wiped several tears from his eyes. "I have never been inside, but I have stood on this very spot. Dreamed that if I remained in the colonies, I might attend this place..." He shook his head, gazed at Massachusetts Hall, and several students that ambled past. "It is familiar, yet it is not. So much has changed."

"Yes, I'm sure it all must be confusing. There probably was much more open land when you saw this campus. Now there are many buildings. Little open space. From the four buildings of the small school of theology you once saw, Harvard has become a full-blown international university. Students from all over come here. It is known as one of the world's major centers of learning. It takes up a great portion of Boston."

"Aye." Noland gazed about and pondered what he was seeing. "There was a road not far from where we stand," he said. "After the parade on the yard, I was introduced to a prominent cleric, who had originally come from Yorkshire—a Reverent Hollingsworth, I believe his name was—who had been informed that I had newly arrived from Newcastle. He seemed interesting and we talked. The reverend told me that five years before, he had been assigned by a missionary council at Cambridge University to teach medieval philosophy at this college in the colonies the council called, 'the church-in-the-wilderness.' That was how he came to be at Harvard. The reverend introduced me to his benefactor, a Mr. Lechmere, I believe was his name. Mr. Lechmere and I spoke, said he was the distiller who provided the British troops with their supply of whiskey. I, of course, nodded in appreciation. Mr. Lechmere then invited me to share the evening meal with his family and Reverend Hollingsworth. This Lechmere fellow provided the reverend with room and board at his home. Since I was given leave from the regiment for the weekend, I accepted." Noland glanced at Dr. Morris, expecting her to provide directions.

"Yes," she said. "Brattle Street. Once known as Tory Row. That is where all the wealthy residents who were loyal to Great Britain lived. It is only a short walk."

Noland and Dr. Morris departed Harvard's Old Yard through Johnson Gate onto Peabody Street and turned south toward Harvard Square. At the square, Dr. Morris said she wanted to contact Dr. Gorski so he could join them for dinner. Dr. Morris found an AT&T phonebooth in the Harvard Square Transit Station.

The doctor exited the phonebooth, looked at her wristwatch, and walked to the bench where Noland was sitting. "It's four o'clock," she said. "Dr. Gorski wants us to meet him at Holli's Seafood on Mount Auburn Street at about six o'clock. That's just on the south side of this square. The chef there is in his reenactors group." She gestured for Noland to follow. "Come, let's look for the place where you had dinner with the reverend from Harvard. Brattle Street is over there." She pointed to the west. Noland followed Dr. Morris across the street and toward the Harvard Coop Bookstore.

"Those historic houses are about ten blocks away," Dr. Morris said. "It's a long walk. Since we won't have much time to play tourist, I'll hail a taxi." She stood next to the curb and waved her arm. Before Noland could understand what she was doing, a yellow vehicle, with a sign that spelled **TAXI** above the windshield, pulled next to her. She opened the rear door, slid in, motioned for Noland to get in, and told the cabby, "Longfellow House."

Traffic was relatively light and in ten minutes the taxi pulled into the driveway of the Vassall-Craigie-Longfellow House. A sign designated the house as an historical heritage site and provided information about the place. The cab stopped at the entrance of the yellowish, white-trimmed, two-story Georgian style mansion. The colonnade had four base-to-roof faux columns, one to each side and two in the middle that defined the entranceway. A triangular gable with a semi-circular window corniced the entry. Nine identical windows, four on each side of the portico and one above the white doorway, delineated the mansion's façade. From the street level, steps to a walkway led to the front door. A white picket fence enclosed the yard. Two dormer windows and a pair of chimneys, projecting from the gray roof, were also surrounded by a low white fencepost barrier.

Dr. Morris leaned forward and asked the driver to wait while they looked at the house. He nodded. She and Noland walked up the front steps and stood by the picket fence.

"I recognize this house," Noland explained. "It looks as I last saw it, when I walked by with the Reverend Hollingsworth. But there was more open land surrounding the manor and there were no trees in the yard. I have never been in the interior of this manor. Of what importance is it?" He stood at the fence and gazed at the house. He turned his head slowly from the right to the left. "Those porches on each side of the building…" he pointed at the two galleries attached to the sides of the mansion, "they were not there when I saw it last."

"The porches were probably added at some later date," Dr. Morris said. "I read the historic sign at the base of the steps and it said Mr. Vassall had the house built in 1759. He was a major in the British army, but in 1774 when revolutionary turmoil began, he and his wife, who was the sister of the governor of the Massachusetts Colony, vacated the house and sailed back to England. Then in July of 1775, General George Washington, who was promoted to commander of the colonial army, made the house his home and headquarters. The general and his wife stayed until April of the next year and then moved to New York City."

"Aye," Noland agreed. "You told me that he was the general who led the colonial army to victory over Great Britain. No one in our regiment had known or heard of this general. He had not arrived in Boston as of yet." The sergeant turned and walked back toward the taxi. He stood next to the vehicle and looked about. "The residence where Reverend Hollingworth lodged is farther ahead. May we proceed." He entered the cab.

Dr. Morris returned to the taxi and got in. "Drive to the Lechmere House," she told the cab driver.

"Yes, ma'am. 149 Brattle Street," the driver answered.

Within about three minutes the taxi stopped in front of a two-story, gray-white-trimmed, colonial mansion. A large oak tree grew on its left, with other trees nearby. The house was slightly smaller than the Vassall Mansion. Four white columns upheld a roof above the entrance. Instead of a classic colonial façade, the first floor had two tall, vertical, two-pane windows without shutters. The second story had a pair of classic-style colonial front windows flanked by black shutters and a taller vertical window over the portico similar to those on the first level, but was bordered by black shutters. Two dormers and a single chimney on the right projected above the light gray roof.

The sergeant looked puzzled. When Dr. Morris came next to him, he said, "I do not recognize this house. There should be a mansion much like the one your general occupied. A large estate with a grand house and outbuildings, and a view of the river." He pointed south. "All I see is an imposing residence, with little land, and many other houses. I do not see the river. Mr. Lechmere, Reverend Hollingsworth's benefactor, lived in the mansion. He took the reverend and me to his distillery, a building behind the main house. I recognize nothing here."

"Two hundred years is a long time," Dr. Morris said. "Much has changed, as you have seen so far. Mr. Lechmere was a prominent man in Boston, but a staunch loyalist. He owned much of the land in this portion of Cambridge. Part of it still carries his name, Lechmere Point. But over the years, the city filled the marshes and grasslands that once grew along the shore of the Charles River. Houses were built. There is relatively nothing here of what may have once been. I'm sorry." She sighed, took a breath, shrugged. "Perhaps we should concentrate more on the present and future." She looked at her watch. "It's nearly five thirty. We're to meet Dr. Gorski at six."

"Aye." Noland tried to listen to Dr. Morris discuss Boston's development as they neared the taxi. But her words dispersed, as he glanced up and down the street. He paused, closed his eyes. *Lechmere had a dream but lost it in the turmoil.* He gritted his teeth. His legs felt heavy when he tried to walk. *I wonder whatever happened to Reverend Hollingsworth. Progress is good, but it can be destructive.*

Dr. Morris turned and asked, "Are you all right?"

"Aye. Only longing for the past."

Reentering the taxi, Dr. Morris told the driver to go to Holli's Seafood Restaurant on Mt. Auburn Street. The rush-hour traffic caused the trip to take twenty minutes. When they arrived, they found Dr. Gorski sitting and waiting on a bench near the restaurant front door.

"Good to see you," Dr. Morris said as she got out of the cab. "Hope you had a good day."

"Probably not as enjoyable as you two have had." Gorski smiled and stood. "Several difficult patients. Sergeant Black, did you enjoy what you saw of Harvard?"

Noland nodded, then dolefully shook his head. "It appears that within a few short days the place from where I came, and knew quite well, no longer exists."

"Noland did remember the chapel, and Massachusetts and Hollis Hall in Harvard's Old Yard," Dr. Morris said. "And don't forget, Noland, you had a McDonald's Big Mac." But Noland looked disappointed. "We tried to find a house on Tory Row where he recently—whoops…" She shrugged, then continued. "I mean in his time, had dinner with an instructor from the college. This house apparently does not exist, though a manor-style house stands on the supposed location. It's several blocks west of the Longfellow House, Washington's headquarters. Noland recognized that house." She tilted her head toward the door to the restaurant. "Should we go in?"

"Yes." Dr. Gorski turned and started to walk toward the doorway. "Lobster, haddock, scrod, raw oysters, or if you prefer, oysters Rockefeller. Chef Charles serves a variety of seafood dishes. He also has great filet mignon as well as other steaks. Everything is quite good here. Charles is also a member of the reenactment team."

Dr. Morris and Noland exchanged glimpses and followed behind Dr. Gorski into the restaurant.

"He's an interesting man," Gorski continued. "His great-great-great-grandfather fought in the American Revolution. Supposedly, he actually knew George Washington; he was one of his spies. Charlie has many interesting stories of his gramps's adventures. Noland, you may have met him. I believe his name was Lieutenant Jack Hollister. He came from Plymouth, England."

"Nay, sir. I have never heard of him."

"I don't suppose you did. Charlie's ancestor, Jack, fought with the colonial army…"

"I do know the Hollister name, however," Noland remarked as they approached the maître d'. "That is the mercantile supplier that provides our regiments with military equipment and supplies."

It took a moment for their eyes to accommodate once the entrance door closed. The attractive young maître d' led the group to a booth opposite the bar. The name tag on her blue-trimmed white blouse noted her name as Ginny. "Your waitress will be here momentarily," Ginny said as she laid down the menus. "May I serve you something from the bar?"

"Thank you kindly for escorting us to our table," Noland said, fascinated by the young lady in the skirted sailor outfit.

Ginny smiled. "You're from England, aren't you? Love your accent."

Noland beamed and nodded.

"A bottle of fine burgundy and three glasses," Dr. Gorski interjected with a grin. He glanced at Noland as Ginny turned and left. "I see you find her attractive."

"Aye. It is unfortunate that the Royal Navy does not procure lovely young ladies into their ranks. Long sea voyages would be far less wearisome."

The three chuckled as they seated themselves. Dr. Morris slid in next to the wall and Noland sat next to her. Dr. Gorski took the opposite bench. The sergeant looked around the dining room.

Though moderately lighted, Holli's décor of plank walls and beam ceiling, tables, chairs, booths, bar, and flooring were finished in dark wood, giving an ambience of a wooden vessel's interior. Antique faux-bronze oil lamps hung from the beige ceiling. Paintings, depicting nautical scenes and sailing vessels and backlighted portholes decorated the walls. Being a Monday, Holli's had few diners. They appeared to be students.

"A very nautical décor," Dr. Gorski said. "Charlie is enamored with his ancestor, who, I believe, had taken part in the first successful naval battle of the American Revolution, a battle before Washington created a fledgling American navy. That is why Charlie decorated his restaurant in the naval theme. Don't think the kitchen is very busy this evening. I'm sure he'll stop by for a chat. So, I'll introduce you. Think he'll find you fascinating, since you are from England."

"You will not tell him I am from the past?"

"No," Dr. Gorski said, "though he was at the reenactment Saturday, when we found you. Only my friend John knows your situation. Charlie is our cook at those meetings. Not being a medical doctor, he'd have been of little use. So, he stayed with the group, while John and I took care of you."

"Is John a surgeon?"

"No. He's a pharmacist," Dr. Gorski answered. "He works with me at the hospital passing out medicines. We've been very close friends since college, and I trust him." Gorski paused and laid the napkin in his lap. "Chef Charlie and I just know each other from the reenactor group."

"This place has a lot of interesting seafood," Dr. Morris said as she perused the menu. "There is also, as you said, the usual beef, pork, and poultry dishes. I see today's specials are shepherd's pie and blue-point oyster stew. What are you guys going to order?"

Dr. Gorski opened the menu and scanned it. "Fresh-caught lobster. Noland, have you had lobster? Or does the British army not serve such a delicacy."

"Nay." The sergeant shook his head. "The herdsmen feed them to the pigs." Looking a bit skeptical, he scratched his head. "They are now considered a delicacy?"

"They are indeed." Dr. Gorski licked his lips. "There is a profitable fishery for that bug. Lobsters are served at the finest restaurants and considered an excellent meal by connoisseurs and tourists. The lobster is a great attraction to diners in Boston and throughout New England. It is caught just offshore and shipped all over the world. The meat is sweet, high in protein, and when dipped in lemon butter…" He touched the middle and index fingers to his lips, kissed them with a distinct smack, and said, "*très bon!*"

Noland chuckled. "Ah, the French, they will eat anything."

"Lobster is very good," Dr. Morris said. "Though it's messy and a lot of work to eat, it is a lot of fun. You should try it." She paused and glanced at Noland. "In fact, I believe I'll have a lobster dinner this evening in celebration of our visitor from another time."

Ginny brought the wine and three glasses and set them on the table. She displayed the bottle's label in front of Dr. Gorski. "Chateau sur le Rocher 71," he read and nodded. Ginny flipped apart a cork-screw and started to open the wine bottle. She moved to the side to al-low the waitress balancing a tray to place a pitcher of water and glasses on the table. The waitress asked for their dinner orders. While Noland and Dr. Morris each ordered a lobster dinner, Ginny poured a tot of wine for Dr. Gorski to savor. He nodded and the maître d' filled the other glasses. Dr. Gorski ordered a pasta dinner of braised scallops in garlic sauce. Completing their tasks, Ginny and the waitress departed.

Dr. Gorski raised his glass. "Welcome to the twentieth century, Sergeant Noland Black." He took a sip. "A fine wine."

Dr. Morris and Sergeant Black followed suit.

"Thank you for accepting and believing in me," Noland replied. "And, for what you both are doing to make me comfortable. I should not be here, nor have I an explanation of how I came to be here. But I'm beginning to enjoy it. The future has become something no one in my time would have ever dreamed of." He sipped his wine.

Almost in unison, Drs. Morris and Gorski shook their heads and replied, "Can't clarify your circumstances either."

The trio chuckled, sipped wine, drank water, but seemed momen-tarily lost in contemplation until Dr. Gorski broke the silence. "I con-tacted a fellow who I know in the State Department. He lives in D.C. Asked what can be done for someone, not a citizen of the U.S., who has lost all documentation of his existence. He's here, but not illegally.

My friend asked how did he get here? I told him, his arrival is complicated and if I tried to explain, you'll never believe me. His answer, 'Sounds like a challenging problem. Let me get back to you.'" Dr. Gorski took a drink of wine. "Typical answer from a Fed. But let's give him a couple of days to call me back. In the meantime, let us enjoy teaching our friend Noland what life is like in the twentieth century. I'm sure Noland can enlighten us about life in the eighteenth century."

Like a light switched on in Dr. Gorski's brain, a smile brightened his face, and he pushed up against the back of the booth. He looked around the table. "Yeah! And he's a British drill sergeant. Teaching recruits. An expert in British army war tactics. What can I say? He's the real thing. And English. Noland, how'd you like to become an instructor for my reenactors?" He fidgeted excitedly, then clasped his hand together and faced Noland. "What'd you say? You game?"

Before the sergeant could answer, Dr. Morris broke in. "He could get paid for what he knows. Will your reenactor group pay him for teaching your guys?"

"Yeah. They'll agree to that."

Dr. Morris continued. "Dr. Gorski, you seem to have many contacts. Noland will eventually have to have some I.D. papers. If he has them, he can expand. Teach others." She stared at Dr. Gorski. "Know any forgers that could create a counterfeit passport or birth certificate?"

Dr. Gorski slouched, but then pushed back again. "No, I don't. But John…I believe he deals with a couple of tough-looking guys who own a bar in Roxbury. Good idea, but not quite kosher." He grinned and nodded. "I'll check with him."

The waitress brought their dinners, while Ginny tied a lobster bib around Dr. Morris's neck. Noland sat quietly and watched. A bewildered look crossed his face when Ginny stepped behind him and began to secure his bib. "It is to be an untidy meal, I assume?"

"Yes." Dr. Morris said with a grin. "But you will enjoy it."

"You two will have to work for your dinner," Dr. Gorski joshed.

Ginny refilled the glasses of water and noticed the wine bottle was less than half full. "Would you care for another bottle?" she asked.

Dr. Gorski looked at everyone and said, "I believe we are fine for now."

"Enjoy your dinners." Ginny nodded, turned, and left.

"Dig in," Dr. Gorski said as he rolled the pasta around his fork.

Dr. Morris showed the nutcracker to Noland and explained what to do with it.

He nodded, but instead of examining the modern-day nutcracker, he tasted the coleslaw. "Cabbage, but favorably done. It is very tasty." He watched as Dr. Morris pulled off the lobster's legs and sucked out the bits of muscle. He attempted to emulate, but an expression of disgust darkened his face and his tongue shot out. "Aarrg! Displeasing. Only salty water," he groaned and took a swig of fresh water.

"Use your teeth to squeeze the leg and suck at the same time; like squeezing toothpaste out of a tube, but using your teeth," she instructed. "There's sweet muscle meat inside, but slightly salty. Give that a try." She sucked on another leg. "Many people don't waste their time with the legs, but I find eating them fun and somewhat relaxing before I attack the claws and tail." She sat back in the chair, wiped her fingers and hands, then grabbed the lobster and twisted off the tail. "I'll show you how to get out the tail meat. Watch." She broke off the tail fins and pushed her index finger into the hole at the tip of the tail. The muscle meat slid out of its skeletal shell and onto the plate. She picked up the knife and fork and cut a bite-sized piece of the tail. "Everything you see in the tail is edible. The green stuff on the front is called tomalley; it's sort of salty-sweet. Some people won't eat it because of the taste and color. Anyway, cut up the muscle and dip the pieces in the lemon butter and pop them into your mouth."

Noland tore off one of the legs with the large claw, picked up the nutcracker, and broke open a knuckle. With the pick-fork, he removed pieces of the joint muscle and popped some in his mouth. He nodded. "Umm. This meat is sweet. It tastes excellent." He extracted the lobster's tail meat, cut it up, stuck a piece with the tiny fork, dipped it into lemon butter, and put it into his mouth. A smile of pleasure enlivened his face. After, the sergeant sipped his wine and drank some water. "A delicacy indeed. I wonder why our cooks have not served them…" he pushed some strands of hair away from his ear and took another sip of wine, "probably because the lobsters are used to feed the pigs. Pigs have a finer meal than do the soldiers. How sad."

"Definitely," Dr. Gorski agreed.

With the bowl of discarded lobster shells nearly filled, Noland and the doctors had almost completed their dinners. Chef Charles Hollister came to the booth where the trio sat. "Good to see you, Dr. Gorski," Charles said. "I hope you have enjoyed your meals?"

Noland nodded as he dipped the last piece of lobster meat into the ramekin of lemon butter.

"We surely have," Dr. Gorski said. "Folks, this is Chef Charles. We can thank him for creating these excellent dinners."

Dr. Morris smiled and nodded. Noland, still swallowing a bite of lobster, grunted his appreciation.

"Thank you." Charles straightened and smiled. "A delight to cook for such a discerning group."

"I really enjoy lobster," Dr. Morris said as she dabbed the moisture from her lips.

"Aye, and so did I," Noland replied after wiping his lips and fingers with his napkin. "The first lobster I have ever had."

"Charles, I'd like to introduce Dr. Carol Morris, an ER surgeon at Mass General Clinic, and her long-lost cousin from England, Noland Black. Noland is studying British military history. A few days ago, he arrived on our shore to research the outcome of the American Revolution."

"Pleasure to meet you two." Chef Charles pulled a chair to the end of the booth and seated himself. He leaned slightly toward Noland. "I'm also very interested in the Revolutionary War. My great-great-great-grandfather fought in that war. Was a spy for General George

Washington, who promoted him to lieutenant. He helped capture the HMS *Margaretta* in Maine during the first naval battle of the war. He also fought in the battle for New York City." Charles stiffened proudly, twisted around toward Dr. Gorski, and nodded at him. "That's why I joined Dr. Gorski's reenactment regiment. I'm their cook. By the way, are we going to meet later this week?"

Gorski nodded. "Yes. Probably Friday or Saturday. At the same location where we met this past weekend. I'll let you know."

"Okay. Perhaps Mr. Black can join us." Chef Charles shifted nervously. "Sorry. Have to get back to the kitchen." He started to turn and leave but stopped and leaned toward Dr. Gorski. "Last weekend. Yeah. You left to take care of some guy who got injured. How'd that come out?"

"Got him to the clinic. Dr. Morris here, took care of his injuries and we sent him home. As far as Noland joining us, I'm sure he'd enjoy that."

"Good. I wondered what happened to the fellow. Hope to see you at Minute Man Park, Mr. Black." Chef Charles continued to the kitchen.

"Want to join us?" Dr. Gorski asked Noland. "You can wear your uniform. You'll fit right in."

Noland nodded noncommittedly. The three diners finished their meals and wine.

Ginny brought the check. Dr. Gorski paid for the dinners. "What's the plan for tomorrow?" he asked as Dr. Morris and Sergeant Black scooted out of the booth and headed for the restaurant's door.

"More sightseeing, if it doesn't rain," Dr. Morris answered. "But first I'm going to sleep in. I took the rest of the week off." She moved through the restaurant's exit. "We've got to catch the MTA back to the Charlestown clinic and pick up my car, which I left in the parking lot."

"Since I've got my vehicle parked just down the street, I'll drop you guys off," Gorski said. "I've got to work tomorrow, but maybe later in the day we can get together. Might have news from the State Department. I'll call if I'm free. Now, let's be on our way."

Tuesday, April 22, 1975

Sergeant Black was awakened from a comfortable sleep the next morning when the telephone rang. He twisted about in bed and lay back. The noise of subtle confusion made its way to the second floor of the house. Noland shoved away the blankets, rose, pushed back his hair, and dressed. He scuttled down the stairs and found Dr. Morris and Norma in the kitchen.

"Good morning. Sorry we woke you," Dr. Morris said.

"Yes. Yes. Good morning, Noland," Norma said anxiously as she fidgeted about the kitchen. "Excuse me. I'll get my things and be on my way."

"Good morning. I hope all is well," Noland said as he stood next to the breakfast table. The increased tension that seemed to fill the kitchen disturbed him.

Norma shook her head and grabbed for the door to the back porch, opened it and exited, then scampered to her cottage. Within minutes she was back in the kitchen, carrying an overnight case. She headed into the living room and out the front door. "Have to hurry. The Greyhound leaves at twelve thirty. I can make it. Call you when I get there…"

"Whoa, lady! I'll drive you to the subway station." Dr. Morris grabbed her car keys from the mantel and followed Norma to the car. Before stepping off the porch, she turned to Noland, who had reached the porch, and yelled to him, "This'll only take a few minutes. Breakfast, when I get back. There's a pot of fresh coffee on the stove."

Muddled, the sergeant stood in the doorway scratching his ear, then his neck where the cross once hung. He watched as Dr. Morris wheeled the VW out of the driveway, onto the street, and squealed away. *The twentieth century is unbelievable. Everyone is in a hurry.* He shook his head, stepped back into the house, returned to the breakfast table, and sat down. In the middle of the table were three tall, narrow, rectangular boxes with colorful images and words; one spelled Wheaties, another Cheerios, and the other, Kellogg's Corn Flakes. Noland picked the Cheerios box and scanned the four sides. "Breakfast food?" he questioned, set the box down and picked up the Wheaties box. "Breakfast of champions." He laughed. "The colonials have become a strange lot, though they are very interesting." Hearing a vehicle outside and, within moments, the front door open and close, he put the Wheaties' box down, rose from the chair, and stepped into the living room.

"Sorry about that." Dr. Morris took off her jacket. "Norma caught the subway to downtown, where she'll catch the Greyhound that will take her to Hartford. The telephone call, that I'm sure woke you, was from a doctor's office. Seems Norma's sister had fallen, injured her back, and had to be taken to the hospital. Her sister is her only living relative. The two are close. So, Norma is going down to take care of her. I believe she'll be gone for a week or two." Dr. Morris removed her jacket, dropped it on the couch, and gestured for Noland to go to the kitchen. She followed.

"We'll have to fend for ourselves," she said. "Did you see the boxes of cereal Norma left on the table? Choose one—or two. That'll be breakfast. Milk is inside the fridge. I'll pour us coffee. I could use some myself right now."

"I saw the boxes." Noland nodded. He also ascertained the word *fridge* meant the cabinet with the cold space and walked around the table to the refrigerator. As he took out the jug of milk, he asked, "What is a greyhound? Is Norma to ride a dog?"

Dr. Morris broke into a laugh. "Good god, no! It is a bus that transports people from city to city, like a stagecoach. The transport business is named the Greyhound Bus Company. Its symbol or coat-of-arms is the greyhound dog, which is supposed to be a fast runner."

"Aye. I understand."

"Now, select one or two—or all three of those cereals. The coffee is ready. And, we'll have breakfast."

With a grin, Noland selected the box of Wheaties. He examined the image on the front. "If I eat this, will I look like the Adonis depicted on the box?" He grinned and poured some flakes into a bowl.

"You already have that physique," Dr. Morris said with a wily smile as she filled two cups with coffee. "Now pour some milk over the cereal. It will soften the flakes. That's the way cereal is eaten."

Noland poured milk over the flakes of Wheaties and spooned some into his mouth. He crunched the flakes. "A very fascinating taste." The crunching and swallowing of the flakes distorted his comment. "Quite appealing." He took a second spoonful. The flakes had softened to the point where he could crush them with his tongue. "Like the gruel Cook serves in the barracks, but with sweetness and more flavor."

Dr. Morris and Sergeant Black finished breakfast, and each had a second cup of coffee.

"I did not wash up after I had awakened," Noland said. "I would like to do so before we begin our day."

"Very well. Take your time. I'll clear the dishes. Give me a yell when you are dressed, and I'll come up and check your wounds. So far, the morning has been cool and rainy. Perhaps the weather will change by lunchtime so I can continue to help you transition into the present.

Dr. Morris finished examining Sergeant Black's wounds, applied an antibiotic cream onto the still-reddish bullet wounds, and bandaged them after he had showered and donned a pair of pants. "You're healing very well," she said. Her hands brushed over his shoulders and she lightly squeezed them. "Dress and come downstairs. It's a rainy, cold day today, so I'll turn the television on and bring some coffee. Perhaps the weather outside will improve after lunch." The doctor collected the medical supplies off the bed. "Unfortunately, the soap operas take up most of the morning hours. You might find watching them entertaining. The actors and actresses are well-dressed, beautiful people."

"Soap, I know. Operas I know," Noland said, "but to me, combining the two words creates a most unusual theatrical..." he chuckled, "group of performers romping and singing about in soapy forth. Aye. Indeed. A comedy. Aye. I would enjoy watching such a performance. Are the actors clothed?"

Dr. Morris began to laugh. "I would love to watch such a performance myself." She took a breath. "No, soap operas are not what you think. They are exaggerated, sentimental, teary-eyed, continuous dramas. I mean they're on television every day. But they started as radio dramas sponsored by soap-manufacturing companies. Listeners began calling the broadcasts soap operas. The name stuck. Some people, who listen to or watch these dramas, think that they depict real family life, mysteries, and problems. They don't. The programs distort real life. Yet, people enjoy watching them and become addicted. Or perhaps, for some it may be a way to escape their own lives for a few minutes a day. Anyway, just wanted to warn you, this is not how most people in America live." She shrugged and headed for the door. "See you downstairs. I'll have the TV on."

Sergeant Black didn't take long to complete dressing himself. After about ten minutes, he ambled down the stairs. Dr. Morris, holding two mugs and a pot of coffee, met him in the living room. The television was on. Displayed on the screen was a group of actors, each sitting in one of nine cubicles that were stacked one on top of another.

The whole formed one large cube. Some were laughing, others dubious or appeared oblivious. A handsome, well-dressed fellow walked on the stage in front of the cube, directing and talking to the individuals in the cubicles. Noland stared at the screen and scratched his head trying to understand what was going on.

Dr. Morris glanced at the screen. *"Hollywood Squares,"* she said as she set the coffee pot and cups on the table. "That's a game show. The man on the stage is Peter Marshall. He's the announcer or host of the show. He asks questions. The actors in the cubicles try to answer. Some give silly answers, other bluff. Eventually, someone answers correctly." The doctor grasped the handle of the coffee pot and poured Noland a cup.

"Aye. Thank you." Noland's eyes remained glued on the screen. He slowly sat down on the sofa.

"The next show is about the same," Dr. Morris said. "There's not much on the television in the morning."

"I should watch." Noland took a sip of coffee and leaned toward the television screen.

"I believe you'll find the morning shows somewhat senseless. There are more interesting and entertaining programs in the evening." Dr. Morris sat down, poured herself some coffee, and took a sip.

Noland started to chuckle.

"You find the program humorous?" Dr. Morris glanced at the screen and the ongoing conflict. She shrugged.

"Aye. The man argues. The woman argues. Does he not realize that he will never win? The woman appears more intelligent, has more sense, and has the upper hand. She is prudent, bold, argues well, which confuses him. His impetuousness will destroy him. Proper argumentation requires reason; he has none." Noland relaxed back against the sofa. "Watching such an encounter is more entertaining than troubling."

Dr. Morris nodded. "You should know. I'm sure the men and women of your time were stronger. They had to face, on their own, many more challenges than today's men and women."

"Aye." Noland lowered his chin, slightly shifted his head to the right, and pushed back his hair. "Indeed. There are more difficulties to survival for those attempting to colonize a new land and develop it in an image they desire. To persevere in wilderness and against unknow hostilities, both men and women have to be courageous and strong. Though I am sure that at this time, there are many challenges that cause dismay, unknown to me, which confront humanity."

"That is for sure. But I believe that the colonists had more forti-tude and confidence." Dr. Morris noticed that the sergeant's attention had returned to the television. "In the evenings there are better shows. Several years ago, Boston's Education Network on the TV's Channel 2, WGBH, became part of the Public Broadcasting Service—BPBS-TV it's called here in Boston. Actually—you'll like this—this public broad-casting service was first started in England sometime in the nineteen sixties by the British Broadcasting Service; it's known as the BBC."

Noland grinned.

Dr. Morris continued. "During the day, Boston's PBS-TV mostly broadcasts educational programs, documentaries, and children's enter-tainment. But recently, on Sunday evenings WGBH features several programs that are produced in England by the British Broadcasting Company or BBC. The one being shown now is titled *Masterpiece Theatre*. The BBC converts classic books written by noted British au-thors into television scripts. The characters in the novels are portrayed by famous English actors. Actually, the present TV play, *Upstairs, Downstairs,* was written by the lead actresses, Jean Marsh and Eileen Atkins. When the play became a success, the screenwriter, John Hawkesworth, novelized the play. It's a drama about the residents and staff of 165 Eaton Place in London's classy Belgravia neighborhood. The story takes place during the unsettled years in the early twentieth century before and after the first world war…"

"John Hawkesworth?" Noland interrupted. "I know of that au-thor. On the voyage I read his accounts of explorers to the South Pacific Ocean."

Dr. Morris shook her head. "It's not the same author. The Hawkesworth who wrote *Upstairs, Downstairs* is alive. He lives in Leicester, England. Alistair Cooke, the host of *Masterpiece Theater*, another Brit, offered a bit of Hawkesworth's life when he introduced the program at the beginning of the series. Hawkesworth is also known for his other novels. I'm not familiar with the John Hawkesworth of whom you speak. Understandable. I don't have much time to read." She took a sip of coffee. "We'll watch *Masterpiece Theatre* Sunday evening when it's on. I'm sure you'll recognize the accents."

"Aye," the sergeant said. He fidgeted as a wave of tension made him uneasy. "I will look forward to watching the show." Noland drank the last of the coffee from his cup.

Though the sergeant's eyes remained glued to the TV, Dr. Morris perceived that he had become reticent. She picked up the empty coffee pot and mugs and carried them into the kitchen.

While activity on the TV screen continued, Noland's mind churned when he tried to rationalize the relationship between Great Britain and the contemporary colonials as he envisioned modern Americans. He shook his head and mumbled, "I do not understand how two adversaries have established such a compact rapport of friendship. The two countries seem to do everything together...." As Sergeant Black ruminated, he glanced about the room. *Great Britain and France have been hostile with each other since I can remember and also, so with Spain. Are two hundred years' time enough to establish such alliances? A time of peace? Or am I being beguiled by what I am being told—by what I am seeing?*

Dr. Morris reentered the living room. "Is something bothering you, Noland?"

The sergeant looked up. "I do not understand this new world I am in. Or, how I got here. You said we are to watch a British show on the contrivance you call a television. My mind has not resolved that the superior forces of Great Britain were beaten by lowly, ragtag colonial militias. America and Great Britain should be adversaries. Yet, you say they are not. What of France? Or Spain? Those countries have been our enemies for as long as I can remember."

Dr. Morris slowly sat down next to Noland. She sucked in her lower lip and raised her eyelids. Her facial features softened as she looked into Noland's eyes. "What Dr. Gorski and I told you is the truth. Except for the shooting war in Vietnam, civil war in Lebanon, and disagreements in ideas and policies with Russia, most of the world is relatively in peace now. England, France, Spain, Germany, and all the other countries in Western Europe are all allied." She nodded and sat back. "How you came to be here, in this time period, is a mystery. I do not know if you will ever return to the eighteenth century. Science has not discovered or invented a means to travel through time. So, Noland, my friend, you'll need to resign yourself to living in the twentieth century. Dr. Gorski and I will do everything possible to help you and keep your origin a secret."

A pensive mood seemed to embrace Noland. He looked down and for a few moments didn't speak. Suddenly his head bobbed and, as if his mind conjured a brilliant notion, his eyes brightened. "Perhaps I was killed on the battlefield. And I am now in the hereafter. Our local parson taught us as youngsters that there was life after death, either in Heaven or in Hell. Since I have not met the Devil, nor seen walls of roaring flames, this must be Heaven. I am in my afterlife…" he looked at Dr. Morris with gravity, "and you and Dr. Gorski are my guardian angels."

Dr. Morris sighed then grinned. "I don't think you should consider us guardian angels. And you weren't killed. This is not Heaven, nor the hereafter. What you are suggesting is that you died and were reincarnated in a new place and time…"

Noland gasped and became agitated. "Reincarnated? I do not know what that means."

"In a sense, it's a similar notion to the hereafter. One dies and comes back to life in a different time and place. Supposedly not in the same body, nor do they remember anything from the past. Memory of their past life, if theoretically any exists in the mind, is lost in the subconscious. You, Noland, know who you are and where you came from. You occur in the same body you had in the eighteenth century. You exist as you did last week, except now, you are in a different time and place."

Noland's hand raised and scratched through his hair. He shrugged and shook his head.

"There are some people who believe in reincarnation," Dr. Morris continued. "In fact, several years ago an account of such a happening made the news. Seems a housewife in Colorado, a Mrs. Tighe, I think, defiantly alleged that in her previous life she was a nine-year-old girl who lived in Cork, Ireland in the early 1800s—1806, to be exact. Her name then was Bridey Murphy. The Colorado housewife was very determined, so some investigators, who were specialized medical doctors, subjected her to what is called regression hypnosis. It's a procedure where the individual is put into a trancelike sleep and the doctors attempt to access information from her subconscious by asking her specific questions. By doing so, the investigators believed that Bridey Murphy could recall her earliest thoughts while she was in a deep sleep. The investigators thought they may have had some success. As the story goes, under hypnosis, Mrs. Tighe in a sense became this Bridey person. Spoke with a strong Irish accent, but when she awoke and was placed under normal conditions, she spoke with no Irish accent. Mrs. Tighe had never visited Ireland. Though as Bridey, she knew the place where she lived in Cork, described the house, named her parents and grandparents, and recounted her marriage, which supposedly occurred in 1815. Under hypnosis, she mentioned that she and her husband, a barrister named Shawn McCarthy, moved to Belfast, because he taught at Queen's University. Bridey died from a fall. Mrs. Tighe, as Bridey, told the doctors that she watched her funeral. She described the inscription on her tombstone and said she was reborn sometime in the early 1900s. And that is where Bridey's story ends. Mrs. Tighe was born in 1923 and, I think, she is still alive.

"Investigators went to Ireland to verify the account Mrs. Tighe presented while she was under hypnosis. They found no evidence to prove that a Bridey Murphy ever lived. There were no birth, marriage, or death records. The house in Cork Mrs. Tighe, as Bridey, described never existed, and Queen's University Belfast had not yet been built when Bridey lived there. In conclusion, the investigators suggested that Mrs. Tighe suffered from what they called cryptomnesia. This is a mental condition where a conjured remembrance returns without being recognized as such by the patient, who believes it is a new and truly original memory. However, the Bridey Murphy story became such a sensation in the media that a book was published and a movie film about it was produced. But it turned out to be all a hoax. But it did create quite a sensation. So far, no real evidence has been found to verify that the notion of reincarnation really occurs."

Noland shrugged. He looked disappointed.

"Let's have lunch. Norma apparently had bought some groceries a day or so ago, so we're well stocked with a variety of things to eat. Would you like tea, coffee, or something cold?" Dr. Morris rose and turned toward the kitchen.

"Tea would be fine," Noland said. "May I help?"

"Thank you, but no. I can handle it. Besides, you're supposed to be recuperating." Dr. Morris started for the kitchen but paused and looked through the window. "Looks like the weather is improving. Perhaps later we'll drive over to Bunker Hill, where you can see how the place has changed. Or we can go into downtown Boston and examine some historical sites that may be familiar to you."

The telephone rang. Dr. Morris answered. She nodded after receiving the message. "Okay. We'll go on our own today. Don't work too hard." She replaced the receiver into its cradle and turned toward the sergeant. "That was Dr. Gorski. He has to work and will not be able to meet with us tonight. We're on our own. I'll make us some lunch and, maybe if the weather continues to improve, we can go into downtown Boston. There are some places you might recognize in the historic district, and I know an interesting pub you might also remember. It's been around for a very long time. We can have dinner there."

"Aye. I would find that interesting." Noland scooted to the edge of the couch. "May I help you prepare our lunch?"

Dr. Morris looked out the kitchen window while she was clearing away the leftovers of the eclectic lunch they had put together. "Looks like the rain has stopped. If we're going to do some sightseeing, we should head downtown. I believe my husband purchased an L.L. Bean rain jacket before he shipped off for Vietnam. I'll try to find it."

Sergeant Black nodded as he finished his coffee and put the cup into the sink. "Aye. I am anxious. Perhaps we will find the barracks that housed my regiment."

Dr. Morris recoiled. "We'll look, but don't get your hopes up. As you realized yesterday, there is little that remains from the 1770s." Dr. Morris scampered up the stairs and searched the closet where she had stored her husband's clothes. In a few moments she hurried back down. "Here it is. Still in plastic wrap." Removing the garment from its package, she handed the orange-colored Gortex rain jacket to Noland.

With an uneasy look on his face, Sergeant Black slipped on the jacket. He gritted his teeth, extended his arm, and glanced at it and down the front of the jacket. "An unusual color. Quite bright."

"Yes," Dr. Morris said indifferently. "I doubt if anyone who sees you will pay any attention. It's a very common color for raingear. David—my husband—was a jogger and bought the jacket to wear during hunting season. He liked to run trails in forests and didn't want to stop during the time hunters were out. The color of the jacket is called hunter orange. Ray bought it for protection. Her head drooped. She shook it. "Sorry. A woeful moment. He never got to wear it."

Momentarily confused, Noland raised his eyes. "What is the season to hunt?" His arm dropped to his side, and he looked at Dr.

Morris. "There were many deer to the north and west of the barracks. The native Americans hunted them all the time. When my regiment wanted fresh meat, we were given permission to shoot one or two. No one cared what season it was. If one wanted fresh meat, one hunted."

"Today that is not so. State governments set specific times in a year that are designated as hunting seasons. And in this day, hunters can only shoot wild animals in selected locations. This allows the game to prosper and reproduce. Most hunting is allowed in the autumn and winter months." Dr. Morris paused for a moment. "Since the city and its surroundings have encroached on the lands where the deer once lived, hunting is not allowed in Boston—too many humans in the line of fire. In fact, the only deer in or near the Boston area are in the zoo. One has to drive miles to find undeveloped land. There they can hunt, when the season is open, in fields and forest where hunting is allowed."

"Ahh, yes," Noland gasped. "I have come to a concerning awareness. Though the colonists fought for their freedom, they have lost some. Also, I have yet to see wild open land in this time." Noland lowered his head.

Dr. Morris sighed and frowned. "The world has become much more crowded in the past two hundred years."

"Aye. I have noticed. Humanity has increased." Noland walked to a full-length mirror on the back of the front door and posed. "I will dismiss the color and accept the jacket's protection from the rain."

"Good. And it will also keep you warm." Dr. Morris grabbed her car keys off the mantel. "Let's get on our way. The station is only a short walk from the clinic. I'll park the car in my space. We'll take the Orange Line into Boston."

"Orange Line? Is it painted for protection? What form of conveyance may that be?"

"Subway." Dr. Morris snickered. "A transport system, I may have mentioned, to rapidly carry people around the city. It runs on rails above ground and underground through the city, and it is powered by electricity. They are also called commuter trains. Boston has four subway lines. They're simple to use. Many Bostonians humorously say the subways were designed for stupid people."

"Aye. A conveyance that moves underground. Amazing. A new experience." Noland moved tensely toward the door, while Dr. Morris picked up her Polaroid camera.

"Can't forget this," she said as she followed the sergeant out the door. "We might want to record what we see."

After parking the VW at the clinic, it took Dr. Morris and Sergeant Black about ten minutes to walk down School Street to the Bunker Hill Community College campus. The rain ended, but a chilly breeze continued.

Noland felt a little conspicuous wearing the orange rain jacket, but the interior lining did keep him warm. He pulled the jacket's collar tighter around his neck as he and Dr. Morris crossed Rutherford Avenue to the stairway and walkway that took them to the Austin Street entrance to the Community College Transit station. Dr. Morris stopped at the ticket vending machine, adjusted the camera strap on her shoulder, and purchased the subway tickets. Then the two walked to the stairway that led to the waiting platform for the southbound Orange Line train.

Because the platform was outside and located below the freeway overpass, the rumble of the traffic above seemed to be amplified. Noland's body tensed from nervousness and amazement. Unconsciously, his fingers massaged his neck. Although it was absent, he could still feel the lanyard from which his Celtic cross hung. He sighed, then gripped the banister tight as he began to descend the stairs to the subway platform. With his eyes opened wide, he scanned the intricate overhead metal girders, the bright ceiling lights and the glossy pillars that supported the highway. He had never experienced such illumination, color, and apparent structural strength under a bridge. An astonished look covered his face. As he walked onto the platform, he became fascinated by the sheen and straightness of the rails in the trench in front of him, the ordered pattern of the crossties and cleanliness of the bedding stones. He walked toward the platform's edge and looked down; then he glanced up and down the tracks. To him they seemed to stretch to infinity.

"Be careful. Don't get too near the edge. Might fall in and get electrocuted or run over by the train," Dr. Morris said. "This station was only opened for service a couple of weeks ago. It is new."

As he stepped back, the sudden appearance of a bright flash in the corner of his left eye startled him. He snapped around to face it. The light grew rapidly and seemed to be coming directly at him. Noland jumped back to the stairway as a wave of forward-rushing air blew past him. Within a moment the train slowed, came to a stop, and the coach doors slid open.

Dr. Morris took hold of Noland's hand and tried to urge him onto the subway. But her attempt felt like trying to get a boy into a barber's chair for his first haircut. "Relax! You'll be okay. Rapid transport, remember. It moves fast. We'll be downtown in less than ten minutes."

Stiffly, Noland walked into the subway car. No sooner did he than the doors closed, and the train began to move.

Dr. Morris pointed to a set of empty seats. "Grab the pole. Hold on and slide into that seat."

Sergeant Black seized the stainless-steel pole next to him as he felt the inertial force tugging him back when the train began to accelerate. He pushed himself toward the seat and slid in. Dr. Morris sat down next to him. Noland glanced out the window and saw nothing but a blur as the train sped to the next station. Within two minutes the scene outside turned black. Before his mind could formulate a response, he felt himself being pushed forward as the subway began to slow on its approach to Boston's North Station. Then suddenly the windows brightened with light. Noland squinted. *This conveyance has entered a barn with intense brightness; it is made not of wood, but of glossy tiles.* The subway stopped and the doors opened.

"North Station," Dr. Morris said. "We've traveled under the Charles River and, from here, we'll continue deep under the city of Boston for two more stops. We'll exit at the State Street Station. We won't have to climb stairs to get out of this tunnel, because there's an elevator, a people lifter, to lift us and other commuters to the street level. Today elevators in Britain are called lifts." She put her hand on Noland's shoulder as the doors closed and the subway accelerated toward the next stop. "Another new experience for you, Noland."

"Aye!" The sergeant nodded. "But not new. My life has become full of new experiences, but 'lifts' I am aware of. In Cornwall and Devon, elevators, as you call them, transport miners into and out of the mines where they dig for tin and copper." Nevertheless, the expression on Noland's face remained bewildered as the subway sped on toward the Haymarket Station. Anxiety surged through his body as the train accelerated. Outside, periodic banks of signal lights flashed his eyes. Side-to-side motion and vibration, and the whooshing sound of the outside air, increased his anxiety. He took a deep breath, tightly clasped his hands together, shoved them between his thighs, and leaned forward.

As the subway slowed on its approach to the next station, tension in Noland's body lessened. And, when the door opened, he felt his shoulders drop. He watched the people scramble off and on. Then with a swoosh, the doors closed, and the train accelerated. His muscles tensed again. Malaise and tautness returned. He glanced at Dr. Morris, who seemed oblivious to the rush. "I have never moved at such speed," he gasped.

As the subway pulled into North Street Station, Dr. Morris stood up and automatically stepped into the aisle as she prepared to exit the subway.

Sergeant Black tried to stand, but his knees felt weak. He grasped the handle on the seat ahead to help himself out of the seat, grabbed the pole in the aisle, and steadied himself. He noticed that Dr. Morris casually exited onto the platform. Noland feebly, but quickly, followed. She led him to a pillar. "Hang on here and relax for a moment," she said, "and then we'll make our way to the street."

As the doors of the subway closed and it began to move away, Noland took a deep breath and nodded. "That indeed was an experience. Let us continue."

Dr. Morris took hold of Noland's left arm. "Okay. Lean on me if you need too. I am your doctor..." she paused and looked at him, "and your support."

Noland smiled, gently nodded, relaxed, and stepped away from the pillar. Feeling secure with Dr. Morris's assistance, he walked along the platform. The two stopped in front of a pair of large, brushed steel panels with a sign above EXIT. STATE STREET. Several other people stood in front of this silvery wall.

Within moments the panels slid apart, creating an opening into what Noland took to be a small, well-lighted, glistening room. A walnut-colored handrail encircled the room. On the room's walls hung colorful posters advertising restaurants and hotels. Noland immediately recognized one poster, the image of the Old State House.

"Boston barracks!" he blurted, which caught the attention of the other commuters, who immediately turned and glared at him. "Aye, the barracks that houses our primary regiment." Without noticing the stares, he walked slowly into the room.

"That's a poster of the Old State House," Dr. Morris disclosed. "That is the building where the Massachusetts General Assembly once met."

Noland took hold of the rail in front of the poster and stared up at it. He did not notice that the steel panels closed or the feeling of momentary weightiness as the elevator began to ascend. "No! Our military removed those rebels. I was..." A quick, intense squeeze on his arm caused him to glare down at Dr. Morris.

She put her fingers to her lips and eased the squeeze. "You should know," she whispered. "You were there. But don't let everyone know."

He stepped back, turned toward the steel doors, blushed, and looked around. Everyone seemed oblivious to his presence. He felt a slight jolt when the elevator stopped. The steel doors slid open.

Dr. Morris and Noland—she still holding onto his left arm—walked into the small station containing ticket vending machines, and through a pair of large glass doors onto State Street. Though the afternoon sky remained overcast, the air cool, and the possibility of rain seemed to still exist, many people flocked about the street.

"Tourists," Dr. Morris said. "This street and its plaza are one of the primary locations of Boston's Historic Walking Trail." She pointed across the street. "There's the Old State House—or military barracks as you called it."

Awestruck, Noland looked skyward and slowly circled in place. "The edifices are touching the sky. I have not seen such structures."

"Skyscrapers, we call them," Dr. Morris explained. "Office buildings. Insurance agencies. Banks."

Noland lower his head and glanced in the direction Dr. Morris had pointed. In front of him stood the Old State House. "Aye, the barracks, but well hidden among these skyscraping structures."

Dr. Morris lightly clasped his arm. "Come. Let us cross into the plaza. I want to show you a sight where an event that provoked the colonial revolution occurred. Perhaps you were even involved in it. It's called the Boston Massacre. A troop of British soldiers killed several protesting colonials."

The sergeant shook his head. "Nay! I was not here, but I was told of this unfortunate provocation. The rebels attacked a solitary British soldier, but his comrades came to his rescue."

"Perhaps so, but it was one of the nails the British added that led to the decline in the relationship between American colonies and Great Britain."

Dr. Morris led Noland across State Street into the tiled plaza on the east side of the Old State House. Roughly in the center of this plaza lay a circle of cobblestones that marked the site where the

Boston Massacre took place on March 5th, 1770. A middle-aged, touristy-looking couple, who appeared to be conversing, was standing near the cobblestone marker. A short distance away stood a group of teenagers and an older woman.

"I'd like a photo of you and me," Dr. Morris said as she removed the camera from her shoulder. "I'm going to ask that fellow over there…" she pointed toward the couple, "if he'd take our picture." She walked to the man and woman.

Noland watched the man nod and then Dr. Morris give him the Polaroid. She then motioned for the sergeant to come and stand with her on the edge of the cobblestone circle where the Old State House would be in the background. "Put your arm around me and smile. Look like you're happy to be here."

Noland grinned, wrapped his arm around Dr. Morris's shoulder, and pulled her close.

"Smile," the man said as he took their picture, then walked forward and returned the camera to Dr. Morris.

Dr. Morris removed the photo from the base of the Polaroid, fanned it, waited a few moments, then preserved it and show it to Noland.

"You visiting Boston?" the woman asked in a heavily accented voice. Reaching into her shoulder bag, she removed a point-and-shoot camera. "Perhaps you would please take picture. Keepsake, I believe you call it. In little while, we return to Warsaw."

"I would be happy to take some photos of you." Dr. Morris accepted the little camera. "Pose yourself near the cobblestones where we stood. The historic building will be behind you." She turned and took hold of Noland's arm and guided him away from the historic marker. Dr. Morris then turned, aimed the camera at the Polish couple, snapped the shutter, and returned the camera. "We…" she looked at Noland and grinned… "we live here in Boston. Just came downtown to have dinner. I hope you enjoyed your stay in our city."

"*Gziękuję Ci*," the woman said, with a momentary sheepish grin, "Thank you. We much enjoy city. Much American history." She glanced at her man. "*Stashu*," she giggled embarrassingly. "Oh my, I should use his American name. It is Stanley. He is professor of history." She paused and looked at her watch. "So sorry. We must go to hotel. Pack, as you say, and go to airport."

"Boston is definitely an historic city," Dr. Morris said. "Thank you for taking our picture. You two have a safe journey home."

"Aye," Noland said and smiled. "Perhaps you should take a taxi to your hotel."

"*Nie*." The man pointed down the block. "Hotel is close. Thank you. We walk." He put his arm around the lady's waist, turned, and the two strolled away.

Dr. Morris chuckled. "Noland, you've become a modern man. You provided information like a present-day Bostonian would. I don't believe taxis were a part of the eighteenth century."

"Aye. But carriages were." He put his hand on her arm. "If I am to be in the twentieth century, I should so act."

Dr. Morris nodded and smiled. "Let's go into the Old State House. It is more of a museum now rather than a place of meeting as it was in your time. I'm sure you'll find something of interest."

They walked around to the front of the red brick building and entered. In the center of the first floor was the spiral staircase that led to the upper floors and tower, a relic from the past. Radiating off the main floor were individual rooms. Some were open to visitors.

Noland strolled past an open room, then immediately back-stepped to its entrance. The sign above the doorway read, "Weapons of the War for Independence." He entered and before him stood three glass museum cases where various muskets and other weapons were displayed. The one in the middle caught his attention. "Brown Bess," he exclaimed, while motioning for Dr. Morris's attention. "The musket we used in battle. Quick to reload, attach a bayonet, and fire. Can hit a rebel at a hundred yards…" Noland pause for a moment, "if the shooter is accurate. It is best used when the enemy is closer. Finest weapon our country has developed."

Dr. Morris looked at the musket and nodded. "Well, I just learned something. You know, I believe Dr. Gorski's reenactors use replicas. We'll need to ask him. I'm sure you can teach the group all about eighteenth-century weaponry. Follow me, I want to show you one of the most important documents of this country. It's why the War for Independence was fought. There is a copy of the Constitution of the United States hanging in the main hall."

Noland followed Dr. Morris out of the weapon display room and on to where the Constitution hung. He examined it. "Similar to the Magna Carta: provides for justice, trials, land ownership, protection from excessive taxes, and other rights of citizens."

"Yes. Similar. But the tenets of the Magna Carta applied to the citizens of Great Britain. They surely weren't extended to the colonials, especially when it came to taxes. Taxes are one of the primary factors that led the colonials to fight for independence from Great Britain—'no taxation without representation,' was their cry. The king and parliament would not listen to the delegates sent to England to present the case for colonists." Dr. Morris took Noland's arm and led him to a nearby wall where portraits of Benjamin Franklin, Samuel Adams, Paul Revere, George Washington, and several others hung. She stopped at the painting. "Benjamin Franklin," she said and pointed to his portrait. "He was the major brain behind the rebellion." She moved and pointed to another portrait. "Samuel Adams, he instigated the Boston Tea Party. And the fellow there is General George Washington. He's the one who led the American army to victory over Great Britain."

"I have not had the pleasure of meeting any of these gentlemen," Noland said, "though the general is quite a handsome fellow. They all must have been men of great bravery and fortitude."

"Indeed."

A young lady came next to Dr. Morris and Noland. "We'll be closing in about ten minutes," she said.

"Thank you," Dr. Morris replied and moved next to the sergeant. "Let's go to the Union Oyster House for dinner. We won't have to wait for a table if we get there early." They started walking toward the Old State House exit. Dr. Morris continued. "The Oyster House is the pub in the area where Boston's founding fathers, as we Americans call them, and colonial rebels, as you call them, used to meet and plan their revolts. I'm sure you'll find this restaurant interesting. It's the oldest eatery in Boston. You might even recognize the building that contains the Oyster House. The building was built some years before the revolution. In the 1700s, Capen's, a fancy-dress dry goods store, occupied the first floor and a rebel newspaper, the *Massachusetts Spy*, was being published on an upper floor when thoughts of independence began to stir. After the dress shop moved out, a seafood-and-oyster public house opened on the first floor sometime in the early 1800s."

"Perhaps so," Noland said. "I may recognize this place where you take me. Here, in this State House, because the staircase leading to its tower I remember from being billeted here for a time, but nothing else inside do I recall ever seeing."

"Yes. There have been many changes in the past two hundred years." Dr. Morris took hold of Noland's arm as the two exited the Old State House.

They strolled up Congress Street to Union Street Park, where they crossed through the park and continued on Union Street. In the waning late afternoon daylight, they headed up the narrow lane. The Union Oyster House was only a short distance away at the end of the block.

When Dr. Morris led Noland into a narrow lane that ran through a dimly lit cavern between the tall warehouse-like buildings, he felt anxious and concerned at the loss of visual freedom they were moving through. But when they reached the restaurant, its setting and façade, which faced Union Street, somewhat comforted him. He seemed to recognize the building that housed the Union Oyster House. Electrified flickering flames from some fake oil lamps, hanging on an old building down another alley, cast dancing shadows and gave the area an eighteenth-century aura. He and Dr. Morris stopped and gazed at the restaurant's entrance and the signage that hung above it.

"Let's go in," Dr. Morris urged.

Noland hesitated, turned, looked up and across Union Street, then down the alley toward the oil lamps. "I have been here. Aye. When I first arrived in Boston, I was quartered in a hostelry nearby." He turned for a moment and raised his arm toward the entrance to the Oyster House. "The harbor, it was behind that building. A disreputable pub is located in that narrow lane." He pointed into the alley. "Blue Goat Inn it is called; believed by the regiment officers to be a nest full of rebels. I was assigned to a patrol that was to search that notorious place. But we found nothing. The alley, I remember, was named Green Dragon Lane."

"Yes. The shore of the Charles River apparently once came nearer to where the Union Oyster House now stands." Dr. Morris nodded. "Cargo vessels were able to anchor offshore and deliver their consignments directly to stores that were nearby. Remember, I mentioned that the building that now houses the oyster house was, in your time, a dry goods store. Cargo ships can no more anchor nearby or come up the river. The debris from digging modern subway tunnels was used to fill the river's marshland and shoals. This narrowed the river but provided more land and expanded the city. By the way, that alley you called Green Dragon Lane is now named Marshall Street. And the inn you speak of no longer exists. Only warehouses are located on that street." Dr. Morris took hold of Noland's arm and urged him toward the entrance to the Union Oyster House.

The maître d' looked up from his notes when the two came through the door. "Today is Tuesday," he said. "There won't be much of a crowd tonight. And they don't start coming in until after six. Sit where you want. A waitress will be with you shortly." He lowered his eyes again toward his notes.

"Thank you," Dr. Morris said.

As they walked toward a cozy corner table, Noland looked at the pictures and memorabilia that hung on the wall they were passing. A framed document caught his attention. He stopped to examine and read the display.

"What's caught your interest?" Dr. Morris asked.

"A page from *The Boston Gazette* printed on 17 December 1773 is in this frame." Noland stood in front of the display of the historic newspaper page. "The sign above it states that the article below is of an historic tea party that took place here in Boston. I know of no such party. The article discusses a dispute over tea being thrown off some vessels. I do not remember hearing of such an argument."

"Oh, you must have," Dr. Morris said as the two seated themselves at the table. "It wasn't so much about tea, but more of a political protest by the colonials, about the taxes they were being subjected to by the British government. The colonials were being taxed without having any representation in Parliament. These settlers felt that their rights as Englishmen were being violated. So, Samuel Adams, whose portrait you saw hanging in the Old State House, organized a group of the patriots to attack the vessels bringing what the colonials called 'king's tea' from London to sell here in Boston. These patriots disguised themselves as Native Americans, boarded the vessels and destroyed the cargo by throwing the cases of tea into the harbor...."

Noland began to chuckle. "Oh. Aye. I now remember. The event happened about a year after I came to this continent." His face livened with Dr. Morris's editorialization of the news article.

"Why do you find the piece humorous?" Dr. Morris asked.

"The cargo of tea did not belong to the king," Noland said with a confident grin. "It actually belonged to the East India Company, a private company. This business was losing money and had an overabundance of tea in their warehouses. It was usual for shipments of tea sent to the colonies to be minimally taxed. But for this particular shipment, Parliament enacted the Tea Act. The Tea Act allowed the East India Company to ship about five hundred thousand pounds of their warehoused tea to the colonies at no commission. This meant that the tea could be sold to the colonials at a discount, thus saving them money. So, the protest was ill-conceived. The Tea Act did not place any additional tax on the tea. Moreover, the vessels that brought the cargo were privately owned American vessels." Noland shrugged, but his smile remained, while he and Dr. Morris seated themselves at the cozy table.

"The patriots actually instigated an act of vandalism against their own people," Noland continued, slipping off the orange L.L. Bean rain jacket. "Though the rebels wore the dress of Native Americans and carried tomahawks, their disguise was not very convincing."

Dr. Morris cocked her head, then nodded. "Yes, that's what we were taught."

A waitress carrying glasses of water and tableware interrupted the discussion. She placed what she brought on the table. "Be right back to take your order," she said, then turned and left.

Noland took a sip of water. "Since the vessels were not British," he said, "nor were any loyal colonials endangered, the British regiments in Boston were not alerted." He took another drink. "I did not learn of the incident until days after, because I was billeted in Charlestown."

"What you say is probably true," Dr. Morris said with a nod and raised eyes. "You were there when it happened. However, I had read somewhere that many of the protesters were angry merchants. They believed that taxes on tea, even though minimal, should not be mandated without colonial representation in Parliament. Also, since taxes on many other commodities were removed several years earlier, but were not on tea, the colonists believed that the new Tax Act was nothing more than a ploy to get them comfortable paying taxes on tea, and then accept any increases that would come in the future." Dr. Morris looked at Noland, then took a sip of water.

Noland's expression became serious. "Great Britain has been at war for many years," he said. "And the country's treasury has been exhausted. Someone must provide support."

"Perhaps so," Dr. Morris answered. "I'm sure the colonists would have been inclined to help if they had had representation in the Parliament. But they didn't. They became more enraged. Especially when King George and Parliament retaliated over the tea outrage that happened in Boston and enacted several more severe acts. Acts that called for the blockading of Boston Harbor, ending free elections of local officials, establishment of martial law in the city, making colonists quarter British soldiers, and posting several other disagreeable decrees. And, these Coercive Acts, as they were called, were passed by the British Parliament without any dialogue with the colonies. These Acts didn't further the colonists' love for Great Britain." Dr. Morris could see the sergeant's face flush with anger.

Noland clenched his fists. "Disobedient colonials—rebels they are—need to be taught a lesson. Colonials are not independent. The Commonwealth of Massachusetts and any of the other colonies established by Great Britain are under the command of King George the Third and governed by the Parliament of Great Britain. All who live on British soil are subject to the decrees administered by the Crown and Parliament. If colonists act like children, they must be treated as children and brought back into the fold." The sergeant tightened his fists and took a deep breath.

"The majority of the colonists were British citizens," Dr. Morris said. "The land where they were living, though on a different continent, was British. All the colonists wanted was to be treated by Great Britain like citizens who lived in the British Isles were recognized, represented, and being treated. The colonists were not unruly children; nor were they the King's or Parliament's chattel. Yet, they were treated as such, like vanquished subjects dominated, controlled, and restrained by armed forces sent by the Crown. The colonists had no representation in Parliament. And that is what angered them the most."

"Aarrgh!" the sergeant grunted. "The colonies are too far removed from Great Britain. Regiments were sent not to conquer, but to protect."

"Protection is good." Dr. Morris took another sip of water and cradled the glass. "But military regiments harassed the colonists. Though the colonists designated or elected minor community leaders—until the Coercive Acts enacted upon Boston in 1774 ended that—most of those who held major governmental positions were assigned by the Crown. The settlers had little to say as to whom their administrators would be." She paused for a moment and set the water glass on the table. "The colonials came to America to escape the restrictions and severities of dictatorship and monarchy. That is why the Continental Congress was formed. The colonists desired self-rule; a democratic government."

Noland fidgeted, spread his hands on the table, and pushed back against the chair. "Colonials are like the residents on the British Isles. They too must be led. And that is why the leaders in Parliament decide the actions of the commoners. It is so in the colonies too. Few individuals have the competences to make decisions for the good of the Crown. To do so, would be opposite to the tenets of God. It is He who ordained King George to attend to the providence of his people."

"What you are saying," Dr. Morris interrupted, "is that the common residents of Great Britain are but peasants, serfs. And so, likewise, are the colonials. So, no matter where any reside, they are nothing more than chattel and subject to the capricious whims of aristocrats and kings. It is also true for the common British soldiers, like you, and British sailors too. Your commanding officers were either aristocrats appointed by the Crown or the progeny of some wealthy landowner who was able to purchase a commission. Besides, most of your officers, I read, were incompetent."

"Aarrgh!" Sergeant Black slammed his hands against the table and shoved his chair away, causing the table to scrape forward. His glass fell over, spilling its water and ice cubes onto the table and floor. He pushed himself up and stood. "Bloody hell," he grunted. "You think your time is so perfect? Perhaps it is. But you did not have to face a rebel menace daily. You were not there...." Noland grabbed the rain jacket, put it on, turned and faced the door, and started toward it.

"And where, may I ask, are you planning to go?" Dr. Morris calmly unfolded her napkin and started to blot the water on the table.

"To my barracks!" he growled.

"You will not find them. Remember, you're two centuries into the future? Most of what once existed, no longer does. I doubt you'll find your barracks."

"You can move to another table if you like," the waitress said as she approached. Using the mop handle projecting from a water bucket, she maneuvered it toward the table. "I'll clean what's been spilled and bring you some fresh glasses of water and take your order."

Dr. Morris nodded to the waitress, rose, and moved to the next table. She looked longingly at Noland.

Noland stood confused; his face still reddened. He shook his head and took a deep breath. "I will find my regiment and be away from this place and time—and you. Though you have been kind, you know little of the time from where I have come. I am sorry for any trouble I may have caused you. Give my regards to Dr. Gorski and others."

"I fear you'll be disappointed," Dr. Morris said. "Landmarks you may once have known are gone. And it's dark outside and you have no money."

"I am resourceful. I will survive." Noland headed out the door.

Dr. Morris sat confused and speechless.

The waitress finished mopping up the water and pushed the bucket back to the kitchen. She quickly returned with water glasses in hand. "May I take your order?" she asked Dr. Morris.

The doctor sighed. Looked at the door. She remained silent for several seconds, anticipating the sergeant's return. Then she looked up at the waitress. "I suppose. Just bring me a cup of coffee. I'm afraid my date decided he had somewhere else to go."

Dr. Morris sat at the table sipping her coffee, looking at the door hoping Sergeant Black would return. She examined her watch. Almost thirty minutes had passed since Noland had left the Union Oyster House. *Where could he have gone?* she wondered. Feeling anxious, and concerned for the sergeant's welfare, she motioned for the waitress to bring the check.

"Your friend has not returned?" The waitress laid the bill on the table. "Can I call you a taxi?"

"No, thank you. I'll walk." Morris reached into her purse, extracted two one-dollar bills and handed them to the server. "That should cover the charge and tip."

"Thank you. Please be vigilant. It's dark outside."

Dr. Morris nodded, shouldered her camera and purse, and headed for the door.

The shades have indeed been drawn, she presumed when she stepped into the tenebrous outdoors. Only a few scattered street lamps spread diffused, yellowish circles of dim light onto Union Street. A pitch-black sky, speckled with a few pinpoints of light, covered the heavens above the building tops. Her muscles tensed. The street appeared deserted. She clutched the straps of her purse and camera, and hurriedly strode toward the Union Street Park.

As she came onto the park, she hesitated. *There are a few benches in there. I'd like to cut across to Congress Street, but it's damn dark. Like walking into a tunnel. But Noland might have stopped to sit and reconsider. He should be able to see me if he's in the park. It's not that far to Congress. It's black in the park. Maybe I should go to North Street and cross over? Brighter streetlights. Traffic. Bus stop. More people.* She contemplated. *Oh hell, barely a half block across.* She clutched the straps that tugged on her shoulder and stepped onto the path that led across to Congress Street. The soles of her shoes crunched the gravel as she defiantly strode into the darkness beneath leafless trees.

I should call his name, she thought. "Noland! Noland, are you here?"

Suddenly a hand seized her left shoulder. "Noland," she gasped and turned to face whomever it was that had come up behind her.

"Name's not Noland, lady," a nondescript, roguish-looking man grunted. "Like that camera. And I'm sure the purse has what I need." His right hand squeezed her shoulder, while his left hand reached behind him and under the black-hooded sweatshirt he wore and whipped out a hunter's dagger and placed it under her chin.

The shot of pain made Dr. Morris grimace and whimper. She tried to twist away.

"I'll just relieve you of your burden and be on my way," the perp snarled as he slashed the knife through the straps Dr. Morris clasped and he released his grip on her shoulder. The tip of the knife cut through the sleeve of her blouse and grazed Dr. Morris's upper arm. The camera and purse dropped to the ground.

"Ow!" she cried out and grabbed her bicep. A warm, sticky feeling oozed between her fingers. "Bastard! I'm bleeding. You've ruined my jacket and shirt." In an instant she twisted around and faced him. Her right leg shot forward and the tip of her shoe struck the perp's shin bone.

He grunted in pain, stepped back, and swung the dagger toward her throat.

Dr. Morris stumbled backward, lost her balance, and began to fall. Suddenly a dark orange flash twisted to her side. She heard the perp scream. Saw his head snap upward, his body twist grotesquely, and right arm do a rapid, unnatural swing around to his back. The dagger hurtled out of his hand and landed in a nearby bush. The perp howled, fell to the gravel path, and rolled to the left. For a moment he lay in a fetal position. Then he kicked out his right leg, flinging bits of gravel into the air as he tried to right himself. Dr. Morris heard him whine when he tried to bring the right arm around to his front. The arm remained locked against his back.

She felt her mouth beginning to dry. *I'm going into shock*, she thought as she sat up and tried to stand. Suddenly two orange-colored appendages dropped in front of her. She felt hands hook into her arm-pits. They began to lift her.

"Good that I was near and saw the attack," Noland whispered near her ear. He pulled Dr. Morris to him, held her tight against his chest, felt her arms tighten around his neck. "Breathe deeply. Relax. You will be sound in a moment." He felt her tension slowly drain away.

Dr. Morris sighed. "Thank you." She relaxed her hold, but still maintained the embrace. Then she took a deep breath and stepped back. "I'm okay." Her left hand continued to clasp Noland's arm weakly as she stumbled to establish her balance.

"Can you stand alone?"

"Yes."

"Good." Noland moved next to the perp, stooped down, and picked up Dr. Morris's purse and camera. He looked down at the squirming man. "Rebel, never attack a woman." With the side of his shoe, he kicked the fellow in his backside. "I take no prisoners." Noland walked back to Dr. Morris and put his arm around her waist. "I believe we should go to the clinic and get you mended."

"Are we leaving him here?" she asked. "We should contact the police."

"Ney," Noland said as he urged her toward Congress Street. "We will leave him. Remember, I am a man with no country. It would be hard to explain myself to anyone." Lifting her slightly, he started walking. "As I mentioned earlier, I will try to become a man of this modern time. I shall get us a taxi."

⌒

When Sergeant Noland Black and Dr. Morris reached Congress Street, Noland stopped on the curb, raised his arm, and waved it toward the light traffic. He felt like a twentieth-century man for his attempt to wave down a taxi. Within minutes a cab pulled to the curb. The taxi driver took the Interstate that crossed from Boston into Charlestown. The trip to the clinic took about fifteen minutes. The speed with which one could move from one place to another within the city impressed Noland. He sat proudly, gazing at the passing night scenery until Dr. Morris brought him back to reality by handing him two ten-dollar bills.

"Use this to pay the driver when we arrive," she said. "Ten dollars should cover the trip and tip. Put the other ten in your pocket for later when you may need some money."

"Aye," Noland said, but the gesture confused him. Nevertheless, he did as she told him.

At the clinic the on-duty doctor cleaned, sterilized, closed the cut on Dr. Morris's arm with a couple of stitches and bandaged the wound. Dr. Morris replaced the bloodied blouse with a T-shirt and a lab coat she had in her locker and put on her jacket. "Let's go home. Can't go trapsing about the city, because I look rather funny in these clothes I'm wearing. Besides, there's plenty of food in the fridge. Between the two of us, we can toss together something to eat. And I could use some wine or something stronger."

"Are you able to drive your motor car with an arm bound as it is?" Noland asked when the two reached the VW.

"No problem. The wound doesn't hurt. Besides, I can steer one-handed, if need be," Dr. Morris answered.

On the trip to the house Noland remained silent. Dr. Morris periodically glanced at him. His hands lay clenched on his lap. He raised his head and looked through the windshield for a few minutes, then lowered it and stared at his lap. It appeared to her that the excitement of waving down a taxi had dissipated. "Is something bothering you?" she asked as she was about to turn into the driveway.

He shook his head. "Nay," he answered softly.

"I get the impression something is bothering you?" Dr. Morris drove into the driveway, stopped the VW, and turned off its engine.

Noland opened the passenger door. He seemed distracted as he slid out of the vehicle. He straightened and stared up at the stars.

Dr. Morris exited the VW and started toward the house. Noland trudged dejectedly behind her.

Once inside the house, before either had time to remove their jackets, Noland took Dr. Morris by the shoulders and turned her to face him. He looked into her eyes. "I acted like a prat at the restaurant," he said. "I—I am so very sorry. I and most of the regiment are not happy for being so far from our homeland. And especially, when we have to confront the colonials. They are Englishmen like us. Our neighbors they could be if we were in England. In time of accord the colonists act properly and are acceptable in all manner…."

Solemnly, Dr. Morris looked at Noland. She nodded.

"But," Noland continued, "we are soldiers, loyal to Great Britain and the King, and we have our orders. Most times we are assigned to missions where we have to exercise authority. But it is not our plan to injure the locals or upset their lives. In Concord we were told of a farmer who had a small cannon buried behind his barn. When we unearthed the weapon, which I learned had been buried some five or more years, I ordered it reinterred. If anyone tried to clean it and attempt to fire it, the weapon would have exploded.

"The farmer's wife graciously provided my troops with bread, cake, and tea. She was happy we did not arrest or punish her husband. As I said, the British army is in the colonies to exercise protection and prudence. Nevertheless, we are viewed by many with disfavor. I fear our officers and perhaps some of our tactics and behaviors may also add to the colonists' dislike. I am having difficulty. My mind is in two places at one time." Noland gently lowered his hands to Dr. Morris's waist.

She looked up at him and could see that he was distraught. She raised her right hand and smoothed his hair. Then she placed her hands against his cheeks. "Noland. Noland," she said while holding his face softly. "I forgive you. But you must remember our minds are separated by two hundred years. I have been taught about the American Revolution, which occurred two hundred years ago, but you are at its beginning, experiencing it in real time. To you the outcome is unknown. To me, the results of this conflict are written in our history, our country's constitution, beliefs, and behaviors. I feel your exasperation and frustration. Hopefully in time, you'll come to understand what the American Revolution was fought for." She laid her head against his chest.

They stood silently, embracing until almost simultaneously they relaxed.

Dr. Morris looked up at Noland and kissed him on the cheek. "Now, let's get rid of the jackets and I'll find us something to eat." She slowly backed away, removed her jacket, and tossed it onto a chair. "I could use a drink. Something stronger than wine." She motioned toward a cabinet against the wall. "There's liquor in there, a bottle of Maker's Mark. Appreciate it if you could pour me a bit of it. There are cocktail glasses in the liquor cabinet also." She lowered her arms and stepped away from him. "I believe we both could use a drink."

Noland lowered his fingers from the spot Dr. Morris's lips touched him. He reached out and clasped her right hand. He nodded with softness in his eyes and smiled.

Grasping his hand tightly, Dr. Morris smiled back, gently squeezed his hand, then released it and turned. "I'll bring us some ice cubes."

Noland watched her leave, then slipped off the orange L.L. Bean hunter's jacket and laid it over Dr. Morris's. His eyes moved to the liquor cabinet. He sauntered to it and opened the door. Inside he found the bottle of bourbon amongst several bottles of wine and other liquors. On the cabinet's top shelf were the cocktail glasses. Taking two and the bottle of Maker's Mark, he poured a tot in each glass. He took a whiff. *Smells strong, sweet, good*, he thought and read the label—Kentucky Bourbon.

Dr. Morris returned with a bowl of ice cubes.

"What is Ken-tuck-ee?" Noland asked as she dropped an ice cube into each glass.

She stood and offered a glass to Noland. "It's a state, mostly west of the Appalachian Mountains and east of the Mississippi River, in the middle of our country."

"This beverage," Noland said, "is new to me. And, I have not heard of the mountains or the state of which you speak."

"It's a whiskey, like scotch, but with a sweeter flavor and distilled in the state of Kentucky." Dr. Morris held the glass up in front of her. "As I mentioned before, the United States is a very large country. Be patient. You will learn. In the meantime, I'd like to propose a toast to my protector. Thank you for rescuing me from that mugger." She raised her glass.

"Aye," Noland said. "The honor was mine."

They each took a sip of the bourbon. Dr. Morris moved closer to the sergeant and again kissed him on the cheek. She then glimpsed into his eyes, closed hers, and backed away.

"Thank you," she whispered. "You came to my rescue—like a knight in shining armor—except all I saw was the color orange. Let's sit."

"Damsel in distress." Noland chuckled, sat on the sofa, and placed his glass on the side table. "Aye. My special damsel."

Dr. Morris sighed and smiled, then looked surprised. She caught her breath. "Noland, I want to ask you a more personal question. Did you leave anyone, a girlfriend perhaps, lover, wife, when you departed England for the colonies?"

A doleful expression crossed Noland's face. A distant look appeared in his eyes. "Ahh—aye," he said as his gaze turned toward a wall. With a contemplative stare, he said, "Aye. I did." His voice cracked for a moment. "Though she no longer is my confidante, she still comes to my mind. Meera is her name, Meera Douglas. We grew up together—played together. She and her family lived in a manor house on a small estate, which bordered the edge of Gateshead, the village where I was born. Her father moved her family from Scotland to escape the rise of the Jacobite confusion. The cottage where I lived was located in the dene below the estate. My father and I, when I became older, tended the Douglas family livestock. And my mother occasionally cooked for the Douglases when they had a reception." Noland turned toward Dr. Morris and sighed.

"We became close. I would saddle her horse and ride with her over the hills and through the dales. Sometimes Mother—my mother—packed us a lunch and we spent the day in a meadow talking of our future. Meera loved to pick flowers and watch birds. She knew the birds and their songs. I watched Meera. She was a lovely damsel, happy, enchanting, and much fun. She had hair that fell beyond her shoulders. Its color auburn, like yours." Noland's expression turned pensive. He reached to the side, lifted his glass, and sipped the Maker's Mark.

"I have not seen Meera for more than ten or twelve years. I should tell you—of our last meeting," Noland said. The volume of his voice decreased. "We were both about eighteen years in age. We had ridden to our favorite location, a green surrounding the ruins of Ravensworth Castle. It was a beautiful day in late spring when the wild lavender was in bloom. Meera enjoyed picking lavender...." His attitude became more somber.

Dr. Morris saw Noland's eyes glisten and a tear ooze from the right one. "You miss her," she said.

Noland sighed and continued. "Aye. I asked Meera if she would be mine forever." Using his index finger, he wiped the tear away. "Instead of the excitement I expected, she became solemn. Laid the lavender flowers in my lap and said that she loved me. Wanted to be mine in the most enormous way. Meera then lowered her head, began to cry, and said that she could not. Her parents had promised her to another, a person of means, who had the possibility of becoming titled. She began to weep. Placed her head against my chest and whispered, 'I do love you, but our life together can never be.' She then removed the necklace she wore and put it in my hand and said, 'Please keep this as a remembrance of my love for you.'"

Noland massaged his neck. "I lost Meera." He sighed. "And I have lost the token of love she gave me, a Celtic cross, a family gift on her sixteenth birthday; that cross became my savior." He paused and pulled himself together.

"Though I visited the Douglas estate several times during the next few months," Noland continued, "I rarely saw Meera. My depression continued and deepened to the extent I had to leave Gateshead

Village. I wanted to get far away." He paused; his eyes wondered. "Yet, if I were able to return, and she be unmarried, I would attempt to renew our relation." Noland sighed, then shrugged. "I volunteered for the military. That is how I came to be in the American colonies. After a five-year tour with the Tenth Grenadier Regiment, I was promoted to sergeant, sent to the Boston area, and put in charge of new, young reinforcements who were being brought to protect the colonies."

Dr. Morris's eyes glistened. "I'm so sorry, Noland. In your time, Great Britain had a social system that separated people by gender and rank. Meera's family believed that you were not of their class. Segregation based on class, gender, rank, or social standing still exists in some cultures, but in this century, it is somewhat infrequent in America, England, and most other civilized nations." She chuckled to lighten the atmosphere. "However, it still exists among the English royal family." She shivered and walked toward the doorway to the kitchen. "How about I get us something to snack on? Feel free to pour yourself another bourbon if you'd like."

Dr. Morris's words did not make Noland feel any better. Nevertheless, he nodded. "Nay. I believe I would rather have some tea."

"Very well," Dr. Morris said.

The telephone rang as Dr. Morris was returning from the kitchen, carrying a tray containing slices of lunchmeat and cheeses, and a basket of bread and rolls. With her hands in total use, she asked, "Noland, would you please answer the phone? Just say hello. Callers will usually identify themselves."

"Aye, Carol." Noland lifted the receiver. "Hello..."

"Noland? Andrew Gorski here. Didn't expect you to answer. Appears Dr. Morris is teaching you well." Gorski paused for a moment. "You two doing okay?"

"Aye, we are. Dr. Morris is here placing the repast tray onto the table. She asked that I answer the telephone..."

"She doin' okay?" Gorski sounded concerned.

"Aye."

"Police brought a suspected mugger to emergency this evening. His face was bruised and right arm dislocated from the shoulder. Police said, he swears he was attacked by an orange monster. The guy's a physical mess. Fixed the disturbed fellow up and the police took him to the precinct for interrogation. They found him in the area where the two of you were supposed to have gone to dinner. There's been a rash of muggings in that area. Just wondered if you guys saw or heard anything?"

Noland took a deep breath. "Aye. That we did. I will let Dr. Morris explain, since I do not feel I had my faculties under control at that time." With widened eyes and clenched teeth, he glanced at Dr. Morris. "It is Dr. Gorski. He knows of this evening's attack." He handed her the telephone receiver.

Dr. Morris sighed. "Good evening. How did you learn about our encounter?"

"As I told Noland, the police brought the assailant to emergency. Since I was on duty, I took care of him. Since the perp had several outstanding warrants, the cops arrested him. So, what happened to you two?"

Dr. Morris explained the attempt to steal her purse and camera, and how Noland rescued her.

"Sorry about that," Dr. Gorski said. "The shin kick left a nasty bruise on the thief's leg. Didn't realize you were such an audacious lady. But it was good that Noland, a trained warrior, was at your side. Got to stay alert in this day and age…" Gorski paused. "Heard from my friend in the State Department. And, he had some promising news. Let's get together tomorrow for lunch and I'll explain it to you. Otherwise, I hope your dinner tonight was good."

"Dinner was kinda disrupted. Tell you about it later, but yes. I was planning to show Noland the Bunker Hill monument tomorrow, so let's meet in Charlestown. There's a pub, The Warren Tavern, on Pleasant Street, just off Main Street. Supposedly, it dates to the Revolutionary War. Washington and Paul Revere hung out there. Do you know of it?"

"I do," Gorski answered. "Can we meet about one thirty?"

"Yes."

"Good. See you guys tomorrow. And don't visit any sleazy areas tonight. Bye."

Dr. Morris chuckled. "I don't plan to. See you tomorrow. Good night." She returned the telephone receiver to its base and turned to Noland. "Dr. Gorski is going to meet us for lunch tomorrow. He talked to his friend at the State Department and learned that there may be a way to get you the identification papers you need to legally be in the United States…"

"That is good news!" Noland clasped his hands together. His eyes brightened and he exhaled. His right hand rose to his neck as he seated himself on the couch. His fingers soothed the area of his neck where the medallion once hung.

"Yes," Dr. Morris said. "But when I return with a pot of tea, I want to hear more about your life before you came to the colonies." She returned to the kitchen.

For a few moments Noland could hear the tinkling of glass as Dr. Morris prepared the tea. *I believe Dr. Morris—ah, she wants to be called Carol. More familiar. Carol seems to have forgiven me for my outburst in the restaurant*, he thought. *I sure hope she has. She is a wonderful woman. I would not want to lose her friendship.* He sighed and shivered with a sense of unease. *She is a pleasure to observe; her auburn hair—yet it does not flow as Meera's does—and those heavenly brownish eyes Carol and Meera have.* He imagined Carol's breasts and sighed. *Hers may be smaller. Ahh, but they appear magnificent…*

The clack of a teacup and saucer being placed on a table, interrupted Noland's warm reminiscence. He looked up and blushed, then grinned.

"Sorry to have disturbed you. You seemed deep in thought." Dr. Morris bent toward Noland and poured the tea.

"Aye." The smile remained on Noland's face as he caught a glimpse of the doctor's diminutive but delectable breasts. "Aye. Warm memories."

The corners of Dr. Morris's mouth rose. Her eyes brightened as she set the teapot down and straightened. She dipped her head slightly to the left and seated herself to the right of Noland, reached forward, and lifted her cup. "Since we missed supper, please make yourself a sandwich, if you like, or eat some of the tidbits I prepared for us."

"Thank you," Noland said. "But I must explain the thoughts I was having."

Carol nodded. "Yes, please go on. I would love to hear your feelings."

"I was thinking of Meera; how much you two are alike. It may be bold of me to compare Meera and you, but your hair color and eye color are similar to hers." Noland took a deep breath. His face flushed. "Meera was lithe, fragile, innocent, and delightful. But so are you. It is almost as if you and Meera were sisters." He lowered his head, embarrassed at what he just said.

"Please do not think me familiar," Noland said. "But Meera is lost to me." Noland kept his head lowered, then raised it. His eyes were teary, and they had a wistful glaze. "I feel disheartened at her loss. So much so, I wanted to get as far away from England as possible. But, with little means of support, my choices of escape were limited. I could go to sea, in which I had little interest. Or volunteer for military service. This I did."

Trying to pull Noland out of his slump, Carol said, "Tell me about that," as she sampled a cracker upon which she piled a dollop of smoked salmon spread. "Great Britain had vast holdings in the world. Were you sent to some exotic place?"

Noland raised his eyes slightly. A peaceful smile lightened his face. He nodded. "After acceptance and training, I was assigned to a dragoon regiment because of my experience with horses. Unfortunately, I remained in the British Isles, posted to Scotland for the next ten years. Though the Jacobite Rebellion had ended fifteen years before, emotions among the Scots ran deep. Jacobite turmoil continued throughout Scotland." He paused as Carol took a sip of tea. "My regiment served in Culloden, Edinburgh, Glasgow, then we were returned to southeast England. There I volunteered for duty in the American colonies, was promoted to sergeant, and in 1770, I set foot in this new world…." He became sullen and seemed to slide back into depression.

Dr. Morris bent toward the table and covered two crackers with salmon spread. She handed one to Noland. "Don't know where Norma found this stuff, but it is really good. Here, taste this spread."

Noland accepted the cracker. But instead of tasting it, he held it to the side and looked into Carol's eyes. "Sorry. My thoughts have returned, Meera—and thoughts of you. Had I been posted elsewhere, I may have never been transported to the future. I would have never met you…"

A warm glow lit up Dr. Morris's eyes. With lowered eyelids, she looked at Noland. Her hands clasped his cheeks and softly, for a moment, she placed her lips on his. Then she put her arm about his shoulders and placed her cheek against his.

Noland felt her warmth. He released the cracker. It fell to the floor. He grasped Carol's shoulders, pulled her to him, and pressed his lips harder against hers.

Dr. Morris gently pushed herself away. "Wait! I shouldn't have kissed you," she whispered. "You're still my patient. Even though I do find you attractive, kissing you was not proper. We've only known each other for a couple of days." She released herself from Noland's hold and twisted to his side.

Surprised, Noland stuttered, "I—I too, have a fondness for you." Noland slid to the side of the couch and sighed. He looked dejected yet felt hopeful for the future. "I believe we went beyond the moment." He sighed and leaned forward, lifted his teacup, and took a sip, then replaced the cup on its saucer. Bending down, he picked up the cracker covered with smoked salmon spread and balanced it on the edge of the dish. "I know I am a burden to you, but I will try not to be. If there is any possibility to remain with you here in Boston, I would like to stay."

"And you shall, until we find some way to establish your residency in the twentieth century. Don't forget Dr. Gorski's telephone call. He may have some good news." Carol looked into Noland's eyes and whispered. "Remember, you are still my patient, though I believe your injuries are about healed." She reached toward Noland and softly patted his right shoulder.

He didn't flinch.

"Now, let's enjoy the snacks and finish our tea." Dr. Morris stood, started to turn, but paused. "By the way, I'll try to stay quiet in the morning, so as not to wake you. I need to go to the clinic for a couple of hours. I'll return to pick you up around lunchtime so we can meet with the good doctor and hear what he has learned."

"Aye." Noland sampled the smoked salmon spread and finished his cup of tea. "Indeed, this will be good. Tomorrow morning, I shall walk about this community alone. My body needs exertion. I like to keep in suitable condition. One never knows when strength and agility will be required."

"Your action this evening was not enough?" Dr. Morris grinned. She turned and walked toward the cabinet, leaned down, and wrote something on a notepad. Then she hesitated. The photo of her and Noland at the Boston Massacre memorial lay next to the Polaroid camera. She lifted it, examined it, and held it out for the sergeant to see. "You are a handsome man."

He smiled.

She laid the photo back on the top of the cabinet, walked to the couch, and handed the note to Noland. "This is my telephone number at the clinic. I want you to have it. I'm sure you have a compass in your head. You won't get lost. But just in case you do, you can telephone me. Don't forget to take the ten-dollar bill and any leftover coins with you. You'll find a Dunkin' Donuts by walking north to Broadway Street. That's not far from here. There you can buy yourself a coffee and donut; it's a little cake with a hole in the middle. Comes in many flavors. Along the way you'll get an idea of what a twentieth-century

American community is like. Be back before lunchtime. By the way, I corrected the date and time on that wristwatch you found on the dresser a day or so ago. Put it on your wrist so you can know what the time is. Might as well use it." Dr. Morris sighed but continued to instruct. "Oh, another thing, when you cross a street, make sure you watch for the traffic. Vehicles are supposed to stop for pedestrians, but many don't. This is not your world. Be careful out there. As I said earlier, I'll pick you up about twelve o'clock." Carol seated herself next to Noland and gently touched his arm. "Now, would you please describe this special medal of yours to me?"

"Aye." Noland looked down. "Thinking of it makes me sad." He rubbed his eyes and raised his head. "The medallion, as I mentioned earlier, is a silver Celtic cross. It looks much like a Christian cross except the upper part of the stem and the flat crosspiece are encircled. There are simple continuous ribands that decorate the face and an emerald gem imbedded at each end of the stem and flat crosspiece. And there is a larger emerald at the midpoint where the flat piece crosses the stem. I hung the medal about my neck with a thin strand of leather. The strand must have broken when I was shot. Perhaps one day someone may find it. I wish I had not lost it. I cherished that gift. It was my savior."

"Thank you, Noland, for sharing," Dr. Morris said. "That Celtic cross also must have been special to Meera. A family heirloom, perhaps. She did love you. It is sad that the two of you could not be together."

"Aye." A shadow seemed to cover Noland's face. He took a bite from a cracker and began to chew it slowly, while he lowered his head and gazed toward the middle of the room.

Dr. Morris's eyes softened. She placed her hand on his knee. "Perhaps, when you obtain some form of identification, you will be able to travel to England," she said. "And if you want, return to places that you remember. Great Britain is better at preserving its traditions and history than we are in America. You might find evidence of what you left behind." She stood and began to pick up the dishes. "Seeing the sun in the morning seems to clear the mind and help establish a course." She started toward the kitchen. "Except for a moment of turmoil and a bit of sad reminiscence, I enjoyed today and have gotten to know you better."

Noland raised his head and smiled. "Aye. I too enjoyed our day. And especially this evening. Though we did not dine at the oyster house, we can go there another day. But I must say, Dr. Morris—oh sorry! I mean Carol, you are a wonderful woman. I have much affection for you also." Noland stood and touched her arm before she stepped away. "Good night." He turned and moved toward the stairway to the second floor.

CHAPTER 13

Wednesday, April 23, 1975

Noland scrambled out of bed when he heard a loud roar moving along the street. He hurried to the window and saw a white, oversized truck with brownish-stains streaking its body, being followed by two rough-looking men wearing black knit caps. The truck stopped next to two large cans sitting at the curb. The men removed the tops, lifted the cans, and dumped their contents into the back of the waiting truck. The men then tossed the cans onto the sidewalk, and each grabbed a handrail protruding from the rear of the vehicle and swung himself aboard. The man on the left side waved his arm outward and the garbage truck gave a vulgar growl, discharged black smoke, and creeped ahead to the next set of cans.

Noland recognized the contents in the cans as daily refuse. He returned to his bed, sat down upon it, and scratched his head. *This future century is indeed strange. Trash is not disposed into a common pit or latrine. Instead, undesirables are dumped into the rear of a monstrous carriage. I wonder where it is taken and ensconced?* He slapped his hands on the bed and bounced up. "Time to explore this modern world," he mumbled, "and see what other bizarre wonders I may find."

The sergeant hurried through his toilette. He dressed in the clothing that Dr. Gorski provided him when he first arrived: a pair of jeans, the sweatshirt with UCONN printed in blue across the chest, and scuffed running shoes. He picked up Dr. Morris's husband's dive watch from the dresser, examined it, and slipped it onto his wrist. It felt cool. He then lifted his arm, admired the watch, and headed for the stairs. *Handsome piece.*

His brain switched to another subject. *It is not raining; I do not have to wear that conspicuous jacket; need to be subtle; look like the others.* He descended the stairs.

When he entered the kitchen, Noland saw that Dr. Morris had put the boxes of cereal, a bottle of milk, and a small jar of sugar, along with a bowl, cup, silverware, and several teabags on the counter. Lying against the cereal boxes, he found a note. It read:

> Pot of hot water on the stove. Take the ten-dollar bill and my telephone number. Watch for landmarks so you can find your way home. Though I don't believe you'll get lost. Being a well-trained soldier, I'm sure you have a compass in your head. Be back here about lunch time. Pick you up then, so we can meet Dr. Goroski for lunch. Be careful and don't get into trouble. Carol.

"Aye, madam. I shall follow your order," he shouted with glee; skipped breakfast, put the milk back into the refrigerator, turned off the stove heating the water, and headed out the door like a child heading for the playground.

Noland stood on the top step and noted his surroundings before stepping down to the sidewalk. To the side of the porch steps grew a bush that shone brilliant yellow in the sunlight but had no apparent green leaves. Across the street was a boxy-shaped, gray, clapboard tenement. *Vivid and dull landmarks. Easy to remember,* his mind noted.

He walked to the sidewalk and turned north. Shortly he passed below two large oak trees and added them to his mental list of landmarks.

The neighborhood seemed older than what he had been seeing the past several days. Built around the turn of the century, the dull-colored single-family and duplex houses were separated by only the width of the driveway between them. Some cottages were decrepit. Other appeared to be well maintained. Entranceways varied from only a stoop on the sidewalk leading to a nondescript doorway, to elaborate roofed porches attached to cottages set back from the street by a small, grassy, rectangular plot. Dr. Morris's cottage fell into the latter category. Reaching the end of the block, he stopped, shrugged, then stepped off the curb. The blast of a car horn startled him. He jumped back. Stumbling about attempting to maintain his balance, he heard the driver yell as the vehicle swished by. "Walkin' about daydreamin' will get-cho-self killed!"

Noland caught his breath, grabbed the street sign pole, sighed, but failed to look up and note the name of the street. Tensed, he stood for a moment peering across the intersection. *I should have heeded Carol's warning about watching traffic.* When relaxed, he looked up and down the street. Seeing no traffic, he darted across to the opposite side and jumped up the curb.

When Noland stepped onto the sidewalk, he realized something was different; he was walking on a smooth sidewalk rather than on a dirt path. Stopping and looking back to examine his trek, from where he had come to where he was, he saw no dirt, gravel, or cobblestone paths to walk upon. He realized that he was not familiar with this material used to construct the path. Everything he walked upon was of a whitish, grayish, or mud-colored material. Though solid and arranged in rectangular, rough or smooth slabs, the route had many cracks, even some with vegetation growing from them. *I did not notice this difference,* he pondered, *perhaps, because the narrow roadways, like the one upon which Dr. Morris lives, are constructed of brick or cobblestone. But the wider one I just crossed, is covered with a smooth, continuous material of a dark substance also unknown to me. And…* he bent down to examine the curb more closely, *these walking paths are raised and separated from the carriageways by borders made from the same material as the pedestrian way. This separation between carriages and ramblers, in my time, is done with bollards or series of posts. I have only seen such separation of roadways in London proper.* "I must ask my mentors about this perplexity," Noland mumbled.

He straightened, looked ahead, and saw that the small residential houses gave way to a brick, commercial building at the end of the block. This building faced a wider street where more cars and trucks were going by. Across the wide street he saw a strip of single-storied structures. *Broadway Street, perhaps?* When Noland reached the intersection of this busy street, he saw the street sign. It read "Medford Street." He stopped. Stood confused, until he heard a dog bark. Noland looked down and saw a medium-sized dog on a leash, being held by a young woman. The dog had stopped about three feet from Noland's leg. It stared up at him and barked again. Noland recognized the breed, a border collie. He stooped and held out his right hand. The dog came closer and sniffed Noland's fingers.

"He seems to have taken to you," the woman said.

"Aye," Noland replied. "I once had one in England. Border collie?"

"Yes. Mostly. But he is not a purebred. I call him Max."

Noland looked directly at Max. "Max has curious eyes. He would enjoy herding geese. That is what my collie did. We did not have sheep." Noland straightened and faced the woman. "Border collies are intelligent dogs. Very loyal to their master and the herd they are entrusted to watch over."

Suddenly, a bus pulled to the corner. Max turned and faced it, his tail wagging rapidly.

"This is our bus," the woman said as she and her dog prepared to board. "Love your accent."

"Thank you. Could you direct me to Broadway Street? I am to find a Dunkin' Donut."

The woman pointed to the left. "Go up a couple of blocks. Broadway's the next major street. Turn left and the donut shop is about a block up. You can't miss it." The woman picked up Max and boarded the bus.

"Thank you." Noland waved as the bus pulled away. He turned and continued walking in the direction the woman pointed, but the opposite side of the street contained some nondescript strips of one- and two-story commercial structures separated by narrow alleyways. These low buildings contained offices, a variety of stores, and specialty shops. Curious, Noland decided to cross to the other side of Medford. But before he did, he cautiously looked in both directions. For the moment the street appeared empty of moving vehicles. He crossed.

Noland saw the word "tax" on a banner of one of the shops cater-corner from where he crossed over Medford Street. He mentally noted this location. The large green letters on the display advertised "H&R BLOCK TAX PREPARATION." He stopped and watched several people enter and exit. *There are taxes in this age also*, he pondered. *No one appears angry or distraught. Taxes must be reasonable.*

In the next block he came upon a larger solitary building with a limited parking area along one side. He recognized the words "GROCERY MARKET" following "ECONOMY..." highlighted in red on the marquee over the entrance. Signs, advertising sales of various items, hung on all the large windows facing the street. He scanned them. *Aye, a market.* He decided to go in and look around.

Inside, he immediately was confronted by two checkout counters. Behind one of the counters stood a woman wearing a white coat. She was feverishly punching the keys on a contraption with the fingers of one hand, while simultaneously with the other hand, pushing a can, box, bag, and various other items toward the end of the counter. Noland had no knowledge of a cash register, but every time a key was depressed, he heard a "ding" and it fascinated him. In the aisle by the closest counter, he watched a strange-looking woman, who seemed to be abstractedly contemplating the ongoing process. Compared to the others in line, holding the handles of their grocery carts, she appeared oddly dressed. A drab but fascinating, thick, knit headband held her straight, mid-length, dirty blond hair off her face and shoulders. She wore a multicolored, loose-fitting blouse that hung below the level of her hips. Noland saw that the blouse was held tight around the woman's waist by an inch-and-a-half-wide leather belt. When the checker told her the cost of her purchase was over eight dollars, she drawled, "Cool, lady. All I got is change." Noland watched as the weird one dumped a bag of change onto the counter; the checker's head twisted about, as if looking for some help. He could also see the frustration of the other customers standing in line behind her.

Noland heard a man, dressed in khaki trousers and a tieless, white shirt, grumble, "Damned goofy hippie." Noland glanced at the man and saw the badge above his shirt pocket. On it was written George White, Manager.

Mr. White looked over at Noland, shrugged, and said, "Hippy bitch has more money than any of us. Yet, she's gotta pay with change." White then faced the checker and yelled, "Count her pennies, Ginny." With a glare in his eyes, the manager walked toward the register.

Noland ran his fingers through his hair and moved away from the chaos at the checkout counters. He walked past a few shopping carts nested in a row, turned, and entered a narrow aisle of shelves filled with a profusion of boxes, jars, cans, and bags of goods and wares. He turned into another corridor and found boxes of breakfast cereals. He recognized the boxes of Kellogg's Corn Flakes and Cheerios. Farther along were breads and rolls. Along the back wall stood a long, glass-enclosed counter that contained a variety of meats. *Where are the clouds of pesty flies?* he wondered. Placing his hands on the glass, he felt the coolness of it as he stared at several bloody hunks of beef. The meats were displayed next to whole chicken carcasses and parts. In a cubby to the side lay a tray of mackerel and cod fillets all arranged in orderly fashion.

"Can I help you?" a voice asked.

Noland looked up. He saw that the voice came from a white-capped head that seemed to float above the top of the counter. When the sergeant straightened, he saw that the head was attached to the shoulders of a man holding a butcher's knife.

"Those are some prime Angus roasts," the butcher said. "Can I cut you one?"

Noland stepped back. "Nay," he said and began to turn away. "Where can I find an apple?"

The butcher drove the tip of the knife into the chopping block and pointed toward a far wall. "Produce, over there."

Astonished at what he had already seen, Noland walked toward the shelves and counters of produce. He took a deep breath. Aromas of spices, oiled wood flooring, coffee, and a myriad of other pleasant smells of the old wooden store tickled his nose. The sweet fragrances of freshly baked goods added to his sensual pleasure and encouraged twinges of hunger as he passed through a small bakery area. Ahead he saw shelves and countertops filled with lettuces and other greens, piles of potatoes, melons, oranges, apples, pears, and trays of different berries. A few colorful displays of cut flowers visually joined his sensual contentment.

A curious look crossed his face when he stood beside the displays of Delicious, MacIntosh, and Granny Smith apples. None were familiar to him. *Where are the red and yellow streaky apples with brown spots that I pick from the trees at the edge of a forest?* He wondered about their absence.

Touching a very red, plump, Red Delicious apple, he felt its firmness. "I shall purchase this one," he mumbled as he took hold of it and made his way toward the front of the store. *This will require a payment.* He reached into his pocket and pulled out the ten-dollar bill Dr. Morris had given him. He saw that the price for a dozen Red Delicious apples was ninety-eight cents. He raised the ten-dollar bill and glanced at it. *This single fruit costs only a fraction of the money I hold.* The earlier scene that involved the hippie flashed through his mind. *Hope this overpayment will cause no turmoil. Hopefully, I will not be compensated for the difference with a mass of coinage.* He shrugged and proceeded to the checkout counter.

The checkout cashier, who was frustrated earlier by the hippie, lifted and rotated the apple in her hand, then scanned the empty counter, and said, "Is that all?"

Noland nodded.

"Eight cents," the cashier said, looking straight into his eyes.

The sergeant handed her the ten-dollar bill, while sheepishly looking at her. Noland noticed that she raised her eyes toward the ceiling and gritted her teeth. She shrugged and punched the buttons on the cash register. The bell dinged as the cash drawer shot out. The cashier inserted the ten-dollar bill and removed a series of bills and coins. She then looked up at Noland and counted the change into his hand. She bagged the apple. "Shall I help carry this to your car?" she chided, while grinning.

Noland smiled and shook his head. "Very kind of you, but thank you, no."

The cashier smiled and winked. "Enjoy the apple."

Outside the grocery store, Noland continued toward Medford Street. He looked at the dive watch on his wrist. *About ten minutes before ten. I have time to find the Dunkin' Donut.* Taking a bite of the apple, he crumbled the little paper bag, inserted it into a pants pocket and increased his pace. The sweet tartness on his tongue invigorated him. In a few minutes he reached the intersection of Medford and Broadway. "Turn to the left, the lady with the dog had said," he mumbled and contemplated his next move.

Strings of trucks and cars moved east and west along Broadway, but a bus facing west was blocking the intersection of Broadway and Medford. Two vehicles on Medford, facing Broadway, were stopped. The one in the left turn lane was gunning the engine. Noland's stomach tensed. He looked across Medford. Stepped off the curb, turned his head left and right, and started across. A man and woman passed beside him.

"Step lively," the man said. "Light's going to turn red. Those guys look impatient."

Noland glanced toward the man, who hopped onto the curb as a car horn blasted. Startled, the sergeant stopped dead, stared at the vehicle a few feet to his side, and swung his hands toward the hood.

"Move your ass—Light's red!" The driver snarled and swung his arm out the window.

As if a bolt of lightning had struck him, Noland snapped around. The apple flew out of his hand as he dashed forward. The Red Delicious exploded into many pieces as it hit the fender of the car. "Beggin' your pardon," he yelled as he jumped onto the curb. His heart racing, he grabbed the light pole and breathed deeply.

"Damned pedestrians! Always in my way," the braggart yelled as he wheeled left onto Broadway.

Noland held onto the light pole and massaged his neck.

"You okay, man?" The African American fellow, who had crossed the intersection ahead of Noland, said. He had seen what happened and had returned to Noland. "Damned lout would rather run you over than give you the right of way."

"Aye. A bit of a surprise, but I will survive," Noland said as he caught his breath.

"You're not from around here, are you? By your accent I believe you're from England. Traffic over there is probably more considerate."

"Aye." Noland released the light pole and stepped to the center of the sidewalk. "Just arrived a few days ago. Almost no traffic from where I come." His breathing returned to normal. "I am off to the Dunkin' Donut."

"Just up the street." The man pointed to the north. "If you move to the curb, you can see the building."

"Thank you for your consideration. I will go there."

"Cities can be dangerous places. Be careful." The man turned and hurried up Broadway.

Noland reached the Dunkin' Donuts building and found it not as glitzy as the McDonald's. Instead, it was a simple, nondescript establishment, with six individual rectangular windows facing Broadway Street. The building actually housed two businesses. The entrance into the building was in the middle. Noland noticed the larger orange sign reading "Dunkin'" hanging above a smaller one with "Donuts" printed in pink. This signage was suspended above the windows to the left of the entrance.

Noland entered the building and found himself in an anteroom with an additional pair of doorways; the door on the left led into Dunkin' Donuts. The one on his right opened into a business whose identity he disregarded.

Once inside, he found the Dunkin' Donuts interior bright and clean, containing several shining, chrome-trimmed, reddish-plastic-topped, centrally located tables and a couple of similar-colored booths. A chest-high counter was situated across the back wall, behind which were shelves of donuts covered in a variety of frostings. The sweet, candied aromas of burnt sugar, cinnamon, and coffee stimulated Noland's desire for some kind of delicious treat. A young woman wearing a white jacket and cap stood behind a waist-high opening in the counter. With a pleasant smile on his face, Noland stepped to the opening.

"May I help you?" the clerk asked.

"Two cakes, with the holes in the middle and a cup of coffee, if you please," Noland answered, shoving his hand into the pocket of his pants.

"We call them doughnuts. What flavors do you want? Plain, or frosted, chocolate, cinnamon, caramel…?"

"Chocolate!" Noland's hand gripped the money in his pocket.

The checker grabbed a pair of tongs, picked up two chocolate donuts, and placed them in a bag. She then poured coffee into a cup, snapped on a lid, and placed the bag and cup on the counter. "Cream, sugar, and napkins on the side, down at the end." The young lady pointed to the left end of the counter. "That'll be a dollar-ten."

Noland gripped the money, locked it in his hand, extended the fist, and opened it. "I am not familiar with your money. Please take the amount required. Thank you."

The young woman removed a dollar bill and dime from his hand, pushed the bagged donuts and cup of coffee toward Noland, turned, and strolled to the cash register. "You are welcome," she said.

The sergeant looked around the area. *I should eat here*, he thought, opened the bag, and sniffed. *Would not want to lose these sweet morsels like I did the apple.* He selected a booth.

As he savored the donuts and sipped his coffee, he watched the people that entered and left. Old and young, they fascinated him by their manner and dress. A young woman with locks of green hair captivated his attention as she sashayed to the counter. The length of her skirt, which ended about two inches above her knees, shocked him. He shook his head and grinned. Shortly after, an elderly couple entered. The man wore a tweed sportscoat, which Noland recognized as a weave typically woven in Great Britain. It appeared to be like the coats he saw as a young man, that old chaps wore to the pub. The tweed-coat man's companion, a bent old crone, wore a dark-colored, heavy-looking overcoat with a sprig of greenery sticking from the lapel. She balanced with a cane held in her right hand and nested her left arm at the old chap's right elbow. They ambled slowly to a table and were greeted by some friends. The entrance door suddenly swung open, allowing a gang of four raucous teenaged boys to swagger through. One boy held a black box at the level of his shoulder. The box blared rackety noise. They pranced to the counter. The kid with the boombox turned it off. They ordered and received their purchase in what seemed to Noland a matter of minutes. The guys then turned, tromped out of Dunkin' Donuts, and turned the noise-producing box back on. Noland could still hear the music as he watched the boys cross Broadway Street about a block away.

"Wow!" Noland uttered, swigged down the coffee, and stood. "What an array of extraordinary bods this modern century has." He dropped the bag, napkin, and coffee into the trashcan as he saw others do. *Supposed to meet Carol.* He looked at the wristwatch. "I must hurry." The sergeant rushed out the door, glanced around, then turned right and walked swiftly down Broadway toward Medford Street. *If I remain on this side, I will not have to cross any large carriageways.*

He reached Medford, turned right, and maintained his quick pace. Periodically glancing to the other side of the street, he finally spotted the Economy Grocery Market. He remembered the word "TAX" in large green letters displayed on one of the shops, slowed, and continued to peruse the shops. He spotted the H&R BLOCK TAX office.

"Aye, there it is." He smiled. "Ah yes, I crossed the carriageway near here. The street where Dr. Morris lives is just beyond." Noland shook his head in disappointment. "Wish I had noted the name of the street on which she lives. It should be where I met the dog, Max."

Reaching the intersection where the bus picked up Max and his master, he stopped, looked around, then turned right and proceeded down the narrow street. In a short distance he noticed that the smooth pavement of the street blended into brick and small residential houses replaced the shops. He came to the block where he was almost run over, crossed it carefully, looked ahead and spotted the familiar forsythia bush loaded with yellow flowers. "Phew! My landmark." He rubbed his right arm across his forehead. *I should have taken a taxi like a modern man would have.* He chuckled and increased his pace.

Dr. Morris turned into her driveway as Noland approached the house. She parked, shut off the VW's engine, and slid out. "I'd like to run in and freshen up," she yelled. "Be back in a moment. Then we'll go and meet Dr. Gorski." She dashed to the house, unlocked the door, and entered.

Driving down High Street, Dr. Morris passed the medical clinic she had left roughly a half hour ago. She continued south toward Main

Street. "We'll be at The Warren Tavern in a few minutes. How was your walk?"

Noland twisted his head away from the side window. He clasped his hands and glanced toward Carol. "It was a rousing experience. Everything—people, conveyances, speech, even time—moves at a much faster pace. Foot travel can indeed be dangerous."

"Did you meet anyone here?"

"Aye."

"And are today's people anything like the colonials you met?"

"They are human. Complicated. Outrageous." Noland leaned forward, peered out the windshield, and pondered for a moment. "I encountered kindness from a woman on the street and vendors in a grocery, strangeness in dress and roistering that in the colonies would have been considered immoral. And belligerence and incivility from individuals who drive the transports. Unlike the colonials, those individuals I met and talked with appeared fiercely independent and do not seem to have any concern of government intervention." He licked his lips, grinned, and glanced back at Dr. Morris.

She chuckled as she slowed, found a parking space on Main Street, and wheeled the VW into it. The entrance into The Warren Tavern was a few feet away, around the corner on Pleasant Street. After turning off the engine and flipping her keys into her purse, Dr. Morris announced, "We've arrived." She gestured for Noland to exit the VW, then opened the door on her side. When both stood on the burnt-ocher-colored brick sidewalk, she moved next to Noland and nested her right arm into his left. "Sounds like you've met some modern Americans. Now, let's join Dr. Gorski." Arm-in-arm, they walked around the corner. Dr. Morris tightened her arm and pulled it back, urging Noland to stop. "That tall, federal-style building in front of us is very historic; considered one of the oldest still-standing buildings in New England. It was built in 1780 after most of Charlestown was burned by the British forces during the Battle of Bunker Hill." They approached the entrance into the tavern. Dr. Morris put her hand on the door handle but paused a moment before she opened the door. "This tavern, The Warren Tavern, is named in honor of Major General Doctor Joseph Warren, a patriot and noted Harvard surgeon. This building has continued to house this pub for about two centuries. Major General Warren was killed during the Battle of Bunker Hill." She pulled the door open and the two entered.

Dr. Andrew Gorski had arrived early. He seated himself at a table for four that was covered with a dull-red tablecloth. The table was located in the dining area, beside a curtained widow, just beyond the left end of the pub's robust L-shaped bar. He realized that it would be difficult to be seen in the dim interior light by anyone entering from the sunny exterior. So, when he saw Dr. Morris and Sergeant Black enter, he raised his arm.

To maintain the ambience of a pub built in the eighteenth century, the walls, beams, and posts of The Warren Tavern were of dark wood. Electrified, pierced-tin revere lanterns hung from the eight-by-eight-inch hand-hewn posts that supported the white plaster-and-beam ceiling. A bit of sunlight diffused through panels of gauzy, laced curtains. The antique lamps added little to the brightness of the interior lighting.

Gorski waved his arm as the two stumbled past the bar.

When Noland's eyes acclimated to the interior lighting, he tapped Dr. Morris's shoulder to alert her, and pointed toward the table where Gorski sat. As they started to the table, Noland was distracted by a photograph hanging on the wall. He moved to the picture and began to examine the image of a pillared building beside a tall obelisk situated atop a hill. Below the photo, a sign noted Bunker Hill Memorial and Lodge.

Dr. Morris came next to Noland. "That place is only a block or two from where we are. It's a memorial essentially to the first major battle between Great Britain and American patriots. The battle occurred in June of 1775, a couple of months after you were mysteriously transported here. So, you don't know of this battle. The British actually won…"

Noland turned and looked at her with a smile. "It is without doubt that my regiment would have fought in that battle. And, had I been there, I would have loyally done my part to assist in the win."

"Perhaps so, but that victory came at a terrible loss of British officers and soldiers," she continued. "Something to discuss over lunch. And after, we'll visit the park. By the way, the lodge at the memorial houses some statues of Boston patriots who were in some way involved in the Battle at Bunker Hill. There is a statue of Major General Joseph Warren. In fact, the lodge was built by the Freemasons of King Solomon, specifically to house his statue. Warren was one of the founders of this group of Massachusetts Masons." She took hold of Noland's arm and urged him to move to the table.

Dr. Gorski stood when Dr. Morris and Noland approached. "Dr. Morris, it is good to see you again." He extended his hand, clasped Noland's, and the two greeted each other.

"Modern America is indeed a strange land," Noland said as he seated himself.

"How so?" Gorski asked.

"Colonial Americans build memorials to enemies who beat them?" Noland frowned, tilted his head, and grinned. "You do not find this strange?"

"The memorial was not built to honor the British," Dr. Morris interrupted as she pulled a chair away from the table and seated herself. "The memorial was built to pay tribute to the patriots who fought in the battle. They might have won the battles had they not run out of ammunition. Britain paid a heavy toll for their victory. The Americans lost only a few men."

Dr. Gorski reseated himself. "What brought on the Battle of Bunker Hill?" he asked.

"Noland saw a picture of the Bunker Hill memorial and read the description next to the picture, which said that Great Britain won the battle. So, he thought it strange that we build monuments to our enemies," Dr. Morris clarified. "Of course, he doesn't actually know about the battle, since he was magically whisked to the future a couple of months before the attack happened."

"Ah yes. Battle happened on June seventeenth; I believe." Dr. Gorski picked up the menu. "Let's order. I've got to get back to the office."

"Okay." Dr. Morris said began to peruse the list of lunch options. "Noland and I are going to visit Bunker Hill after lunch. He says his barracks was located nearby on Ferry Hill. Going to see if we can find any evidence of it." She frowned and looked up at Noland.

He nodded.

"Doubt you'll find anything," Gorski interjected. "The Charlestown Navy Yard and modern development obliterated most of what was once there. Don't even think Ferry Hill still exists. The only ferries operating from the wharfs over there are for sightseeing. Most of the area is owned by the navy. Oh yes, the USS *Constitution* is also anchored there. If you have time, you should visit it. That ship was built and launched in 1797. Noland, you should recognize the design. The *Constitution* looks like the frigates you Brits had back then. There's also a museum on that property."

"Can I take your order?" a waitress interrupted.

Everyone seemed to be on the same page. They all ordered clam chowder, a hamburger, and French fries. With an urge from Dr. Gorski, Noland also ordered a pint of dark beer. The waitress departed.

Dr. Gorski adjusted himself in his chair, looked up at Noland and Dr. Morris. "On this problem we have—establishing Sergeant Noland Black's legality in the United States—my friend in the State Department called back. He told me of several possibilities: temporary travel visas, Brits don't really need one, but they need a passport. Immigrants from Great Britain, its commonwealth and territories, and countries in Europe and Asia can get temporary work visas, green cards, refugee status, etcetera, etcetera. But all of these require verification of where the individual came from. So, I don't know. My friend said he'd continue working on the problem." Gorski placed his hands on the table and shrugged. "Guess we'll play it by ear…" An amused look crossed his face. He then glanced at Dr. Morris and started to chuckle. "Of course, you two could get married."

Dr. Morris grimaced. Noland tilted his head to the right and raised his left eyebrow.

"Guess you guys are still maintaining a doctor-patient relationship," Gorski humorously whispered. "Thought, because of the close quarters, you may have developed a more intimate relationship."

"I believe your mind has fallen into the gutter." Dr. Morris's chide was interrupted by the waitress bringing the food.

"Sorry," Dr. Gorski said as he unfolded his napkin, then savored a French fry. Lifting his gaze from the bowl of clam chowder, he grinned at Dr. Morris. "Didn't mean for my comment to sound suggestive." He tasted the chowder.

The three ate in silence for a few minutes.

"This porridge is quite tasty," Noland said as he finished off the chowder. Then he raised his head and glanced across the table. "Dr. Gorski, I would like to thank you for the effort you are expending to find a way for me to live in this century. I know I must be a productive individual if I am to be of any use. You have my gratitude."

"I'm sure there is a way." Dr. Gorski glimpsed at his watch. "And it will be found." He crunched the napkin, dropped it on his dish, and motioned for the waitress. "I'll get the bill, because I'm going to have to go." He reached for his wallet. "See you tomorrow morning at Hartwell Tavern. It's our reenactment site. It's not far from where we found you. Dr. Morris knows how to get there. She'll bring you. Be there at around ten thirty. Oh yes, wear your uniform."

"That's not far off the Concord Road in the national park, is it?" Dr. Morris asked.

"No, it's not. We meet about fifty yards from the tavern."

The waitress came to the table and Dr. Gorski paid the check. He rose, brushed off his sleeve and started toward the exit. "See you both, tomorrow."

"He's in a hurry. Must be something serious." Dr. Morris finished eating her French fries and pushed her dishes toward the middle of the table. "There's always an emergency in the emergency room. There are never enough doctors to handle the broken patients. Gorski's dedicated." Dr. Morris stood. "It's getting late. Let's head over to Bunker Hill."

Noland swigged down the remaining beer, used the napkin to wipe his lips, pushed back from the table, and raised himself from the chair. He sighed. "That was an enjoyable meal."

Dr. Morris turned the Volkswagen into the lane that ran along the south side of Monument Square Park. "If you look to the right and up the hill, you'll see the obelisk pictured in the news article you saw at the Warren Tavern, the Bunker Hill Battle memorial. The building to its side, with the pillars, is where the statue of the general that tavern was named to honor, Major General Warren, is located." She continued slowly along the lane that circled around Bunker Hill. "As soon as I find a place to park, we'll visit the memorial. Ah, there's a couple slots." She turned the VW into an angled parking slot.

"I am anxious to learn about the battle we won, although, for me, it has yet to occur." Noland immediately opened the door and jumped out of the vehicle.

Dr. Morris remained in the VW a few moments before exiting to brush her hair. Noland stood against the car, looking up at the Bunker Hill Memorial, when a vehicle flashing red and blue lights pulled up behind the VW. A man in a blue uniform exited the right side and approached. "You're parked in a restricted zone," he announced. "You need a permit to park here."

As Dr. Morris opened her door and swung her feet out, she heard the man in blue ask Noland in an authoritative voice if he had any identification.

Dr. Morris stood and looked over the top of the car to face the policeman. "What's the problem, officer?" she asked as Noland stood looking befuddled.

"Sorry, but I do not have any," Noland answered quietly.

"He's my cousin visiting me from England," Dr. Morris piped up. "He left his papers at the house. He's here to research the Bunker Hill Battle. We'll only be here less than an hour."

"Yes, ma'am. Can I see your driver's license? You are parked in a restricted parking zone. You'll have to move this vehicle, or I'll have to ticket you."

Noland's stomach tightened. He straightened and clenched his fists but realized the man in blue had a weapon holstered to his belt. Dr. Morris came around the VW and handed the policeman her driver's license.

He started to examine it when his partner exited the police cruiser. "Hang on, Sam. I recognize this lady," he said. "She's a medical doctor. Works up the road at the clinic. Took care of a couple of druggies we brought in a couple of months ago. What's her name, Sam?"

"Carol Morris. Lives in Somerville."

"Gonna be here long, Dr. Morris?" the second policeman asked.

"Less than an hour," Dr. Morris answered. "My cousin, Noland, wants to look at some of the displays at the memorial. He believes an ancestor fought in the battle."

"Sam," the second officer said, "write them a warning. Dr. Morris, we'll be back through here in an hour. I expect you will be gone by then."

"Yes. Thank you," Dr. Morris replied.

The second officer nodded. "My ancestors took part in that battle—and others. Militia men they were. Fought for independence." He turned and started to walk toward the police cruiser. "You have a pleasant visit. Nice meeting you, Noland. Hope you have an enjoyable stay in the States."

His partner handed Dr. Morris the warning and returned to the cruiser. With the flashing emergency lights off, the policemen went on their way.

Noland's tension subsided. He sighed. *Good that I did not confront those men. I might have created trouble. They respected Dr. Morris.*

"What's on your mind?" Dr. Morris asked as she and Noland climbed the stairs to the base of the Bunker Hill Monument.

"Those men respected you. They are allowing you to leave the vehicle here, are they not?"

"Yes," she answered. "Boston policemen. Nice of them to compromise. Probably, since you are a tourist, and also, because maybe today is not a busy day. Whatever, they're not bad guys."

The two reached the base of the obelisk. Dr. Morris looked at her watch. "It's getting late. We should skip climbing to the top of the obelisk. Over two hundred steps. It'll burn us out. We can catch it another time." She put her hand against his arm. "Let's go into the lodge. You can see the statue of General Warren and a couple other memorial items. Then we'll walk over to the museum in the old library. It's just down the hill. Not much to see, but enough for you to learn something about the battle that took place here. Then we can go to Constitution Park and see the frigate. You might find that more interesting. There's a museum at the park that provides evidence on how the Royal Navy lost its dominance of the seas. It's not far, and I know a parking area there where the police won't bother us."

Few people were inside the Bunker Hill Lodge. The interior was a subdued, dismal, forlorn space. The sergeant shivered. To him it was like walking into a tomb. Noland quickly spotted the statue for whom the lodge was constructed.

Housed in an open alcove defined by a wooden-colored ingress, the elaborate, highlighted, white marble statue of General Warren faced the lodge's main entrance. It stood on a black marble pedestal, in front of a white faux entranceway and framed between two white pillars. Several decorative flags, the Stars and Stripes, King's Colors, and others, stood on the floor in front of the statue. The entire exhibit was ringed by a brass guardrail.

Noland and Dr. Morris walked to it.

Drawn to the statue of General Warren, the sergeant examined it. "So, this is the individual for whom the tavern, where we dined, was named." Noland turned toward Dr. Morris. "He surely is not presented as a military man. But he must have been important to the people of Boston." He returned his attention to General Warren's statue.

"Indeed, he was," Dr. Morris said. "Dr. Joseph Warren was a physician, man-of-letters, member of the Charlestown Freemasons, the president of the Massachusetts Provincial Congress, and an unfaltering patriot. Several days before the Battle of Bunker Hill, General Israel Putnam, who was in charge of the Colonial Army, encamped on Bunker Hill and held the northern portion of Charlestown Neck, appointed Dr. Warren as a Major General. Instead of immediately accepting, Warren volunteered to aid in the battle and accept the appointment after the fighting ended. Unfortunately, when the Colonial Army retreated, the redoubts on Breed's Hill—by the way, the battle actually took place on Breed's Hill, the hill upon which we now stand; Bunker Hill is to the north—Warren, being one of the last to evacuate, was fatally wounded. However, in tribute to Dr. Warren, his appointment to the rank of Major General was awarded posthumously.

"A regrettable loss…" Noland said, "but an understandable one. When an untrained militia faces a highly skilled military force like the British military, considerable casualties would be expected." Straightening and crossing his arms against his chest, the sergeant stood proud.

"Perhaps so," countered Dr. Morris. "In this case you are wrong. Though the British technically won the Battle of Bunker Hill, their losses were greater than those of the colonial militia. The British attacked with over three thousand men and lost over one thousand, about eighty of whom were officers killed or wounded. The militia had less than a thousand men. The number of rebels, as you call them, killed or wounded was only around four hundred.

"Aye. A victory resembling Pyrrhus's defeat of the Romans. King Pyrrhus took heavy losses." Noland's head drooped. "When did the Bunker Hill Battle take place?"

"June seventeen, 1775," Dr. Morris said as she lowered her chin and furrowed her brow. "Who's this King Pyrrhus?"

"He was the king of the land of Epirus, which was located near Greece. He ruled that kingdom about three hundred years before Christ."

"Where did you learn that?"

"I have always been interested in ancient military history." Noland raised his eyelids. "As a young man in Gateshead Village, the vicar of our church taught me to appreciate the classics. He allowed me to read many of his books. Then in the military, during my free time, I borrowed books kept by my officers. There is not much to do while crossing the Atlantic. The captain of our vessel gave me freedom to use his library. His books were mostly of naval expeditions."

"I didn't expect you to be an intellectual, but I felt you had a more-than-average education. Since you've been here, your true intellect hasn't really surfaced." Dr. Morris arched her eyebrows and smiled. She pressed her hand against his arm. "Let's skip the rest of this place and the library and go visit the USS *Constitution*. I'm sure you'll find the old vessel and its history more to your interest."

"Aye. This Battle of Bunker Hill, in my mind, has not yet occurred. I did not know it was even to happen. But if I returned to my time and knew of this battle, I would try to inform my commanders of the futility of their mission and urge them to be more receptive to the wishes of the colonials."

The drive from the Bunker Hill Monument to Constitution Road took about five minutes. Dr. Morris drove around the area and found an empty slot on the edge of Paul Revere Park where other cars were parked.

"No signs," she said. "Should be safe to leave the VW here. It's only a short walk to those buildings over there, the Hoosac Stores, three large old naval warehouses." She pointed ahead and to the left.

From where Dr. Morris parked her vehicle, it was only a short walk to First Avenue, then once past the warehouses, Noland was able to get a relatively close and complete view of the USS *Constitution* tied to the wharf.

Noland walked between the buildings toward the slip where the frigate floated. He stopped and looked at the vessel. Suddenly, an internal sensation, a feeling of discernment, a twitch of anxiety. He quickly turned and attempted to look back at the city, but his view was obscured by the warehouses, barriers to an elevated roadway, and nearby trees. His body shivered and his stomach quivered. *I know this place, when only the brush and trees grew along the river's edge.* He swung around, felt faint as his graze returned to the *Constitution*. *There were no wharfs; no buildings; only shoreline vegetation and water.* His arm drooped.

Dr. Morris saw him wobble. She grabbed him by the arm. "Are you all, right? You were standing there. Then you looked as if you were about the fall." She felt him tremble, then gasp. In a few moments she felt his body cool, relax. She looked him in the face and released her hold, but she maintained a grip on his arm.

"Aha, I am all right. I know this place. But what I see is not what was here." He again turned and looked toward inner Charlestown. "There were no structures. Only wild vegetation, shoreline." He pointed to a dock on the right. "The barracks, my barracks, were just a short distance away, up a small rise. Ferry Hill, it was called…" Noland continued to point to the west, toward Chelsea Street. "Charlestown, the village where the people subsisted, its boundaries began maybe a half mile from here."

"What you have seen and experienced was two hundred years ago," Dr. Morris said. "Ferries still operate from the docks near the historic vessel and naval yard. They do cross the river, but they are not used as a means to transport people across the rivers, though some do. Today, most of Boston's ferries are for tourists, sightseers who want to get a look at Boston's waterfront and nearby islands. Bridges and subways get everyone else across the river much more efficiently and rapidly." Dr. Morris glanced in the direction Noland had pointed. She pondered his vision for a moment. "What you saw in your time, has been obliterated by the expansion of the modern city of Boston. By the way, this is the shoreline where the British forces came ashore to attack Bunker Hill."

"Aye, for a moment I seemed to have forgotten I had come into the future." He shook himself and took a couple of deep breaths. "We should go on. That vessel does look like a British ship-of-line."

Dr. Morris and Noland walked onto the USS *Constitution*'s wharf to which the vessel was tied and slowly made their way to the gangplank. Approaching, they noticed very few people on board. But they saw several people exit the vessel. Dr. Morris read the sign at the base of the gangway. She looked at her watch.

"Visitation of this ship closes at five o'clock. The last guided tour began about an hour ago. I believe we've missed going aboard." She put her hand on Noland's shoulder. "We got a glimpse. I know you probably wanted to go aboard. This vessel is not going anywhere. So, the next time we visit, we'll allow more time. It's worth a tour."

"Aye." Noland strolled along the dock toward the frigate's stern.

Dr. Morris followed close behind.

Periodically, Noland stopped and perused the hull. "She seems to be a strong vessel. Well-armed. Many gunports…"

"Yes. I believe she has somewhere near forty cannons." She sidled next to Noland. "The hull is very strong. During battles, cannonballs fired by a British ships-of-the-line harmlessly bounced off the *Constitution*'s sides, while the British vessel sustained great damage from her shots. After the first battle, the crew of the USS *Constitution* cheered their win and began to call their vessel Old Ironsides; today she is better known by that battle name."

Noland cocked his head and grinned. "A fascinating name, though she is made of wood." He continued his amble. "I do not know of this vessel. The rebels had vessels, but they were no more than an irritant to our naval force."

"The USS *Constitution* was launched in 1794," Dr. Morris remarked. "The battles I mentioned occurred during the War of 1812, the second war between the United States and Great Britain. When this war ended, Britain was no longer the world's dominant naval force. The Americans had taken that crown."

"So, the Royal Navy is no longer a notable force?"

"To the contrary. It surely is. Like the United States Navy, today's Royal Navy is a force to be reckoned with. But America and Great Britain are allies. Other countries in the world also have strong navies. Some are allying with us and some are not."

Noland and Dr. Morris reached the end of the dock.

A variety of small pleasure crafts buzzed about. To his left, up the river, a pair of racing shells seemed to be competing against each other. Several sailing dinghies scooted along the far shore. "The world has changed considerably in two hundred years," Noland said while staring at the Charles River and chewing on his lower lip. *A couple of days before we marched on Concord, four British frigates and a dozen gunboats floated on this river.* A tap on his right shoulder interrupted the sergeant's reminiscence. He looked to his side and saw Dr. Morris excited and pointing south, toward Boston's open harbor. Beyond the McClellan Highway bridge, he saw a large, gray, sleek vessel, her stack trailing a turbulent column of grayish-black smoke and her bow aimed for the open sea.

"A modern-day frigate," Dr. Morris said, "or, what it's called today, a destroyer."

"An unusual ship," Noland said. His elbows raised and hands clasped the back of his neck as he watched the destroyer churn a foamy, white path through the bay. "It has structure amidships, a complex mast and yardarms, but no sails. The hull has no gunports, yet it appears dreadful and fast."

Dr. Morris grinned. "It is well armed. It is some distance from us, so its guns are hard to see. But the structure with two large pipes you see at the front end of the ship are rapid-fire cannons." She squinted and tilted her head forward. "If you look carefully, you'll also see another cannon mount in the rear. There are also many smaller cannons called machineguns." She paused for a moment. "The entire vessel is made of steel. Highly maneuverable. And it can cruise at a speed of around twenty-five knots, and probably faster. We don't know, because the military keeps that kind of information secret from the public. The mast you mentioned is covered with an array of electronic sensing instruments to aid in the ship's navigation, gun control, enemy location, and supposedly other things."

The destroyer turned to the south and cruised out of view. Noland continued to gaze in the direction the destroyer disappeared. "I would so much like to visit such a ship. Perhaps that can happen?"

Dr. Morris fidgeted. "Yes, that is possible. Occasionally, when a naval ship arrives in the harbor, the captain allows an open house for several days. Somewhat of a festive occasion to allow the public to tour the vessel, obtain information and meet the crew."

"Aye, I have attended such events in London and Portsmouth. Many of these fetes were presented to glorify life and travel in the Royal Navy to tempt young men into service. Probably, it is still now a means of attraction."

Dr. Morris sidled to the edge of the dock and glanced at the water below. "I'm sure that it is still a technique the military uses to lure the fascinated." She turned and looked back at Noland. "You joined the Royal Army…"

"That I did. But it was not for the glories of the service. Then I wanted to leave England and never return. Now, with what I have seen and learned, I would like to return." For a moment Noland mused at what he had just said. "Not to the past, but the present. I would enjoy seeing how two hundred years has changed England."

"Yes. But first you must become real—legal, accepted here and in the present." Dr. Morris shrugged; she nested her arm at Noland's elbow. "Once that happens, you'll be free to travel wherever you like." She gazed back toward the USS *Constitution*. "It's getting late. Let's head for home. On the way we'll stop and pick up something for supper; something that is more modern, something that people today enjoy eating."

On the way home, Dr. Morris swung off Main Street onto a side lane where she knew of an Italian grocery store that also served a variety of takeout meals. "Going to pick up a couple of Italian grinder and beer for supper."

"What is a grinder?" Noland straightened, lifted his chin, turned and, with wide open eyes, gazed at Dr. Morris.

"Boston's full of Italians, who are known for creating very tasty foods. They've improved the sandwich. You know what a sandwich is, don't you?"

"Aye." Noland nodded and raised his eyebrows. "Meat or jam placed between two pieces of bread; a simple delicacy to satisfy hunger. The barracks' cook provided them for our excursions."

"The Italians make their version of a sandwich. Instead of sliced bread, they use a roll, a kind of Italian baguette. Slice it in half and add cuts of their dry, spicy meats: pepperoni, salami, prosciutto, and others that I don't know. Then they add slices of provolone cheese, shredded lettuce, sliced peppers, tomatoes and olives, and sprinkle the delicious, peppery mess with salt and olive oil. The grinders are then heated, wrapped in paper, and bagged." Dr. Morris licked her lips as she parked her car along the curb. "I'm sure you'll find eating a grinder enjoyable. It'll rattle your taste buds; bring them into the twentieth century. The flavors are very different from what we've eaten up to now." She opened the door and stepped out. "I'll buy a six-pack of English ale, bag of potato chips, and a carton of gelato; a dessert that will cool the mouth. Be back in a minute."

Noland scrunched in his seat. Crossed his arms over his chest. Momentarily squirmed, then relaxed, gripped his hands together, and laid them in his lap. He stared at the Italian grocery store. The interior of the street-facing windows was framed in leafy vines adorned with bunches of dusty-looking red-wine grapes. A green, white, and red-striped flag was splayed above the entrance. *I have never met an Italian. Nor have I eaten their food. Believe they live in southern Europe, near Rome. Make good wines, well flavored, but lack sweetness.*

The spicy, savory fragrances emanating from the bags Dr. Morris brought into the VW and placed in Noland's lap, caused his stomach to churn. His mouth overly moistened. He sighed deeply and used his fingers to dry his lips. The aroma that filled the interior of the little German vehicle gave a pleasant but riveting sense of hunger. Noland looked at Dr. Morris and believed she too was responding similarly to the smells. They both had eaten an early light lunch and the hour was approaching six o'clock.

Dr. Morris wheeled the VW into her driveway and turned it off. "The smell has made me very hungry. Let's get into the house and eat."

Noland gripped the bags and exited the vehicle. He bent back into the VW and retrieved the six-pack of beer that Dr. Morris had set at his feet. She slid out the driver's side, headed straight for the front door of the house, unlocked it, and entered. Noland followed, carrying the groceries.

Within a few minutes, she had laid out some dishes and glasses, tore open the bag of potato chips, and dumped them into a wooden bowl. "There's a bottle opener next to the sink. If you would open a couple of bottles of the Newcastle Brown Ale I bought. It's a beer brewed in your hometown."

Noland found the bottle opener. It was a simple one: a wooden handle with a metal ring at one end. He had no idea how it worked. So, for a moment, he rotated it a couple times, then put a finger through the ring and felt the flat tooth on the inside edge. Almost immediately he understood what was needed to pop the cap off the bottle. "Aye." Noland grinned and nodded as he grabbed a bottle of ale. He placed the ring of the opener on top of the bottlecap so the tooth would slip under the cap's edge. He lifted the handle of the opener and the cap popped off. The beer fizzed up the bottle's neck, shot through its mouth, down the bottle's side, and over Noland's hand. "Oh, my lord!" he exclaimed.

"Should have warned you." Dr. Morris chuckled. "Those bottles are warm. Inside pressure builds, causing the beer to foam up. Not a problem. When you open the other one, hold it over the sink. And pour each of us a glass."

Noland cocked his head and smiled. "We received our ale in a mug. Never in bottles." He grabbed a second bottle of Newcastle Brown Ale, held it over the sink, and popped off the cap. The beer foamed out the bottle's month, but not to the extent as the first. Setting the bottle on the counter, Noland shook his beer-wetted hand, flipped on the sink spigot, and rinsed it off. Wiping his hands, he then removed two glasses from the cupboard and carefully filled each with ale. "I am anxious to taste…" he cocked his head slightly to the side, tussled his hair and grinned, "one of those grinders. The smell of them is rumbling my stomach."

"I've put them on a plate," Carol said. "Grab it and the bowl of potato chips, then go and seat yourself on the couch." She placed the glasses of ale on a platter. "I'll bring the beer."

As Dr. Morris seated herself on an armchair across from the couch, Noland took a bite of the grinder.

Carol straightened, pushed back her shoulders, and glared at him. "Well, what's the verdict?"

Noland chewed, furrowed his brow, swallowed, looked up, and smiled at Dr. Morris. "Most delectable." He licked his lips. "The grinder, spicy, tastes much like the aroma it emits and—its flavors stay in my mouth. Never have I experienced such substances and textures. Indeed, most unusual." He took another bite, then popped several potato chips into his mouth. "Richly salted, the chips are. They enhance the flavors from the grinder." He lifted the glass of ale, took a healthy swig, and sighed. "Ahaa, what a treat. Regimental foods were never like this. And the ale is wonderful."

"Yes," Dr. Morris agreed. "You've never tasted Newcastle Brown Ale, since it was not brewed until the mid-1800s."

For the next few moments Dr. Morris and Noland enjoyed the grinders and ale in silence. When they finished, they pacified their mouths with scoops of gelato. Noland sat back and rubbed his lips with the pointing finger of his right hand.

"My god, I forgot to bring the napkins. Sorry." Carol scooted forward and started to stand.

"Please do not concern yourself," Noland said. "I would rather you tell me more of this Battle of Bunker Hill. If the British won, there should have been elation among the troops. The battle should have ended the revolution. But it did not."

Carol sighed and scrunched back into the armchair. "There's not much to say about the battle, except that it considerably increased the colonists' displeasure with Great Britain." She leaned forward. "I'll turn on the television…"

"No! I do not want to watch the television. I want to hear why Britain lost the war."

Dr. Morris took a deep breath. "Perhaps your commanders were delighted by their win at Bunker Hill, but I'm sure their excitement was short-lived. Prior to that battle, there were many skirmishes between Great Britain and the American army. Great Britain lost many of these, some of major importance. For example, the loss of Fort Ticonderoga and the capture of several naval vessels. The British tried to secure their hold on Boston by attacking Charlestown and the American encampments on Breed's Hill. This infuriated the colonials, who made life for the British in Boston miserable. So, it's a good thing you are not there."

Noland leaned toward his glass of ale, lifted it, and took a drink. "How so?"

Dr. Morris readjusted herself in the chair and sipped her beer, then set the glass down. "After Bunker Hill, American patriot groups harassed the British in Boston to the point that it became difficult getting supplies, food, ammunition, lumber, and other necessities into the city. Life for all became wretched. Then winter came and the military had to burn furniture because of the scarcity of firewood. Many loyal to Great Britain devested their possessions and vacated the city…"

Noland's anxiety rose. He clenched his fists. Straightened and leaned forward. "Even those who lived in the manor houses we visited—the place you called Tory Row?"

"Yes, I'm sure. Your friend the Reverend Hollingsworth, the Lechmere family, and other loyalists who owned mansions on Brattle Street. And many who lived in the city of Boston. They fled, some to New York City, others to Halifax, Jamaica, and other British-held islands in the Caribbean."

"Not the British army?" Noland grumbled. His face began to flush with anger.

"No, they did not. But they were stuck in Boston. The rebels, as you call them, surrounded the city. Essentially blockaded it, even though the British enforced Boston Neck, the only land entrance into the city."

"Aye." Tenseness had gripped Noland's body. He wiggled forward on the couch until he was ridged on its edge. "Aye, I knew they would never retreat but stay and put down the rebellion."

"No, they eventually did leave." Dr. Morris took another sip of beer. "Noland, please relax. It all happened two hundred years ago. There is nothing that anyone can do. It's history."

Noland leaned back, took several deep breaths, tried to release the stress that had tightened his muscles and stirred his stomach.

"You see," Dr. Morris continued, "tensions in the city increased further with the arrival of General George Washington. He was put in command of the colonial American army. Another general, Washington's artillery specialist, General Henry Knox, came up with a plan to move the cannons—there were fifty-nine of them—and ammunition from the recently captured Fort Ticonderoga to Boston." She looked at Noland, who seemed to have calmed and seated himself more comfortably. He became more attentive. "Now remember, this is the winter of 1775. Lots of cold, snow, and ice. The patriots marched about three hundred miles to the fort on Lake George in New York, built some sledges, loaded the cannons and ammunition, and transported everything back to Boston. Only one cannon was lost. Knox and Washington had the cannons placed at strategic locations around the city and pointed at the harbor. By the spring of 1776, your generals in Boston realized they had been outwitted. In March of that year, the British troops evacuated the city of Boston."

Noland lowered his head and grasped it in his hands.

"Now don't get maudlin on me," Dr. Morris said. "The British officers and troops sailed off to Halifax, Nova Scotia and sat around for a few months. Then in August of 1776, reinforcements arrived, and all sailed back, attacked Long Island and New York City, and kicked George Washington and his rebels out." She watched Noland raise his head. A grin appeared on his face.

"How long did the war last?"

"About eight years. The Americans would have been defeated had it not been for the alliances they established with France and Spain. France, primarily. I believe Dr. Gorski mentioned that the last major military engagement had occurred when the colonials, directed by Washington, joined forces with the French military at Yorktown, Virginia. The French Navy was commanded by the Marquis de Lafayette, while the French army combined with the colonials, engaged in a surprise land attack led by Comte de Rochambeau on the British. Your General Charles Cornwallis surrendered. The Battle at Yorktown, which occurred in October of 1781, was the last major engagement of the American Revolution. It was a decisive battle. Though conflicts didn't end until representatives of King George signed the Treaty of Paris in 1783. The treaty ended the war and British rule in the colonies, which led to the total evacuation of British troops and Loyalists from New York City."

Noland sat silently, staring at the fireplace and pondering what he had been told. Then, with confidence, but a circumspect expression, he said, "It is too bad that King George and his minions could not foresee the future. I am glad I am not there anymore. I am astonished and enthralled by what the consequence of that war created. My hope is that Dr. Gorski and you will find a way for me to be a part of this century." Noland finish his ale, sat back on the couch, and looked at Dr. Morris.

She smiled. "Can I get you another ale?"

"Nay. I believe I am in the right state of mind to enjoy where I am and who I am with."

Dr. Morris nodded. "Me too."

The two regarded each other as if time had stopped. After a few moments, Dr. Morris looked up, closed her eyes, unconsciously took a deep breath, and sighed. She opened her eyes and looked down at the empty dishes scattered on the table. "I should get these into the kitchen. You have a big day tomorrow with Dr. Gorski. He wants us to meet him at the Hartwell Tavern in the Minute Man National Historical Park. Your uniform is ready to wear. Since your original blouse was destroyed when Dr. Gorski and John removed it after they found you, I put out one of my husband's white shirts. You can wear that. Your red coat will mostly hide it. It has been a long evening. I'm tired."

"Aye, it will be interesting to meet the others, reenactors, as Dr. Gorski calls them." Noland raised himself off the couch. "May I help remove the leavings from our meal?" He bent down and picked up several dishes.

"Thank you," Dr. Morris said. "Just put them next to the sink. I'll clean them in the morning." She collected what remained and carried it into the kitchen.

Noland followed.

"Now, you go and ready yourself for tomorrow and get some sleep." Dr. Morris kissed him on the cheek, stepped back, and waved her arm toward the stairs. "I'll see you in the morning."

Noland felt a warmness from Carol's gesture. "Before I go, I would like to say, you are an intelligent, enlightened, and capable surgeon. You successfully treated my injuries. They have healed nicely. In my time, only men were trained in the art of medicine. No women. The thought was that women could not tolerate the repugnance of blood and entrails from broken and diseased human bodies."

"That's what men thought back then," Dr. Morris said. "But that is a myth. In many cases women can endure such abhorrent, disgusting conditions better than men. I have never felt faint at the sight of gore."

"Aye, you are indeed a strong woman, who is also a conversant historian."

Dr. Morris chuckled. "I have lived most of my life in Boston, which by many is considered the root of American history; this city is part of me. And you, Sergeant Noland Black, are a living part of this city's history too." She moved closer to Noland, embraced him, again kissed his cheek, and pulled away. "Now go to bed. And may you have pleasant dreams."

The ardor Dr. Morris had shown him, titillated Noland's body as he climbed the stairs. He sighed. *She has become a fondness of my affection, an enchantment of my dreams.*

CHAPTER 14

Thursday, April 24, 1975

During the night, Noland woke, rolled about in bed, pulled the banket to his chin, and stared at the ceiling. His chest heated and dampened as apprehension spawned a foreboding premonition of an unknown source or consequence. He closed his eyes. His brain churned. *Could it be that meeting and interacting with a group of twentieth-century men is causing me this unease?* He sighed. *No! I have faced such vulnerabilities before. The outcomes were largely successful.* Noland's chaotic thoughts assembled another possibility. *Carol? A wonderful woman. I do have a strong attraction for her. She seems to feel the same, but I am uncertain.* Noland sat up and mumbled, "I should tell her. Yes! A romantic dinner," he whispered. "This evening, by ourselves, then I will express my feelings." His shoulders suddenly dropped. The anxiety returned. "I have no means of payment for such an attempt. No American dollars. Only a useless shilling or two I have in my coat." He looked to where the dollar bills he'd received as change yesterday lay and shook his head. "That is not sufficient for a fine dinner. Carol pays for everything." He lowered his head onto his knees. Then his worries were interrupted by Dr. Morris.

"Are you awake?" she yelled up the stairs. "It's getting late. We're to meet with Dr. Gorski's group in about two hours."

"Aye," Noland yelled. "I am awake and will be dressed in a short time." He kicked off the blanket, rotated himself, and bounced off the bed. *I will need to dress in proper uniform for this meeting.* As his feet padded down the hall to the bathroom, his body momentarily shivered. He stepped into the bathtub, pulled the shower curtain closed, turned on the water, adjusted its temperature, and pulled up the shower lever. "Aah!" he gasped as the warm spray hit his body. "This warmth will ease my distress."

After hurrying through his toilet, Noland returned to the bedroom, closed its door, and glanced at his now-clean uniform, which hung on a nearby chair back. He slipped on the socks, white combat trousers, belt, Dr. Morris's husband's white shirt, and boots. Accepting his image in the mirror, he stepped to where his red coat hung, brushed his hands down its front, and examined the right shoulder and backside for the bullet holes. They were properly mended. Removing the coat from its hanger, he grinned when he noticed the orders for the Lexington/Concord mission stuck out of the inside pocket. *A memory from the past.* Pondering the remembrance, he paused, pushed the order out of sight, clenched his fists, and sighed deeply. *I do not want to return to the past.*

Noland donned the red coat, moved to the full-length mirror on the back of the bedroom door, and again glanced at himself. Pausing for a moment, he adjusted the red coat to cover the collar of the modern white shirt. He took a deep breath, tightened his chest muscles, straightened, and placed his arms akimbo. Stiffening his jaw, he turned his head to the right and left, while seriously examining his image. "I do believe I can do well in this future time," he mused as he moved to the dresser and picked up the photo of Dr. Morris and himself taken at the Boston Massacre Memorial. "Dr. Gorski will enjoy this photo," he mumbled. He pocketed it in the red coat along with the change from the ten-dollar bill he used yesterday.

Opening the bedroom door, Noland stepped toward the stairs. "Be ready to meet a British Grenadier from the past," he called to Dr. Morris and marched down to the first level of the house.

After finishing a breakfast of several bowls of Cheerios and strawberries, Noland and Dr. Morris left for Minute Man National Historic Park. "You look spiffy, very British," she said as the two walked out of the house to the Volkswagen parked in the driveway.

"Thank you." Noland's face glistened at her comment. He then scratched his head. "I do not know spiffy. Do I look proper?"

"You sure do. Sorry. 'Spiffy' is a recent expression. It means smart-looking, handsome, well-dressed, and so forth."

"Ah. A modern word." Noland puffed up his chest and smiled. "Thank you for the compliment."

"It'll take us about thirty minutes to get to Hartwell Tavern," she said as she backed the VW onto the street and pointed the vehicle toward Medford Street.

Medford would take them to Broadway Street, which would blend with Massachusetts Street, Highway 2A. As they neared the park, the highway name changed to the Great Road. In roughly twenty minutes Dr. Morris would turn off onto Virginia Road. Hartwell Tavern, the reenactors' meeting place, was a short distance from this turn.

"This is the road your regiments marched upon from Lexington to Concord," Dr. Morris mentioned as they cruised toward Virginia Road. "Since your troops passed the Hartwell Tavern, you may recognize it. But remember, two hundred years ago the place and area must have looked quite different."

"Indeed," Noland said, while curiously looking out the window. "I do not recognize anything. The land has been trimmed and dressed. It was not so when we marched to Concord. This highway looks nothing like the Bay Road or Boston Road, as some call it, our regiments moved upon to reach Concord, Lexington, and locations further to the west."

In a short time, Dr. Morris turned onto Virginia Road. "The tavern is about a mile away."

Noland glanced into a meadow where people seemed to be milling about. Ahead he saw a modernized clapboard building surrounded by a rail fence with a gravel parking lot to the side that contained a collection of vehicles. Closer now, in the meadow beyond the fencing, groups of men wearing red coats and white trousers, and others in red-trimmed blue coats and khaki-colored breeches rambled about. All wore tricornes and looked very military. Moving among the uniformed soldiers were individuals dressed in more plebeian garments, brown waistcoats, worn leather jackets, dark- and light-colored duck pants, and a variety of belts from which hung packs and canteens. Some of these men covered their heads with narrow-brim tricornes, various styles of knitted caps, or were bare-headed. From the waistbelts of a few uniformed individuals hung a sword, while most officers carried a musket. Some of the commoners also held muskets, but others totted pitchforks or other pieces of perilous farm implements. Noland also noticed several field tents were scattered about, where women in period dress dawdled about.

Dr. Morris turned into the lot and parked the VW. "We're here."

Before exiting the vehicle, Noland glanced out the windshield. "I do not recognize this tavern. I do remember passing a dark brown, board-sided building along our route, but this looks larger and much like a private dwelling. We never visited this tavern on our expeditions to or from Concord."

"Yes," Dr. Morris replied. "This is Hartwell Tavern, built in the early 1700s. After the original owner passed on, the place was sold, and it became a residential dwelling. I'm sure that much of this building has been added to or altered in the past two hundred years. This dwelling was purchased about ten years ago by the National Park Service, which plans to restore it to its original tavern appearance. That has not yet been done. Let's go and find Dr. Gorski." They exited the VW.

Dr. Morris and Noland wandered into the meadow where the reenactors were meeting. As the two meandered among the groups, Noland noticed that individuals and small clusters of persons would turn and look at him. As they moved through, a man spoke out. "The coat you're wearin' seem awfully warm. Looks like it's made of wool."

"Aye," answered Noland. "'Tis indeed warm. But one learns to tolerate it." He and Dr. Morris continued walking. Then Noland turned back to the man and asked, "We are in search of Dr. Gorski. Might you know where we might find him?"

The man pointed to a white tent with the Union Jack hoisted above it.

"Much obliged." Noland nodded. He and Dr. Morris headed toward the tent.

They found Dr. Gorski in the tent sitting at the head of a table, bent forward perusing some papers. Three other men were also seated next to the table, two on one side and one on the other. All were dressed in red coats adorned with buttons, facing, and medals signifying their rank. To Noland, they seemed disengaged, but they occasionally glanced at Gorski. They appeared to be waiting for a comment, information, or orders from the senior officer, who Noland assumed to be Dr. Gorski. The three looked up when Dr. Morris and Noland entered the tent.

"Ah, good." Gorski put down the paperwork. "You made it. Good to see you two. We're planning for the Fourth of July. It's going to be a major event. Hope to have representatives from the five military services in attendance. So, we've got to get things right. Pull up some chairs and make yourselves comfortable." He lifted his arm over the table and pointed to an individual sitting to his right. "Noland, you know my friend John. Jim Kirby is seated next to him and Patrick O'Connell is across from them. We have several other board members, but they were tied up today with work. One of them you and Dr. Morris have met, the owner of Holli's Seafood, Chef Hollister. He's, our cook." Gorski then stood and waited for Dr. Morris and Noland to seat themselves.

Dr. Gorski nodded at Noland. "Gentlemen, I'd like to introduce Sergeant Noland Black and Dr. Carol Morris. Sergeant Black has come to us from England, Newcastle upon Tyne…" he looked at Noland, "Is that correct?"

"Aye," Noland verified. "I am actually from Gateshead Village, which is across the river from Newcastle."

"Our other visitor is Dr. Carol Morris from the Mass. Medical Clinic in Charlestown. Sergeant Black is Dr. Morris's cousin. Came to Boston for a visit, had an encounter with some muggers, who absconded with his money, ID papers, and most of his clothes. John and I found him and took him to the clinic. His visit came as a total and happy surprise to Dr. Morris. She and Noland had met as very young children and have never seen each other since. It being Saturday and she being the only surgeon on duty, Dr. Morris had to put him back together…" he glanced at Noland, "We're pretty informal here; do you mind if I call you Noland?"

"Aye. 'Tis fine."

Gorski continued, "Noland wants to remain in the states, so Carol invited him to stay with her until he can establish himself in this country. I invited him to join our reenactors group. A previous drill sergeant, and now, honorably discharged from the British military and a student of early British military history and strategy. I'm sure the sergeant can provide us with information that will help improve our performances." Gorski amiably grinned at Dr. Morris.

She smiled back at him.

"Luckily, his uniform, which is an authentic eighteenth-century one, only got slightly damaged and was easily repaired." Gorski looked at Noland. "Am I correct with what I'm saying? And you would like to join us?"

Noland nodded but looked somewhat distressed. "In that encounter I had with those you called muggers, I lost all my funds. I am without money, and I feel bad having others support me." He glanced at Dr. Gorski. "You mentioned I might receive a stipend for the services I provide the reenactors. Is this possible?"

Dr. Gorski looked up and sighed. "That will have to be discussed with our board members. But I'm sure they will agree. In the meantime, we can take up a collection that will provide you with some cash until the board agrees or you find some other means of employment." He glanced at the other three. "What do you think?"

John nodded. Jim Kirby raised his arm and waved a thumb's up. Patrick O'Connell scrunched forward and reached for his wallet. "Yeah!" he uttered.

"Figured you'd all agree," Dr. Gorski said as he seated himself. He collected the paperwork into a neat pile and looked up. "Let's adjourn this meeting. We've got plenty of time to plan the events for the Fourth. I'd like to introduce Sergeant Black to the group that is here. Try to get them to contribute a buck or two to support the sergeant's immediate lack-of-cash plight."

Everyone but Dr. Gorski pushed away from the table, shuffled about, and stood. Patrick O'Connell extended his arm across the table toward Noland. Noland reached over to shake his hand. Patrick handed him a ten-dollar bill. John and Jim Kirby did likewise. But, when Dr. Gorski reached across the table to hand Noland a ten-dollar bill and insist that he accept it, Noland refused and handed the money already in his hand to Gorski.

"I am already greatly indebted to you and Dr. Morris," Noland replied. "You two have been my support since I arrived."

"Thank you, but I'll add my contribution to whatever may be added," Gorski said. "You'll never know I gave it to you."

As John, Patrick O'Connell, and Jim Kirby left the tent, Noland turned to Dr. Morris and handed her the two ten-dollar bills. "Please keep these for me," he said.

She nodded, took the money, and put it into her purse. The two stood and readied themselves to leave also.

Dr. Gorski pushed back in his chair and motioned to Noland and Dr. Morris. "Please stay a moment. I have something to tell you." He paused for a moment and took a breath. "My friend Josh in the State Department called earlier with some possible good news. He said that he had found a probable way that could provide Noland the identification papers he will need to become a certified United States immigrant. Josh explained that the process is a bit complicated to discuss over the phone, but the procedure does not require any verification from his homeland. Josh said he will be traveling to Boston next week for a meeting and would like to meet with us. Said he'd clarify what needs to be done. I told Josh we'd be happy to meet with him."

Momentarily astounded, Noland's body shook. He fisted his hands, strongly swung his arms up and down, and whooped, "Bloody incredible!" A huge grin lit his face and his body moved as if he were about to dance a jig. "How wonderful. I may be accepted, able to stay in this modern time."

Dr. Morris placed her hand across her mouth to stifle a shout of joy.

"Glad to see that this news makes you both happy," Dr. Gorski said with a grin. "But let us not get ahead of ourselves. The government works in mysterious ways. We'll cheer and party when Noland receives the city key to Charlestown. Now let's go outside, and I'll introduce you to some of the reenactors. Being a weekday, only about half of the group is present. In a few weeks, we'll hold a full-blown rehearsal for the Fourth of July presentation." He patted Noland on the back as they began to exit the tent. "Most of the fellows that are here are younger members and new to our group. Being a drill sergeant, you should feel comfortable with them. I too will have to get to know them."

Outside, Noland, Dr. Morris, Dr. Gorski, and his friend John ambled through the regiment of reenactors for about thirty minutes, introducing themselves and engaging in small talk. During this time, Noland seemed uncomfortable. He moved about as if bewildered, chewing on his lip and furrowing his brow.

"Is something bothering you?" Dr. Morris asked as Gorski excused himself to talk to four young men who appeared to be carelessly handling their muskets.

"Aye," Noland answered. "I do not know the importance of the Fourth of July. What is the significance of this date to the Revolutionary War for which this group is to portray? Secondly, Dr. Gorski's reenactors appear oblivious of their duties. They show no military discipline. Dr. Gorski is their leader. They do not treat him as an officer but as if they were of equal rank. I do not understand. This is supposed to be a military regiment, but it appears more of a frolic."

"They are not military," said Dr. Morris. "They are actors, but not in performance. When they do perform, these men will do everything that is expected of someone in the military: march in rank, address their superiors with respect, salute, fall in battle, feign death when shot, everything military. As for the Fourth of July, that is the date in 1776 when the fifty-six members of the Second Continental Congress signed the Declaration of Independence drafted by Thomas Jefferson. This declaration liberated the thirteen American colonies from Great Britain's rule. This date is celebrated with much pomp and circumstance throughout the United States. And, of course, Dr. Gorski's reenactors put on their great show. Ah, here comes Dr. Gorski. I'm sure he can explain more about the significance of the Fourth…."

Suddenly, as Dr. Gorski approached, a musket blasted, startling everyone. He wheeled around and looked back at the group he had just left. A cloud of white smoke rose above them and one of the members lay huddled on the ground, holding his face. His buddies twisted about in mixed confusion. "What in the hell happened?" Dr. Gorski shouted as he rushed back to the cluster.

Noland's mind created an image of his men falling in battle. He momentarily shuddered, but a quick shake of his head dissipated the disturbing vision. He and Dr. Morris hurried toward the group. When they reached the injured reenactor, they saw one of his buddies, named Norm, breathing deeply, trying to calm and pull himself together.

They heard him say, "Bobby brought his grandfather's antique musket and tried to fire it. It exploded!"

Dr. Gorski knelt next to Bobby. "Move your hands. Let me see your face."

Bobby did as he was asked.

"You have a facial burn," Dr. Gorski said as he held Bobby's chin and moved his head to the left. "Don't appear to have any shrapnel wounds. Pupils dilated. Flash pan exploded. Blew fragments to the right." He examined the boy's right arm. "Powder burn and might have some metal pieces above the wrist." Gorski gently lower the boy's arm, looked up and saw that John, Jim Kirby, and Patrick O'Connell had joined him and Dr. Morris and Noland. "Will a couple of you take this young man to the clinic? He needs some repairing." Dr. Gorski helped Bobby to stand.

"I have a van," O'Connell said. "We can use it."

Noland looked around and saw several of the other reenactors hurrying toward them; one was totting a stretcher. *No doubt that is the same one they carried me on to that screaming metal monster,* he thought.

The stretcher bearer, carrying the litter, laid it on the ground and unrolled it to accommodate the victim. "Please lie down on this," he said, "and we'll carry you to Mr. O'Connell's vehicle."

"I'll assist you guys," Jim Kirby said.

The bearers secured Bobby to the stretcher, lifted it, and followed Patrick O'Connell toward his vehicle. Jim Kirby and Gorski's friend John tailed behind the group.

Bobby's friends stood by, appearing concerned, confused, and helpless, while they watched from a distance as the litter was slid into the back of O'Connell's van.

"Gentlemen," Noland said as he joined Bobby's friends. "The weapon must have deteriorated, or too much powder was put in the flash pan. Whichever, both would cause an explosion." He looked at the muskets the three others held and noticed that they resembled the Brown Bess weapon his troops relied on. "I would like to demonstrate how such a musket is loaded and fired properly in battle. I do not think any of you would want another accident to occur."

"Excellent," Dr. Gorski said. "A demonstration should calm the air. And perhaps show how the British soldiers prided themselves in the speed that they could load and shoot. I believe a good marksman could load and shoot at least three rounds in a minute. Is this not correct, Sergeant Black?"

Noland nodded as he, Drs. Gorski and Morris engaged Bobby's friends.

"Gentlemen…" Dr. Gorski said as he took the lead and introduced Noland, "this is Sergeant Black, a grenadier from her majesty's Royal Army. He has come over to join us as a consultant. I've asked him to show you the way an eighteenth-century British soldier loaded a musket during the heat of a battle. It had to be done quickly to allow him to shoot a series of rapid shots." He looked at Noland. "Sergeant, the audience is yours."

Noland gritted his teeth and swallowed as he faced the three men. "I see that the muskets you hold are what appear to be the primary weapon a British foot soldier would have carried into battle. Do any of you know what the musket was called?"

"Brown Bess," one of the fellows alleged and another echoed.

"Aye, 'tis indeed. How it received its name, is unknown. The name really does not matter. What does matter is that the Brown Bess was the most advanced military weapon of its time. The weapon was in British service for over fifty years by the time Great Britain entered the American Revolution. An innovative flintlock or firing mechanism made it extremely effective in battle. Ammunition was standardized and the proper amount of powder for a single shot was packaged in a paper cartridge. This eliminated the need to carry separate containers of loose powder and shot. To load, all a soldier required was a single paper cartridge, containing powder, shot, and plug.

"The Bess's barrel has a bore of seven-tenths of an inch and takes a shot of six-ninths of an inch—all standard. For hand-to-hand combat, a bayonet could be attached in less than five seconds. The Brown Bess was a well-trained soldier's appendage; in a sense, he was married to his weapon and could…" Noland took a breath, "fire off three to four shots in a minute or less." Noland glanced to the side and extended his hand toward the musket one of the fellows held. "If you allow me, I shall demonstrate. May I borrow your weapon?"

The young reenactor handed his musket to Noland.

"Do any of you have paper cartridges?"

The same fellow who provided the musket reached into his pocket. When he pulled the hand out, he extended it toward Noland and unrolled his fingers. Four, two-and-a-half-inch-long, narrow paper packets fell onto the sergeant's open hand. Two others fell into the grass. "Excuse me, sir." The fellow moved forward and bent over to pick up the escapees. "Sorry."

"Aye. Leave them," Noland said as his fingers arranged the four cartridges in his right hand and closed it over them. "Now I will demonstrate loading and firing while in battle. Watch me carefully, for a soldier moves rapidly when being shot at."

The newcomers locked their eyes on the sergeant. While his left hand gripped the musket, they saw the thumb of his right hand dart under the fingers, shove a single packet upright against the index finger, and clamp down on it. Simultaneously, they observed the thumb on his left hand half cock the musket's hammer and raise the frizzen, the cover that provides access to the flash pan. The fellows then saw Noland snap the hand holding the cartridge to his mouth, bite off the packet's end, and spit out the piece.

Noland paused to explain as he raised the musket and held it horizontally. "With the paper cartridge open," he said, "pour about a third of the powder into the flash pan. Make sure it is directed toward the vent." He demonstrated. Then, using his left thumb, he flipped the frizzen closed and rotated the musket into a vertical position. "Make sure the frizzen is closed before you rotate your musket and set the stock on the ground," he cautioned. The sergeant's left hand maintained a grip on the musket's barrel and held it upward. "Now, pour the rest of the powder down the muzzle and stuff in the remains of the paper cartridge. Then use the ramrod, attached under the barrel, to give the shot a good strike so it seats in the breech. Remove the ramrod from the barrel and place it back in its holder under the barrel…"

"When do you load the shot?" one of the recruits naively interrupted.

"It is already in the barrel. Falls in with the powder." Noland finished the maneuver, and scanned the area down range. *Area clear.* He carefully raised the musket with the hand holding the extra cartridges and seated the weapon's stock against his shoulder. Concurrently, he used the left thumb to fully cock the hammer and placed his left hand under the barrel to balance the weapon; he aimed and fired.

Dr. Morris removed her fingers from her ears as Noland lowered the musket. "Forgot how loud a musket blast is."

The sergeant looked away from his students and grinned when he heard what Dr. Morris said. He also noticed that other reenactors had gathered around them.

Dr. Gorski chuckled. "Love your explanation. I believe you mentioned that a well-trained soldier could, if the enemy was in full charge, load and shoot many rounds accurately and in a hurry. Can you show us how that is done?"

While fingering the three paper cartridges he had left in his hand, Noland stood for a moment and then slowly nodded. "First let me say, soldiers in the Royal Army, when faced with imminent death or injury, remain calm, totally absorbed, and they do what is necessary. To them, distractive thoughts place them in danger. Their concentration on the action around them has to be complete." He raised the musket and walked away from the gathering. "I will need some targets," he called back. "I have three shots."

Two of the student reenactors each had empty soda bottles. They held them up and looked toward Gorski.

"Anyone else have an empty bottle?" Gorski asked. "We need one more." A reenactor standing nearby brought the doctor one.

"Thank you." Dr. Gorski walked to one of the students holding a bottle and handed it to him. The doctor swung his arm out toward a low hillock. "The bottles will be the targets. Set them below that hill. That's about forty paces from where Sergeant Black is standing. Separate them about two or three feet apart. Make sure they're visible and then, get back here."

The boys followed Gorski's orders and returned.

"Can you see the bottles?" the doctor called to Noland.

"Aye," the sergeant shouted and waved his right hand. He scoped the targets, then looked back at Gorski. "I am ready."

Using her finger, Dr. Morris again plugged her ears.

Dr. Gorski fidgeted and looked at the minute hand on his wristwatch. All the observers stood silent. They saw Sergeant Black shake himself, take a deep breath, raise the musket to a horizontal position, bite open the end of a paper cartridge, spit it out, and load the weapon. Then he mesmerized the crowd by quickly morphing into a frolic of loading, aiming, and firing. With each shot the reenactors heard the blast, saw fire eject from the barrel, and a bottle shatter. Within what seemed only a moment, all ended and a cloud of white smoke curled upward. Then all heard Dr. Gorski yell, "Forty-nine seconds!" as Noland relaxed and pointed the musket barrel toward the ground. He then turned and walked back to an applauding audience.

"My god, that was one hell of a demonstration," Gorski cried.

"Breathtaking," Dr. Morris complemented as she removed her fingers from her ears.

Several in the group shouted, "Huzza!"

"Thank you, all," Noland said as he joined the group. He then looked at the student reenactors, who stood awestruck. "To do what I did takes practice and concentration."

"Let's go to lunch," Dr. Morris said as she walked to Noland and put her arm around his waist. "Dr. Gorski, would you like to join us? We're going to Helen's in Concord."

"Yes, I'd enjoy that. But first, let me do a moment of supervising. Excuse me." Gorski strolled to a group of men.

Noland heard him say, "Be back after lunch to help dismantle today's event. If you need to leave, don't forget we're meeting Saturday."

Then one of the men asked, "Are you bringing Sergeant Black?"

Dr. Gorski glanced at Noland and answered, "Absolutely, if he wants to come."

"Let us take the Volkswagen," Dr. Morris said as she and Noland headed for her vehicle. "I've eaten at Helen's Restaurant several times. The food is good."

Dr. Gorski nodded and followed.

When they reached the VW and Gorski attempted to enter, he pushed the passenger seat forward and grunted several times as he finagled himself into the rear seat. Being of medium height and not overly robust, he was able to utilize the rear seat in the little vehicle. Outside, everyone heard Gorski sigh as he seated himself and stretched his legs across the width of the car. "I'm in," he shouted. "It's only about four miles to the restaurant. I'll survive. Get in! Let's go!" He grabbed the top of the passenger seat and pulled it back to the upright position, allowing Noland to enter. Dr. Morris slid into the driver's seat and started the engine.

Carol drove out of the parking lot and turned right onto North Great Road. Within less than a minute, she reached the intersection with Virginia Road. She stopped and was about to proceed onto Concord, but Gorski suggested that she turn right onto Virginia and follow it toward the village. "I would like to show Noland where we found him."

When they reached the curve where Virginia Road becomes Old Bedford Road, Gorski pointed and spoke, "Over there is the burial site of some British soldiers who were killed at this tight curve. This is Bloody Angle curve. No one is sure who the soldiers were, because there are no headstones or markers." He moved his arm up between the two front seats and pointed to the left. "Noland, we found you over there about fifty yards up this road, lying in a shallow depression."

Dr. Morris slowed as she drove around the Bloody Angle curve.

"On our return," Noland said, "I would like to stop, look at the site, and proclaim my condolences to the spirits above. I am sure several of those buried there were members of my regiment."

"We can, and shall, do that," Dr. Morris replied as she drove on, returned to North Great Road, and continued onto Concord. She turned onto Main Street in Concord and parked. She and Noland exited the VW and waited for Dr. Gorski to wiggle himself out.

Dr. Morris pointed. "Helen's Restaurant is across the street, located in the middle of that complex of buildings."

They crossed Main Street and entered the restaurant. The maître d' seated them at a table near the large, convex-shaped, paneled window that faced the street. She left menus and said, "Your waitress will bring water and take your order."

Noland scanned the dining room's modest early American theme. Dark wood paneling contrasted with the beige interior. A few paintings hung on the walls. A group of booths contained behind a low, white, wainscoted panel created an aisle that separated the booths from additional tables. Helen's Restaurant was about half full of patrons.

"I bet you've never had southern fried chicken?" Dr. Morris raised a menu for Noland to see. "This is a specially here."

"Jungle fowl," he replied, "from Asia. Only nobles enjoy chicken, as you call the bird. I have never eaten it. But I have been told that its meat is quite palatable."

"Amazing," Dr. Morris said. "I always thought the masses thrived on this fowl. It is so common. In fact, I believe the chicken and its eggs are considered one of the most staple foods in the world."

Noland looked up from the menu. "Peasants cannot afford to raise the jungle fowl as they do cows, pigs, and sheep. The birds require special grains to feed upon. While cows, pigs, and sheep can be left to graze on local vegetation, there is little cost to feed those animals."

"Well, times have changed," Carol said with a grin. "The costs for beef, pork, and lamb are less affordable for the masses. But not so for chickens. The jungle fowl, as you call them, are raised by the thousands for their eggs and meat. They are fed corn and other grains, which are produced in great abundance. I do believe you should give southern fried chicken a try."

"Aye," said Noland. "A new cookery. Why is it southern?"

"Because it is cooked by a procedure that was developed in the southern part of the United States in the last century. The bird is not baked but is cut into parts and covered in flour and spices, and deep fried in oil. Makes a very flavorful crisp coating on all the parts. I believe I'll also order that. Haven't had southern fried chicken since I was in Atlanta." Dr. Morris licked her lips, shifted about in the chair, and made herself comfortable. "And what are you having, Dr. Gorski?"

"A haddock burger," he answered. "I'm not a fan of chicken. Had too much of it when I was a kid. My mother served it in a thousand different ways."

The waitress arrived, carrying three glasses of water, and set them on the table. "Are you ready to order? Or will you need a few more minutes?" She stared at Noland, then glanced over to Dr. Gorski. "Love those red coats you guys are wearin', you havin' a reenactors' party?"

"Yes, we are," Gorski said and looked at the others at the table. "I'm ready to order. Need to return and help dismantle the tents and clean up the area. And, it'll take a few minutes to allow Noland to stop and view the site where we found him."

Dr. Morris ordered. "Southern fried chicken." She glanced across the table. "Noland, if you're having the same, you'll need a few more pieces." She saw Noland nod; she then looked at the waitress. "Why not bring us a plate with a couple of thighs, drumsticks, breasts, and wings. What sides come with the chicken?"

"French fries or mashed potatoes, and a vegetable," the waitress answered as she wrote down the order. "Your vegetable choices are listed below the entrées."

"I'll have French fries and broccoli. Noland, what are you having?"

The sergeant looked at the side selection of vegetable choices. He cocked his head in confusion. "I have never heard or eaten vegetables. They are unclean and not cooked. Cause indigestion and are not served in England. Beans and peas, sometimes, but they are cooked. Most on this list—I do not know what they are."

Dr. Morris grinned. "Noland, you've had tomatoes. Some call them a vegetable." She then glanced at the waitress. "Bring my friend a dish of onion rings. Also make up a small vegetable sampler dish. You know, broccoli, carrots, cauliflower, some pickled beets, a dilled pickle, cucumbers slices, peppers, celery…. You can forget tomatoes. He's eaten them before. Can you do that?"

"Yeah. A salad that's not a salad. Will that be all?" She shuffled around to Noland's side. "Where don't they serve vegetables?"

"In the Sahara," Gorski answered before Noland could. He lowered his eyelids and coughed. "Our friend here has just returned from a top-secret mission with the Foreign Legion."

"Wow! That's cool."

Impatiently, Gorski shook the menu. "I'll have a burger with everything on it and fries."

The waitress scribbled down Gorski's order and flipped the notepad closed, shoved the pencil behind her right ear, and scampered off toward the kitchen.

"Where did you come up with that story?" Dr. Morris asked.

A curious look crossed Noland's face, then it morphed to a grin.

"I couldn't have told her that our British time traveler just left the Revolutionary War." Dr. Gorski flipped his napkin open and laid it in his lap. "Had to tell her something. People seem to believe the preposterous rather than the truth, even though in this case, the truth is more outlandish. Let's change the subject." Dr. Gorski straightened against the back of his chair. "My friend John was to tally the contributions that were collected from the group when he returned from delivering the injured young man to the hospital." He looked at Noland. "Hopefully he's done that. The contributions will provide you with spending money. So, my friend Noland, you'll have a few bucks in your pocket."

The sergeant snapped up his head. "I do not feel it proper to accept a donation. You two have done so much for me. But I have no way to repay you for your kindness…"

"Whoa!" Dr. Gorski blared. "You have provided us with the most unusual experience that has ever happened to a human on this earth—you have appeared in our life from the past, from a time when our country was being born and at the beginning of its war for independence. I don't believe anyone has ever had such an experience. You owe us nothing. But you are an outlander. Hopefully, come Wednesday, that may change. When it does, you'll have the identification that is needed to function as a resident of the United States and a little spending money."

Noland sighed, placed his hands on the table, clasped them, and lowered his head. "To me, I feel that is not correct. When I become an American, I can gain employment. At that time, I will be able to return your kindness."

"That will be acceptable." Gorski moved the eating utensils to provide space for his meal. He looked up at the waitress, who had arrived.

Dr. Morris smiled at Noland and nodded.

The waitress placed a platter of chicken and a basket of onion rings on the table. She then set Gorski's hamburger and fries in front of him and glanced at Noland, then quickly turned and scampered back to the kitchen. "Almost forgot," she said when she returned and set a plate of assorted vegetables near Noland. "That's a bit of everything we had in the kitchen." She smiled and looked around the table, picked up the pitcher of water, and refilled everyone's glass. "Wow! It's sure neat to serve a member of the Foreign Legion. Can I get you anything else?" she said as she turned, readying to leave.

"Thank you. No." Dr. Morris scanned her meal, breathing in the appetizing aroma. "I believe we're all fine."

"I'll check back later." With an ear-to-ear grin, the waitress returned to the kitchen.

"We'll give her a good tip," Dr. Morris said. "She went out of her way. A good vegetable sampling platter. She even included some dipping sauces. They're in those little condiment bowls. Looks like French, Thousand Island, and ranch or sour cream and dill. I'll have to taste them. Enjoy, Noland." She positioned her dish in front of her, then, with a pair of tongs, took a couple of pieces of fried chicken and put them, along with a serving of French fries and several onion rings, onto the plate.

A curious grin crossed Noland's face. He picked up a carrot stick, dipped it into the orange-colored sauce, and bit off a piece. Chewed and nodded. He stuck the carrot into the whitish paste. Sampled it. Then tried the pinkish-colored dip. "My heavens, they are all good. I have never tasted such flavors." He licked his lips. Picked up a celery stick, stirred it into the white sauce, and stuck it into his mouth. He nodded and smiled. He continued to savor the various vegetables.

"Many people eat a salad, which is a mixture of leafy green vegetables decorated with a variety of other colorful ones, like tomatoes, carrots, peppers, olives, beets, and so forth," Dr. Morris clarified.

"Thank you," Noland said, "for explaining. I did not know what a salad was." He nipped off the end of a dill pickle. Immediately, he grimaced, his tongue shot out, and he wanted to spit, but flung the napkin to his mouth. "Vinegar! And too much salt. Not good."

"Drink some water." Dr. Morris pushed his water glass to him. "Not all vegetables are to our liking. Brussel sprouts and cooked asparaguses are not my favorites. But vegetables are an excellent source of nutrients," Dr. Morris explained. "And they are washed to rid them of dirt, sand, and any toxic products before they are eaten. So, you're not going to get indigestion. Now, dig into the chicken and tell me what you think."

Noland picked up a well-crusted drumstick and took a bite. He chewed for a moment, then paused. His eyes closed as he savored the flavors; then he swallowed. "I have tasted the food of aristocrats." He opened his eyes and took another bite.

Dr. Gorski chuckled. "Hate to disappoint you, Sergeant Black, but you've just savored the primary meat of the masses. Everyone—in the whole wide world—royalty, aristocrats, and peasants now, all eat chicken. It can be prepared in hundreds of different ways."

After enjoying several more bites of fried chicken, Noland pushed back from the table with a look of concern. "Aye, that is understandable. The chicken is extremely good." He glanced at Gorski and Morris. "It would be sad if I were not allowed to stay in America. Being here, in this time, is a delight."

"Well, I can't see how you can get back to your time," Gorski remarked. "A way to travel through time, as we have told you, has not been discovered. As far as staying in America, where else would you go? For now, let us enjoy our time together and cross the bridge to legal residency when we get to talk to my friend from the State Department. He'll be here Wednesday."

A smile crossed Noland's face. "Aye. I will try to contain my anxiety and concern." He finished off most of the vegetables and stripped the meat off the last drumstick on his plate.

Dr. Morris completed her meal. "You seem to like staying at my place, don't you?"

"Aye."

"Then you have little to concern you. I'm not going to throw you out. You can stay for as long as it takes to get you settled, and beyond if you like." Dr. Morris looked up and scanned the table. "Dr. Gorski needs to return to his reenactor group and you, Noland, want to visit the place that was once Wright's Tavern. I believe you said you had lunch there several days ago. Is there anything else we need to discuss?"

Noland raised his napkin and wiped his lips. "Thank you, Dr. Morris. I too, have a fondness for you and our relationship, and would like to show my gratitude. But I have no way to do so."

"But you do," Gorski piped up. "Remember? I told you that our company donated you some spending money. You can take Dr. Morris out to dinner this evening."

Noland's body tensed and his face reddened. "I am beholden to the two of you, but not to the reenactors, though they are a kind group. My ethics do not allow me to accept a gift for something I have not earned."

Dr. Gorski nodded. "You are a man of morals. But in this case, you did provide a service. You showed the men how to load and fire a musket. And you demonstrated that such a weapon can be fired rapidly by a well-trained soldier. The money the group provided is pay for your service. It is what you earned. When we return to our event site, I will pay you what you have made."

"Very well." Noland relaxed and placed his hands on the table. His fingers fidgeted. "I will accept my pay. But I would like to show my appreciation this evening to you both with a grand feast of excellent food and wine." He scratched his ear. With a quizzical expression, he continued. "I know of no pub that offers fine cookery."

"The evening will be for you and Dr. Morris," Dr. Gorski said as he folded his napkin and laid it over his plate. "I appreciate your invitation but will not be able to join you. I need to be in New York City tomorrow to meet with some colleagues from Bellevue Hospital. Seems there is going to be an opening in their primary care services clinic this fall. And they want me to consider it. I'll be back Saturday in time for our reenactor Fourth of July rehearsal. Dr. Morris and you can have a fine evening. I feel that there is a more lasting relationship brewing between you two. Anyway, Dr. Morris knows the city well and can suggest a nice, quiet, plush restaurant." Gorski raised his arm to attract the waitress.

Dr. Morris softly laid her hand atop Noland's. "We'll have a wonderful date," she whispered. "It will be a wonderful evening. And, tomorrow, we will continue to get to know each other better."

The waitress took Dr. Gorski's credit card and returned with the bill. After signing it, Gorski rose from his seat, pushed back the chair, and started toward the door. Dr. Morris took Noland's hand and the two followed.

Outside, Dr. Gorski started to head for Dr. Morris's vehicle.

"Wait!" Dr. Morris said. "Noland wanted to see Wright's Tavern. It's only about a hundred feet up the block. It's that old brownish-red clapboard building on the corner. It'll only take a few minutes. No need to go inside. All is changed. Though the building is a registered National Historic Site, it is no longer a tavern. Its exterior, except for a side addition, has been maintained. The building now houses the offices and meeting rooms of the First Parish Church of Concord. The actual old church is behind it on the right. I believe they handle their outreach and educational programs in the old tavern. Anyway, let's take a gander around to the front and let Noland get a look at it."

Gorski sighed and nodded. "Okay, let's do it."

Noland and Dr. Morris strolled down the block to the front of the old tavern. She looked at the façade and then glanced at the sergeant. "So, this is where you brought your regiment to get a meal?"

"Aye." Noland felt uneasy as he scanned the building. He envisioned his men milling about, which in his time occurred only a few days before. He shook his head and sighed. "It is difficult for me to stand here where I did two hundred years ago. Except for that small addition to the right, the tavern appears not to have changed, though recently painted. I would expect at any moment my men exiting and relaxing in this yard. And Mr. Amos Wright, with his soiled apron hanging down his front, standing in the doorway wishing us a safe march back to Charlestown." Noland wiped his forefingers across his eyes. "If only I had heeded his words of the minutemen visit, bloodshed might have been avoided."

Dr. Morris placed her hand atop a metal sign. "This historical marker indicates that Concord's Minutemen visited this tavern before your troops came to refresh themselves and left when they heard the courthouse bell being rung. Did you know that the ringing of the bell was a signal that the British troops were approaching?"

"Aye. No one heard the bell. Noise of the march," Noland grunted. "Word must have reached Concord that colonials were killed in Lexington. No doubt a messenger on a fast horse. Boston Road is not the only route to Concord." Noland scratched his head. "Or there is a spy among our ranks."

"Probably a messenger from Lexington," Dr. Morris said. "But Mr. Wright knew that the minutemen were in the tavern earlier. Did he not mention that they were there?"

"Nay. He just wished us a safe trip back to our barracks." Noland fisted his hands. "But now I know. Wright knew of the coming attacks. His words were a covert, a placation to keep us off guard. Had I known what lay ahead, I would have placed my men on alert." He took a deep breath. "We walked into a massacre."

Dr. Morris saw Noland's face flush in anger. "I'm sorry," she said as she took hold of the sergeant's arm. "Anger brings on terrible events. There is little you can do about it now. It's all history. Let's go back to the car. I believe we've seen enough. I don't want our day to be ruined. I'm looking forward to our evening together. I haven't been on a date for a long time." She caught Dr. Gorski's attention and signaled him that she and Noland were returning to the VW.

Dr. Morris turned off Lexington Road onto Old Bedford Road to take her, Noland, and Gorski back to the Hartwell Tavern reenactment site. In a short distance she came to where the road bent right and became Virginia Road.

"Stop here. Pull off to the side," Dr. Gorski ordered from the backseat. He pointed to the left across the road toward the meadow at the edge of a thin forest. "Noland, this is where we found you last Saturday. You asked to see the site."

"Aye, that I did."

Dr. Morris pulled off the asphalt onto the narrow gravel apron and stopped. Noland scrambled out the passenger door, tripped, and fell against a rock fence. A twinge of anxiety squeezed his stomach when an image of a woman dressed in unusual clothing holding a bicycle appeared. He shivered. The image vanished.

Dr. Gorski pushed the passenger seat forward, wiggled out of the back of the VW, and stumbled into a growth of briers. He pulled himself free and grabbed Noland's arm. "You okay, my friend?"

Noland nodded, then looked up as he heard the whining roar of a low-flying 727 airliner, passing over their heads.

"We must be under the approach into Logan," Gorski said.

"Aye, an amazing machine." Noland continued to watch as the airplane descended eastward. "Perhaps, one day I will travel to England aboard such a craft."

"For sure, my friend. I am certain that very soon you will have the necessary identification." Gorski tightened his grip on Noland's arm and urged him to move across the road.

Dr. Morris exited the car with poise, crossed the road, and stood, gazing at the freshly cut meadow. "What's taking you guys so long?"

"Airplanes heading into Boston," Gorski said as he and Noland walked up next to her.

They scanned the area from the edge of the road. Noland turned and looked back at the remnants of the rock wall. He visualized his men hunkered down behind it. The reminiscence conjured images of them lying on their backs, loading their muskets, then twisting over and crouching just above the edge of the wall, and firing at unseen targets. He shook the hallucination from his mind.

Dr. Morris put her hand on Noland's shoulder. "You, okay?"

Noland nodded and looked around.

Carol pointed to her left toward the bend where Old Bedford Road became Virginia Road. "In that meadow across the way that Dr. Gorski pointed out earlier, about twenty or so British soldiers, who were killed here at the Bloody Angle battle, are buried. If there were any grave markers, they didn't survive. But evidence of their burial was found, and the area is marked as a British cemetery."

Noland looked toward the cemetery where some of the men in his regiment might be interred. He sighed and lowered his head. After a moment he looked up and scanned to the right. "Where is Dr. Gorski?"

But before Dr. Morris could answer, Noland saw Dr. Gorski across the way, standing on a dark green mat of early growth sedges. "This is the depression where we found you," Gorski yelled. "Seems water from rain and melting snow collects here. It supports the growth of these aquatic grasses where I'm standing." He tromped around the basin. "It's dry now. Haven't had any rain lately. But Noland, your uniform was wet and stained with mud when we rescued you. So, this ditch was wet when you fell into it."

Noland observed as Gorski moved about. The doctor stopped. Bent down, appeared to search through some clumps of vegetation, then he picked something up. Noland watched him straighten, wipe what he discovered against his pant leg, and start to return to where he and Dr. Morris stood. Gorski removed a handkerchief from his pocket, wrapped the cloth around the item, and rubbed it between his fingers.

Gorski's boots crunched as he strolled up to the road. "Noland, I believe I may have found what you lost," he said as he approached. He lifted the object to his lips, blew off some of the remaining grains of dirt, and held it up for all to see.

Noland raised his right hand. Unconsciously his fingers massaged the skin on his neck. He squinted as he glared at Gorski. A twinge tightened his stomach. He took a deep breath, exhaled, and started toward Dr. Gorski. But Dr. Morris had moved ahead and was already standing next to her colleague.

"My god…" she cried, "it's the Celtic cross!" She grabbed the cross from between Dr. Gorski's fingers, then turned and faced Noland.

"It's the Celtic cross, Noland! Your protective medallion! What you've been looking for! Dr. Gorski found it!" She rotated the pendant. Held it in front of her. "It's a beautiful keepsake. I'm so glad it's found." Dr. Morris held the cross out for Noland to take.

When Noland touched the cross, his fingers seemed to become attached to it. Suddenly his body felt weightless. He looked down at the medallion. It began to glow. He glanced at Dr. Morris and saw her eyelids expand; her mouth opened as if she were trying to scream. Yet he heard nothing. She flung her arms out toward him and tried to grab him, but he felt nothing. Then Dr. Gorski appeared next to her. To Noland both seemed totally crazed.

"What the hell's happening!" Dr. Morris shrieked. "He's become an image of bouncing particles." She dropped onto her knees and exhaled a terrifying cry.

Swiftly the particles spun into a dust-devil-like spiral and vanished. Overhead, the roar of another airplane broke the eerie silence.

"What the hell happened!" Dr. Morris screamed. "Where is Noland?" Her hand clasped her face. She fell on her knees and lowered her head.

Dr. Gorski took a breath and exhaled loudly. He attempted to compose himself, put his hands on Dr. Morris's shoulders, and bent down nearer her. "I believe he's returned to his time," he mumbled.

CHAPTER 15

Thursday, April 24, 1975

Drs. Morris and Gorski returned to the reenactment site. While in the VW, neither spoke. Carol rode with her head depressed, but periodically raised it and stared empty-eyed out the front windshield. During the short trip, Gorski glanced at her and noticed tears and a blank expression on her face. He slowly maneuvered the little car into the parking lot.

Immediately, Dr. Morris exited. She slammed the door and fell back against it. She clasped her hands over her face and lowered her head. After a moment, she audibly exhaled, straightened, turned, and looked over the vehicle's roof at Gorski. "Thank you for driving. I could not have done it," she stuttered and sighed. "What in the hell did we just witness?"

"I'm not sure," Dr. Gorski answered. He faced Dr. Morris and rested his hands on the vehicle's roof. "It appeared that the time portal, if there is such a thing, was active or activated. And, Noland stepped into it. Hopefully, as I mentioned, he may have been sent back to his time."

"That Celtic cross!" The middle of Dr. Morris's brow furrowed; her fists clenched. "As soon as I handed that cross to him, he dissolved before my eyes." She thumped her fist on the VW's roof. "That cross must have caused him to vanish. If I didn't give that damned object to him, he might still be here." With her head lowered, she walked around to the front of the car and stood, staring in the direction of Bloody Angle curve.

Dr. Gorski watched her. He saw Dr. Morris spread her hands open and place them against her midriff. It appeared she felt sick. Trying to distract and comfort her, Gorski spoke softly, "What happened to Noland is a mystery. We'll probably never know what caused him to come to the twentieth century or what ended his visit. Just because time portals are predicted by a bunch of theories, do they really exist? No one knows. But maybe they do. Perhaps one day someone will prove that they are real and do exist." He walked to Carol and put his arms around her. "Don't feel guilty. You didn't do anything. Giving Noland his cross was a natural move."

Carol laid her head against Gorski's shoulder. He could feel her tremble. "I thought I found someone really special, different," she mumbled. "I'm not going to lie. I was fascinated by him. A fascination that developed into affection between us. Really wanted to get to know him better."

Dr. Gorski held her and let her cry. "Your relationship had become obvious to me at Helen's Restaurant."

Dr. Morris pulled herself away from Gorski and took a couple of deep breaths. "A romantic relationship is difficult to hide," she said, removing a handkerchief from a pocket and wiped her eyes. "Thank you for comforting me. You are a good friend." She shook herself, sighed, and turned to look in the direction of the remaining reenactors some distance away. "I don't know what I'm going to do with myself." Rubbing her hands down her sides, she straightened. "Let's return to the group. There will be some explaining to do."

The two walked together, but separately, toward some of the costumed individuals scurrying about dismantling the reenactment site.

Dr. Gorski, trying to reduce the tension of their situation, broke the silence between them. "Too bad the Park Service won't let us leave things together for a couple of days. Sure would save us some time on Saturday. Guess they don't want to be held liable for any vandalism." He shrugged.

"I should have never let myself become infatuated with Noland," Carol said. "It was silly of me. I should have known. It's usually the patient that develops a foolish love association with their caregiver. A doctor should not do so."

As they approached a group of men, someone yelled, "Thank God, you finally returned. I have some curious information that you might want to hear."

Gorski quickly piped up with a chuckle. "Okay, John, did someone steal the money that was donated?"

"Nah! Where's Noland?"

"In a moment," replied Gorski. "Long story. What did you want to tell us, John?"

"After we dropped off the kid who was injured by that exploding musket, I returned to my office. Saw my answering machine blinking. The message was from a librarian I asked to get me some information on ship movements in Boston Harbor around the time of the Battle of Concord and Lexington and after. She found some interesting stuff. So, I went by her office and picked it up." John stepped back and tilted his head slightly to the side. His eyes locked onto the two doctors in front of him. He could see from the expression on Dr. Morris's face that she was troubled. He asked again, "Where is Noland?"

"He's no longer with us," Dr. Morris blubbered.

"What did you find out?" Dr. Gorski grunted.

John, the only other person who knew Noland came from the past, straightened and exhaled. "I'm not surprised Noland didn't return with you two. Had he, he would have missed the boat." John reached into his pocket, brought out a folded piece of paper, and began to open it.

"What do you mean, he would have missed the boat?" Dr. Morris pursed her lips and glared at John.

"The librarian found that in the early 1700s the *Boston Gazette* published manifests and sailing information of ships entering and leaving the harbor. She gave me copies of these lists published in 1775. I scanned them all and the manifest from one vessel caught my eye. The HMS *Avalon*, a British frigate, sailed from Boston Harbor on April the twenty-seventh bound for England. Besides some varied cargo, the vessel also was transporting the soldiers who were seriously injured in the attack that occurred on their return to Boston from that battle." John sighed. "Sergeant Noland Black's name was on the list. So, if that vessel made it to England, Noland returned to his homeland."

Dr. Morris sniffled and pursed her lips. "Well, that information is somewhat comforting. At least we know that Noland returned to his century, but we don't know if that ship ever got to England. Also, I didn't realize he was seriously injured."

"Well, if Noland had told his superiors," Dr. Gorski commented, "where he had been, what he saw and experienced, and especially, if he said that Great Britain would lose the war against the colonial rebels, they wouldn't believe him. They'd consider his assertions preposterous. Remember, we're speaking of the eighteenth century. To us their mores are considered primitive. There was no modern medicine. And, medically, very little was known about how the mind works. A brain injury in that time was essentially a person's dead-end. A doctor's diagnosis then would be that the sergeant sustained a brain injury and would no longer be suitable for military service. So, he was sent home to be discharged.

"Oh, that's sad," Dr. Morris cried. "Noland is an intelligent man. He's not crazy. His head was grazed by a bullet, but the injury was superficial." Her hands fisted. "At least we know he was put on a ship for England. But we still don't know if he ever got there." She glanced toward the sky. "I'm going to miss him. If I ever get to England, I'm going to see if I can find anything about Noland's life."

CHAPTER 16

Monday, April 24, 1775

Sergeant Noland Black sat with his head lowered and forehead clasped in his right hand. Obliviously, he gripped the Celtic cross he held in his left hand. Though a slight breeze wafted, it produced in him no sensation. He heard no sound until the raucous call of a blue jay followed by a series of chickadees chirping caught his attention. Noland lowered his hand and raised his head. A cold wetness penetrated his clothing and chilled his body. He momentarily shivered, then opened his eyes and tried to scan his surroundings. But a fleeting blur screened his vision, and he felt the edges of the Celtic cross pressing into his palm. Unconsciously, he opened his hand and pushed it into a pants pocket, releasing the cross. Shaking his head, he rubbed his eyes. They focused on several purple skunk cabbage flowers. His mind questioned. *Where is the carpet of short, young sedges?* He raised his knees and placed his hands flat on the ground. Cold wet mud oozed between his fingers. Pushing down, he rose to a standing position. Instinctively, he wiped the muck from his hands onto his pants and coat.

Sergeant Black took a deep breath and glanced at the land that encircled him. Instead of seeing a manicured parkland behind where Dr. Gorski stood moments ago, there now spread a deep mixture of flowering weeds that extended to a dense mature forest. He turned and looked toward where he and Dr. Morris had stood. Instead of asphalt, the roadway was now covered with gravel scoured by wooden carriage wheels and horses' hooves. Beyond stood the rock wall, the one he had fallen against when he exited the VW. Only now, the stones appeared fresh and devoid of briars and other vines. Instead, a mixed bed of white and blue flowers grew along its base. Behind the wall rose a field of boulders interspersed with mature trees.

His body shook. "What the bloody hell just happened?" he shouted.

Though his vision oscillated between being blurry and moments of clarity, he stepped forward and staggered to the road. Anxiety and caution trembled his gut. He scanned the boulder-strewn forest. His mind raced with warning. *Rebels hiding.* A hurried attempt to move forward caused Noland to stumble and fall to his knees. *Need a walking stick.* Looking up toward the rock wall, he saw that if he hurried, he could be protected from any potential musket shots by the trunk of a massive oak tree. He scuffled toward it. Several fallen limbs were scattered near the oak. One lay propped against the wall. When the sergeant reached the rock wall, he sat down beside the fallen limb with his back concealed by the trunk of the tree.

He sat, breathing deeply and rubbing his eyes. After a few moments he glanced at the limb. It was about fifteen feet long with a diameter tapering from about three-quarters of an inch to three inches at its broken end. *That center portion would make a good walking stick,* he rationalized. Grabbing the bough and still protected by the massive tree trunk, he stood, pulled the limb over the wall, and swung it around toward the road. Lifting the branch, he pushed the thin, tapered portion over the rock wall until the limb's diameter reached about an inch. Then placing it against the sharp edge of a rock, he broke the thin upper end off. Drawing the branch back over the rock's cutting edge for about six feet, he bashed it against the sharp edge. After several thwacks, the bottom end of the limb broke away. "Aha, I have a walking stick."

Gripping the walking stick, he moved onto the road, pushed himself erect, looked up at the sun, and set his heading eastward. Though the walking stick helped maintain his balance, his knees and thighs felt weak. He continued to stagger for about twenty yards. By then he began to feel more in control of his body. He took several breaths, glared forward, and forged ahead in a controlled, steady stride.

Suddenly he heard a continuous crunching of gravel and the snort of a horse behind him. He grabbed the walking stick in both hands, raised it to chest level, and felt several painful stings in his right shoulder. *Damn musket wounds still sensitive. Thought they had healed.* Nevertheless, he whirled around. Using the walking stick as a barrier or weapon, his arms shot forward. Tense and alert, his body readied for battle, he could almost feel the hot breath of the horse. The horse and wagon were about twenty feet away and approaching slowly.

"Whooa, nag," Noland heard the driver command.

"Sorry for surprisin' you," the driver yelled in a slow drawl. "You look like a leftover from the battle a day or so ago. Gonna be a long, dangerous stroll if'n you're on your way to Charlestown. You seem a bit tattered, but movin' along smartly."

"Aye, the battle," Noland responded. "What day is today?"

"Monday the twenty-fourth of April." The driver remained calm and seated in the wagon. "If you're a headin' for Charlestown, as I said, it is a long and dangerous jaunt. Would not mind the company, since I'm a headin' to Charlestown…."

Noland stared at the driver. *My god, I am back in my time, talking with a rebel.* He held his stance and the walking stick at the ready.

"If'n you decide," the driver continued, "you need to remove that red coat. Makes the folks about, angry. And there's snipers. Don't need them shootin' at me." He reached behind himself and pulled a weathered jacket from under the seat. "Wear this an' there be no questions."

"I will ride with you," Noland said with caution. "But I am keeping my walking stick." Lowering the stick and releasing his left hand, the sergeant walked to the side of the wagon, laid the walking stick against the seat, removed his red coat, and climbed aboard. He shoved the coat under the seat and covered it with straw that lay in the bed of the wagon. He then put on the weathered jacket. Its aroma of mud and manure made him gasp.

The wagon driver snapped the reins and shouted, "Move on." The horse jerked the wagon into motion.

Noland's senses acclimated to the odors of grass, trees, clean air, and a twinge of manure as the two rode silently for a time; *those smells are not part of the twentieth century*, he thought. His eyes widened and locked onto Hartwell Tavern as they passed it by. He recognized the building, sans the gravel parking lot. "Hartwell Tavern. I have been by this tavern several times, but never in it," he reminisced.

"Ni-der have I," answered the driver. "It is not close to Concord. Friends and I raise our pints at Wright's Tavern. Breakfasted there this past Wednesday, 'fore your troops arrived."

"Aye. Amos Wright is a proper host." Noland squirmed in his seat. "Fed my men well when we stopped there before returning to our barracks." Feeling uneasy, the sergeant tightened his clasp on the walking stick. "You a member of those minutemen that attacked us?"

"Supporter," the driver answered. "My farm takes most my time. Too dangerous to get involved. But, Wednesday, when I joined my friends at Wright's, we was asked to hassle some British at North Bridge. There was about a dozen of us. Got to the bridge early. When the British troops arrived, there were too many. And they shot with more accuracy. We scampered when two of our men got shot. Heard that a larger militia force came later and did more damage."

"So, you were not involved in the Bloody Angle massacre?"

"Nay!" The driver straightened and slapped the reins harder across the back of the horse.

Apprehension tensed Noland. He gripped the walking stick tighter and clenched his left fist.

"Heard the British took a real beating o'er there."

The sergeant nodded. "Aye, we did. Got myself shot in the back and head. Lost consciousness. Do not know how many men I lost."

"Sorry to hear you and your men was injured," the driver said. "Not what I wanted. The forces of Great Britain are strong. I am afraid that what happened Wednesday will throw us colonials into a war, a war we have not a chance of winning. Most of us came to this new land to live our lives in independence and peace. I do not believe it is going to turn out that way."

Noland relaxed. "Aye. That is a noble desire. Do not lose it." He scrunched forward on the seat and lowered his head into his hands. "If only you knew," he whispered. "I believe Great Britain has met its match." He looked at the driver. "How long did the battle at Bloody Angle last?"

"I was told that within a matter of two or three hours the British reinforcements arrived." The driver scanned the fields and forests ahead. "Though I believe the colonials had many men, I don't believe they were ready for a major encounter. The militia and minutemen ran away, returned to their homes and towns."

The two rode in silence as the trip continued. East of Lexington they were stopped by several men on horses. The leader of the horsemen recognized the driver and asked him what was taking him so far from his farm. The driver explained that he and his helper were traveling to Cambridge to obtain some bags of grain and farming supplies. Since the leader had never seen Noland before, he seemed a bit suspicious. The driver clarified by introducing Noland as Grady, his wife's nephew, who was a sailor and lived near Falmouth in the far eastern portion of the Massachusetts Colony. The driver told the leader that Grady wanted to give up the sea and come and live with him and his wife. Satisfied, the leader nodded, and he and his men rode off.

"Did you know someone named Grady?" Noland asked the driver.

"Aye, I did," the driver said. "My best friend, when I was a youngster many years ago. He enjoyed the sea and wanted to enlist in the

Royal Navy. In Boston he was successful and sailed away. I never heard from him again."

Silence returned between the two men as they continued on toward Charlestown. Noland sat back and shoved his hands into his pants pockets. His left fingers touched the Celtic cross and removed it from the pocket. Noland glared at the talisman as his fingers softly stroked it. Suddenly the wagon lurched, and Noland gripped the bottom edge of the seat. The Celtic cross fell out of his hand. He looked down. It lay under the seat, stuck between the floorboards. Bending forward, he picked it up, straightened, and scanned the meadows and fields as the sun lowered toward the western horizon. Unconsciously he fondled the amulet. His thoughts turned to Carol, Dr. Gorski, and the twentieth century. He shoved the cross back into his pocket.

"Should arrive at your barracks 'bout sunset," the driver said. "Passed the five-mile marker a short time ago. Guess we have 'bout another hour's travel."

Noland, oblivious to the driver's remark, gazed at the wildness that they were passing through. In disbelief at the scene that surrounded him, he shook his head. Forlornness began to cloud his mind and upset his innards. He closed his eyes. *Earlier today, Carol and I traveled to Hartwell Tavern, there was no wild. She lived somewhere near here. There are no houses, buildings, markets, people, motor vehicles, crossroads; wildness is all around. Two hundred years have yet to come.* He sighed, opened his eyes, and glared at the meadows and trees. In the distance he saw several buildings. The slow, rhythmic clomp of the horse's hooves and crunch of wagon wheels increased his sadness, especially when he began to think about his feelings for Dr. Morris. *There was no opportunity to say goodbye. Will I ever see Carol again? What does she feel?* His melancholy and sense of loss deepened. *This war no longer excites me. The colonials will be victorious and create a new world.* He shoved his hand into his pockets. His fingers caressed the Celtic cross. *Perhaps there is a way I can return to the future.*

"O'er yonder…" the driver said and pointed toward a hill on the horizon, "is Bunker Hill. Heard that men of the Massachusetts militia started fortifying that hill, since they learned that you Redcoats attacked Concord and Lexington. Heard that a major general from Connecticut was put in charge. Name's Putnam. Some men of the Connecticut militia followed him."

"My god." Noland grunted. "News sure travels fast…" He shook his head. *And telephones do not exist.*

"Aye, it does." The driver snapped the reins to urge the horse to trot a little faster. "Rider on a fast horse can cover the distance from Lexington to Charlestown in about an hour or two."

The farmer's remark pulled Noland out of his depression. He looked toward Bunker Hill and noted the absence of human structures. He remembered seeing the memorial obelisk with Dr. Morris, reading the newspaper clipping that hung in the Warren Tavern, and gazing at the statue in the memorial lodge of the only American officer lost in the battle. "Know that hill. In the near future the British are going to attack it, Breed's Hill, and burn Charlestown," Noland mumbled. "They are going to win but lose many men."

"How'd you know that?"

"You would not believe me if I told you." Noland squirmed.

"You a warlock or something?"

"Nay." Noland mulled over what he had just told the farmer. *Of course, he questions me. Though I am a British soldier, but not an officer, I should not be aware of military plans for the future.* "Common sense, think not?" Noland continued. "The British army and navy, the mightiest military on this earth, will not tolerate a rebel fortification on a nearby hillside. They will destroy it."

The driver nodded. "Aye," he grunted and, with a disdainful expression, snapped the reins again. "Your barracks is near Ferry Hill; not far from where the road turns toward Cambridge. We can part there; be 'bout a half-mile walk to your barracks from there."

Noland pushed his hand into his pocket and felt the two shillings. He removed them, touched the driver's shoulder, and handed the coins to him. "A small gratitude for your courtesy and trouble. Many thanks."

The driver remained stern-faced, nodded, and accepted the shillings. "Take care of yourself. Do not wear your red coat. Snipers. Keep the jacket I gave you." The farmer tightened the reins. "God be with you."

At the junction in the road, the driver halted. Noland reached behind himself, grabbed the red coat, turned it so the inside dark lining would be visible, and pulled it across his lap. He then rolled it into a bundle, took hold of his walking stick, and climbed off the wagon.

An ancestor of future Americans, if that rebel survives the American revolution, Noland thought as he watched the horse and wagon disappear around a forested bend. He turned and gazed up the road. It ascended for about fifty yards. He pushed the medallion deep into his coat pocket and, using the walking stick, trudged up the low hill.

At the top he paused. The confluence of the Mystic River and Charles River lay to the northeast. The dwindling sunlight highlighted the crowded skyline of Boston across the Charles River. Noland noticed his landmark, the white steeple of the North Church. It glowed orange. Two British frigates were anchored offshore. Beach vegetation progressed to a sand-and-rubble shoreline. Some piers jutted into the Charles River on his right. Charlestown Point projected seaward on the left. *The Americans will build their navy yard along that shore where their mighty frigates will float at peace.* He shook off the reminiscence and looked inland to his left. His barracks lay in the shallow valley between where he stood and Bunker Hill.

Pushing the walking stick against the ground he started to descend on the gravel road that led to the British garrison. The Union Jack fluttered at half-mast. Anxiety tensed Noland's insides when he noticed something unusual. Though the gate into the compound was open, only two sentries patrolled the camp's grounds. There usually were six or more, at least one at each compass point and two on patrol. And, except for the solitary soldier standing near the privy, the parade ground seemed unoccupied. "Snipers," he grunted. Nervously, he scanned the area. *Not much cover. Only a few low clumps of bushes.* Shoving his bundled red coat under his left arm and tightening his grip on the walking stick, he continued toward the gate.

Upon reaching the entrance, he was confronted by the guards. Both pointed their muskets at his chest.

"Sergeant Noland Black, Grenadier, Tenth Regiment," Noland stammered.

The sentries examined the jacket Noland was wearing. "Where have you come from?" The taller one, a corporal, said as he glared at Noland with a furrowed brow and narrowed eyes.

"Concord! The massacre."

"That was five days ago. Did you walk?" The corporal glared at Noland's face and the clothes he wore. "Clean shaven. Pants wrinkled, a bit muddy, but mostly pressed. No blood. No damage. And, that shirt you are trying to cover with that dirty jacket…" he shook his head, "unusual. Never have seen such a shirt. Not regulation."

Noland chewed his lower lip. *It is true. I do not look as if I were in a battle. I cannot tell this fellow because he will not understand.* Unbundling and exposing the red coat, he laid it over his arm. "This is regulation. I was brought to the crossroad beyond the hill in a wagon. The farmer who drove lent me his jacket."

"A rebel farmer, no doubt." The two sentries pointed their muskets toward Noland. "You had no encounters with rebels or snipers along your journey? Seems a long way through enemy territory without incident." The corporal momentarily backed off, paused his interrogation, and seemed to ponder Noland's answers. Then he stepped forward and pushed the musket barrel to within inches of the sergeant's chest. "You, dear sir, are probably a spy!"

"The farmer and I did meet some horsemen, but the farmer explained my presence. Told them I was a visiting relative." Noland took a breath and expanded his chest. "No, I am not a spy. I cannot tell you where I have been or what I have experienced. You would not believe me."

"Let us take him to Colonel Smith," the corporal said. "He will know what to do."

The smaller sentry held his position and kept his musket aimed at Noland. The corporal swung his musket barrel toward the barracks. "Move ahead. Keep your arms up," he ordered.

"I would like to put on my uniform coat," Noland said, while he removed the farmer's jacket and tossed it onto a nearby post. He paused, donned the red garment, and raised his arms. He followed the corporal through the barracks door. The interior was dim and had a putrid stench. He paused. His eyes accommodated and focused on about a dozen men lying in the bunks. Several had their heads bandaged, one had a binding over his eyes, and others had dressings wrapped on shoulders, arms, or legs. Those who could, glared in his direction.

The corporal poked his musket barrel into Noland's side to nudge him ahead.

"I assume these men were injured on the march back?" Noland asked as he started to walk down the aisle between the bunks.

"Aye," the corporal grunted. "They're waiting to be ferried to Boston." He prodded Noland. "The lieutenant colonel's quarters are at the end."

Noland gauged his steps as he moved past the injured soldiers, scrutinizing each man, hoping to recognize someone from his regiment. One individual, with a bandage covering the left side of his face and having an exposed, bandaged stub of a left leg, grunted. He attempted to raise his right arm, but Noland had already passed his bunk without noticing him.

The small sentry knocked the end of his musket barrel against the lieutenant colonel's door.

"Enter!"

The three strode into Smith's office as he watched from behind his desk. His eyebrows lifted and his cheek muscles tightened.

The corporal snapped to attention. "Stopped this man at the gate, sir!" he announced. The barrel of his musket stared at Noland's back. "Believe he is a rebel spy, impersonating a British sergeant, sir!"

"Aha! Sergeant Noland Black," Smith asserted with a huff. "You have returned." He pushed back against the chair and glared up at Noland. His face remained stern. "Thank you, corporal. You and your comrade are dismissed."

The two sentries snapped to attention, lowered their weapons, made an about-face, and marched out of the lieutenant colonel's office.

"Remove your coat, sergeant," Lieutenant Colonel Smith said. "The day is warm, then please sit."

Noland did as ordered then folded the coat and laid it in his lap.

"You have been missing for five days," Smith continued. "Your body was not found by the regiment dispatched to collect the dead and wounded." The Lieutenant colonel scanned Noland. "You appear not to have even been in the battle, though one of your men swore he saw you fall after being hit by several musket shots. Have you an explanation, Sergeant Black?"

Noland hesitated. "I am not sure I do, sir." He shook his head, fisted his hands, and placed them on his lap. "You will not believe me if I do try to explain," he said.

Lieutenant Colonel Smith reached behind himself and retrieved a decanter partially filled with an amber fluid and placed it on his desk. "Perhaps a tot of rum will ease the tension."

"I would rather have some water, sir."

Smith again reached around himself and picked up two glasses and a jug of water. "As you wish, sergeant." He filled one glass with water and the other with rum. He pushed the glass of water across the desk toward Noland, who immediately drank it as if he had just returned from the Sahara Desert.

"Except for a bit of dust you picked up on you journey," the lieutenant colonel said, "your uniform appears to be clean and pressed. However, I do not recognize the blouse you are wearing. I have never seen such a design; it has a flat collar around the neck and pearly buttons down the front. The shirt is not regulation." The lieutenant colonel took a sip of rum.

"A friend gave it to me, since my shirt was badly damaged and soaked with blood from the wounds I received." Noland took a deep breath. "It is of a future design. One day it will be as common as dandelions are in weed beds."

"Are you trying to be facetious, sergeant?"

"Sorry, sir. No, I am not."

"Except for the abrasion on your forehead, you do not appear injured. I would like to see your wounds." Smith finished what remained in his glass and poured himself another shot of rum.

Noland stood and lifted the coat in his lap by its shoulders. He rotated it to expose the area where the musket shots had entered. "Sir, my coat will show where it has been mended."

"I see the threads. No doubt sewn by a rebel's wife." Smith sat back in his chair and swigged the rum. "Now, take off that shirt, sergeant!"

Noland nodded. He draped the coat across the seat of the chair, then unbuttoned the shirt and removed it. He then turned his back toward Lieutenant Colonel Smith.

"What I see are wounds that are well healed," Smith grunted. "It has only been five days since you were supposedly shot. And, if you were so injured, I would expect to see reddened, festering lesions. You are showing me old wounds." His chair scraped the floor as he pushed away from his desk. "Sergeant, where have you been for the last five days?"

Noland put the shirt back on, turned, lifted the coat, and sat down. He again laid the coat in his lap and unconsciously slid his hand into the exposed pocket. His fingers felt the Celtic cross. He removed it, brought his hand around, and glanced at the medallion.

His thumb pressed against the pendant while his fingers closed over it. He sighed deeply and looked straight into Smith's eyes. "I am unsure of where I have been or how I got there. But one thing that is certain is that two hundred years from now, the descendants of the colonists, which we now regard as rebels, in Boston and across the United States of America, will be celebrating their independence from Great Britain. Next year in Philadelphia, the Continental Congress will sign a Declaration of Independence from Great Britain. The Revolutionary War that has just begun will continue for some seven more years and Great Britain will lose." The sergeant straightened and inflated his chest. The fingers of his right hand played with the cross. "Sir, I received two musket shots on the Lexington Road..." Noland twitched his right shoulder, "one in the shoulder, one below in the back, and a load of scattershot. The wounds were treated with antiseptic elixirs to thwart bacteria. This allowed my injuries to heal rapidly. The shot that grazed my head was not severe. It was not treated."

Disturbed and astonished, Lieutenant Colonel Smith glared at Noland in shocked disbelief. He bent forward and took a swig of rum. He sat silently and stared. Then he fisted his hands and slammed them on the desktop. He bolted upright. His chair flew back against the wall. "You know damn well," Smith growled, "there is not a country on this earth that can oppose Great Britain's military force!" His face reddened. He took a deep breath. "Who treated you? Where were you? I do not know of such medicinal elixirs. And bacteria. What the bloody hell is that?"

"I am sorry, sir. You will not believe me if I tell you where I was, how I came to be there, or how I was treated. I, myself, do not understand what happened to me. But, if I must, I will try to tell you." Noland dropped the Celtic cross. He leaned down, picked it up, and put it into his pocket.

Lieutenant Colonel Smith righted his chair and returned it to its proper position, sighed, and sat down. "I will try to remain calm," he huffed.

Noland nodded. "When I was shot, I fell to the ground, unconscious. When I awoke, everything was different. In some mysterious way, I had been transported into the future, lying exactly on the same spot where I fell, but two hundred years from now."

Lieutenant Colonel Smith shook his head and stared directly at Noland. "I do believe the shot that grazed your head has jostled your thinking." Smith leaned forward, moved a piece of writing paper toward himself, and started to write.

Noland began to chew his lower lip and dispassionately said, "I believe you are wrong, sir. Within less than a year, land access into Boston will be blockaded. General Howe and the British troops will evacuate the city. I do not believe that you—King George or Parliament—can comprehend the vastness and extensiveness of this nation, and the colonists' capabilities and strong desire for independence. This land, which we call America, comprises one-third of the North American continent. The colonists, their offspring, and the future immigrants from all nations, will populate this land because they all want to live where their independence is sacred and with minimal governmental influence. Almost immediately after this conflict, which will involve all thirteen colonies, ends and our British troops vacate, the people of this country will create a great democratic nation that will prosper far beyond our imagination. It will become the most dominant force on earth."

"Enough!" Smith slammed his fist on the desk. "Any more of this fantasy, Sergeant Noland Black, and you will be hanged as a traitor. I believe your head injury has caused your madness." The lieutenant colonel picked up the pen and wrote rapidly, while Noland watched. "Tomorrow morning you will be taken, along with the others who were injured, to the HMS *Avalon*. This armed transport will sail for England on the afternoon tide. I have written the order," Smith held up the communiqué, "for you to be treated during the voyage as a soldier wounded in battle. You will be discharged once the vessel docks in Greenwich. As for now, return to your quarters, collect your personal items, and prepare for the voyage. Then get some sleep. You are dismissed."

Noland stood. "I am sorry you do not believe me, sir. Where I was is beyond anything I could dream of. I did not want to leave—and, if it were at all possible, I would return. The future of this country is going to be astonishing."

Lieutenant Colonel Smith glared at him.

Noland came to attention, saluted, did an about-face, and walked out of Lieutenant Colonel Smith's office.

Feeling disturbed and rejected, Noland walked slowly to his quarters. He looked at the cot and dresser. Nothing had been changed, but the room stifled him. It lacked the delicacy, comfort, and warmth of the bedroom that Carol Morris had provided. He went to the dresser, pulled out a drawer, rummaged a moment, and found a cord. Reaching into his pocket, he retrieved the Celtic cross, slid it onto the string, and tied the string's ends together, creating a necklace. He flipped the lanyard over his head and pulled the cross down to his neck. "I need some air." He fingered the amulet. Looked at it. "I need your help." He punched the door to his room open, stood for a moment gazing into the hallway, and lowered his head. His fingers unconsciously rubbed the cross. "I need to return to 1975. I will do whatever is necessary."

Sergeant Black hobbled out the back door of the barracks, found a bench against the wall, and slumped onto it. He stared across the Charles River. The waning sunlight still highlighted the North Church steeple and some rooftops in Boston. Dispirited, he closed his eyes and slouched forward. With his face buried in his hands, his brain filled the blackness with an image of Dr. Morris. Noland shook his head. *I cherished her*, he thought. *I am here. She will not exist for another two hundred years.* He felt a tear roll down his check. The sergeant raised his head and opened his eyes. His fingers automatically wiped away the dampness.

"I am to be returned to England…discharged. I will return to Gateshead." He moaned, then sighed. "It has been fifteen years. Do my parents still live? What will I do there?"

Distracted by a pair of seagulls tussling on the empty shoreline below, Noland watched them scuffle. Within moments his mind recalled that two days ago, in a different time, he stood on a wharf admiring the hull of the American frigate *Constitution*, or as Dr. Morris called the vessel, "Old Ironsides." His head drooped. "I will never have the opportunity to see or go aboard that ship." He clenched his teeth, looked up toward Bunker Hill and the uninhabited land that descended to the edge of the Charles River. He muttered, "The United States Navy will build on that shore—the Charlestown Naval Yard and the city will encircle it with lodgings, commerce, highways…." His hands covered his ears. He rubbed them, collapsed back against the barracks' back wall, and thought of the determined colonials who were entrenched on Bunker Hill. He scrunched forward and straightened. "That futile battle! To happen in two months!" Noland shook his head. "A tragedy it will be!" He slouched back and mumbled, "I will not be believed if I tell anyone."

Noland stared straight ahead as if in a trance. He gazed upward. A cloak of darkness covered him. His mind filled with conflicting thoughts. He dismissed the glistening pinpoints of lights that were beginning to appear overhead. Finally, his body shivered. He sighed. His thoughts had jelled. *There is nothing I could do or say. The destiny of the American colonists lies in their revolution for independence from Great Britain. For whatever reason, fate has given me the opportunity to see its outcome. And the results cannot be changed. The outcome will be as it will be.* The grenadier relaxed and looked to the sky. "It is best I return to England as an injured soldier, away from the madness Great Britain has created." A smile crossed his face, and he closed his eyes.

D r. Morris became married to her career after Noland's exodus and Dr. Gorski and his friend John moved to New York City. Eventually, Dr. Morris's supervisors recognized her medical proficiency and, in 1982, transferred her to the Massachusetts General Hospital Emergency Room in Boston. There, her prudent administrative and strategic insights bettered working conditions in the ER, which improved patient care, and she was promoted to Chief Physician of the ER. Such distinction in a major hospital complex opened the door to medical celebrity. The achievement brought requests to present at numerous local and national medical meetings. In 1989, one invitation caught her eye. The British Medical Association asked if she would chair a session on emergency room improvements at their annual national conference which was to be held at the University of Newcastle upon Tyne in June of 1990. The BMA request also included a stipend to cover travel expenses. Almost immediately after reading the invitation a fourteen-year fog dissipated from her mind, and Sergeant Noland Black popped to the forefront.

Dr. Morris completed her stint as chairperson of the session on Emergency Room Strategies and Procedures at the BMA Conference and went to lunch in the University of Newcastle upon Tyne center's dining room. There she met with three colleagues and several students. They discussed medicine and the history of the area. Morris asked about the town of Gateshead and learned that it was just across the river from where she was. The students began to provide historic and touristy information. One mentioned that the Romans had established an outpost in Gateshead in the sixth century. Another, who was from Gateshead, mentioned that the town received its village charter in the twelfth century. Back then, he said, Newcastle was important for coal mining and Gateshead, because of the Tyne River, became an important harbor. And, from then on, the city's population blossomed.

"Do any of you know if the name Black has any historic importance in the city?" Dr. Morris asked.

Several students glanced at each other, seemed at a loss for words and shook their heads. Her medical colleagues seemed oblivious to her query.

"How about the name Douglas?"

"Don't know anything about the place," the student from Gateshead said, "but there's a bed-and-breakfast called the Douglas Inn. It's a manor somewhere in the Ravensworth area."

Noland mentioned a ruined castle named Ravensworth; Dr. Morris remembered. She finished her lunch, paid her tab, excused herself, and returned to her hotel.

In the hotel lobby Dr. Morris met with the concierge. "I'm trying to find information on an individual who lived in the eighteenth century. He came from Gateshead," she said. "A student from the conference mentioned that there is a charming B&B named The Douglas Inn in that city. Could you get me a room there for two nights? My suite here is paid for the week, so please don't cancel it. I'll be returning."

The concierge nodded, picked up the telephone, dialed, and within five minutes, hung up the receiver. "I have you a room," she said.

"When you are ready to leave, please call down and I'll secure a taxi to take you there."

"Thank you," Dr. Morris said and walked to the elevator. As she waited, she noticed a rack of tourist brochures. Scanning it, she found a leaflet advertising The Douglas Inn. She folded it and stuffed it into her pocket. Within about forty-five minutes the doctor had packed an overnight bag, telephoned the concierge, and returned to the hotel's lobby. Her taxi awaited out front.

After a short distance the cabby announced that they were crossing the Tyne Bridge, "…over the river that links Newcastle to the world," he commented.

On the motorway, Dr. Morris retrieved The Douglas Inn leaflet and began to peruse it. It listed the amenities offered, plus a postcard image of an attractive, gray stone manor house sitting in a manicured English vista. She read the manor's brief history, which included being built in 1698 by a Scotsman named Eric Douglas who became the first lord of the manor. He died in 1719. His son, Chester Douglas, inherited the property and became the second lord of the manor. The house remained in the family until the death of the last lord of the manor, Andrew Black, in 1926. Neglected until after World War II, the Douglas estate was purchased by an American conglomerate, registered as an historical heritage site, restored, and converted to a bed-and-breakfast. The business owners found it prudent to maintain the property in the name of the original owners. Reading the leaflet set Dr. Morris on pins and needles. *The last lord was a Black. May he have been related to Noland Black?* she pondered.

The taxi slowed, turned, and passed through an open-gated entry onto a gravel driveway that was canopied by ten large beech trees, five on each side.

Dr. Morris scrunched forward in her seat to gaze out the front windshield at the manor house surrounded by the picturesque grounds.

The cabbie followed the driveway around to the left and pulled to a stop in front of the manor's entrance. "We have arrived, miss." He exited the vehicle, took hold of the doorhandle on the back left side, and opened the door to allow Dr. Morris to exit. He then stepped to the back of the taxi, opened the trunk, and removed her overnight bag. "Not much luggage," he said as he placed it next to her. "Reception area is in the main hall," he said as he positioned it next to her. "Enjoy your stay."

"Thank you." Dr. Morris paid the fare, lifted her bag, and headed for the entrance. She paused for a moment and looked around. *Where are the servants who are supposed to greet me?* she thought, then chuckled.

Once inside, she entered a medium-sized hall mostly illuminated by daylight passing through several tall, ornate windows. In the middle stood a large dark desk with two brightly lighted desk lamps. Two young women were at the desk; one wearing a cable-knit sweater was seated and the other, dressed in a wool tweed sportscoat, was standing, but looking down at the registration book.

"I am Dr. Carol Morris," she said as she approached the desk. "I have a reservation."

"Yes, we've been expecting you," the woman in the tweed coat looked up and said in a pleasant voice. "I'm Vicki, the concierge. Welcome to the Douglas Inn. Your room is ready. Please follow me and I will show you the way."

As Dr. Morris turned to follow, she noticed five portraits—four men with austere expressions and one somewhat attractive woman— all staring intently into the hall, hanging on the wall in the space between two large windows. All were dressed in black. *Could one possibly be an image of Noland?* she wondered. "Please wait a moment," she said as she turned and pointed toward the portraits. "May I ask who those people are?"

"Yes," Vicki said. "They are the former lords of the manor, except for Lady Black, who inherited the estate after her father, Lord Chester Douglas, died. I believe, he passed away sometime in the mid-1700s."

"I'd like to look at them." Carol stepped to the pictures. The concierge followed.

Carol examined the brass information tags below each portrait. The tags identified the individual and the length of their service to the manor: Lord Eric Douglas, 1698 to 1720; Lord Chester Douglas, 1720 to 1762; Lady Meera Douglas-Black, 1762 to 1820; Lord Mortimer Black, 1820 to 1854; and Lord Andrew Black, 1854 to 1926. She nodded to Vicki. "It appears that the lords changed from Douglas to Black," Dr. Morris commented. "I assume Lady Douglas married someone named Black?"

"Suppose so. I don't really know," Vicki said. "Those portraits were found scattered about the house after it was purchased. The decorators suggested that the owners save and hang them for clients to see. They believed that old portraits and art by classic British artists…" she pointed across the hall toward a medium-sized oil painting, "like that Gainsborough over there—added a semblance of elegance and nobility to old manor houses." The two women returned to the reception desk.

"Yes," Dr. Morris said. "Guests from away, like us Americans, expect to encounter vestiges of old-world culture and tradition when we visit." She braced herself against the desk. "I have a friend who is researching the fate of British soldiers who were attacked by American colonials during their march from Concord and Lexington, the battle that began the American Revolution. One of the soldiers was named Noland Black. Would anyone at this residence have any information on this individual?"

Vicki contemplated Carol's question, cocked and shook her head. "I don't believe so. Except perhaps the man who Lady Douglas-Black married may have been someone nearer her age, or she may have known him earlier."

Dr. Morris could see that Vicki looked hesitant, but still seemed to want to help.

"That event you speak of took place over two hundred years ago," the concierge continued. "The only place that might have information, marriage certificates and such, is the Church of St. Mary the Virgin over at quayside. It is the only church in Gateshead that existed back then. It is now a heritage site, and they have volunteer genealogists. But one needs an appointment to enlist their help for a search. I'm sure there is a donation involved. Might this be an interest to you?"

Dr. Morris nodded. "Absolutely!"

Vicki moved next to the young woman seated behind the desk, bent over her shoulder, and said, "Ann, please call St. Mary's and try to get an appointment for Dr. Carol Morris with one of their genealogists." As Ann dialed the telephone, Vicki straightened and looked toward Carol. "St. Mary's is next to the river. They also have an archive and an old graveyard. If that person lived in Gateshead, he might be buried there. Religious services ended at St. Mary's in the early 1800s, when the village grew and churches of other denominations were built."

Ann hung up the telephone and smiled. "Dr. Morris, you have an appointment tomorrow with the head curator at half ten in the morning. I mentioned that you were interested in material from the beginning of the American Revolution. There will be a taxi at the door when you finish breakfast."

"Thank you both; I'm ready to go to my room now."

The next morning Dr. Morris finished breakfast and left the dining room. As she passed the reception desk, Ann, the young woman at the desk, said, "Your taxi awaits you out front."

"Thank you," Dr. Morris acknowledged, turned toward the exit, went through the hotel doorway, and entered the taxi.

In twenty minutes, the cab rounded a rotary intersection onto Abbots Road and immediately turned left into St. Mary's Square. On her left, Dr. Morris saw the gray stone and brick medieval gothic church that now housed the Heritage Center. The cabbie entered the Heritage Center parking lot and stopped in front of a nondescript entryway that led to the vestibule. To Dr. Morris, the entrance appeared as if it were the back door to the church. Unlike classic gothic cathedrals and churches, where the entries are situated between the clock/bell towers, the single tower of St. Mary's rose at the opposite end of the building, facing the south approach to the Tyne Bridge.

"St. Mary's Heritage Center, miss," the cabbie said as he exited the vehicle and opened the left rear door.

Thanking the driver, she paid the fee, walked to the entrance, and entered the Heritage Center. The vestibule appeared bright, comfortable, and inviting. Cushioned armchairs and settees arranged in conversational groupings, and several study tables located along the side walls, were colorfully illuminated by internal lighting and beams of sunlight passing through a large stained-glass window. Dr. Morris approached the small reception desk and introduced herself. "I have an appointment to meet with the curator," she said.

"Yes," the young woman replied with a smile. "Vicar Mcleod is expecting you."

Dr. Morris nodded and looked up. She saw an elderly, professorial-looking man wearing a dark suit, beige shirt, and red tie, approaching. He had a neatly trimmed beard and a tonsure, a monk-styled haircut. As he approached Dr. Morris, he extended his right hand. "Vincent Mcleod, at your service," he said. "Most about here call me Vicar. I'm retired and enjoy my time volunteering as the curator for this establishment."

"Dr. Carol Morris," she said, as Mcleod and she shook hands.

"Yes, yes. You're here in search of soldiers who fought during the Battle of Concord and Lexington." Mcleod glanced at the receptionist and back to Dr. Morris. "We do not have very much. Perhaps a few documents, some letters, and family bibles. You see, St. Mary's was built in the thirteenth century. The building was damaged during the English Revolutions that took place in the 1600s and there have been several fires since. Many of the earlier documents and artifacts have been destroyed or lost. However, I did lay out some historic pieces from that time period." He could see a shade of disappointment in Carol's eyes. "There were relatively few soldiers from this area who took part in the early days of that war. Most were sent when our troops attacked New

York City. But there was a box of historical objects deposited in the church sometime in the late 1940s, after the sale of the Douglas estate. That box had been at the estate since the seventeenth century."

Dr. Morris's eyes brightened.

"I have the box in my library." The vicar pointed toward a hallway. "Please follow me."

Vicar Mcleod headed down the corridor. Dr. Morris followed. They entered a dimly lighted room with shelves full of books, stacks of papers, and several small boxes. The room contained a long central table illuminated with desk lamps. Four metal folding chairs were randomly arranged around the table. In one corner of the room, an overhead lamp hung above a comfortable but well-worn armchair. On an opposite wall was a desk with two lamps, and piles of papers and books. The curator directed Dr. Morris to the table. "The box in the middle contains the material from the Douglas estate," Mcleod said as he removed the cover. He gestured for Dr. Morris to take a seat.

Reaching into the box, the vicar removed a scroll and a bundle of folded documents. "These are the legal testaments of the lords of the Douglas estate. There were five of them, starting with Eric Douglas, who purchased the land and built the manor house sometime back in the 1680s and finally ending with Andrew Black, who had no heirs and died in 1926."

"Why did the lords with the Douglas name change to Black?" Dr. Morris asked.

"Aye." Mcleod unfolded one of the wills and scrolled through the pages as he narrated. "Chester Douglas, Eric's son, only had a daughter. Her name was Meera. He left the estate to her, because Eric did not have any male relatives. Meera married an elderly fellow in 1755, but the gentleman died after three years. Meera remained a widow for eighteen years, but in 1776, she married a Mr. Noland Black."

Carol's right hand snapped up to stifle a gasp. She felt her heart skip a beat. Her mind reeled. *Noland, I've found you.*

Vicar Mcleod paused, glanced at Carol, took a breath, then continued his narration. "Mr. Black was a soldier who had returned from the American colonies. The two married. Lady Meera Douglas—Lady Douglas-Black after the marriage—continued to supervise the workings of the estate. Since Black was not a nobleman, the estate maintained the Douglas name, but because of Black's queer behavior and prognostications, the manor became known as crazy Black's manor. As the years passed, Lord and Lady Black's offspring inherited the estate. The name Black remained with the manor until the present owners decided that it would be prudent to return the manor to its original name, Douglas."

Vicar Mcleod slid a sheet of paper from the bottom of the bundle that he was holding and raised his eyebrows as he examined the document. "This may provide more clarification and Mr. Black's condition. Supposedly, he suffered from a brain injury sustained in America and was considered eccentric and sometimes mad."

"No! He…" Carol blurted, then caught herself and took a deep breath. "Sorry."

Mcleod glanced up at Dr. Morris. "Are you all right?"

She nodded. "Yes. Please continue."

The vicar lowered his eyes, laid the wills on the table, and removed a small bundle of documents from the box. "These are letters from the family, neighbors, and friends. They mention that her husband attempted to foretell the future. He wrote and spoke of many wonders that the future would bring. In one letter that caught my eye, an individual wrote to others '…Mr. Black predicts that the forces of nature will be harnessed.' For example, he wrote that '…electricity supposedly from lightning will be used to illuminate homes, cities, move objects, produce heat, transmit images over long distances, and so forth….'"

Mcleod unfolded another letter. "This one is from Meera's close friend, written shortly after her marriage to Black. The friend apparently attended a court hearing where she heard Mr. Black tell the local magistrates that the Americans would win their independence from Great Britain. Meera's friend stated that the justices considered his remark as that of a madman." The vicar shook the letter, laid it on the table, and removed another one from the box. He scanned the message and looked up at Dr. Morris. "This one was written a year after the war in the colonies ended. It states that Mr. Black was correct. Britain did lose the war." Mcleod smiled and refolded the letter. "Most of the other letters refer to Black's other predictions." He looked up at Dr. Morris. "I examined all these papers before you came today. Interestingly, his prophecies have all come true. But, in Mr. Black's time they were considered the preposterous imaginations of a madman. It is still a mystery how Mr. Black could have known all that did happen."

Mcleod reached into the box and retrieved a small ornate chest. He opened it. "Some unusual and inexplicable artifacts were found among Mr. Black's belongings. For instance, an American five-dollar bill, several monetary coins dated from early 1970s..." He removed a slip of paper. "This piece of paper has the numbers 724-8135 written on it, and here is a folded, tattered photo, which had been torn in half. It has the image of an unrecognizable female on it." He handed the photo and slip of paper to Dr. Morris.

She looked at what the vicar had given her. She gazed at the numbers on the slip of paper and gasped. *That was my telephone number at the Massachusetts Health Clinic in Charlestown.* She looked at the tattered photo, chewed her lower lip, then sighed. *This is the Polaroid of Noland and me when we posed at the Boston Massacre Monument. The Old State House is in the background. If my memory is correct, the photo was taken by those Polish tourists we met. Wonder why Noland's image has been torn away? Guess I'll never know.* She furrowed her brow. *Can't tell this vicar what I know.* "Too bad the woman is not recognizable," she told Mcleod. "Wonder how the photo and those modern things got into that chest? Cameras weren't invented until the mid-nineteenth century."

"They weren't indeed," Vicar Mcleod commented. He massaged his bald spot, then reached into the chest and brought out another letter. He unfolded it. "This is a letter, written to Lady Meera. It's in Mr. Black's hand. Probably in response to the question some wives ask of their husbands; did they have any love attractions while away? In Mr. Black's case, may he have been smitten by anyone in the colonies? His reply to

Meera reads, '…yes, I developed an affection for a lovely lady, but that is of no consequence. I was not able to further the relationship, for she has yet to be born….'" Mcleod raised his eyelids and looked at Dr. Morris as he refolded the letter. "A strange answer, don't you think, Dr. Morris? It was almost as if he had been in the twentieth century and experienced everything he prophesied." The vicar shrugged as Dr. Morris stood and appeared to wipe a wetness from her right eye. "Sometimes the contents of archival boxes get mixed," he said.

An impulse made Dr. Morris bend toward the chest, but from where she stood, she could not see into it. *What happened to the Celtic cross?* she wondered. She straightened and glanced at Mcleod. "Mr. Black was a soldier. Perchance, are there any military medallions or pieces of jewelry in that chest?"

Vicar Mcleod lifted the chest, turned it upside down, and gave it a shake. Nothing fell out. "I'm afraid not. Such items are easily lost, stolen or…" he pondered while he set the chest back on the table, "perhaps sometimes they are interred with the owners or given to their relatives." He returned Noland's artifacts to the chest and closed it. "I hope this small amount of information will be of some use."

"Thank you for your help, Mr. Mcleod," Dr. Morris replied as she reached into her purse and removed a check, she had written earlier for one-hundred-pounds. She handed it to Mcleod. "Please accept this donation."

"Thank you," Mcleod said. "This is very generous of you."

"What you provided will make my friend in the States happy to know that Sergeant Noland Black really did exist," Dr. Morris said as she turned and started to walk toward the door. She stopped for a moment as a thought came to mind. *If this vicar only knew. Oh, what difference will it make if he does know? He probably won't believe it.* She took a deep breath, turned to face Vicar Mcleod, smiled, and said, "By the way, Mr. Black really did visit the twentieth century."

www.ingramcontent.com/pod-product-compliance
Lightning Source LLC
Chambersburg PA
CBHW020652120726
47906CB00001B/233